Winning Becca

Book 4 in the Northwoods Adventures Series

By Amy A. Corron

Copyright 2008 by Amy A. Corron

Winning Becca
By Amy A. Corron

Printed in the United States of America

ISBN 978-1-60647-774-8

All rights reserved solely by the author. The author guarantees all contents are original and do not infringe upon the legal rights of any other person or work. No part of this book may be reproduced in any form without the permission of the author. The views expressed in this book are not necessarily those of the publisher.

Unless otherwise indicated, Bible quotations are taken from the New King James version of the Bible. Copyright 1982 by Thomas Nelson, Inc.

Contact the author at
amycorron@northwoodsnovels.com

www.xulonpress.com

Tom and Lynn,

Merry Christmas 2008

God bless you always!

Amy A. Corron

This book is a work of fiction. Although Atlanta, Michigan — located half-way between Alpena and Gaylord — is a real place, I have taken extreme liberties with the setting for the sake of the story. All characters portrayed in this novel are figments of my overactive imagination. Any resemblance to real people, living or dead, is merely a very strange coincidence.

For my beautiful daughter, Katy. It has been a blessing and a privilege to watch you grow into the lovely young woman you have become. I still remember you as a five-year-old swinging on the swing, begging me to push you higher so you could "swing all the way up to Jesus." May you always have your eyes on heaven. And remember, no matter how grown up you become, you'll always be my little girl. I love you so very much!!

CHAPTER ONE

The hot August sun beat down relentlessly, burning through Becca Weaver's straw cowboy hat and searing the top of her head. Sweat gathered between her shoulder blades and trickled slowly down her back. Becca fought the urge to squirm. She knew better than to move a muscle. Instead, she kept her eyes trained on Bailey's Irish Delight. The quarter horse gelding had dozed off in the heat.

From the corner of her eye Becca watched the judge, dressed in slim black jeans, white button-down shirt and white cowboy hat, make one last pass down the line of horses. Becca snapped to attention and smoothly transitioned from one side of Bailey's head to the other as the judge strode past. Finally he stopped, scribbled something on a piece of paper and passed it to the ring steward.

Static echoed from the loudspeaker. The air was split by the ear-piercing squeal of feedback, making Bailey raise his head in surprise. Someone tapped the microphone.

"We have the results of western showmanship, sixteen years and over."

Becca's shoulders tensed. Bailey immediately felt the change from his end of the lead line and began to quiver.

"In first place we have number 27, Toby Sinclair and Rocky."

Becca squeezed her eyes shut and grimaced. If she were a different kind of girl she would have sworn. Toby and Rocky trotted toward the gate to receive their blue ribbon. Becca could practically feel Toby's smirk clear across the show ring.

"Second place goes to number 16, Becca Weaver, and Bailey's Irish Delight."

Becca could hear her sister Rhonda's piercing whistle above the clapping of the crowd. She forced a smile, clucked to Bailey and headed toward the exit gate. She accepted the red ribbon gracefully then moved away toward the cool shade of the horse barn.

"Tough luck, Red," Toby said, falling into step beside Becca. His buff-colored felt hat shaded his eyes, but Becca knew there was a triumphant gleam shining in their brown depths. "Looks like Rocky and I are headed for the grand championship once again."

"The fair's just started," Becca replied tartly. "I wouldn't go counting your ribbons before they're won."

They reached the blessed coolness of the barn. The horses' hooves echoed hollowly as they were led to their stalls. Becca swung open the gate to Bailey's stall and led the gelding inside, breathing a sigh of relief when Toby continued down the aisle. She unsnapped Bailey's lead and he quickly buried his muzzle in his water bucket, slurping noisily. Becca patted the sorrel's shoulder lovingly before slipping out of the stall. She hung the second place ribbon on the gate just as two shadowy figures entered the barn pushing a baby stroller.

"Hey, Bec." Rhonda gave Becca a hug. "You got robbed," she whispered in Becca's ear.

"I thought you had it all the way," Rhonda's husband, Wes, agreed.

Becca took off her hat and tossed it on a lawn chair. Her hair was soaked with sweat.

"Yeah, well, I wouldn't care so much except this is my last year to compete at the fair and I wanted to beat Toby just once."

She removed a wash cloth from her tack box, took a bottle of water from a nearby cooler, unscrewed the top and emptied the cold contents onto the rag. She quickly buried her face in the refreshing coolness.

Rhonda reached down and lifted her one-year-old son Brendan from the stroller. His red curls, so much like his mother's, were plastered to his head.

"Well, the fair's a long way from being over. It's just one class," Rhonda encouraged.

"I know. That's what I told Toby when he started bragging."

Rhonda took Brendan over to the stall and let him get a closer look at Bailey who was now dozing, head hanging down. The little boy reached for the red ribbon on the gate, clasping the scarlet silk in one small fist.

"He just razzes you because he has a crush on you," Rhonda said with a smile, extricating the ribbon from Brendan's grasp.

"Bite your tongue, Ronnie!" Becca threw herself down in a lawn chair. "He's the last person on God's green earth I want having a crush on me." She reached up and pulled the pins from her hair, untwisting the bun and letting the strawberry blond mass fall around her shoulders. "Wes, can't you put the fear of God in him or something?" She looked pleadingly up at her brother-in-law.

"Sorry, kid." Wes put a placating hand on her head. "I have a hard enough time protecting my reputation around here as it is." He ruffled Becca's hair. "You want a lemonade or something?"

"That sounds heavenly," Becca sighed.

"Be right back then." Wes sauntered out the double barn doors where the sounds of the Montmorency County fair, Calliope music mixed with laughter, drifted in.

Rhonda moved away from Bailey's stall. She lifted Becca's hat from the lawn chair, setting it on Becca's head before settling herself and Brendan in the chair. Becca tilted the hat down to cover her eyes and slouched low in the chair. The heat made her feel as sluggish as a sloth.

"So, what do you think the difference was?" she asked.

"Between you and Toby?"

Becca nodded.

"The judge prefers Arabs," Rhonda answered. "I heard a few people talking in the stands. They said this guy judges on the Arab circuit."

Becca groaned. "I'm toast then. If he's an Arab judge, there's no way he'll place Bailey above Rocky, no matter how good I ride. He probably recognizes Toby from when he showed on the circuit. I swear I have the most rotten luck."

"Hey now," Rhonda protested. "You've got me for a sister, and Brendan for a nephew..."

"And me for a brother-in-law."

A cold cup was pressed into Becca's hand. She sat up and bumped the hat back on her head, smiling up at Wes.

"Now that's the best!" She lifted the lemonade in a silent toast before taking a long drink. "I love you, Wes."

"I know you do kid, but don't tell Rhonda." He winked at his wife.

Brendan began to squirm. Wes lifted him from Rhonda's arms.

"When's your next class?" Rhonda asked, pushing herself up from the chair.

"Not until after lunch."

"I think we'll take the little guy home then and get him out of this heat. I'll come back later."

"Okay. See ya." Becca settled back in her chair and watched Rhonda and Wes disappear. Pulling the hat back down over her forehead, she closed her eyes and held the icy cup against her cheek.

Winning Becca

Toby Sinclair closed his horse's stall with a silent click and crept soundlessly down the barn aisle. He stopped short of Becca's tack box and just stared for a moment at the wilted figure slouched in the chair like a rag doll, cowboy hat pulled low over her eyes. Toby knew without looking that her eyes were the same color blue as the chicory flowers that grew all along the back roads of northern Michigan. Those eyes had been snapping with temper when Becca came out of the show ring with that red ribbon.

Two quiet steps and he was standing practically in front of her. She still hadn't budged. Toby plopped himself down in the lawn chair Rhonda had vacated.

"Shouldn't you be getting ready for our next face-off?"

Becca started, sloshing lemonade down the front of her blouse.

"Son of a..." She pushed the hat off her head and glared at Toby.

"Preacher man," he finished for her with a grin. Becca kicked out at him, the pointed toe of her cowboy boot connecting solidly with his shin. "Ow!" Toby yelled, grabbing his throbbing leg.

"Toby, you are *such* an idiot." Becca jumped from her chair, plucking the sticky blouse away from her chest. She cast another hate-filled glare at him before spinning to enter her 4-H club's curtained-off dressing area.

"Hey, I'm sorry," Toby apologized, trying to sound contrite despite the smile that still split his face. He couldn't help it, it was so much fun to get

Becca riled. "I really didn't mean to make you spill all over yourself."

"Yeah, well, lucky for you I've got plenty of show clothes here or else you'd be in deep doo-doo." A few moments later Becca emerged from the dressing room buttoning the last buttons of a baby blue cotton blouse.

Toby looked up at her and let out a low whistle. "I like that one much better anyway. It brings out the color of your eyes."

"Oh good grief, shut up. You're going to make me barf and then I'll have to change again."

Becca turned away and tucked in her shirttails. Toby admired the view of her backside in close fitting, midnight-blue jeans. Glancing over her shoulder, Becca caught him staring and stuck out her tongue.

"Why don't you take a picture, it would last longer."

"Would you let me?" Toby replied, grinning.

"Not in a million, bazillion years." Becca turned back around, grabbed her hat and strode toward the barn doors without so much as a fare-thee-well.

Toby launched himself from the chair, his long strides quickly eating up the ground between them.

"Hey, where you going?"

"Lunch," she answered succinctly.

"Sounds good. Mind if I come too?"

"Yes, Toby, I mind very much." Becca stopped in her tracks and glared up at him. "I don't want my appetite ruined. Not to mention the fact that I have no intention of breaking bread with the enemy."

Toby lost some of his bravado as he stared down into her snapping blue eyes.

"I'm not your enemy, Bec."

"Oh, Toby." She patted his cheek. "You've *always* been my enemy." Turning on her heel, she quickly strode away.

Hands on hips, Toby watched until Becca was swallowed by the crowd milling around the midway. He hung his head for a moment before turning back to the horse barn. He leaned against the gate to Rocky's stall. The dapple gray gelding turned, hanging his head over the stall door. Toby absently rubbed the dished face, his mind still on Becca.

"That girl sure doesn't like to lose," he confided to the horse. "Course, I guess I can't find fault with that. I don't like to lose either. And I don't plan to. Not in the show ring or out of it. You'll see, Rocky. In the end, we're going to win the grand championship *and* the girl."

Becca balled up the wrappers from her grilled cheese sandwich and French fries. Tossing them in the nearest garbage barrel, she headed back toward the barn. She shouldn't have eaten. Between the heat and her nerves, her lunch was now sitting like a boulder on her stomach. Glancing down at her watch she was disappointed to find there would be no time for a quick little nap on the cot in the dressing area. She had to get ready for her next class. Her next "face-off" with Toby Sinclair.

"Lord, I know this is a totally selfish thing to ask, but couldn't I place above him, just once?" Becca beseeched the Lord quietly as she strode toward the barn.

"Hey, Becca! Becca!"

Becca stopped, searching the fair crowd for who had called her name.

"Becca!"

Her friend, Violet Compton, pushed around a couple of older gentlemen who were looking at the ATV the animal shelter was raffling off. Becca waited while Violet, bulgingly pregnant, made her slow way across the grass. Violet's boyfriend, Vince, slunk a few steps behind. Becca eyed the young man with his long, black hair warily. Something about Vince Schmidt always gave Becca the creeps. She never could understand what Violet saw in the guy, but Vi declared it was "true love," as if she could possibly know at eighteen. Now the two were expecting a baby any minute.

"I'm glad I caught you," Violet said, stopping to catch her breath. "Where are you going in such a hurry?"

"I have to get ready for my next class. I'm in halter after the lunch break."

"We'll walk with you then." Vi motioned toward Vince and the three started walking together. "How'd you do this morning?"

"Second." Becca couldn't help the dismal tone that seeped into her voice. "Toby got first, of course. Turns out the judge has a thing for Arabians."

"Aw, that's too bad," Violet sympathized.

"What are you doing here, anyway?" Becca asked, stopping near the poultry barn. The cacophony of geese, ducks and chickens squawking drifted out on the hot air. "You look like you're about to pop and it feels like a hundred and ten in the shade. Aren't you miserable?"

"Oh, no," Vi said with a laugh. She brushed her bottle-blond hair back over her shoulder. Her face, which was normally all angles and planes had been softened somewhat by pregnancy. "I'm not due for another three weeks. We wanted to come see you, cheer you on. Didn't we, Vince?" Violet glanced at her boyfriend.

Becca did the same. To her horror, Vince had fished a cigarette out of his pocket and was in the process of lighting it.

"No smoking around the animal barns," Becca informed coldly, pointing to the warning sign tacked to the outside of the barn. "Fire hazard."

Vince just shrugged lazily, a greasy half-smile crossing his face.

"Sorry."

He didn't sound it. Not the least little bit. His beady black eyes clashed with Becca's.

"Vi, I'm gonna head over to the show ring, catch a smoke over there."

"Sure baby. I'll catch up with you in a minute."

Becca watched Vince scuff away and had to repress a shiver.

"Vi, are you sure about this whole thing?" she asked. Violet just laughed, her trademark tinkling giggle.

"It's a little late to be asking that, silly," she said, placing a hand atop her round tummy.

"I don't mean about the baby. I mean about him." Becca hooked a thumb in the general direction of the show ring.

"Becca, we've had this discussion before. Vince is a good guy. I don't know why you can't see it. He is, truly. And he's excited about the baby. We're going to see how it goes for the rest of this summer. If his job holds steady and things are working out okay, we'll probably get married in the spring."

"Well, if you're sure that's what you want."

"I know you think I'm crazy. But I'm not like you. You've got this wonderful future ahead of you, with college and a career. Me, you know I was never any good in school. All I've wanted was to have a real family. That's what we're going to be, Vince, the baby and me."

Becca didn't have the heart to burst her friend's romantic bubble. But there was no way Vince Schmidt was going to settle down and become some twenty-first century version of Ward Cleaver, coming home from work every day to his pretty little wife and children. Becca looked into Violet's shining eyes and gave a small smile.

"You'd better go find some shade before you melt in this heat."

The loudspeaker screeched to life.

"First call for halter horse, ages sixteen and under."

"I've gotta go get Bailey curried and to the practice ring." Becca moved away from her friend and toward the horse barn. "I'll see you later, Vi."

Inside the dark barn, Becca blinked several times, waiting for her eyes to adjust to the lack of light after being in the bright sun. When she could finally see, she looked around for Toby. Thankfully, he was nowhere in sight. She moved toward her club's tack area where several other riders were dragging out show halters and curry combs. She beamed with pleasure to see her parents in front of Bailey's stall.

"Hey Mom, Daddy." She leaned forward to give them both hugs.

"Hi, honey," her mom said, giving Becca a brief squeeze. "Sorry we missed your first class. Your father was having some trouble with the irrigation system and it took longer than he thought to get it fixed. We see you took second, that's good."

"Not good enough," Becca muttered. Her parents shot her questioning looks. "It's not like I'm being greedy or anything," she defended. "But do I have to lose to Toby Sinclair every year?"

"You promised us this was only for fun, remember? When you talked your father into buying Bailey, you promised us you just wanted to enjoy showing 4-H, that you weren't going to get broken hearted if you didn't win big trophies or championships."

"I know." Becca hung her head. "But this is my last year. For three years in a row I've come in second to Toby. Is it really that wrong of me to want to go out on top in my final year of showing?"

"No baby, it's not." David Weaver wrapped his daughter in a bear hug. "If it was me, I wouldn't like playing second fiddle to Toby either. So, let's get that nag out of his stall and brush him till he shines."

CHAPTER TWO

The bright lights of the midway lit up the night. Music blared as the Ferris wheel made its slow rotations. Roadies called out, enticing young and old alike to draw near and try their hand at a game of skill or chance. The smell of popcorn and fried foods hung heavy on the still night air.

Toby navigated his way through the crowded midway, around young couples pushing baby strollers, parents carrying tired or crying children and teens walking with their hands in each others back pockets. He finally spied Becca up ahead with a group of other kids from her North Ridge Riders 4-H club. She had changed out of her show clothes and now wore a pair of hip-hugging, flare legged jeans with a wide belt around her slender waist. The air had grown chill with the setting of the sun, but all Becca wore to ward of the cold was a filmy cardigan over a curve-hugging t-shirt. Her coppery hair hung down between her shoulders.

Pushing around the people in front of him, Toby trotted the last few steps until he was side by side with Becca. She glanced up at him from the corner of her eye as he draped an arm casually over her shoulders.

"Hey, Red. I was beginning to think I would never find you." Toby had to practically yell to be heard over the carnival din around them.

"Did it ever occur to you that maybe I didn't want to be found?" Becca asked, pushing his arm off her shoulder.

"Oh, come on. You can't still be mad. We're one and one now. You bested me in the halter class, so can't we call it even?"

"There's still two more days of showing left to go."

"Come on, Bec. Can't you just forget this silly competition?" Toby urged. "I'm the reigning champ, three years running. You really think you have a chance at dethroning me your last year?"

Becca stopped dead in the middle of the midway. People continued to flow around them.

"Yes, Toby, I do think I have a very good chance of dethroning you. Even if your parents did stack the deck against me by talking the fair board into hiring that judge from the Arabian circuit."

"Whoa, hold on there." Toby grabbed her arm before she could turn and walk away. "My parents didn't have anything to do with which judge they hired. I don't need to sink to cheating to win. You know that better than anyone," he added with a smirk.

Winning Becca

Becca shook off his hand and continued walking.

"You know what your problem is, Toby?"

"I'm sure you're all-fired ready to tell me," he answered, falling into step beside her.

"You lack humility. God likes humble people, like me. I think God's on my side."

"Oh ho, you do, huh?" Toby laughed, looking down at her. "Seems to me God's got an awful lot on His plate. I would think the Montmorency County Fair would be a little under His radar."

"God's eye is on the sparrow. If He's watching the sparrows, that means He's watching us, too. The Bible says God resists the proud, but He gives grace to the humble. And since I'm humble and you're full of yourself, I'm thinking that gives me the advantage."

"Well, I guess we'll just have to wait and see about that, won't we?"

The crowd had stopped in front of a ticket booth. Toby decided to wait in line with the others and when he got up to the window, he dug into his jeans pocket for a wad of bills. He passed a ten across the counter and took the long strip of tickets from the teller.

"Come on." He grabbed Becca by the hand and pulled her toward the Tilt-O-Whirl. "I'm going to get you so dizzy you won't be able to sit upright in the saddle tomorrow."

"I thought you said you didn't have to cheat," Becca challenged. "And I'm not going on that stupid ride with you. It makes me throw up."

"Okay then." Toby changed directions. "How about the Ferris wheel? It's more romantic anyway."

Winning Becca

"Oooh, gag. Now I really am going to throw up." Becca made a face at him but allowed herself to be dragged along, much to Toby's pleasure. A few minutes alone with her, up near the stars, that was pretty near heaven in Toby's mind.

The carnival worker watched as Toby secured the seatbelt around them before lowering the bar and sliding the safety pin into place. The Ferris wheel lurched backward, stopping abruptly to fill the next seat. Becca slid as far to the side as she could manage and sat stiffly, arms crossed. Why in the world had she allowed Toby to drag her on this ride? Had she totally lost her mind?

She spared him a quick glance from the corner of her eye. His short brown hair stood up in damp spikes above his forehead, as if he had splashed water on his face and slicked it back over his hair. His once enviably straight nose sported a pronounced knot on the bridge from when he had broken it the year before.

Becca could remember perfectly the chilly fall evening, the stands of Atlanta High School packed for the Huskies' homecoming game against Hillman. Toby was playing tight end and somehow lost his helmet during a tackle. The crunch of a well-padded shoulder plowing into his nose could be heard all the way up in the stands. Ever since, Toby had carried his scar with as much pride as if he had won the Medal of Honor in combat.

The Ferris wheel jerked and moved again. Toby's eyes reflected the bright lights of the midway as he turned to her with a flirtatious smile.

"Whew, it's chilly up here." He gave an exaggerated shiver. "What are you doing all the way over there? Don't you want to slide over so I can put my arm around you and keep you warm?"

"Not in a million, bazillion years. You so much as lay one finger on me and I'll start screaming bloody murder," Becca warned. "Then I'll break your nose again. And *do not* rock the car," she ordered as Toby began to make the buggy sway.

"Man, Bec, you take all the fun out of everything," he groused. "Okay, I'll behave myself. Look at those stars." He glanced up. "They're just sprinkled across the sky, just like the freckles on your cheeks."

Becca started making gagging noises in her throat.

"I swear Toby, you say the most retarded things."

"I thought girls were supposed to like that stuff. It's supposed to be romantic."

"What's got you on this stupid romance kick all of a sudden?" Becca wanted to know. The Ferris wheel had picked up speed. Their car went over the top, leaving her stomach momentarily suspended before they made the downward turn. "I'm gonna have to tell Miss Sandy to start watching what you're taking out of the library. Seems you've been hitting the Harlequin section pretty hard these days."

"Speaking of love, I saw V and V nation were here today," Toby commented.

"Violet and Vince?" Becca asked, sparing him another glance.

"Yeah. Could Vi get anymore preggers?"

"Her pregnancy hasn't exactly been a secret, considering she was nearly seven months along at graduation."

"Do you suppose Vince said lots of cheesy, romantic things to Violet before he got her in the family way?"

"I highly doubt it. With Vi it probably didn't require much effort. I don't understand it. There's nothing Vince could ever say that would convince me to allow him to lay so much as a finger on me. I think he's slime from the pits of..." Becca caught herself and snapped her mouth shut.

"If he ever laid a finger on you, I'd break a heck of a lot more than his nose," Toby said quietly.

Becca turned her head to look at him. His soft brown eyes were very serious. This time she didn't make gagging sounds. Instead she went back to staring straight ahead, figuring it was safer that way. After all, Toby was still her enemy. At least for two more days.

"Violet has visions of family bliss dancing in her vacuous head," Becca continued. "She thinks they're going to get married and live happily ever after."

"Ha!" Toby barked out a laugh. "Happily ever after with *Vince*?" He grabbed his midsection and leaned forward, laughing hysterically. "I'm sorry." He gained control of himself and sat back. "I know you and Vi are friends, but living happily ever after with Vince?" Toby started to laugh again. Several seconds passed before he could speak. "She's whacked," he finally finished.

"Yeah, I think so too," Becca agreed. "But she's *in love*," Becca said with disdain. "You can't tell her anything. And think about it, the way she grew up. Her dad drinking all the time, her mom sunk in depression. And you know, her brother…" Becca bit her lip.

"Her brother what?"

"Never mind. You don't need to know. It's just that, Violet has her reasons for wanting so badly to be loved. I can't judge her. All I can do is pray that she finds the happiness she's looking for."

"Yeah well, I can tell you it ain't going to be with Vince Schmidt."

"You never did answer my question." Becca pursed her lips and looked at Toby from the corner of her eye. "What's got you talking all this romantic nonsense?"

"Hey." Toby slouched low in the seat. "A man gets to a certain age, he starts thinking about the future."

Becca couldn't swallow the snort of laughter that burned her nose.

"What?" Toby's head swung lazily to look at her.

"Man? Toby, you're barely past 18. You've got plenty of time to worry about your future love life."

"Vince is the same age I am and he's about to become a father. Does that make him a man?"

"I've already told you what I think Vince is," Becca reminded with disgust. "I don't believe man is the word I used."

The ride gradually slowed. Soon it was their turn to exit and Becca hopped off, Toby right at her side. He put his hand on her elbow to steady her.

She quickly shook it off. If Toby had romance on the brain, he was going to have to think about it with some other girl.

"What do you want to go on next?" Toby asked.

"I can't. It's getting late and I need to get home." Becca headed toward the parking lot, not daring to look up. Toby grabbed her shoulder, forcing her to stop. She sighed heavily and dared to meet his hopeful eyes. "Look, I've got a big day ahead of me tomorrow, trying to dethrone the reigning champ."

"Good luck with that." Toby grinned down at her. "I'll walk you to your car."

Toby tried to walk slow, eking out every possible second with Becca, but her quick strides ate up the ground. His mind scrambled through possible stall tactics.

"Hey, you want some cotton candy before you leave, or popcorn?"

"Nah, I'm good."

Toby saw how the male carnival workers gave Becca the once-over as she walked by. Several tried to get her attention, holding out stuffed animals to entice her to step up to their booth. Becca ignored them all. Toby fought the urge to put a fist into a carnie's face when the man let out a wolf whistle as Becca strode by. The blood in Toby's veins pumped up to a near boil. He longed to put a protective arm around Becca, but if she realized she was the focus of so much male ardor, she gave no sign of it.

"What about Bailey? Don't you want to check up on him before you head home?"

"He's all taken care of," Becca assured. "Chris pulled barn duty, so Bailey's in good hands. Unless, of course..." She halted and looked at Toby with suspicion. "You plan to sabotage my tack or something?"

"I told you, I don't have to cheat. By the end of the week that big purple ribbon and huge gold trophy will be mine, fair and square."

"Hmph. There you go with that pride again. I told you Toby, you'd better be careful. God's watching."

"Whatever." Toby waved a dismissive hand as Becca continued on through the crowd.

As they neared the exit gate, Becca suddenly squealed and launched herself at a tall man dressed in the brown uniform of a Montmorency County Sheriff's deputy.

"Nate!" She laughed as he scooped her up in a bear hug. The two other deputies nearby smiled knowingly.

"Man Nate, even married you still got the chicks throwing themselves at you," the one said, shaking his head.

"Eat your heart out guys," Nate replied and set Becca back on her feet. "How's it going?" he asked, ruffling Becca's hair in brotherly fashion.

"Okay." Becca tugged at the hem of her sweater. "I'm just heading home. Can you do me a favor?"

"Sure." Nate nodded, his blue eyes sparkling. "What do you need?"

"Can you arrest this guy for harassment?" She hooked a thumb toward Toby who started to smile. The smiled quickly vanished when Nate's laser-blue eyes turned on him full-force.

"Ha, ha. Very funny, Bec. Hey, Nate, I was just making sure the lady got safely to her car. Honest." Toby held up his hands in surrender as all three deputies leveled hard eyes on him.

"So which one is it, Becca?" Nate asked, relaxing into a hip-shot stance. "Is he bothering you or playing knight in shining armor?"

"What if I said he's bothering me by playing knight in shining armor?"

"Then I can't help you. You got pure intentions Toby?"

"Yes sir! Of course." Toby straightened his shoulders. "I would never hurt Becca, and I'd never let anyone else hurt her, either."

"Well then, looks like you've got a knight to escort you to your car. You two have a good evening." Nate touched the brim of his cap and moved away, the other two deputies following suit.

"Geez Bec, that wasn't funny!" Toby shoved Becca's shoulder as she burst out laughing. He followed her into the field that was full of parked cars. "I about had a heart attack when Nate looked at me like he would eat me alive."

"You should have seen the look on your face," Becca managed between giggles. "That's what you get for beating me this morning."

"Do I have to keep reminding you that you beat me once, too?"

Becca stopped next to her car and fished the key out of her front pocket.

Winning Becca

"Hey, I have an idea," Toby said, leaning against the back door of the car while Becca unlocked the driver's door.

"Toby, you're scaring me."

"No, really. How about something to make the competition between us more interesting?"

"Like what?" she asked skeptically.

"How about a little bet? A friendly wager," Toby suggested. He crossed his arms, drumming his fingers on his biceps while he thought. "I'm thinking the prize could be a date. Say, if I win, you go with me to the bump-and-run car race Saturday night."

"That's supposed to make the competition more interesting?" Becca shook her head and slid behind the wheel of her car. "What if *I* win?" she asked, looking up at him.

"Then you get to pick the place of the date."

"Oh, no. I don't think so Toby. If I win, you promise to never speak to me again. How's that?" Becca slammed the car door and the little engine roared to life. As she drove away, Toby set his chin and watched her taillights fade in the distance.

"Well then Becca, I most certainly *won't* be losing," he muttered to the dark night.

CHAPTER THREE

The grandstand was filling up with spectators for the horse pulling competition. Becca sat half-way up in the covered, bleacher-style seats surrounded by others from her 4-H club. She took a deep breath and stared out at the sun just beginning to set beyond the Rattlesnake Hills. Becca knew that Atlanta, Michigan was mid-America nowhere to most people, but she had to believe there wasn't a fairgrounds in the United States that had a prettier view. The beauty of the familiar landscape helped ease some of the hurt that still lingered after losing the championship to Toby earlier in the afternoon.

Huge horse trailers were parked around the perimeter of the arena below, their owners unloading the massive draft horses that would be competing to see which team could pull the most weight. Becca looked over each pair with a critical eye, determining which team she would root for. Her heart plummeted when she saw Toby climbing the bleacher steps, taking them two at a time.

"Hey guys, what's up?" Toby greeted, plopping himself down next to Becca.

"You come to rub it in?" Becca groused, scooting away from the hip that was pressing a little too close to her own.

"Rub what in, Bec?" Toby asked, his eyes shining with innocence. "Oh, are you talking about the championship? The fact that you weren't quite able to dethrone me?"

Becca bit down hard on her lip and resisted the urge to turn and slap the self-satisfied look right off Toby's face.

"Too bad about that one tiny little point that separated us, huh?" Toby continued. "Guess God must have been watching the sparrows during that last class. But hey, reserve grand champion isn't anything to sneeze at, you know. And if you have to come in second place, better to do it to real winners like me and Rocky."

"Oh look, there's Bobby!" Becca jumped up and stuck her pinky fingers in her mouth, splitting the air with a shrill whistle. "Bobby!!" She windmilled her arms in the air. The young man walking behind a huge team of Belgian draft horses looked up into the stands and smiled. Becca careened down the bleachers to the fence that separated the spectators from the arena.

"Hey Bobby," she greeted somewhat breathlessly. She could almost feel Toby's eyes burning a hole in the back of her t-shirt. She glanced over her shoulder to verify her instincts were right on target. With a little smile she turned back to the young man with his

Winning Becca

tousled blond hair. He was wearing a faded orange t-shirt under a pair of old-fashioned bib overalls. "I didn't think you were competing again this year."

"Changed my mind." Bobby gave a self-conscious shrug. "How'd you do this year?"

"Second over-all," Becca answered flatly.

"Toby again?" Bobby asked, his eyes scanning the stands.

"Yep. What can I say? Will you have time for a lemonade after the pull? If you win, I'll even buy."

"Sounds good." The horses shook their heads impatiently. "Gotta go. Wish me luck."

"Luck," Becca whispered. She turned and climbed back into the stands, satisfied to see that Toby no longer wore his haughty smirk.

"Was that really necessary?" he asked after she had settled back onto the hard bleacher seat.

"What?"

"All that. Bobby!" he mimicked in a high-pitched voice, waving his arms in the air. "As if the two of you were long-lost lovers. It's horrible of you to play the poor hick like that."

"Bobby is not a poor hick, as you so rudely put it. And I'm not playing him. We're friends, not that it's any business of yours. We're going to meet after the pull. Maybe go on a few rides, have some lemonade. You know, have fun together," Becca goaded.

"But what about our date?"

"The bump-and-run isn't until tomorrow night. You won the grand champion ribbon and trophy, Toby, but you didn't win me. It would do you well to remember it." Becca set her jaw and focused on the dirt being stirred up in the arena.

"You're pouting," Toby accused, bumping his shoulder lightly against hers.

"You're bragging," Becca returned, pulling away.

Just then the loudspeaker hummed to life, splitting the air with the screech of feedback. Becca clapped her hands over her ears.

"Man, when are they going to get that thing fixed?" she complained, shaking her head to clear the ringing in her ears.

"Ladies and gentlemen, welcome to the Montmorency County Fair and the draft horse pulling contest. The fair queen and her court will be coming around accepting donations that will offset the cost of this event. If you care to donate, see one of these lovely ladies."

Becca watched as Melissa Mehan entered the grandstand. A glittering crown sat upon her sun-streaked blond hair. A silk sash was draped over a midriff-baring top that left enough of Melissa's belly exposed to make Becca uncomfortable. She was followed by a group of girls ranging in age from thirteen to eighteen, each wearing a sash designating them as part of the queen's court. Each girl carried a coffee can with a slit cut in the plastic lid. Melissa's eyes scanned the crowd. She smiled and started up the steps.

"Uh-oh Toby, looks like the queen has found some honey," Becca said, grinning.

"Would you like to make a donation?" Melissa asked, stopping at the end of their row of seats. Her tanned tummy was right at Toby's eye level. She held out the can, her eyes never once resting on Becca. Instead her gaze latched onto Toby as if he were a life preserver and she a drowning woman.

"Sure, I'm in." Becca dug into her jeans and pulled out some change. She reached over Toby to drop the money through the slot. It plinked as the coins hit the bottom of the can. "Come on, Toby." She elbowed him in the chest. "Ante up."

"Congratulations on the championship, Toby," Melissa said in a breathy voice as Toby lifted his hip from the bleacher seat and pulled out his wallet. "If you want to celebrate later..."

"That's an excellent idea, Toby!" Becca agreed, eliciting a confused look from Melissa. Toby swung his eyes toward Becca. She saw pure displeasure in their brown depths which only increased her own level of satisfaction. "After the pull you and Melissa should go hit the midway to celebrate your victory. But I must warn you." Becca leaned around Toby and met Melissa's hopeful blue eyes, speaking in a stage whisper. "He's got romance on the brain."

"Miss! Oh Miss!" someone called from farther up in the grandstands.

"I have to go. See you later, Toby." Melissa continued to climb the bleacher steps.

Becca fell over. Laying on her side on the hard bleacher seat, she clutched her stomach, laughing until a sharp slap on her backside had her rocketing up-right.

"Hey!" she complained.

"Serves you right!" Toby glared at her. "That was not funny."

"That was hilarious," Becca disagreed, as another fit of laughter bubbled up. "Serves *you* right. Toby and Melissa sitting in a tree," she sing-songed. "K-I-S-S-I-N-G."

"Geez Bec," Toby stood. "When you are you going to grow up?" He stomped off down the bleachers, shoulders stiff.

"Not today," Becca answered with a giggle as she watched Toby push through the incoming crowd to the exit. "Not today."

"Why does she have to be so stubborn?" Toby asked, running a brush over Rocky's gleaming, dapple-grey hide. The horse didn't need currying, but Toby felt the need to work off his agitation. "She knows darn well that Melissa's been chasing my tail since the sixth grade. I swear sometimes I could throttle that girl."

"I know the feeling."

Toby looked up to see Tyler McGillis standing outside the stall gate. He was dressed in dark blue pants and t-shirt, the white tri-township rescue logo emblazoned on the breast. A two-way radio was clipped to the shoulder. In his arms he held a little girl with dark, wispy hair in braids that were unraveling. Tyler's wife, Emma, stood beside him, smiling. Another couple that Toby vaguely recognized stood just beyond the stall.

"You Dr. Doolittle now?" Tyler asked with a grin. Toby shook his head.

"Just blowing off steam," he answered with a shrug.

"Congratulations on the grand championship," Emma said. "Four years in a row, that's pretty impressive."

"Thanks. Becca gave me a run for my money, that's for sure. It really was just a fluke that I came out on top this year. We were awfully close in the points."

"Can I pet the horsy?" The little girl asked.

"Can Tiffany pet your horse?" Emma asked. "She's been wanting to pet all the animals and it's driving her nuts that all the signs say don't touch."

"Sure." Toby reached out and unlatched the gate. "Bring her on in. I just picked the stall, so you don't have to worry about stepping in anything. Rocky's gentle as a lamb, aren't you boy?" Toby rubbed the horse's face lovingly.

Tyler entered the stall. Tiffany reached out to run her fingers through Rocky's snowy mane, then hesitantly touched his withers.

"He's soft," she whispered.

"Here, you want to brush him?" Toby asked, holding out the soft bristled brush he had been using. Tiffany took the brush from him and awkwardly ran it over the horse's back. Rocky stood still as a statue, his training evident. "She can sit on him if she wants to," Toby offered.

"Oh no, that's quite alright." Tyler took the brush from Tiffany's hand and gave it back to Toby.

"Maybe some other time. Thanks, Toby. Tiffany, tell Toby thank you."

"Thank you," the little girl repeated obediently. The two moved out of the stall and back into the center aisle of the barn. Toby followed, latching the gate securely.

"You know my brother, Trevor?" Tyler asked, pointing to the couple standing with Emma. "And his wife, Kelly."

"I've seen you around." Toby nodded and held out his hand. "Nice to meet you."

"I'm still curious about the girl you want to throttle," Trevor said, giving Toby's hand a firm shake.

"Yeah, well, it's not important." Toby waved a hand dismissively.

As if reading his mind, Tyler asked, "Have you seen Becca around?"

Toby chewed the inside of his cheek. "She's over at the horse pull," he answered curtly. Probably whooping and hollering for Bobby Fitzgerald, he added silently, jealousy gnawing at his gut.

"Isn't she good friends with Violet Compton?"

"Yeah, why?"

"I heard over the radio she went into labor. Must have been some sort of complication because they took her by ambulance to Alpena Regional. I thought Becca would want to know so she could be praying."

"I'll pass the message along, if I run into her." Toby turned to put the brush away in his tack box as the two couples left the barn. "And if she's with Bobby I just may throttle *him*," he muttered.

Toby waited until he was sure the horse pull was over before heading out of the barn to the midway. He carefully avoided the entrance to the grandstand arena, not wanting to chance running into Melissa Mehan and her royal court. The last thing he wanted was to have Melissa attached to him like a barnacle on the bottom of a boat.

The sun had set, leaving only a faint, rosy glow on the western horizon. The midway blazed with electric lights, the air thumping with the music that blared from strategically placed speakers. Toby cautiously scanned the crowd, ready to duck behind the nearest cover if Melissa appeared.

"Well, if it isn't the superstar of the show ring." A hand clamped down on Toby's shoulder and spun him around, bringing him face to face with several other boys from his Thundering Hooves 4-H club.

"What's up guys?" Toby asked, exchanging a series of handshakes and slaps with the group.

"Nothing much, Tob," Brad Archer, who had his herd of prized dairy cows at the fair, answered for the group. "We're just hanging out, looking for some action. What's the stud of the stable doing cruising the midway solo? Thought you would have a groupie on each arm tonight after your big win."

"Yeah, Toby," Heath Everett chimed in. "You know Melissa Mehan would give up her royal robes for you anytime." The boys snickered and slapped each other's shoulders.

"Lay off guys," Toby commanded. "You know what I think about her royal highness."

"We also know who you've got your eye on, but you don't have a snowball's chance." Brad shook his head sadly.

"I thought Becca was gonna explode like an IED when the point totals were announced," Mike Newhouse said with a chuckle.

"Now that would have been fun to see," Heath agreed with a laugh. "Would serve the stuck up witch right."

"Hey." Toby's hand shot out, grabbing Heath by the front of his t-shirt. "You watch your mouth."

"Sorry, Toby, sorry man." Heath grabbed Toby's wrist but Toby refused to loosen his grip.

"Toby, let go man." Brad pried the two apart. Toby took a step back, his blazing eyes still pinned on Heath.

"Geez Heath, you got a death wish or something?" Mike muttered.

"I think we all need to chill out," Brad observed. "I've got something in my camper that will help us do just that." He headed for the area behind the animal barns where many of the fair exhibitors were camped for the week. "You coming Toby?" Brad stopped and looked over his shoulder. From the corner of his eye Toby spied Becca walking up the midway, Bobby at her side.

"Nah, you know how I feel about that stuff."

"Suit yourself." The three boys moved away through the crowd.

Winning Becca

When they had disappeared, Toby backed into the deep shadows created by the side of the funhouse. From his hiding spot he could clearly see Becca and Bobby as they stopped before one of the carnival booths. The roadie behind the makeshift counter pointed to a large stuffed puppy hanging above his head. Becca and Bobby exchanged a glance, laughed and then Bobby dug into the pocket of his overalls. Toby rolled his eyes. Several minutes later the two strolled away from the game, Becca holding a much smaller stuffed animal. As Toby watched, Bobby reached out and put a possessive hand on Becca's back. Stifling an oath, Toby stepped from the shadows and crept up behind the couple, fighting the urge to do just what he had threatened, throttle Bobby Fitzgerald.

"Becca!"

Becca hesitated at the sound of her name, then recognizing the voice she kept moving forward.

"Becca!" Toby called again.

With a sigh and a roll of her eyes, Becca stopped and did an abrupt about-face.

"What?" she asked in exasperation.

Bobby turned also, standing shoulder to shoulder with her. She took perverse pleasure at the shadow of jealousy that flitted across Toby's face. Becca made an exaggerated show of leaning around Toby to the left and then the right.

"Where's Melissa?" she asked, staring at Toby with wide-eyed innocence. "I thought the two of you would be off in some corner celebrating. Her crown and sash, your ribbon and trophy. Sounds like a winning combination to me. Do you need me and Bobby to help you look for her?" Becca stood on tip-toe to scan the crowd, searching each face. "Hey, I think I see her over there." She threw up an arm, ready to call out Melissa's name. Toby quickly yanked her hand down.

"Don't even think about it," he warned, standing nearly chest-to-chest with Becca. His strong fingers encircled her wrist.

"Let go," she commanded.

"Back off, Sinclair." Bobby wedged himself in front of Becca, forcing Toby to release his grip. Becca stepped out from behind his broad back in time to see Toby draw back a tightly balled fist.

"Toby! Don't be stupid."

"Oh, come on Becca, let him take a swing at me." Bobby, who was nearly a head taller and a good deal thicker across the shoulders and chest, grinned at Toby.

"Do you really want to mar your perfect winning record by getting in a fight?" Becca hissed. Toby unclenched his fist. She smiled reassuringly at the people who walked around them, casting curious looks at Toby and Bobby. She reached out and grabbed Toby by the arm. Yanking him off the midway, Becca dragged him behind a trailer selling elephant ears and corndogs. "What is your problem?" she demanded. "Can't you take a joke?"

"Oh, was there a joke?" Toby asked, rocking back on his heels. He crossed his arms and tilted his head to the side. "I don't recall hearing anyone tell a joke.

By the way," he said, motioning toward Bobby with his chin. "How'd the bumpkin do in the horse pull?"

Becca rolled her eyes. "Now who's the one who needs to grow up?" she asked. Toby just glowered at her. Becca squeezed the stuffed animal in her hand so hard that had it been a real kitten, she would have strangled the life right out of it. Her heart beat in time with the music blaring from a nearby speaker.

"You're a jerk, you know that? I should have let Bobby deck you." Becca turned to leave, throwing over her shoulder, "He came in second, same as me. Maybe that's why we get along so well." She headed back toward the midway.

"Becca, wait!"

Becca hesitated, taking a deep breath before turning back around to face Toby. She hitched a lock of hair back behind her ear.

"What, Toby? What do you want? You beat me in the show ring, now why can't you just leave me alone?"

"What about our date tomorrow night?"

"You have got to be kidding me." Becca shook her head slowly. "After the way you acted today, you still expect me to go to the bump-and-run with you?"

"We made a bet. You can't welsh on it."

"Oh, can't I? We didn't even shake hands, so it wasn't a real bet. You've got your grand championship, why can't you be happy with that? That's what you wanted, wasn't it? Go find your friends and celebrate but *leave me alone*." She spun on her heel and headed back to Bobby, who was waiting patiently by the merry-go-round."

"Wait!" Toby called after her.

"I'm through talking to you, Toby," Becca answered, not slowing her pace. "If you bother me again I'm going to find Nate and this time I'm not going to be kidding." She reached Bobby and purposefully put her arm through his.

"I've got a message for you from Tyler," Toby spoke from behind them. "It's about Violet."

Tilting her head back, Becca looked at the bright stars in the velvety sky. She counted ten stars before turning once more to face Toby.

"What about her?" she asked, her voice strained.

"Tyler said he heard over the radio that she went into labor. He said there must have been some sort of complications because they took her by ambulance to Alpena."

"What kind of complications?" Becca asked, her annoyance replaced in a heartbeat by concern.

"Don't know." Toby shrugged. "He didn't say. Just said to tell you so you could be praying." Becca searched his eyes, which seemed sincere.

"Okay, well, thanks. I'll be praying. But there's nothing else I can do for her, so let's go, Bobby. I still owe you that lemonade." Becca tugged on Bobby's arm and he fell into step beside her. She could feel Toby's glare burning a hole in her back and knew if he had superpowers that both she and Bobby would have been vaporized by now.

"You okay?" Bobby asked. His blue eyes shone with concern.

"Yeah, I'm fine."

"I take it you and Toby have butted heads a few times this week, huh?"

Becca sighed. "Toby and I have been butting heads our whole lives." She looked down at the gravel crunching beneath her sandals and felt an odd sense of regret that she couldn't understand.

"This Violet that went into labor, she a friend of yours?" Bobby stopped at the lemonade stand and reached into his pocket. Becca put a hand on his arm.

"It's supposed to be on me, remember?"

"Only if I won," Bobby answered, smiling down at her. Becca couldn't help but smile in return. He passed the bills across the counter and took two large cups of lemonade, handing one to Becca.

"Vi's my best friend. I hope she's okay." Becca worried her lip. "Complications, that doesn't sound too good, does it?"

"Nope."

"Here. Let's stop and say a prayer right now, then I'll feel better." Becca stopped in the middle of the midway and closed her eyes.

Dear Lord, be with Violet right now. Be with the baby and with the doctors. Let everything be okay, in Jesus' name, amen, she prayed silently.

"Okay," she said, opening her eyes. The bright lights of the fair still shone all around her. Her heart felt lighter.

"Just like that, huh?" Bobby was still grinning.

"Yep, just like that." Becca smiled in return. "Hey, what are you doing tomorrow night? You want to come to the bump-and run?"

"Sounds like a plan," Bobby replied in his easy manner.

"Good. Sounds like a plan to me, too."

CHAPTER FOUR

Everything was packed. The field that served as a parking lot was packed, the midway was packed, the grandstands of the arena were packed to overflowing. The bump-and-run, part stock car race, part demolition derby, was by far the biggest draw of the entire fair. Toby sat at the very top of the bleacher seats, close enough to touch the iron rafters that held up the metal roof over the grandstand. It was the only place where you could actually see what was going on in the arena below. The sky was heavy with clouds and there was a chill in the wind that spoke of fall fast approaching.

Brad, Heath and Mike sat shoulder to shoulder, hunched into heavy, hooded sweatshirts. They each held a 20 ounce bottle cradled in their hands. Toby knew the bottles held more than cola. He had gotten a whiff of the sweet smell of liquor on their breath. They were his friends, but Toby honestly didn't know why he hung around with these three. Besides 4-H and sports, what did they have in common? He wasn't wild and rebellious like they were, living on the edge, experimenting with drugs and alcohol. Toby knew that stuff led to a dead end. He wanted more out of life than that.

With his back pressed against the cement block wall behind him, Toby stared glumly at the crowd below, unconsciously searching for golden red hair. He couldn't believe how badly he had blown it with Becca. How had he managed to screw things up so completely? He heaved a heavy sigh and thumped his head back against the wall in frustration. He had looked forward to this night all week and now...

"Here Toby, have a drink." Brad held out the pop bottle.

"No thanks." Toby gave his head a little shake and dug his hands deeper into the pockets of his green and white letterman jacket.

"Hey, isn't that your girl coming up the steps?" Brad asking, pointing with the neck of his bottle at two people pushing their way up the bleacher steps, like trout trying to swim upstream.

Becca, wearing a fuzzy blue sweater and low slung jeans, made her way slowly up each step carrying a box of popcorn in one hand and a hot pretzel in the other. Bobby was close behind, trying to keep two paper cups full of lemonade from spilling. Toby chewed the inside of his cheek.

"Seems like everyone knows she's your girl, except her. And maybe Bobby Fitzgerald," Brad continued with a chuckle.

"Shove it, Brad," Toby growled. He stared off across the dark arena, trying not to watch the two as they searched for empty seats. But his eyes were drawn back to Becca, like a compass searching for true north.

"Lighten up, Tob." Brad lightly slapped Toby's knee and took a swig from his bottle. After a quick swallow he continued, "I don't get it. Why tie yourself up in knots over a girl who doesn't want you, when you've got Melissa practically throwing herself at your feet?"

Toby had asked himself that very same question more than once. For six years now Melissa had made it plain that she thought the sun rose and set on Toby's shoulders. On the other hand, he and Becca had been continuous rivals for everything from blue ribbons at the fair to scholastic achievement awards. They had constantly locked horns as they tried to best each other. Even the church youth group had turned into a competition of who could raise the most money for missions, or who could bring the most friends. Both girls came from good, stable families. Melissa was pretty, in a flashy "look at me" sort of way, while Becca seemed completely oblivious to her own beauty. Why was he so set on winning Becca? Why didn't he just give in and ask Melissa out? Toby knew she would be more than willing, in more ways than one.

"Maybe it has something to do with man's primordial instincts for hunting and conquering," he finally answered Brad's question.

"Huh?" Brad gave him a blank stare.

"You know, the excitement of the hunt. Melissa's been after me since sixth grade. What fun is there in

Winning Becca

that? There's no challenge. It's not really winning if the other side surrenders before the contest begins. Becca, on the other hand, has presented a constant challenge. She's a worthy opponent. When I finally win it will be a hard-fought victory but worth it."

"You're whacked." Brad shook his head in disgust. "What sane man goes out hunting when there's fresh meat laid right at his doorstep?"

"Maybe I want more than just meat. I want the whole banquet. All those delicious delicacies they serve at royal weddings. Melissa may be fresh meat, but Becca's a whole feast."

"You really are whacked." Brad took another sip from his bottle. "You been reading too many Hallmark cards or something."

"I just know what I want, that's all." Toby got up and slapped Brad on the shoulder. "I'm the reigning grand champ. I believe in winning and this is one contest I plan on coming out on top of." Brad gave him a lecherous smile, making Toby regret his choice of words. "Just save my seat for a minute."

Becca and Bobby had found seats several rows down from the top of the grandstand. Toby took the steps two at a time then squeezed his way down the row of seated spectators.

"Scooch over," he said, nudging Becca's shoulder. She looked up, scowling. Bobby, too, turned his head and looked at Toby with a malevolent glare.

"What do you want, Toby?" Becca asked, staying firmly planted in her seat.

"I just want to ask you a question. I'm not going to cause any trouble, Scout's honor."

"You were never a Boy Scout and I highly doubt you have any honor," Becca replied, taking a slow draw on the straw in her lemonade.

"Come on, Bec. Just scoot over before I start making a scene." With a grimace, Becca scooted closer to Bobby, leaving just enough room for Toby to straddle the bench seat, facing her. "How's Violet?"

Becca slid him a look from the corner of her eye. "She's fine. I went to see her this morning."

"What'd she have?"

"A monkey. What do you think she had?"

"Ha ha, very funny." Toby smiled at the joke. "I meant did she have a boy or a girl?"

"A girl. She named her Nicole Anne. She's beautiful and so tiny!" Becca became more animated and turned to look square at Toby. Her blue eyes shone, making Toby's heart jump into his throat. "She's got these teeny little seashell hands. And she's got Vi's little pointed chin and this goose down hair. I even got to hold her. I don't think I even got to hold Brendan when he wasn't even a day old yet."

"Everything's okay then?" Toby asked, feeling warmed from head to toe by Becca's excitement. "There weren't any complications?"

"Well, there were." Becca nodded and took another sip of lemonade. "I guess Violet went into labor and was walking around the house and her blood pressure must have dropped and she passed out. Her mom called 9-1-1 and when the paramedics got there, her heart beat was really erratic and the baby's was, too. They were scared the baby's heartbeat had dropped too much so they called the ambulance and took her to the hospital. But God answered prayer and everything turned out okay, she didn't even have to have a C-section, so that's good."

"Was the proud papa there for all of this?"

"No," Becca spit out in clear disgust. "He never showed up for the birth, and he wasn't there this morning when I was there. Vi was pretty distraught over it. I couldn't very well tell her good riddance to bad rubbish, but believe me, I was thinking it. It turns my stomach to think of that precious baby being raised by Vince."

"Maybe he'll stay out of the picture for good," Toby suggested.

"Maybe. I think it would be for the best. But that's just my opinion." Becca shrugged.

Motors began to rev in the staging area outside the arena, making conversation impossible.

"Well, I gotta get back to the guys," Toby leaned in close and yelled into Becca's ear. She glanced at him and he motioned to the top of the bleachers. "Have fun!"

"Yeah, you too," she yelled back.

Toby stood and made his way back down the row and up the steps to where Brad waited. Brad, resting his leg up on the bleacher seat, dropped his foot to the floorboards to make room for Toby.

"What was that all about?" he leaned in to yell above the roar of car engines.

Toby smiled. "Just putting out a little bait is all," he answered, tapping his temple. "A smart hunter knows what kind of bait will lure his prey closer."

Winning Becca

Becca stood and watched the melee of cars as they sloughed around the arena, over the mogul humps built up around the track, into each other and the outside wall. Every person in the grandstand was on their feet, making it impossible to see if you sat down. Between the roar of the engines and the screaming of the spectators, talking was out of the question unless you wanted to yell yourself hoarse.

Popping a few more kernels of popcorn into her mouth, she glanced up at Bobby. He raised both fists in the air and let out a primeval yell as a beat up, black car t-boned an equally dented white El Camino. An odd sense of guilt crept up her spine. She *was* supposed to come with Toby. No matter how angry he made her, she shouldn't have gone back on her word.

Not that she really had given her word, Becca argued with herself. And if *she* had won the championship, she knew there was no way on God's green earth that Toby would have stood by the bet and never spoken to her again. Unfortunately. He seemed to like nothing better than trying to get her goat.

Becca slowly glanced over her shoulder, risking a quick peek at the uppermost bleacher seat. Toby stood, along with his friends, his eyes glued to the action taking place in the arena below. She quickly turned to face the front, breathing a sigh of relief. Toby seemed to have forgotten that she and Bobby even existed.

"Praise the Lord for small kindnesses," she whispered to herself.

When the race was over, Becca plopped down on the hard wooden bleacher seat, watching the waves

Winning Becca

of people hurrying for the exit. She saw no reason to rush. Funneling this crowd through the exit gate would take awhile. A cold wind smelling of rain gusted up under the roof of the grandstand. Becca shivered.

"You okay?" Bobby asked. He propped one booted foot on the bleacher and leaned over, resting a forearm on his jean-covered knee.

"Yeah." Becca nodded and rubbed her arms. "Just cold."

"Here." Bobby unzipped his thick, hooded sweatshirt and shrugged out of it, placing it around Becca's shoulders. It was warm from his body and smelled like Old Spice. Becca gratefully clasped it closer.

"Thanks." She gave him a smile and admired his bulging biceps beneath his t-shirt. "But now you're going to be cold."

"Nah." Bobby shook his head and smiled. "You gotta remember I'm a farmer, used to working outdoors in the wind, rain, snow or heat. Cows don't milk themselves, remember?"

Becca scanned the thinning crowd. She caught a glimpse of green and white heading down the steps and looked over just in time to see Toby raise a hand in farewell. She didn't wave in return. Bobby straightened and looked around.

"Looks like everybody's just about out. Guess it's safe to leave now. You want to go on some rides before I take you home?"

"No." Becca shook her head. "It's too cold and I think I'm about faired out."

"Okay. I don't suppose you want to head over to Hillman to the Dairy Queen? We could get a hot fudge sundae."

"That sounds good," Becca agreed. Bobby held out his hand. She put her own into it and he hefted her up from the seat, draping an arm over her shoulders as they clomped in unison down the steps. Becca knew she should protest his arm around her, but it felt nice. Warm and safe. So she let him keep it there.

As they exited the arena another strong gust of wind blew up, bringing with it a few sprinkles of rain.

"This will put a damper on the midway," Bobby commented, leading the way toward the parking lot.

"Yeah, I guess the race got over just in time, huh?"

The sprinkles quickly turned into a steady rain. Becca lengthened her strides to keep up with Bobby. She yanked the hood of his sweatshirt over her head just as the rain turned into a downpour. They ran the last few steps to Bobby's battered Chevy truck.

"Get in," Bobby ordered, yanking the door open for her. Becca gladly followed orders, climbing in and slamming the door. She turned her head to watch Bobby go around the back of the truck. He paused at the rear tire on the driver's side. Becca heard him spew out an oath as he slammed a fist down on the side rail of the truck bed.

"What? What is it?" Becca opened the door and hopped down into the squishy grass. "What's wrong?" she asked again.

"Flat tire," Bobby answered shortly. "Get back in the truck. You're going to be soaked to the skin."

Becca did as she was told. Moments later Bobby jumped in the driver's side door. A gust of cold rain followed him into the truck before he could slam the door closed.

"No point in trying to change it in this deluge," he said. "I'll wait a few minutes and see if this blows over."

His t-shirt clung to his skin, outlining the contour of every muscle. A deliciously foreign sensation curled up from Becca's insides, setting her heart to tripping and warming her from the inside out.

"Here, have your sweatshirt back," Becca offered. Was that her voice that was quavering? she wondered as she swung the sweatshirt off her shoulders and held it out to Bobby.

"That's okay, I've got another one in here somewhere."

Bobby knelt and rummaged around in the back seat. He came up with a t-shirt in one hand and a jean jacket in the other. Settling himself behind the steering wheel, he wiped his face with the dry shirt, then leaned forward and slowly peeled the wet one over his head.

Becca watched, entranced as Bobby's bare back was exposed, then his chest as he reached over to toss the sopping shirt into the back seat. He was a massive expanse of well-defined muscle all the way down to the waistband of his jeans. An odd, shimmering feeling set Becca's stomach to quivering.

She had never been in such close proximity to a half-naked male who wasn't family before.

She couldn't turn away as Bobby pulled the dry shirt over his head and covered what Becca decided was an extremely nice chest. Much nicer than those guys that graced the perfume ads in magazines. Her heart continued to thump heavily as she watched Bobby shrug his broad shoulders into the jean jacket. Becca shivered, but she wasn't entirely sure it was from the cold.

"I'd turn on the heater, but I don't have a whole lot of gas. I was running late to pick you up and didn't have time to stop. Figured I'd take care of it on the way home," Bobby explained. He held out a hand. "But if you come over here we can cuddle up real close and keep each other warm."

Their breath had steamed up the windows, adding to the feeling of isolation. Bobby's hand clasped her shoulder, encouraging her to scoot across the bench seat. The warmth of his fingers seeped through Becca's sweater. She stared at him, wide eyed. His blond hair stood in wet spikes all over his head. His blue eyes sparkled as lightening lit the sky. Becca's eyes fell to his lips and she felt the first sweet taste of temptation. Instinctively she leaned toward him. Bobby's arms drew her closer. Her hands found the hard plane of his chest as his lips descended on hers. Becca lost all perception of time and place as the kiss deepened.

Thunder pealed loudly overhead, startling her back to reality. Becca automatically pulled back.

Pushing away from Bobby's chest she slid across the seat and hugged the door.

"I don't think this is such a good idea." Becca watched the rain streaming down the windshield and tried to catch her breath. The cab seemed to be filled with the roar of the storm and her own heartbeat.

"Making out's always a good idea," Bobby replied. "Haven't you ever parked out in the woods somewhere and made out with a guy?"

"Um, that would be a no," Becca answered, sparing him a short glance. "I'm not that kind of girl."

Oh, but she could be, Becca realized, horrified. A picture of Bobby's naked chest flashed before her eyes and she could once more feel the sensation of his lips pressed to hers. Give her a few more minutes and a little more coaxing and she most certainly could be.

"Wow. I'm impressed, Becca, really." Bobby settled himself back behind the steering wheel. "I respect you. Not too many girls make it all the way through high school untouched. I suppose I should apologize for kissing you like that," he sounded sincere. Becca's heart tripped at his lopsided grin. "It just seemed like the right thing to do. But I don't want you thinking I've just been waiting to jump your bones or something."

Oh, Bobby, Becca thought, would you still respect me if you knew how much I wanted you to do just that?

Someone rapped on the passenger side window, making Becca jump. She reached for the crank and rolled the window down.

Winning Becca

"Something wrong?" Toby asked. Relief made Becca's heart take wing. She had never been so glad to see Toby in her life. Rain had plastered his hair to his head.

"Flat tire," Bobby answered. Draping a wrist over the steering wheel, he leaned across the bench seat toward the window. "I'm waiting for the rain to slow to change it."

"Don't think it's suppose to stop for awhile," Toby said, glancing quickly at the sky and back at Becca. Lightening flashed. Thunder boomed. Becca's teeth chattered as rain blew in the open window. "You look like you're freezing," Toby observed.

"Bobby's low on gas, he didn't want to run the engine to get the cab warmed up." Becca realized she hadn't even felt the cold until now.

"Here." Toby reached into his pocket and pulled out a set of keys. He dangled them in front of Becca. "Run over to my Bronco." He motioned with his chin across the parking lot. "Start the engine and get yourself warmed up."

Becca tossed a quick glance at Bobby before grabbing the keys. Toby yanked open the door and she nearly tumbled out on top of him. Slipping and sliding in the wet, muddy grass, Becca ran across the field toward Toby's car. With trembling fingers she fit the key into the door, barely able to see past the rain streaming over her eyes. Within seconds she had the engine running, the heater cranked up full-blast. Rubbing her hands together for warmth she peered all around, looking for something she could dry off with. A few stray, tan napkins littered the floorboards. Becca picked them up gingerly and shook them before wiping them across her face.

The driver's side door opened and Toby climbed inside. He took one look at Becca and began peeling off his coat.

"Here." He tossed it her way. "It's dry on the inside and you look like you're about to freeze to death."

Becca's teeth clattered together in response.

"What about Bobby?" she asked, shaking as she peeled off her sopping sweater and pushed her arms into the warm sleeves of Toby's coat.

"I told him I would take you home."

For once, Becca didn't argue.

Toby drove slowly through the storm toward the Weaver farm. His headlights cut a dim swath through the darkness as the wipers struggled to keep up with the downpour. Something was definitely wrong. Becca hadn't even given him sass about driving her home. She sat huddled in his coat looking small and defenseless, her hair a lank, wet mass around her face. A dull ache settled in Toby's chest.

"So, what was going on back there?"

"Nothing!" Becca answered a little too quickly, refusing to meet his eyes. "Bobby's truck had a flat and we were waiting for the rain to slow so he could change it. Wait a minute." She turned to glare at Toby. "Did you have something to do with this? Did you slash Bobby's tire?"

"Absolutely not!" Toby denied. "You think I want you steaming up the windows in someone else's truck?"

"What's that supposed to mean?"

"Nothing." Toby chewed the inside of his cheek. Jealousy burned like acid in his stomach at the thought of Becca making out with someone else. "It was just the kind of situation that a guy would take advantage of, that's all. Stuck in close quarters alone in the dark."

"Well, Bobby wasn't taking advantage of me or the situation," Becca defended. She crossed her arms and stared, stone-faced, out the windshield.

"If nothing happened then why did you jump out of that truck like there was a skunk in the cab and it had just raised its tail?"

"You exaggerate."

"You know if he touched you I'd beat the tar out of him, right?"

Becca snorted. "You couldn't beat the tar out of Bobby. He's twice as big as you."

"Now who's exaggerating?" Toby asked.

"I'm not exaggerating. Bobby's arms are as big around as your thighs."

"Oh ho, you been busy checking out my legs, Bec?" Toby grinned.

"Not in a million, bazillion years," Becca grumbled, resting her head against the side window.

"You still haven't answered my question," Toby prodded.

"For the love of all that is holy!" Becca exclaimed, slapping a hand down on the cracked, vinyl seat. "I told you nothing happened!"

"Look, I may not be next in line for the FBI, but I'm not a complete moron. The past few times when you've had a choice between me and Bobby, you chose Bobby without batting an eyelash. Now tonight you come barreling out of his truck cab like you got a momma black bear chasing you. Something happened, so do us both a favor and stop lying about it."

"I'm not lying." She passed a weary hand over her face, tucking stray strands of hair behind her ear. "Nothing happened. We, uh, we just…"

"You just what?" Toby asked between clenched teeth, dreading the answer.

"We just kissed, that's it."

A volcano erupted inside Toby, spewing hot lava into his veins.

"That good-for-nothing, stupid farmer!"

"Hey!" Becca sat up straighter and glared across the seat. "My daddy and my brother-in-law are both farmers. You watch your mouth!"

"I don't care. I should break his arm for touching you!"

"Bobby didn't touch me, not in the way you're imagining," Becca defended. "And he apologized for the kiss. He said he respects me. I don't think he'd ever hurt me. Not in a million, bazillion years." She grew quiet, her face turned away from him. Thunder rolled overhead. "You really want the truth, Toby?" she finally asked, still peering out the window. When she turned back to look at him, Toby saw the fear and confusion in her eyes. "When I got out of that truck in such a hurry, I wasn't running from Bobby, I was running from myself."

"What's that supposed to mean?" Toby's hands tightened on the steering wheel. He waited for her answer, unsure if he wanted to hear it or not.

"Have you ever made out with a girl?"

"What kind of question is that?"

"Just answer me. Have you ever parked out in the woods and made out?"

"You know I haven't," Toby answered, wanting to tell Becca she was the only one he would ever want to do that with, anyway. "And I know for a fact neither have you."

"How do you know that for a fact?" she challenged.

"I just do, that's all."

"Well, you're right." Becca sighed heavily. "It never even crossed my mind until tonight. Tonight, with Bobby, I was tempted for the first time in my life."

A fist grabbed hold of Toby's gut and squeezed. He spared a glance toward Becca. She sat toying with the ribbed cuffs of his letterman jacket.

"It scared me," she whispered the admission and refused to meet Toby's eyes. "It would have been so easy to get carried away. I always thought I was different from Violet. Tonight I realized we aren't so different after all."

"Don't even say that!" Toby erupted, trying to erase the mental image of Becca getting carried away with Bobby Fitzgerald. The thought left him nauseous. "You and Violet are as different as night and day."

"No, we aren't." Becca shook her head sadly. "We're both human, both capable of making mistakes. The Bible calls it sin."

"Well, you didn't sin, right?" Toby insisted. "You said nothing happened except the kiss. I don't think kissing qualifies as a sin. Doesn't the Bible say that it isn't sin to be tempted, just sin if you give into it, right?"

"Yeah, something like that," Becca agreed quietly. Toby saw the glint of tears in her eyes.

"Then I say avoid the temptation. Stay away from Bobby Fitzgerald," he ordered.

"Oh ho, that would make you happy, wouldn't it?" Becca rose to the challenge. "You aren't the boss of me. I'm not about to stay away from Bobby because you said so."

"That's better." Toby smiled at her. "I like it better when you're arguing than when you're on the verge of tears."

Becca's eyes narrowed. "I really do hate you, you know that?" She flounced back against the seat.

"No you don't, you enjoy the game as much as I do."

"I don't know what you're talking about." Becca waved a dismissive hand.

"Yes you do. But seriously, Bec, you aren't going to go out with him again, are you?" Toby's heart remained suspended as he waited for her answer.

Becca's eyes glinted in the dark, but not because of tears this time. She grinned knowingly.

"Who knows, Toby. I just might."

Toby pulled into the Weaver's driveway and put the Bronco in park. Becca began to shrug out of his coat. Toby put a hand out to stop her.

"Keep it," he suggested. "It'll give me a reason to come back."

"Not in a million, bazillion years." Becca laid the coat on the seat between them and opened her door. "Thanks for the ride."

Quickly she slammed the door shut and hurried through the rain to the front porch of the farmhouse. Toby watched her disappear, chewing the inside of his cheek.

"Okay Becca," he spoke to the rain falling on the windshield. "You threw down the gauntlet and I'm accepting the challenge. There's no way on God's green earth that I'm gonna let you give into temptation with Bobby Fitzgerald."

He shifted into reverse and backed out of the driveway. He threw it into drive and the Bronco fishtailed on the muddy road as he stomped down hard on the gas. The rained drummed above his head as Toby drove home, contemplating the next step in capturing the heart of his prey.

CHAPTER FIVE

Becca sat at the scarred, wooden table in the farmhouse kitchen. Textbooks were spread around her, some laying open, some stacked on top of one another. In front of her was a spiral notebook, its blank page staring up at her accusingly. Sighing, Becca dropped her head onto her hands. College was certainly a lot harder than high school. Two weeks into it and she was already feeling swamped by homework. And math had never been her strong subject. Toby had bested her in it every year, no matter how hard she had studied.

Squaring her shoulders, Becca pulled the statistics book closer and read the problem again. She didn't know why she had allowed her counselor to talk her into taking this class. The woman had *promised* that statistics was easier than algebra. Becca now knew that was a flat-out lie. And why did she have to take all this math anyway, when she was majoring in early childhood education? Becca didn't think she would be teaching statistics to three-year-olds!

The graphing calculator sitting at her elbow had yet to be any help. She could go in the family room and ask her father for help, but his mathematical knowledge didn't extend much beyond bushels per acre. Becca glanced toward the phone. She could call Toby. He wasn't in her statistics class at Alpena Community College. Being a math whiz, he had chosen to take the much more difficult calculus class, having tested out of just about everything else. It really wasn't fair, Becca groused silently. Did God *have* to use up all the mathematical brain cells on Toby? Couldn't He have left just a few for Becca? Someday she was just going to have to accept the fact that Toby was better than her at just about everything. The thought left her grinding her teeth and reading the math problem again. She was bound and determined to get an A in this class, even if it killed her.

Light tapping sounded on the back door. Becca looked up, listening. The tapping came again. Rising from the table, Becca walked across the kitchen. She glanced into the family room. Her parents were oblivious, her father hidden behind the daily paper, her mother engrossed in the crossword puzzle. Curious, she headed for the back door.

The mud room at the back of the farmhouse held the usual assortment of muddy boots, barn coats, baseball caps and old buckets. Becca navigated through the maze to the back door at one end. She was surprised to see Violet, holding a baby carrier, standing on the step.

"Vi! What are you doing here?" Becca asked, holding the door open. "Come on in."

Winning Becca

"No." Violet shook her head and looked over her shoulder. There was a desperate gleam in her eyes. "I can't come in. I can't stay but a minute."

"Okay." Becca stepped out the door and closed it behind her. The night air held the chill of fall. Becca crossed her arms, hugging her sweater close. She glanced down at the baby seat. If there was a baby in there, Becca couldn't tell. The entire thing was covered with a fuzzy blanket. "Should you have the baby out in the night air like this?"

"I didn't have any choice. Becca, I, I need a favor."

"What kind of favor?"

"I need you to keep Nikki for a couple of days."

"Keep Nikki? Are you crazy? I can't! I've got class and..."

"I don't have any choice!" Violet interrupted. "Vince, he took off. I have to go after him, Becca. I have to convince him to come home so we can be a family! You're the only person I can trust."

"This is ridiculous, Vi. You don't need to be traipsing all over the state looking for that good-for-nothing Vince. He's bad news anyway. What do you care if he comes back or not? You and Nicole are better off without him." Becca's anger boiled over, chasing off the chill of the night.

"Don't say that! A baby is never better off without a father," Violet defended. "And Vince isn't bad news. I don't know why you hate him so much but..."

"For doing things just like this!" Becca spat. "He wasn't even there when Nikki was born, for Pete's sake!"

"But he's been real good with her since I came home from the hospital. I know he loves her. And he loves me, too. He's just scared right now, that's all. Becca, please," Violet pleaded. "I can't leave Nikki with my parents. My dad's drop-dead drunk most of the time. Last night he nearly set the house on fire. And my mom's not much better. You know about babies. You're real good with kids. That's what you're going to school for, right?"

"Which is why I can't keep her," Becca stressed. "I've got class, Vi. And on the weekends I'm working for Emma at the Spot of Tea. I don't have time to take care of a baby."

"It's just for a couple of days," Violet assured. She set the baby seat down on the brown grass then swung a diaper bag off her shoulder before backing away. "I have to do this, Becca, I just have to. You have to understand."

"Violet, don't you dare!" Becca warned, jumping off the concrete back step and rushing after Violet's retreating form. "Don't you leave this baby with me." Violet ignored her. "I'll call children's services, Vi, I swear I will. They'll take Nikki away from you, and then where will you be?"

"No you won't." Violet turned and gave Becca a half-hearted smile. "You won't call children's services. You're my only real friend. You wouldn't do that to me, and you wouldn't do that to Nikki. She needs her mommy, and her daddy. Together. That's why I'm doing this. To give Nikki the family she deserves. It will only be a couple of days. Vince went to his uncle's down near Detroit. I'll find him tonight. Who knows, we'll probably be home tomorrow."

"Violet, don't!" Becca held up a hand to stop Vi, but she had disappeared into the dark. A car door slammed. The baby began to whimper and wiggle in her seat. Becca sighed and looked up at the stars that were spread like sequins across the velvety night sky. "O Lord, help!"

Picking up the baby carrier in one hand and the diaper bag in the other, Becca marched up the porch steps, through the mud room and straight into the family room. Her mother looked up from the crossword puzzle book in her lap, her eyes going wide at the sight of the baby seat. Nicole picked that moment to let out a lusty bellow. David Weaver lowered his newspaper and stared at Becca across the expanse of the room.

"Did Violet stop in for a visit?" Mary asked.

"Not Violet, just Nikki," Becca answered, fury still clinging to her words. Mary Weaver raised an eyebrow in question. "Vi has gone off on some fool's errand to get Vince to come home. She expects me to take care of the baby until she gets back."

"But you've got school and work," Mary reminded.

"I know that, Mother," Becca snapped.

"Becca," the warning in her father's voice told Becca she had better watch her tone.

"I'm sorry," she quickly apologized. Setting the baby carrier on the floor, she knelt to unwrap the baby and lift her from the seat. A pacifier was tucked beneath the blankets. Cradling the baby in one arm,

Becca held the pacifier to her lips. Nicole immediately latched on and grew quiet. "I didn't mean to snap, Mom. I'm just mad, that's all. I told Vi I have class, and my job at the teashop. She wouldn't listen. She just set Nicole on the grass and walked away, as if that miserable Vince Schmidt is more important than her own child."

"Well then, I guess we'll just have to call children's services. They'll charge her with child abandonment," Mary said.

"We can't call until tomorrow, and Violet said they'll probably be back by then, anyway. But I've still got class in the morning. Could you take care of Nikki while I'm at school?" Becca asked, hopeful. The look on her mother's face told her the answer.

"Absolutely not. I've got to take care of the quilt shop and I've got five women coming to take the new class I'm offering. I can't teach quilting and take care of a newborn at the same time. Besides." Mary leveled her serious eyes on Becca. "Violet is *your* friend. I warned you over and over about associating with her, but you wouldn't listen. Now look at the pickle it's gotten you in. You're just going to have to figure out how to deal with it yourself."

"What about Rhonda?" David suggested, always diplomatic. "She's home during the day. I'm sure she'd be willing to help you out tomorrow, if it's only for one day."

"Thanks, Daddy." Becca went across the room and placed a kiss on her father's weathered cheek. "I'll go over there right now and ask her." This seemed the type of thing better explained in person than over the phone.

"And take the baby with you." Mary motioned toward the baby carrier. "I've done my time raising children."

Dismay filled Becca as she pulled into Wes and Rhonda's driveway to find Nate's Jeep parked there. She glanced in the rearview mirror at the infant carrier in the backseat. She couldn't let Nate know about Nicole. He would immediately insist on calling the authorities.

Before she could throw the car in reverse, Wes came out the front door. He casually trotted down the porch steps and over to Becca's car door. Slowly she rolled the window down.

"Hey, I thought I heard a car pull in. What are you doing just sitting out here?"

"Well, I, um…" Becca's fingers drummed the steering wheel. "I needed to talk to Rhonda, but I see you have company."

"That's okay, it's just Penny and Nate."

"No, I don't want to bother her if she's entertaining."

Wes barked out a laugh. "Entertaining? We aren't in New York City, kid. We aren't entertaining, just having some coffee and desert."

A soft mewling sound issued from the back seat. Wes went perfectly still then turned to glance into the rear window.

"Becca, there's a baby in your back seat."

"Thanks Matlock, you just solved the mystery! I wondered what that thing was back there."

Wes pierced her with his cool, gray stare, his chiseled mouth unsmiling.

"Look," Becca continued. "I sort of have a situation here. That's what I needed to talk to Rhonda about."

"Then we'd better get your situation inside."

Wes opened the rear door and expertly extracted Nicole and her seat in one swift move. Carrying the baby seat he motioned for Becca to proceed ahead of him into the house. She tried to swallow the lump in her throat as she made her way toward the warm kitchen. Rhonda, Penny and Nate looked up from the table as Becca and Wes entered. Becca took note of the coffee mugs and the half-eaten chocolate cake that sat on a plate in the middle of the table.

"Hey, Bec," Rhonda greeted. "Wes thought he heard someone pull in."

"It's those Army Ranger ears of his," Nate commented. "I swear he can hear a footstep in the woods from a mile away."

"Some survival instincts die hard, I guess," Wes replied, setting the infant seat on the table.

Nikki began to squirm and fuss in her carrier. Becca moved quickly to loosen the harness and pull back the blanket the baby was swaddled in.

"Oooh, what have we here?" Penny rose from her seat and moved around the table.

Becca saw the look of pure longing that crossed Penny's face as her golden gaze feasted on the baby. She reached out and touched Nikki's downy hair with a gentle finger. Becca knew the unfortunate story, how Penny and Nate had been trying to have a baby for nearly three years now with no success. How their grief mounted as first Emma and Tyler, and then Rhonda and Wes had started families.

"Who's baby?" she asked, lifting Nicole from the seat and cradling her in her arms. Nikki opened her eyes and stared up at Penny with unfocused eyes.

"My friend, Violet Compton's," Becca answered. "Her name's Nicole, Nikki for short."

"She's so tiny," Penny observed, picking up one of the baby's star-like hands and letting the fingers wrap around her own. "She can't be very old."

"Not quite a month old I guess," Becca responded, her misery mounting with each passing second. She felt Nate's gaze linger on her, questioning without words.

"So what's she doing with you?" Rhonda finally asked the question that was obviously on everyone's mind.

"Well." Becca sighed. "I, um, well, I'm watching her for a bit." Becca carefully kept her eyes trained on the baby in Penny's arms. If Wes could hear a sound from a mile away, then Nate Sweeney could spot a lie from the same distance. "Only for a day or two. Violet had a family emergency she needed to take care of."

"And she didn't take her newborn baby with her?" Rhonda's voice echoed with the same disgust Becca felt.

"Look, I don't know all the details. Violet was very sketchy about it all. I just know that she couldn't leave Nikki with her parents." At least *that* was the truth, Becca thought. "I'm the only one she trusts. But I've got class in Alpena tomorrow and if Vi doesn't get home by the end of the week, there's my job at the Spot of Tea."

Becca broke off and stared at the floor, trying to figure out how her life had been turned upside down in the space of a few minutes. And she thought statistics was complicated!

"Mom's tied up with the quilt shop and her classes, so I was wondering, Rhonda, if you could help me out."

"For how long?" It was clear from her tone that Rhonda wasn't keen on the idea. "Brendan's a big enough handful, I'm not sure how I can deal with him and a newborn. Not to mention we're getting everything ready to open the orchard the first of October."

"Hopefully it will just be tomorrow." Oh, please Lord, please let Violet get back tomorrow! Becca prayed desperately. "But if this emergency takes longer to straighten out…"

"I could help," Penny interjected. She settled herself back down in her chair and arranged the baby comfortably in her lap.

"Could you?" Becca asked, hopeful.

"Penny…" Nate simultaneously warned.

"No, really, I would love to help take care of her," Penny insisted. She looked straight at her husband and Nate immediately softened. "I've got Thursday and Friday off. I think it would be fun. And I bet my mom would enjoy it, too."

"Well, Violet will most likely be back by then," Becca said. "But if not, even though I don't have class on Friday, I work a full shift at the Spot of Tea."

"No problem. You can drop her off at the house on your way to class or work. Just let me know the time and I'll be ready."

"That still leaves tomorrow and Wednesday," Becca said, looking imploringly at Rhonda.

Rhonda and Wes exchanged a glance. Wes just shrugged.

"It's up to you," he said, taking a sip from his coffee mug. Rhonda took a deep breath.

"Okay, I'll give it a try. Who knows, maybe this will let me know if I want to give Brendan a baby brother or sister or not."

When she returned home, Becca was faced with a whole new dilemma. She unpacked the diaper bag, finding several prepared bottles, a can of powdered formula, diapers and little sleepers. Nikki fussed and rubbed her eyes.

"Looks like that baby is hungry and then needs to go to bed," Mary commented, coming through the kitchen to set a mug in the sink.

"Bed." Becca scrunched up her face. "Where's she going to sleep? She can't stay in that seat all night."

"There's the port-a-crib I use when Brendan's here. It's set up in the living room." Becca was amazed that her mother almost sounded helpful. "You'll have to take it upstairs to your room so you can get up and feed her in the middle of the night."

Becca's heart sank. "My room?" she asked weakly. "And how often will she wake up during the night?"

"Yes, your room. If you put her in Rhonda's old room, you'll never hear her when she wakes up. It will be easier if she's in the same room as you are. It will keep her from waking up your father and I. And she probably needs fed every two or three hours."

"Two or three hours?" Becca wailed in dismay. "How am I ever going to be able to function at school tomorrow if I don't get any sleep?"

"It's a little late to be asking that now." Mary bustled around the kitchen, setting up the coffee maker for the morning. "You should have thought about that before you agreed to this hair-brained arrangement."

"I didn't exactly agree," Becca argued. "I told Vi I couldn't do it. She just left. What was I supposed to do? Chase her down the road?" Becca turned on the hot tap and filled a pan with water, setting the bottle in it to warm. She lifted the fussy baby from the infant carrier.

"Well, if she doesn't come tomorrow I expect you to call the authorities. You're in no position to be taking care of an infant. Violet got herself into this sordid mess, now she can live with the consequences."

Becca looked down at Nikki. Her little fisted hands held each side of the bottle as she nursed. She didn't look like a sordid mess, or a consequence. She looked like a beautiful little angel who never asked to be brought into this world. But here she was. Becca vowed she would do the best she could while she had the chance. After all, someone needed to be looking out for this innocent baby who wasn't responsible for the actions of her parents.

It was much harder at 3 a.m. to remember her vow. Nikki took her bottle but then continued to fuss, even after she had been burped and changed.

"Come on, baby, you've got to go back to sleep," Becca cajoled, pacing the floor with Nikki held to her shoulder. "I can't deal with English composition on only two hours of shut eye."

Nikki let out a weak cry in response and Becca jiggled a little more. Finally, she collapsed into her creaky rocking chair by the windows. She arranged Nicole in her lap and rocked gently, staring out the window at the waxing moon.

"Okay, Lord, you know what I'm hearing?" Becca whispered. "I'm hearing that emergency siren. You know, the one where the voice comes on and says 'this is a test, this is only a test.' I take it that's what this is, Lord. A test. I want to pass, truly I do. But I need Your help. I'm not ready to be a mother yet. I know how close I came to crossing the line with Bobby. I've asked Your forgiveness for that, and I've been avoiding temptation where he's concerned. And this is one of the reasons." Becca looked down at Nikki, who's eyes had finally closed. "I've got plans and dreams, Father God. Things I want to accomplish for You. But You've given me this cross to bear, and I'll do it with as much grace as You give me. But I'm asking, please Jesus, send Violet home today. This baby needs her."

CHAPTER SIX

The September sun was shining on a glorious fall morning as Becca pulled into Wes and Rhonda's driveway. Turning off the ignition, she sat for a moment, staring at the clear, blue sky. Becca closed her eyes, imagining saddling up Bailey and spending the day riding the power lines. She would pack a lunch and ride all the way to Avery Lake. Now that would be heaven.

With a sigh she opened her eyes and pushed open the car door. She didn't have enough strength to heft a saddle onto Bailey's back, even if she did have the day free. After getting up with Nicole every two hours all night long, Becca felt like she had been "rode hard and put away wet" as her father liked to say. Somehow she had to make it through a full day of classes, then come home and pick up Nikki and start the whole routine all over again. Yeah, wow, this certainly was a day to look forward to.

"Please, Lord, let Violet come home today," Becca begged, looking up once more to the cloudless sky.

Hefting the infant carrier and diaper bag from the back seat, Becca made her way around the neat stone farmhouse. She let herself in the back door, through the glassed-in mudroom and straight into the kitchen. Brendan sat in his high chair, banging a spoon on the tray. Rhonda turned from the sink, a smile of greeting on her freckled face.

"You sure you're up to this?" Becca asked, turning to set the carrier on the table. She came to an abrupt halt at the sight of Toby sitting there, a 20 ounce bottle of Mountain Dew in front of him. "What are you doing here?" she asked coldly, setting Nikki and the baby seat on the table.

"Wes hired me to work for him through the harvest." Toby rose from his seat and came around the table to stare down at the baby. "You been keeping secrets from me, Bec?"

"Yeah, Toby. I didn't even know myself. Imagine my surprise when I went to the bathroom and a baby popped out."

Toby gave her a confused look, eyebrows raised.

"Don't be a moron." Becca swung the diaper bag off her shoulder and plopped it down next to the baby seat. "Violet has gone off to God knows where, chasing after Vince who I guess decided the dream of wedded and baby bliss was really a nightmare after all."

"I thought you said she had a family emergency." Rhonda came across the kitchen with a wet cloth and began wiping pureed peaches off Brendan's face. The toddler squirmed in his high chair, trying to avoid his mother's ministrations.

"Yeah, well, Nate was sitting right here. I didn't think it wise to blurt out the whole story and have him jumping up to call children's services."

"So, you lied," Rhonda stated.

"I didn't lie. I said Vi had a family emergency. In her book, Vince taking off and leaving her with this baby was an emergency. Although, if it were me, I'd be calling it a gift from God."

"How long is this little arrangement supposed to last?" Toby wanted to know, wagging a finger between Becca and the baby.

"I'm praying Vi will be back today. Not that it's any of your business," Becca reminded him.

"But what about your classes?" Toby sounded genuinely concerned, which did not soothe Becca a wit.

"That's why I'm here," Becca stated between clenched teeth. "What's your excuse? How can you work for Wes and be at class at the same time?"

"Most of my classes are in the evening, or on-line. I scheduled them that way on purpose so I'd have a better chance of working while going to school."

"Well, bully for you. I've got to go." Becca turned her full attention on Rhonda. "I guess everything you'll need is in here." She patted the diaper bag. "Not that I would know."

"Don't worry about it." Rhonda sounded much calmer than Becca felt. "If it's not in the bag, I'm sure I've got it here in the house somewhere."

"Great, thanks Ronnie. I owe you one." Becca gave Rhonda a hug, dropped a kiss on the top of

Winning Becca

Brendan's red curls, then headed for the door. "Gotta run. I should be back around 3:30 or so."

Becca hurried out of the house, purposely ignoring Toby as she shot out the back door. She spotted his Bronco parked in the shade of the barn. How could Wes have done this to her? Now she was going to be stuck seeing his haughty face every time she came over between now and Thanksgiving. Thankfully, her classes and work, and Nikki, would be keeping her too busy to worry about Toby Sinclair!

"So, what's this all about?" Toby asked as Rhonda lifted the baby from her seat. His heartbeat was finally returning to normal after the surprise of Becca walking in with a baby in tow.

"I wish I knew," Rhonda said, bending to kiss Nikki on the top of her downy head. "You heard what Becca just said. My feeling is that Violet is doing what Violet does best, using someone else to get what she wants."

Toby peered over Rhonda's shoulder at the sleeping infant.

"She sure is a pretty little thing," he observed.

"The baby or my sister?" Rhonda angled a knowing glance up at him. Toby smiled in reply.

"Both," he answered. "Do you think she'll ever forgive me?"

"For beating her in that last class at the fair?" Rhonda asked. She balanced Nikki in one arm while rummaging through the diaper bag with her other hand. She extracted a pair of full baby bottles and headed toward the refrigerator. "I doubt it."

Winning Becca

Toby's smile slipped away. Hope drained out of him one heartbeat at a time.

"Hey, Toby, sorry to take so long." Wes entered the kitchen, stuffing his arms into a flannel shirt. "I had to proof that ad for the Tribune and e-mail back the changes. I want to make sure everything is perfect for the big opening of the orchard and pumpkin patch."

"No problem," Toby said. If Wes hadn't been running late, then he never would have gotten to see Becca, no matter how briefly.

"Let's get to work." Wes dropped a quick kiss on Rhonda's mouth, tousled Brendan's curls, then strode toward the back door. He turned, one foot in the mud room. "You going to be okay with these two?"

"I think I'll manage." Rhonda smiled. "Like I said, this will be good experience for me. By the end of the day I'll know if I want another baby or not. But if you hear me screaming, come running."

"Running in the other direction maybe." Wes laughed and continued out the door.

Toby matched Wes stride for stride as they walked toward the rusty red, hip-roofed barn situated a good distance back from the house. A herd of black angus cattle stood near the gate of a pasture off to the left, looking expectant as the two drew near.

"Okay, this is what I want you to do," Wes instructed. "Take the tractor and the wagon down to the pumpkin patch. Go all the way to the northern edge. That patch we're going to pick and haul the pumpkins up to the hill above the orchard. We'll sort them there by size. I've made some stakes with prices to drive into the ground near each group. The other patch closest to the orchard will be for pick-your-own. Got it?"

"Yeah, I got it." Toby's voice held a decided lack of enthusiasm.

"You okay?" Wes asked, stopping just inside the barn door. Toby stared at the dirt between his boots.

"Can I ask you something, man to man?" He risked a quick glance at Wes, whose eyebrow rose over one clear, gray eye.

"Sure Toby," he replied slowly. "Man to man."

"Rhonda says that Becca is never going to get over the fact that I beat her for the grand championship," Toby's voice reflected his inner misery. "How can I get her to forgive me?"

"If you'da been smart, you would have blown a lead or something in that western equitation class."

"No way." Toby shook his head adamantly. "If Becca would have beat me fair and square, that would have been one thing. But I wasn't going to lose on purpose. I've got pride, you know."

"Yeah, well, you've got pride, but you don't have Becca. How's that working for you?" Wes gave him a pointed look before moving farther into the barn.

"Come on, Wes. Help me out here," Toby begged. He leaned against the John Deere tractor's huge tire as Wes climbed up into the seat, checking gauges. "Even if I wanted to, I can't go back and undo the past. Not that I think it would do any good. Becca would probably hate me even more if she thought I threw the championship on purpose. And it's not just the championship that's between us. Becca also thinks

Winning Becca

she has a thing for Bobby Fitzgerald." The thought of Becca and Bobby kissing left Toby wanting to punch something. "What can I do?"

Wes jumped down from the tractor, brushing his hands together. He pinned Toby with a serious stare.

"You really want to know?"

"Yes. I really want to know. I'll do anything."

"You've got it that bad, huh?" Wes smiled and shook his head. Toby remained sober. "Okay, this is what you do. Be her friend, the best friend she's ever had. Then, when she needs it, be her hero."

Becca squinted into the late afternoon sunshine as she drove toward Atlanta. She tugged a pair of sunglasses from the visor above her head and slipped them on. She couldn't help smiling in satisfaction as she thought of the 'A' that was written in bold, red ink atop her first college English paper. Maybe she would survive higher education after all, despite statistics class. The smile faded away as Becca realized she still had to finish her statistics homework. It had been hard enough last night before Violet showed up and dumped Nikki on the Weaver doorstep. How in the world would she ever concentrate on it now with a baby to take care of?

Maybe Violet and Vince would show up tonight, Becca thought hopefully. They could take the baby and go be one happy little family again. And Becca could get on with her own life. Maybe Bobby would call and they could go over to Gaylord to the movies this weekend. After this little experiment in childrearing, Becca knew she wouldn't be tempted to cross the line with Bobby again.

The interior of the car grew warm and Becca rolled down her window, breathing deeply of the fresh air. She rested an elbow on the door and sang along with the radio, enjoying these few brief minutes of freedom before reality and responsibility set in. She knew that as soon as she pulled into Wes and Rhonda's driveway the party would be over.

Her little green sedan bumped over the rough dirt road that led to the Cooper and Weaver farms. Becca slowed as she approached Wes and Rhonda's driveway. A huge green tractor and wagon were parked on the lawn. Orange pumpkins were spread over the hill above the orchard. A shirtless Toby, his chest glistening with sweat, wrestled a large pumpkin from the back of the wagon and carried it across the lawn to deposit it on a pile. Becca saw the muscles across the back of his shoulders ripple with the exertion and she felt a funny shimmy in her stomach.

Groaning, Becca pulled into the driveway and parked behind Wes' pickup. She was turning into a shameless hussy! First Bobby's bare chest had caused fireworks to go off and now Toby. And it wasn't as if she hadn't seen Toby's a million times before. Toby, Becca and their gang of friends had spent nearly every summer day for the past several years at Crooked Creek beach. She had seen Toby in nothing but swim trunks more times than she could count and it had never caused this bizarre reaction to her insides.

Becca rested her head against the steering wheel and tried to pray.

Lord, keep me pure of heart and mind. Forgive me, Father for these wayward thoughts and feelings. I don't know what's gotten in to me lately, Lord. Please make it stop!

"Hey, you okay?"

Startled, Becca looked up to find Toby peering in the open window. His bare chest seemed to fill her vision. Becca squeezed her eyes shut.

"You sick or something, Bec?" Toby asked, sounding worried.

Yes, yes she was definitely sick, Becca decided, if she was feeling this weird attraction to someone who had been her arch enemy for years.

"No, I'm fine. I was just praying," she said, opening her car door and stepping out. "Getting myself psyched up for another night of no sleep." Becca headed toward the back door. Toby followed closely behind. She cleared her throat. "Shouldn't you, uh, get dressed or something before coming in the house?" she asked, her eyes steadily on the doorknob.

"Why? Is the sight of my chiseled physique setting your heart all aflutter?" Toby asked with a knowing smile.

"No. The smell of your stinky sweat is making me nauseous," Becca complained. She yanked open the back door with more force than was necessary. "Go find a shirt."

"Your wish is my command," Toby replied, jumping off the back step and trotting around the house.

Becca huffed out a breath, squared her shoulders and entered the farmhouse kitchen. She was just tired, that's all, she reasoned. Lack of sleep was definitely wreaking havoc with her ability to respond properly to half-dressed men.

"Hello, anybody home," she called.

"In the living room," Rhonda answered.

Becca quickly walked through the kitchen, into the large, comfortable living area. The afternoon sun sparkled through the big, back windows. Rhonda sat on the floor with Brendan, an assortment of toys and cardboard books spread around them. The rhythmic tic-tic-tic of the baby swing filled the room. Nikki slept peacefully as the little seat swung to and fro.

"How'd it go?" Becca whispered. Brendan smiled at her and held out his arms. Becca gladly lifted him from Rhonda's lap and spun him around. His giggle caused a catch in Becca's heart.

"Fine. Nikki's as good as gold. She slept most of the day," Rhonda answered.

"Well, of course she did. She barely slept a wink all night!" Becca replied.

"That's what babies do." Rhonda hefted herself up off the floor. "Thankfully it doesn't last forever. Brendan was sleeping through the night by the time he was six months old."

"Well, thankfully I won't have Nikki that long. I'm hoping and praying with all my might that Vi gets home tonight. I've still got statistics homework to tackle." Becca passed Brendan back to Rhonda and bent to stop the baby swing.

"I'll get the diaper bag together so you can get home then," Rhonda offered.

Becca carefully lifted the sleeping infant from the swing. Nikki didn't even open an eye. She merely cuddled closer as Becca clasped the baby to her chest. Becca couldn't resist kissing the light fluff of hair on Nikki's head as it rested just below her chin.

"You really need to wake up, you know," Becca chided quietly. "I can't have you sleeping all day and then being up all night." She carried Nicole into the kitchen and placed her in the infant carrier, making sure the buckle was latched securely before tucking the blanket all around the baby.

"Here you go." Rhonda handed Becca the diaper bag. "If Vi doesn't show up tonight, I'll keep Nikki again tomorrow. But really Becca, you need to be thinking about the future. If Violet isn't back by the weekend, you really should call children's services. You aren't the one who got pregnant. It's not fair that your life should be put on hold for a baby that doesn't belong to you."

"I know." Becca looked down at the angelic face that peeked out above the fuzzy pink blanket. "I'll think about it. Hopefully it's a non-issue. Vi will probably be home tonight." Becca slung the diaper bag over a shoulder and lifted the carrier. "Thanks Ronnie, I really do owe you. I swear I'll help with the orchard. I'll do pony rides or whatever you want to pay you back for this."

"Oh, don't worry about it." Rhonda waved a hand. "That's what family is for."

Becca moved toward the back door but before she could reach for the knob it swung open. Toby stood on the other side, a dirty, white Atlanta Huskies t-shirt now covering his chest.

"Here, let me help you with that." He reached out and plucked the baby carrier from Becca's hand.

"Toby, I can manage just fine," she protested. Toby ignored her as he walked down the back steps and around the house to Becca's car. He opened the back door and placed the carrier on the seat.

"Not like that!" Becca corrected. She shoved around him and turned the carrier so that Nikki was facing the back window. "They have to face backwards. For safety," she explained, putting the seat belt securely in place.

"Oh. Sorry. I haven't had too much experience with babies." Toby backed away and looked sheepish.

"Yeah, well, I'm sorry I snapped at you." Becca slammed the door shut and risked a look up at Toby. "I'm just tired. I didn't get very much sleep last night and I've still got statistics homework that's due tomorrow and I can't make heads or tails of it."

"You want some help?" Toby offered.

"Oh ho, you would like that huh? Rub my nose in the fact that you were always better at math than me?"

"No." Hands on hips, Toby shook his head. "I was just thinking you might need some help, that's all."

"Well, I don't," Becca denied.

Winning Becca

"You know, I seem to remember back during the fair. This girl there, she gave me this lecture about humility. She told me I was prideful. But she said she was humble. She told me God liked humble people." Toby squinted up at the sky. "I was just thinking that humble people accept help if they need it. Isn't it prideful to say you don't need any help when you really do?"

Stung, Becca's shoulders slumped and she hung her head.

"You're right," she whispered.

"I'm sorry, what was that?" Toby asked, cupping a hand around his ear. "I didn't quite hear you."

"Criminey, you are insufferable!" Becca bit out.

"I know." Toby leaned indolently against the side of the car. "But I'm really good at math."

"Okay, fine. You want to help, be at my house at eight." Becca yanked open her door. "But for the love of Pete, take a shower first." Slamming her door closed, she started the engine and quickly backed the car around and headed down the drive, fuming all the way home.

CHAPTER SEVEN

Be her hero, be her hero, be her hero.

The words echoed over and over again in Toby's head as he drove toward the Weaver farm. He wanted to be Becca's hero. The question was, would she allow him to be? Would she lay aside her pride long enough to notice that he was trying to be? Toby had tried to play the hero when he carried the baby out to her car and Becca hadn't even said 'thank you.' All she had done was complain and correct him. Obviously carrying a baby wasn't heroic enough. Was it possible to win a girl's heart by helping her with math homework? Toby was certainly praying that it was.

Pulling into the Weaver driveway, he parked behind Becca's car and turned off the Bronco. Toby took a deep breath before opening the door and hopping to the ground.

"Here goes nothin'," he muttered. "Supermathman to the rescue." He took the porch steps in one stride and wiped his hands down the sides of his jeans before reaching out to knock. The front door swung open and there stood Becca. Her hair was pulled back in a ponytail, making her look about ten years old.

"Hey," she greeted.

"Here I am," Toby said, his arms held wide. "All showered like you asked." He raised an arm and sniffed his armpit. "I even put on deodorant."

"You're such a dork." Becca spun on stocking feet and headed toward the kitchen, leaving Toby to follow. He swung the door closed and quickly made his way down the hall. Becca stood in front of the refrigerator. "You want something to drink?"

"I don't suppose you have any Dew?"

Becca shot him a look that said 'get real' as she pulled open the fridge door.

"Sorry. There's milk, tea, water." Toby pulled a face. "Or fruit punch."

"Fruit punch? What are we, six?"

"Hey, I happen to like fruit punch!" Becca defended. "If you don't like any of those choices, there's always baby formula." She held up a full bottle.

"I'll take fruit punch." Toby looked around the kitchen. Becca's textbooks and notepads were spread out on the table by the windows. "Where's the rug rat?" he asked. "Did Violet come and get her?"

"No." Becca's voice had gone cold. "I left five messages on her voice mail. She's either out of range of her service or she's got her cell phone turned off." She brought two glasses of fruit punch over and set them on the table before sliding into a chair. "Nikki's upstairs sleeping. Hopefully she'll stay that way until you finish explaining this confounding homework to me."

Toby shrugged out of his windbreaker. Hanging it on the back of a chair, he sat down across from Becca and pulled the statistics book in front of him.

"Why did you take statistics anyway?" he wanted to know.

"Because my advisor *lied* to me. I told her math was my weakest subject. She told me statistics would be easier than algebra and I fell for it."

"Why were you so afraid of algebra? You took it in high school and did okay."

"Okay?! I got a 'B'! It totally ruined my grade point average. And that was after poor Wes spent night after night trying to tutor me in it. He got so frustrated with my frustration that I thought he was going to pull out his gun and shoot us both just to end the misery."

"Well, I'm here now. And as much as I like Wes, I think I'm probably a little better in math than he is."

"Hmph." Becca sat back and crossed her arms. "That's the problem. You think you're better than everyone at everything."

"That's because so far, I have been." Toby grinned at her.

"Well, if you're so all-fired great then why aren't you off studying at Harvard or Yale or someplace fabulous? Why are you taking on-line classes through the community college?"

"If I was off at some Ivy League school, then I wouldn't be here to help you," Toby stated. "Now, are you going to sit there and pout or are you going to show me what's got you stumped about statistics?"

"Okay, fine," Becca sighed and leaned forward. She flipped the statistics book open and pointed to a problem. "I've read the four basic steps for determining the value of any quartile at least a dozen times and…" A soft mewling cry issued from above their heads. Becca dropped her head into her hands. "Great, just great." She glanced at the clock as the cry grew stronger. "She's probably ready for her bottle. I swear that kid eats more than a moose."

"Go get her. I'm not going anywhere." Toby tried to let his eyes convey his full meaning.

Becca just stared at him for a moment before pushing herself up from the table and disappearing down the hall. Toby heard her tired steps as she climbed the stairs. His heart seemed to thud in time with her footfalls. Trying to get his mind off Becca, he scanned the math problem. It was really elementary statistics work. The kind of stuff he could do in his sleep. How could he explain it to Becca in a way that would make it come alive and make sense?

Moments later Becca returned to the kitchen carrying a bundle wrapped in a fuzzy pink blanket. Toby watched as she went to the sink and turned on the hot tap before opening the refrigerator and pulling out a bottle. The whole thing was done with an efficiency of movement that made Becca look like a natural mother.

"You're pretty good at that," Toby complimented. "You look like you could really be Nikki's mom."

"Bite your tongue," Becca retorted, carrying the baby, bottle and burp cloth over to the table.

"Here." Toby moved over a chair. "You'd better sit on this side of the table so I can explain this stuff to you while you feed the baby."

Becca sat, arranging the baby in a comfortable position. Before Toby could blink, Nikki was sucking away contentedly, her tiny little fists holding each side of the bottle. A curiously warm sensation wrapped around Toby's heart as he watched the baby nurse.

"She sure is a precious little thing, isn't she?" he asked.

"Yeah, well, you can say that because you aren't the one getting up with her at two o'clock in the morning."

Toby reached out and touched the sleeper-covered feet that stuck out from beneath the blanket.

"Has she made you, you know, think about being a mother?" he asked timidly.

"She's reminded me why girls my age should avoid temptation," Becca replied.

"Speaking of that, how's it going with Farmer Fitzgerald?"

"That's really none of your business." Becca removed the bottle from Nikki's mouth and slapped it down on the table. She lifted the baby to her shoulder and began patting her back as Nikki's head bobbed and weaved. "He's been pretty busy with the harvest and I've been busy with school."

"So he doesn't know about Nicole?"

"No! Why should he?" Becca gave him an exasperated look. Nikki began to fuss. Becca laid the baby back down and offered her the bottle once more. "I thought you were here to amaze me with your math genius, not interrogate me about my love life."

"You don't have a love life with Bobby Fitzgerald," Toby stated with certainty.

"Oh ho, that's what you'd like to think!"

"No, it's not what I think, it's what I know. If Bobby were the love of your life he'd be here helping you with your homework, and he would have been the first one to know about Nicole."

"He's got some nerve," Becca fumed as she laid Nikki on the bed to change her diaper. "Thinking he knows so much about me and Bobby. What does he know? Nothing!" she answered her own question.

Nikki smiled and kicked her legs. Becca zipped up the sleeper and lifted Nikki into her arms.

"You seem awfully chipper now that you've had your dinner," she observed. "You also look wide awake. I don't suppose there's any hope you'll go back to sleep?" The baby stared back at her with wide-open eyes. "No, I didn't think so. Well, I guess you'll just have to come back downstairs with me. I don't suppose there's any chance that *you'll* understand statistics?"

Becca held the baby close to her face and planted a kiss on her tiny nose before grabbing the infant seat and heading back down to the kitchen. Toby had angled his chair slightly away from the table. His long, lanky frame was sprawled out, the statistics book held in his lap with one hand while the other reached for a bowl of popcorn. He looked up when Becca entered, the baby in one arm, the seat in the other. He jumped up.

"Here, let me help you with that." Before Becca could utter a protest he took the carrier from her hand and placed it on the island counter.

"I don't think she's going to go back to sleep just yet," Becca explained. "She's wide awake now that she's eaten." She moved to place the baby in the seat. Toby laid a hand on her arm, stopping her.

"Um, can I hold her? I mean, it seems like she's in that seat an awful lot. It's probably not the most comfortable thing in the world."

"You sure?" Becca hesitated. "You said yourself you don't have much experience with babies."

"I don't think you need much experience to hold one. I mean, all we're doing is sitting here at the table. I think I can handle that. And if she starts to cry, I'll just hand her to you." Toby smiled.

"Typical male," Becca replied. "Okay, here ya go." Toby held out his hands and she carefully placed Nicole in his arms. "The most important thing is to…"

"Support her head," Toby interrupted with a nod. "I know that much."

Becca watched in amazement as Toby cradled the baby to his t-shirt covered chest. Something inside her squeezed tight at the sight of his broad hand on the back of Nikki's downy head. He walked back to the table and slowly took his seat, rearranging the baby more comfortably in his arms. Nicole looked up at him with wide eyes and then smiled and kicked her feet.

"I think she likes you," Becca said, resuming her seat beside Toby. "Where'd you get the popcorn?"

"Your mom made it for me. I think she likes me, too." Toby slid a grin her way.

"Yeah, well, Nikki's too young to know any better and my mother's too old," Becca retorted.

"So what's your excuse?" Toby asked.

"My excuse?" Becca laid a hand on her chest and stared at him wide-eyed. "My excuse for what?"

"For liking me," Toby whispered, leaning toward her.

"I don't like you," Becca said, drawing back. Her heart tripped several times.

"Sure you do," Toby countered. "I told you before, you enjoy this little game of ours as much as I do. And once you ace your statistics homework, you'll like me even more."

"Just so you know, I already aced my first English paper and I did that without any help from you, Mr. Know-it-all."

"That doesn't surprise me. You're an extremely intelligent woman." Toby reached for the statistics book with his free hand and pushed it toward her. "I've never doubted that for a minute. You do know that, right Bec?"

"Know what?" Becca stared into his brown eyes, feeling as if she were being sucked into a vortex.

"That I've always thought you were extremely intelligent," Toby explained, his gaze never wavering from hers. "You gave me a run for my money, year after year. If it hadn't been for you nipping at my heels, I never would have been as good a student as I was. You made me try harder, study more, take harder classes. But Bec?"

"Yeah?" Becca waited, breath suspended.

"We aren't in high school anymore. We're all grown up now, so can we drop this competition and stop trying to out-do each other?"

A slow grin spread across Becca's face.

"Aw, Toby. You said it yourself. We both enjoy the game. If we give it up, what fun would there be in that?"

Nikki had fallen asleep in his arms. Toby's hand was numb from the lack of circulation, but he didn't want to say anything. Becca's head was bent over the statistics book, as she concentrated on the last problem. She pulled the notebook to her, scribbled some numbers, punched several buttons on the calculator then smiled at Toby in triumph. His heart slammed hard against his ribs.

"There!" She held the notebook up for him to see.

Toby glanced down at the problem in the textbook, then once more at the solution Becca had written on her paper.

"Excellent. I knew you could do it." He smiled into her glowing eyes.

"Well, I hate to admit this, but you really are a good teacher." Becca slapped the notebook closed and quickly stacked the books into a neat pile. She pushed up from the table and reached to take Nicole from his arms.

"And unlike Wes, I never wanted to murder you even once." Toby shook his arm trying to restore blood to his hand. Pin-pricks ran up and down his arm.

"Yeah, well you have to remember that Wes is *trained* to kill people, not teach them algebra." Becca turned and laid the sleeping infant in her seat. "You really should consider going into education Toby. You're a much better math teacher than any of the ones I had in high school."

"As much as I appreciate your vote of confidence, teaching is the last thing I want to do with my life." Toby stood and shrugged into his windbreaker.

"Oh, thanks a lot!" Becca spun around to face him, hands on her slender hips. "What does that say about me, then?"

"What?" Toby stared at her blankly. "It doesn't say anything about you. I thought we were talking about *me*."

"We are, but the way you said it, that teaching is the last thing you want to do, sounded as if it is a complete waste of someone's time. Since I plan to go into teaching, I was wondering what you must think of me."

"Becca, you already know what I think of you, and believe me, it's all good. Going into preschool teaching is a whole different ball game than teaching high school algebra. For one thing, I don't think you have to worry about drugs and weapons in a preschool. I know how passionate you are about little kids. I've seen you work with them at church. I know you love it and you feel it's your calling in life. Me, I want to be an engineer. After my two years at Alpena, I hope to get into U of M. I don't feel any calling to be a teacher." He stepped forward and brushed back a lock of hair that had fallen from her ponytail, tucking it gently behind her ear. "Except for you. I'll be your teacher, anytime."

"Yeah, well, I think I'm good now." Becca crossed her arms stiffly. "I appreciate the help, but don't think I'm going to get in the habit of calling on you to help me with my homework."

"Hmm, do I hear that old pride rearing its ugly head again?" Toby smiled and bent his head toward Becca's, barely resisting the urge to drop a quick kiss on her mouth. Instead, he satisfied himself with merely touching his forehead to hers. "Anyway, you're welcome for the help." Toby headed toward the front door.

"I didn't say thank you," Becca argued from behind him.

"I know, that's so rude." Toby turned at the door and gave her a grin. "Didn't your parents raise you better than that? Anyway, your thanks was implied in your new-found hero worship of me. Anytime you're in distress, just call Supermathman."

"Oh good grief!" Becca pretended to stick her finger down her throat, making gagging noises. "The only one who hero worships you is *you*."

"Now Becca," Toby sighed heavily as he reached for the door knob. "We both know that isn't true. But if you still want to play hard to get, that's fine with me. Like I said, we both enjoy the game." He gave her a wink as he stepped out on the front porch. "See you in the morning."

The door slammed behind him, making Toby grin. He whistled as he strode through the frosty air to his Bronco. Being Becca's hero was going to be easier than he thought. A little help with math homework, a little help with the baby. He could do that. And he could be her friend into the bargain. Sure, Becca would give him a merry chase, but the battle was already won. Toby knew it. Becca knew it. But in the meantime he planned to enjoy every minute of the game until Becca finally gave in and admitted he was the only guy for her.

CHAPTER EIGHT

The driveway leading back to Nate and Penny's log home on the river was long and winding. The oak and maple trees along the banks of the Thunder Bay shimmered with the beginnings of deep fall color while birds darted in and out among the cedars. Becca had her window rolled part-way down, breathing in the crisp morning air.

Parking behind Penny's silver SUV, Becca got out and pulled her hoodie closer around her, warding off the fall chill. She opened the rear door and pulled out the still sleeping Nicole. With the baby carrier in one hand and the diaper bag in the other, Becca headed toward the wide front porch. The front door swung open before Becca's foot landed on the first step.

"Are you sure about this, Pen?" Becca asked, carrying her load through the living room. "Hey, Miz Scott," she greeted Penny's mother, who sat wrapped warmly in a quilt in a wide side chair by the fireplace. Penny's mom, disabled by a stroke, smiled and nodded in reply.

In the large, sun-lit dining room and kitchen area, Becca set the baby and bag on the table. Beyond the sliding glass doors was a wide deck. Chickadees, nuthatches and tufted titmice took turns at the bird feeders placed strategically around the deck.

"Just to warn you, she didn't sleep for beans last night," Becca complained. A huge yawn emphasized her lack of shut-eye. She dug into the diaper bag and pulled out several bottles while Penny unbuckled Nicole from the seat and lifted the baby into her arms. "I think she's missing her mommy."

"Poor baby," Penny murmured, cuddling Nikki close. Nicole sighed and snuggled closer.

Becca headed toward the refrigerator with the bottles. As she opened the door, she glanced back at Penny, the baby tucked securely under her chin. She stopped and stared.

"What?" Penny asked, tossing her long curtain of honey-colored hair over her shoulder.

"Nothing." Becca shook her head, trying to clear away the image. She set the bottles in the fridge and pushed the door shut.

"It must have been something. You had the weirdest look on your face."

"It's just..." Becca busied herself sorting needlessly through the diaper bag. "Nikki, she, uh, she looks a little bit like you."

"You think so?" Penny glanced down at the face nestled against her chest.

"Just a little bit."

Footfalls sounded on the stairs and Nate strode into the room, adjusting his tie. His tall frame in his brown uniform seemed to fill the room. The frown pulling down the corners of his mouth told Becca exactly what he thought of this little arrangement.

"Violet still isn't back?" His blue eyes bored into Becca's and it was all she could do not to squirm.

"Not yet. Probably by the weekend," Becca answered, silently calling down fire and brimstone on Violet's head for putting her in this uncomfortable position.

"Becca says Nicole looks a little bit like me," Penny chimed in, moving closer to Nate. The furrow between his brow deepened.

"All babies look pretty much the same," he said gruffly. With deft hands he checked the equipment on his belt, dropped a quick kiss on Penny's mouth, then headed across the kitchen to the door that led to the garage. "Gotta get to work. I'll check in later."

The door slammed. Seconds later the hum of the garage door opener vibrated through the room.

"He doesn't seem very happy," Becca stated the obvious.

"He's just worried about me," Penny said, moving to stare out the sliding glass doors. "It's hard, wanting something so much and having God say no." She pressed a gentle kiss to the top of Nikki's head. "Acting mad is his way of hiding the hurt. He's worried I'll get attached, or start longing again for something I can't have."

"I'm sorry." Becca bit down hard on her lip. "I should have thought about how hard this would be for you."

"Oh, it won't be hard, will it baby?" Penny held Nikki away from her chest and jiggled her slightly. "We're going to have a grand old time."

"She's got plenty of diapers and clean sleepers in here." Becca patted the diaper bag. "I fed her before I came over, so she should be set for a few hours anyway." A quick glance at the clock told Becca she had to hurry or risk being late for class. "I've got to run, if you're sure you'll be okay…"

"We'll be fine. Go." Penny waved Becca away. As she headed out the front door, Becca heard Penny say, "Mom, look who's come to visit for the day."

Out on the porch, Becca paused to take a deep breath. Bird chatter filled the quiet morning. Becca felt like a protective mother, worried about leaving her child with a sitter. How silly. She hadn't worried in the least about leaving Nicole with Rhonda. Penny was perfectly capable of taking care of a baby. But what if Nate was right? What if Penny became too attached?

She wouldn't have time to become attached, Becca reminded herself, striding off the porch. Violet would be coming home, hopefully today. Nicole would be back with her mother, where she belonged, and Becca and Penny could go on with their lives. Please, Lord, send Vi home today, Becca prayed as she lowered herself into her car and slammed the door.

Toby couldn't quite hide his disappointment when Becca didn't show up at Wes and Rhonda's. Since Wes had cracked the whip and had him working sunup to sundown, Toby had missed her the day before, as well. Maybe Vi had come home. Maybe Nicole was safely back in her mother's arms, along with that no-good Vince. Toby craned his neck to stare once more down the deserted dirt road. Wes socked him a hard one.

"Ow!" Toby rubbed his bicep and stared at Wes.

"Pay attention!" Wes ordered. "You just put four two dollar pumpkins in the five dollar pile."

"Sorry," Toby muttered and moved to correct his mistake.

"She's not coming today, so you can stop looking and keep your mind on your work," Wes informed.

"I don't know what you're talking about." Toby continued to arrange the pumpkins in large rectangular piles. Wes merely snorted and pounded a stake into the ground in front of the pile of smaller pumpkins.

"I'm pretty sure God says something in the Bible about lying," Wes said, choosing another price stake and moving on to the next pile.

"I just thought Becca would be dropping the baby off this morning, that's all," Toby amended. "I didn't get a chance to talk to her yesterday and I was wondering how she did on that statistics homework I helped her with."

"Uh huh. Homework. I'm sure that's all you've been thinking about." Wes shot him a look that said 'keep on lying.'

"So, why isn't she coming? Did Vi finally show up and reclaim her child?" Toby asked, curiosity finally getting the better of him.

Winning Becca

"Not that I know of. Penny's watching the baby today and tomorrow."

"Oh." Toby felt suddenly deflated.

"Which means I might actually get some work out of you. If I had known this obsession with Becca was going to cause me so much trouble I never would have hired you in the first place."

Toby got the point and immediately doubled his efforts. But all too soon his mind wandered back to its original subject.

"I sure hope Violet gets back here this weekend. I'd like to beat the tar out of her and Vince for what they're doing to Becca and that baby."

Wes cast a glance his way and continued pounding. "Becca should just turn the baby over to the authorities and be done with it."

"She won't ever do that," Toby defended. "Becca's the most loyal person I know. She'll stick by Violet to the end, no matter how badly Vi's using her."

"Yeah, well, she'd better hope Nate doesn't get wind of what's really going on. One phone call to the right people and Becca could find that baby taken away, no matter how loyal she wants to be to its mother."

"Becca just wants what's best for Nicole. I think she really cares about that baby. She's good with her. She's going to make a great mother someday."

Wes snorted. "And you'd like nothing better than to be the one to make her a mother, I'd guess."

"What's so wrong with that?" Toby demanded.

"Toby." Wes just stared at the ground and shook his head slowly. "You're only eighteen. You've got the whole world at your feet. You're a smart kid. I can see you going places in this world. Marriage and babies should be the *last* thing on your mind."

"Well, Wes." Toby stood and brushed his gloved hands together. For a moment he stood, staring out over the hay field across the road. "You went all the way around the world, and where did you end up? Right back here at home." He finally got the courage to look Wes in the eye. "If everything I really want is right here, what's the point of going out into the big, bad world? I'm just gonna come right back here anyway."

Later that afternoon Toby was toiling at the bottom of the hill, picking up windfall from the orchard floor. He glanced up in time to see Becca's green sedan slow down on the road. He straightened and lifted a hand in greeting. The car stopped so Toby jogged out to the road. Becca leaned across the front seat and rolled the passenger-side window down. Toby bent at the waist to peer into the car.

"Hey," he greeted, his breath ragged. He must be getting out of shape, he thought. He shouldn't be winded from that short jog. He ran a knuckle over his sweaty brow.

"I just wanted to thank you," Becca said hesitantly.

"Really?" Toby asked in feigned surprise.

"Yes, really." Becca rolled her eyes, making Toby grin.

"So, my superior math skills must have helped."

"Well, a little bit. I got a 95 on my homework."

"Only a 95? Becca, you do disappoint me."

"Oh shut up! It's still an A." She reached over to roll the window back up, but Toby curled his hands over the top of the glass, stopping her.

"I'm proud of you Bec, really. You'll be as good as me at math in no time."

"I wouldn't go that far. I know my limitations. But like I said the other night, you are a pretty good teacher, even if you don't think teaching's a worthwhile profession."

"I never said it wasn't worthwhile. I just said it wasn't for me. Don't twist my words around to shield yourself from my charms."

"Oh good grief. I'm perfectly safe from your so-called charms," Becca refuted. "I have to get home. I've got chores to do and the munchkin back there will be needing fed again soon." She put her foot on the gas and the car eased forward, forcing Toby to let go of the window and take a step back. The little green car was soon swallowed up in a cloud of dust.

Turning, Toby slowly made his way across the browning grass to the cool shade of the orchard. Leaning down he snagged up the apple picker and set back to work, a smile turning up the corners of his mouth. He loved it when Becca denied her attraction to him. He just wondered who she was trying to convince more, herself or him.

"I'm serious, Vi. You need to get home and you need to get here now!" Becca hissed into the phone. She twisted the cord around her fingers and stared stonily out the kitchen windows.

Winning Becca

"I know, I know," Vi sounded desperate. "It won't be much longer."

"What do you mean, it won't be much longer? Have you found Vince or not?"

"It's not that simple..."

"Yes, it is that simple. Vi, I can't believe this!" Becca rubbed her temple, trying to ease the pounding that had erupted there. "It's a yes or no question. Have you found Vince?"

Silence echoed over the phone line.

"Vi..." Anger infused that one simple word.

"Yes, I found him," Violet finally answered. "But like I said, it's not that simple." Laughter erupted in the background.

"Where are you?" Becca questioned. "Are you at a party or something?" Becca swore her head was going to explode.

"No, not a party. Hold on." A door slammed. "Sorry. I'm outside now. Vince's uncle's place, it's small. And there's a million people in and out. Becca please, just listen."

"I'm about done listening Vi. Do you understand the seriousness of this situation? Pretty soon everyone in town will know I've got Nikki. I'm having to scramble to find people to watch her while I'm at work and school. I can't go on like this indefinitely. You *have* to come back home, with or without Vince."

"I know, I know. And I will, soon. Just as soon as I can."

"That's not good enough, Vi. I need a day. I need a time. If you don't give me one, then I'll give you one. If you aren't back in Atlanta by Monday then I'm calling children's services."

Violet's sharp intake of breath echoed over the phone line. "You wouldn't."

Becca squeezed her eyes shut, praying that she wouldn't have to find out if she could follow through with her own threat.

"Yes, I will. I've had it. What you're doing isn't fair. It isn't fair to me and it most certainly isn't fair to Nicole. I'm not the one who got knocked up, remember? I've got plans for my life, and they don't include becoming a mother at eighteen. You get home by Monday or Nikki will become a ward of the state."

"I can't promise that, Becca. I'm trying. You have to believe me. I'm doing the best I can. Tell Nikki I love her."

"No, you don't!" Becca exploded. "You don't love her. If you did you would be here, taking care of her, not chasing after her slime-bag father!"

"I do love her, Becca, I do. It's because I love her that I'm doing what I'm doing. Trust me, please. It's all going to work out, you'll see. Just be patient a little longer. I know I'll be in your debt forever. I appreciate what you're doing for me, and for Nicole. I know you love her, too. And because you do, you won't call children's services. I'm counting on you to take care of my baby."

The phone went silent. "Vi? Vi, are you there?" Becca practically yelled. No, it was obvious Vi was not there. Becca hung up the phone, pressing her forehead against the kitchen wall.

Lord, she prayed, *I know You said thou shalt not murder, but right now I would like nothing better than to kill Violet Compton. Forgive me, Father, and help me through this. Show me what I'm supposed to do.*

CHAPTER NINE

"Mom, Nikki's out of diapers, and formula, too," Becca called down the stairs. Mary Weaver appeared at the bottom of the steps, laundry basket propped on one hip.

"Then I guess you'd better make a trip into town and buy some," Mary stated simply before disappearing into the kitchen with her basketful of clothes.

Becca spun on her heel and stomped back to her room. Her mother had not wavered an inch in the five days Nicole had been in the Weaver household. Though she was kind to the baby, she refused to baby sit, give her a bottle or change a diaper. Mary Weaver's opinion of the matter was etched clearly on her face: children's services should be called immediately. It had taken all of Becca's best efforts to keep her mother from doing just that.

Nikki gurgled in her baby seat. Becca stared first at the contented infant, then at the pile of books on

Winning Becca

her desk. She had a ton of homework to do. Her head hurt, her feet hurt, and she was exhausted.

Collapsing onto the edge of her bed, Becca allowed herself to indulge in a moment of self pity. She didn't want to play mommy anymore. She wanted Violet home and she wanted her home yesterday. Becca squeezed her eyes shut and thought about the conversation with Vi the night before. Why did she have this sinking feeling in her gut that Violet would not be home by Monday? The realization made her angry all over again, especially when she remembered her conversation with Bobby just a few minutes after Vi had hung up. Bobby had asked her out to the movies and she had to say no. She had to explain about Nicole and how she was already tapping out all available babysitters for her class and work schedule. There was no way she could ask someone to watch Nikki so she could go out on a date. Bobby had sounded disappointed but understanding. He said Becca should call him when Violet got back to town. Whenever that might be!

Good Lord she hated this. This was a hundred times worse than when she had to carry that automated baby doll everywhere for a month for her child development class. If that experience hadn't been enough to scare her away from the possibilities of teen pregnancy, then this little experiment in unwed motherhood certainly had! Why, oh why hadn't that class project frightened Violet enough to keep her from getting pregnant? But Becca remembered the way Vi had responded to that fake baby, how she had thrived on having something to love and care for, even if it

Winning Becca

was an automaton. Then why wasn't she here now, taking care of this real baby that God had given her to love? And why had God given Nikki to Violet if He knew she was just going to run off and abandon the poor thing when He refused to give a baby to Penny and Nate who would be wonderful parents?

The vagaries of the Lord and His ways always had Becca stumped. Better to not think about it too much. Sighing heavily, she pushed her sore and tired feet into her tennis shoes then reached for the infant carrier.

"Come on, lets go get you some clean drawers and some food. Good grief, I bet you've gained five pounds already. No wonder, eating every three hours," Becca groused as she tromped down the stairs and out the front door to her car.

The grocery store in town was sparsely populated on this Saturday evening. Becca set Nicole's carrier in the cart and headed toward the baby care aisle, thankful the store was relatively deserted. She was tired of explaining to people who's baby she had and why.

As she stood comparing prices on the half-dozen different brands of diapers, the hair on Becca's neck suddenly stood on end and goose flesh formed on her arms. She looked around, having the oddest feeling of being watched. She turned to look down the aisle, but she seemed to be alone in the store. She spun to look in the opposite direction. Had someone just disappeared around the end cap? Becca blinked several times to clear her vision. No one was there. She shook her head and chuckled.

"I'm definitely not getting enough sleep," she said to Nicole as she plucked a pack of diapers from the shelf and tossed them in the basket beside the baby seat. She pushed the cart a few paces farther to the formula.

"Hey, Becca."

Becca tensed at the sing-song voices in chorus. Turning, she faced Heath Everett and Mike Newhouse. Both had been all-star athletes on every Atlanta Huskies sports team. Both had been offered hefty scholarships to Central Michigan University, and both were friends of Toby's.

"Hey," Becca answered. "What are you guys doing back in town?"

"Just came home for the weekend," Heath said.

"Really? That's weird. I thought you guys were playing North Dakota State tonight. Won't you get in big trouble for missing the game?"

"Yeah, well." Mike scratched the end of his nose. "There was this little *incident* last week and…"

"Hey Mike, check this out," Heath interrupted, moving around Becca to look at the baby in the cart. "Seems like holier-than-thou Becca Weaver has been doing the horizontal disco."

Mike grinned. "Funny, but you didn't look preggers at the fair when Toby kicked your butt."

Becca's temper, which had been building to a slow simmer all day, began to boil over. She pushed herself between the two football players and turned around to face them, guarding the baby lest she be violated by their mocking eyes.

"The baby isn't mine, morons," she ground out. "She belongs to a friend, not that it's any business of yours. And need I remind you that Toby did not kick my butt at the fair, he beat me by one lousy point!"

Toby was headed straight for the cooler of twenty-ounce drinks, thinking about nothing but getting his caffeine fix when he heard a familiar voice that was a mere decibel away from being shrill. He abruptly turned on his heel and headed across the store, looking down each aisle as he went.

"Oh man, Heath, this must be Vince's spawn." There was no mistaking Mike Newhouse's permanently off-pitch voice.

"She's not a spawn!" Becca spit out the words just as Toby turned down the aisle filled with diapers and jars of baby food. Her eyes glittered with fury and her cheeks were as red as the apples in the Cooper orchard. "I swear, what kind of education are you getting at that fancy college downstate?"

"A heck of a lot better than what you're getting, I bet," Heath sneered. "Where are you going again? Oh yeah, the University of Alpena." Both boys snickered.

"Hey guys, long time no see." Toby came up behind Heath and Mike, slapping each of them on the shoulder a little harder than necessary.

"Toby, my man!" Heath greeted. The three exchanged a series of hand slaps and knuckle bumps. "What are you doin' here?"

"Just got off work. Came to get my Dew," Toby replied, looking at Becca. Angry sparks were still flying from her eyes. "Then I heard the distinct sound of a damsel in distress."

"I was not in…" Becca spluttered.

Heath nearly fell in the aisle laughing. "Becca? A damsel in distress?" he managed between snorts of laughter. "Man, Tob, you nearly got me there."

Toby pierced both boys with a serious stare, unsmiling. Mike reddened and took a step back, scratching the end of his nose. Heath, not realizing the danger of the situation, hooked a thumb toward Becca and the baby.

"Hey, wait a minute. Maybe this isn't Vince's spawn. Maybe it's yours, Toby!"

"Good grief! Why don't you go crawl back under the rock you slithered out from," Becca snapped. She grabbed two cans of baby formula and tossed them in the cart. With a quick jerk she spun the cart around and hurried toward the checkout lanes. Heath continued to snicker at her departing back.

"Guys," Toby said quietly. He reached out and grabbed them each by the collar, pulling their heads in close to his. The laughter died on Heath's lips. Mike stared at the floor. "You ever, I mean *ever*," he emphasized with a little shake, "harass Becca again, I will personally hunt you down and skin you alive. We clear?"

"Sure Tob," Mike agreed with a quick nod.

"Hey man, we were just funnin'" Heath defended.

"Yeah, well, go find your fun somewhere else." He released the two and pushed them away, watching as they hurried down the aisle.

By the time he got to the cash register, Becca was nowhere to be seen. Toby hurried out of the store, forgetting what he had come in for. He caught Becca as she was tossing her purchases into the trunk of her car.

"Hey Bec, you okay?"

"I did not need rescuing!" she spat.

"Oh," Toby huffed out a laugh. "I'm sure you didn't. It's just that..."

"Do you know what those two dung beetles said? They said you kicked my butt at the fair!" She slammed the trunk with far more force than was necessary, rocking the little compact. Nikki yowled her displeasure from the back seat. A look of frustration and fury fluttered across Becca's face. Toby swallowed a chuckle

"They, uh." He cleared his throat and bit down on the inside of his cheek to keep from smiling. "They were just trying to rile you up. You're, uh, you're pretty when you're all snappy with temper. Looks like it worked."

"Go jump." Becca brushed around him and reached for her car door.

Toby laid a gentle hand on her arm, remembering Wes's advice to be the best friend she'd ever had.

"What gives?" he asked quietly. "You're way more flaked out than Heath and Mike warrant. Something's got you stressed to the max."

"Let's see." She stared off across the top of her car and blinked quickly. Toby saw the sheen of tears and something squeezed his heart and held tight. He fought the urge to wrap his arms around her. "I've got homework stacked to the ceiling, I'm getting about zero hours of sleep a night, I've got my mother breathing down my neck every second about calling children's services and I'm about sick to death of playing house."

"Then why don't you?"

"Why don't I what?" Becca threw him a blank look.

"Call children's services."

"I can't!" she wailed. She laid her arms across the top of her car and dropped her head onto them. "I can't do that to Vi, and most of all I can't do that to Nikki. I've heard all those horror stories about children trapped in the system. I can't make Nicole another victim. Not that I didn't threaten it." Becca's voice was muffled by the sleeves of her sweatshirt.

Toby moved behind her and kneaded the tight cords of her neck. Her hair felt like spun silk beneath his fingers. Surprisingly, Becca didn't complain or pull away.

"So you talked to Violet?"

"Yes." Becca sighed and turned around, forcing Toby to drop his hands. She leaned back against the side of the car. "I finally got a hold of her last night. It sounded like she was at some sort of party, but she said it was just Vince's uncle's house was full of people. I told her if she wasn't here by Monday, I would call the authorities." Becca shrugged tiredly. "She pretty much called my bluff."

A beat-up, black car cruised slowly through the parking lot. Becca straightened and followed the car's progress with her eyes.

"What is it?"

"Nothing," Becca answered slowly. She slumped back against the car and scrubbed her hands over her face. "I'm just tired. I keep thinking I see...someone. But it's just my exhausted brain playing tricks on me."

"Becca, I'm worried about you. I know Vi's your friend, but she's using you. She brought Nicole into this world. It's her responsibility to care for her, not yours. It's not fair that you're paying the price for her mistake."

"Is that all Nikki is, a mistake?" Becca asked. She bent to look in the window. "My mother called her a sordid mess and a consequence. But to me she just looks like an innocent baby, a baby who deserves better than this."

"So do you, Becca, so do you. What are you supposed to do, put your life on hold indefinitely?"

"I don't know. I just keep praying that Vi will come home. The sooner, the better. At least you'll be glad to know I had to turn Bobby down. He called and asked me out, but I told him I couldn't go because of Nikki. There's no way I was going to ask Rhonda or Penny to baby sit while I went out on a date."

Toby felt an odd mixture of resentment and relief. Nicole's cries increased in volume.

"I've gotta go." Becca spun and yanked open her car door, lowering herself into the seat with one quick motion.

"If you need anything," Toby offered lamely.

"Yeah, well, if you have any sanity I can borrow..." Becca turned the key and the car roared to life.

Toby stepped back, watching as she drove from the parking lot and disappeared around the corner. His mind was already working in overdrive, planning on how he could be Becca's hero one more time.

The chime of the doorbell echoed down the hallway of the Weaver farmhouse. Becca glanced at the clock on the kitchen stove and pushed herself tiredly from the table. She padded down the hall to the front door, not even bothering to peek out the window before swinging the door wide. Toby stood on the front porch.

"What are you doing here?"

"Well." Toby smiled shyly and looked down at his feet. "Since you had to opt out of your date with Bobby, I thought I'd try and make up for it. I brought a movie to watch." He held up the DVD in its heavy plastic box. "And snacks." He held up the bag in his other hand.

"Toby, don't try and fool me. You weren't the least bit upset when I told you I had to turn Bobby down. You were probably doing cartwheels all the way across the parking lot of the IGA after I left."

"I can't deny that Bobby's loss is my gain," he replied. Becca narrowed her eyes. "Come on, cut me some slack here." He shook the movie in its box. "It's the latest pirate movie. I *know* you have a thing for Orlando Bloom."

"Oh good grief, you're so infuriating." Becca spun away from the door and padded back down the hall toward the kitchen. She heard the door close and the squeak of Toby's tennis shoes as he followed her.

"Why, because I'm right all of the time?" Toby asked, stepping into the kitchen.

"You are not right all the time," Becca returned, plopping down at the kitchen table. "Like tonight for instance. I wouldn't have been able to go out with Bobby anyway, because I have too much homework to do." She motioned to the books spread out in front of her. "I don't have time to sit around watching movies, with Bobby or you, so there."

Toby set the DVD on the table and picked up a text book.

"This is English comp. You can do this stuff in your sleep," he argued. "And you've got all afternoon tomorrow to work on it."

"But the baby is sleeping now."

"All the more reason to take advantage of this time and relax. Becca." He leaned down, his brown eyes burning into her own. "You are stressed to the limit. You need to take a little time for yourself and unwind. Where's your folks?" he asked, looking around.

"Over at Wes and Rhonda's, as if you didn't know."

"I didn't know. What?" He looked at her, eyebrows raised. "You think I'm spying on you now? Oh, well, maybe Wes *did* mention something about them coming over for dinner tonight." A grin suddenly split his face and Becca found herself smiling in reply. He reached for her hand. "Come on, a couple hours staring at Orlando will have you feeling good as new."

Winning Becca

Becca found herself being pulled into the family room and didn't have the energy to resist. Toby pushed her down onto the sofa then went to the television. Crouching down in front of the entertainment center, he popped the video in then headed back to the kitchen. Minutes later he returned with a bowl of popcorn in one hand and two twenty-ounce drinks in the other.

"Mademoiselle, your *boisson*," he said, handing her a bottle of cola. Becca made choking noises in her throat.

"Now you're speaking *French*?" she asked with a snort of laughter.

"I did take two years of it in high school you know," Toby replied, looking hurt. He plopped down beside her and placed a bottle of Mountain Dew on the floor between his feet.

"Just don't go getting any ideas about *amour* during the movie, got it?" She looked at him pointedly. "I know you, Toby, and you've had amour on the brain for months now and if that's what you're thinking you can just march right out of this house and over to Melissa Mehan's."

"Get over yourself, Bec." Toby reached for his drink and twisted it open with a quick flick of his wrist. "I'm just here as your friend. Now quit yapping and turn on the movie."

Twenty minutes later Becca reached for the remote and hit 'pause.'

"Hey!" Toby complained, pointing at the TV screen.

"Shhh!" Becca commanded, putting a finger over her lips. The cry came again. "I thought so. Nikki's awake." She made a move to get up but Toby put a restraining hand on her knee.

"I'll go get her." He quickly stood.

"You don't know where…"

"I'll follow the sound," he said, tugging his ear.

"But she's in my…" Becca began. Toby waved away her protest and quickly left the room. She heard him hurry up the stairs. Moments later he returned carrying the baby. "You shouldn't have gone into my room!" Becca complained.

"Why? Didn't want me to see those posters of Orlando and Johnny plastered all over your walls?" Toby asked with a smirk. "Here." He set Nicole in her arms.

"She needs her bottle." Becca went to get up.

"I know. I watched you do it the other night. I think I can figure it out. And here." He thrust a diaper at her. "Figured you'd probably need one of these, too."

"Good golly, Miss Molly, you are insufferable!"

"Now Becca," Toby stopped in the doorway and screwed up his lips. "We both know what insufferable means. It means unable to be suffered or tolerated, and that is certainly not true of me. I'm being helpful and astute, what could you find intolerable about that?"

Toby left the room. Becca pulled her knees up and rested the baby against her thighs.

"He is insufferable," she said to Nikki. "He thinks he's so blasted smart! And did I ask him to be helpful? No. We've been doing just fine, haven't we, without his so-called help."

"Don't be filling her head full of lies now," Toby ordered, returning with a bottle in his hand. Becca snatched it from him and lowered Nicole so she could nurse.

"What lies?" she said sweetly, looking Toby square in the eye. "I wasn't telling her any lies."

Toby resumed his seat and reached for the remote. The movie came to life once more.

"I don't think this movie is baby appropriate."

"Becca, she's what, a month old? I doubt she's paying any attention."

Toby slouched low on the sofa, his head lolling now and then to watch Nicole take her bottle. Becca could feel his cheek as it brushed her shoulder and told herself to pull away, but for some reason she couldn't make herself do it. It felt oddly comforting, having Toby here. Almost like they were a real family.

The thought had Becca bolting upright. Nikki gave a start and let out a cry. Becca took the bottle from the baby's mouth and lifted her to her shoulder to burp. The motion gave her the perfect opportunity to scoot slightly away from Toby. This was not her baby, they were not a family, and Becca had far too many dreams to ever allow herself to think about "playing house" with Toby Sinclair!

"Everything okay?" Toby asked, shooting her a questioning look.

"Yeah, sorry. The movie, it just made me jump, that's all." What had been on the screen? Becca realized she hadn't even been watching. "I scared Nikki when I started like that."

She laid Nicole back down and held the bottle to her lips. Toby shifted in his seat. Leaning on the arm of the sofa, he pulled a pillow under his head. Becca should have been relieved to have the space between them, but it suddenly made her feel cold and lonely, which only made her feel annoyed. She wasn't about to feel *amour* for Toby, not in a million, bazillion years.

CHAPTER TEN

᭢

Becca was not the least bit surprised when Violet did not show up on Monday. At least she did call, even if the conversation left Becca feeling more frustrated than ever, especially since it sounded distinctly like Vi was calling from a bar.

"Are you still at Vince's uncle's house?" Becca asked. There was a long pause.

"Actually, no," Vi was slow to answer. "Vince took off again. His uncle thinks he could be headed to a cousin's house, down around Kalamazoo. I'm calling from a truck stop."

"Kalamazoo! Violet, are you *insane*? You can't go traipsing all over the state. Get back here this instant and take care of your daughter!" Becca wished she could crawl through the phone and slap her friend upside the head.

"Soon, Becca, I promise."

"Yeah, right! Your promises mean nothing. Vi, I can't go on like this forever. My sister can't keep babysitting, she has her hands full with Brendan and the orchard opening next weekend. If I ask Penny to keep watching her, then Nate is going to get even more suspicious than he already is. The Elk Festival is this weekend, too, and Emma's got me working open to close. You have to get home!"

"I have an idea. Let me call you right back."

In an instant the phone went dead. Ten minutes later it rang again.

"Okay," Violet said. "I talked to my Aunt Connie. She's the only one around there that I trust, besides you. She'll watch Nicole while you're at class or work, but she can't keep her past four because that's when my uncle gets home and he'll blow a gasket if there's a baby in the house when he comes in wanting his supper. Do you remember where my Aunt Connie lives?"

"Vaguely," Becca answered without enthusiasm. She could barely picture the house, but she could remember perfectly the intimidating form of Violet's Uncle Joe, who had always scared the living daylights out of her, even when he was sober as a judge.

"They've got that old brick farmhouse down McMurphy Road, pretty much right on your way to school. And not far out of your way on the days you work."

"Great, Vi, just great. Why do I get the distinct impression that you aren't planning on coming home anytime soon? Do you have any idea what you're doing to Nikki, not to mention me and the rest of us who are forced to deal with this mess you've left behind?"

"I'm sorry, Becca, really I am. You're the best friend, better than best, and I know you hate me right now for this. But you have to believe me, I'm doing this *for* Nikki."

"No, Violet, I don't believe you. Because right now I don't think you're doing this for Nikki, I think you're doing it for yourself."

This time it was Becca who hung up the phone. Tomorrow she would drop Nicole off at Violet's aunt's house, and pray the whole way that she didn't run into Joe Compton.

For God has not given us a spirit of fear, but of power and of love and of a sound mind.

The Scripture from Second Timothy floated through Becca's tired brain. She squeezed her eyes shut, trying to absorb that simple truth.

But if God hadn't given her a spirit of fear, then why did she feel so frightened, for herself, and Violet and most of all for Nicole?

She sighed. Wasn't the second part of that verse something about a "sound mind"? Well, it was obvious she didn't have one of those, or else she wouldn't be in this predicament in the first place. If she had a sound mind she would have turned the whole matter over to the authorities days ago. If she were of a sound mind she would never set foot on Joe Compton's property.

Lord, have mercy! It was a pleading prayer straight from Becca's heart.

In her room, Becca stared down at the sleeping Nikki who was blissfully unaware of the storm of emotions and controversy swirling around her tiny form. Becca tried to harden her heart against the love that was blossoming for this innocent little angel.

How could any mother run off and abandon her child the way Violet had? Nicole wasn't even her child and Becca couldn't fathom setting her in the grass and just walking away. But tomorrow she would have to leave her with Violet's Aunt Connie.

"She is not my child," Becca reminded herself, putting emphasis on each word.

But what if…?

The question tugged at the corner of Becca's heart.

What if she had allowed herself to get carried away with Bobby?

What if Nicole was really her child?

What if Violet never came home?

Shaking her head to clear it of such thoughts, Becca turned resolutely to her desk and the ever-present pile of homework. With grim determination she shoved aside thoughts of tomorrow and what if's. Didn't the Bible say something about not worrying about tomorrow, because tomorrow had enough trouble of its own? Something like that. Becca sat down at her desk and just stared at the textbooks stacked in front of her, her mind still on the verse. She thought it was from Matthew. As if pulled by a puppet string, Becca got back up from her desk and went to her bedside table. She picked up her Bible and thumbed to the book of Matthew, looking for the familiar verse that she knew was underlined. It was easy to find, under the heading 'Do Not Worry.'

Becca read aloud softly. "Therefore I say to you, do not worry about your life." She paused, staring out through the window to the setting sun glittering on golden cornfields, ready for harvest. That was a profound word right there. Do not worry about your life. For a moment Becca closed her eyes, allowing the Lord's peace to settle quietly into her heart. She quickly scanned the remaining verses in the sixth chapter of Matthew, about the birds of the air and the lilies of the field. She stopped once more when she got to verse thirty-three, the verse preceding the one she was actually looking for.

"But seek first the kingdom of God and His righteousness, and all these things shall be added to you," Becca read.

Had she been seeking God at all in this situation with Nicole and Violet? Becca easily answered her own question with a resounding no. She had only been consumed with how this was affecting *her*. How it was messing up *her* plans for *her* life.

"Forgive me, Lord," she prayed quietly. "Help me to see Your hand in this. Lead me to know what is Your will where Nikki is concerned and to stop worrying about myself."

Glancing back down at the Bible in her hands, Becca finished reading verse thirty-four. The familiar words of Jesus telling His followers, "Therefore do not worry about tomorrow, for tomorrow will worry about its own things. Sufficient for the day is its own troubles."

Okay, Lord, I won't worry about tomorrow. I'm leaving this situation in Your hands. But please, can we keep the 'troubles' to a minimum?

Winning Becca

The farmyard of Connie and Joe Compton was neat as a pin. Becca parked in the drive and looked around, curiosity warring with trepidation. The brick farmhouse, though old, was in good repair. Off to the right of the driveway was a chicken coop, surrounded by a well-maintained fence. Inside the chicken yard, an assortment of white hens scratched in the hard earth while a red rooster kept watch. Becca's blue eyes took in the woodpile next to the house, amply supplied for the winter. The only vehicle in sight was a 1985 Buick parked near the front porch, its navy blue paint faded from time but the car appeared to be in good condition.

Do not worry, do not fear, do not worry, do not fear.

The mantra played over and over in Becca's head as she removed Nicole's carrier from the back seat and walked up the step to the front door. At her timid knock, the door swung inward on well-oiled hinges.

"Hello Becca," Connie Compton greeted, her voice soft but warm.

"Mrs. Compton." Becca nodded, realizing that Violet's aunt hadn't changed at all in the five years or more since Becca had seen her last. She still wore her reddish-brown hair in the same short, permed style. Her solid form was dressed in brown corduroy slacks and a cream cable knit sweater that Becca judged to be at least ten years old.

"Come in, come in." Connie held the door wider and Becca stepped across the threshold, into the warmth of a small parlor that smelled of bee's wax and Pine-sol. "Let me meet my new great-niece."

Winning Becca

The baby carrier was whisked out of Becca's hand and in mere moments Connie had unbundled Nicole and sat rocking the infant in a solid oak rocker near a small wood burning stove.

"I didn't realize you hadn't seen the baby yet," Becca finally managed to squeak out.

"Shouldn't really surprise you much, considering the crazy Compton family ways." Connie smiled and Becca was encouraged to walk farther into the room, depositing the diaper bag on a nearby settee.

"Well, I'm sorry to inconvenience you this way."

"It appears dear child, that you are the one being inconvenienced," Connie stated. "Unfortunately, Violet's apple didn't fall far enough from the family tree."

"Oh, Violet's okay," Becca defended. "She's just in love, you know. And girls in love do crazy things sometimes."

"Yes, I know," Connie answered slowly, a note of sadness creeping into her voice. Her eyes stayed steadily on Nicole.

"It's awfully kind of you to help out this way."

"Oh poo, not so kind really," Connie waved the compliment away. "Just selfish. Steven moved to Arizona and Charles is in Pittsburg. Joe's not big on traveling, so I don't get to see the grandkids much. It will be nice to have a baby around for a bit. But Violet did tell you…"

"Yes, I know. Pick her up before four o'clock." Becca answered quickly. "Don't worry. I don't want to…" She bit her lip to stop the flow of words. "I

Winning Becca

don't want to wear out Nikki's welcome, so I'll be here between 3 and 3:30. Everything she needs is in here." Becca motioned to the diaper bag. "She's due to eat again around 10 or so. I've got to hurry or I'll be late for class. Thank you again, Mrs. Compton, for helping me out like this."

Back out on the front porch, Becca stood still, listening. For what? Becca realized she was holding her breath, waiting for Nikki's now-familiar cry. How silly! She tried to shake off the feeling of...what? Not unease really. Then she recognized it, the same feeling that had assailed her when she left Nicole with Penny. That odd feeling of anxiety and longing that must come with leaving your child...

Stop! Becca commanded herself. She raked her fingers through her hair, pulling it away from her face and holding tight. She *is not* your child! She yanked slightly with each word, as if that would help the truth sink into her hard head. With a heavy sigh she jumped off the porch and headed for her car. As she drove to Alpena, Becca kept up a running conversation with the Lord.

"Jesus, Nicole isn't my child. She isn't really even Violet's child. She's Your child. You say in Your Word that You know the plans You have for her. Plans to give her a future and a hope. Father God I ask that Nicole's future would include being part of a happy family. Having a mommy and daddy that will love her and care for her, who will teach her Your Word. I know deep in my heart that I am not that person. You've put Nikki in my care for now, for whatever purpose. But somehow I know that I'm not supposed to fall in love with her as a mother does with her child. Guard my heart, Lord. And if it's Your will, bring Violet home today."

Movement in her rearview mirror caught Becca's eye and she glanced up. A black car was riding her tail. What in the world? Becca looked at her speedometer. She was going the limit. She looked ahead. There was plenty of room to pass if the driver was in such a hurry. Why wasn't he going around her? She glanced again in the rearview mirror, trying to see who was behind the wheel. Was it one of her friends trying to be funny? Becca didn't think so. She didn't immediately recognize the face behind the reflective sunglasses. The dark ball cap pulled low over the brow didn't help, either. Something about the car struck a cord of familiarity, but Becca couldn't put her finger on where she had seen it before. She slowed down as she approached Hillman, and as she passed through town, the car turned left, heading north.

"Good, let him go tailgate someone else," Becca muttered, relieved. But for some reason she couldn't shake the ominous feeling that settled over her soul. And this time, it had nothing to do with Nicole.

Yesterday had been the big day. Toby stared down the road toward Becca's house and wondered if Violet had come and gotten Nicole. Becca hadn't seemed any too certain that her threat would bring Vi home. But here it was, well past nine and Becca and the baby were nowhere in sight.

A shrill whistle split the quiet morning air and Toby turned, not sure if his boss was whistling for him or for Ranger, his giant German shepherd. Ranger frolicked like a pup at his master's feet, but Wes was certainly waving for Toby. Hunching his shoulders deeper into his sweatshirt against the chill, Toby trotted toward the barn.

"I got the stuff just like you told me to," Toby said, not wanting his boss to think he was slacking off. "The back of my Bronco is stuffed to the gills with every size and color of Indian corn. The guy down in Fairview gave us a really good price."

"Good." Wes nodded. Toby knew Wes was pleased, even if he didn't show it outwardly. "We'll see how it sells this year and if it looks like a money maker, I'll put a couple acres of it in come spring."

"Rhonda says a lot of people going to the pumpkin patch want the whole experience now. It's not just about buying a pumpkin anymore."

"That's right. If they just want a pumpkin, they'll buy it at the grocery store. Young families now, they want one-stop shopping. Apples, pumpkins, Indian corn, gourds, crafts. You name it. But one thing at a time. I don't plan on diving into the deep end until I know this thing will float. Let's see how the Indian corn does this year and if it's a big seller, I'll plant my own. Then next year we'll try something else. Next thing you know Rhonda will be saying we need carnival rides."

"I did hear Becca offer to do pony rides."

"Yeah, we thought about it. But I looked into it with my insurance agent. The liability for something like that is huge. It's a big enough gamble doing the hay rides. I'm planning to put you in charge of that, if you think you can handle it."

Toby straightened his shoulders. "Of course, no problem."

"That will just be a weekend thing, Friday, Saturday and Sunday. It's too late to get the word out to the schools now, but next year we're hoping to talk to the schools, maybe get some field trips coming in. Today though our job is to work on this barn, get it ready to host a whole bunch of people wanting hot cocoa, cider and donuts."

"Okey-doke." Toby rubbed his hands together and looked around the cavernous barn, wondering where they could start. Wes went over to a work bench and began packing tools into boxes. Toby followed suit, his mind drifting back to their conversation. "Too bad about the pony ride thing. Becca's great with kids. She would have had them eating out of her hand in no time, and their parents emptying their pockets."

"Is that who you were looking for?" Wes asked.

"When?" Toby carefully placed a ratchet set in the box he was packing.

"Ten minutes ago. Standing up there in the driveway, staring down the road."

"No. Well, um…" Wes threw him a look. Toby chewed the inside of his cheek. "I wasn't really *looking* for her. It's more like I was wondering."

"Wondering what?" Wes scooped up an armload of motor oil bottles and deposited them in a box.

"If Violet showed up yesterday to get Nicole. Becca gave her an ultimatum. Said if Vi wasn't here by Monday she would call children's services."

"Well, I don't know if Vi came back or not," Wes said. "All I know is that Becca didn't show up here, so I guess that could mean she doesn't have the baby anymore. I don't know who else she would get to watch her."

"The college campus has a daycare," Toby observed.

"They don't let just anyone drop a kid off," Wes argued. "You have to have papers proving who you are. You have to have shot records and all that. Becca's not Nicole's legal guardian or anything, so there's no way she could enroll her in daycare."

"What do you think will happen if Violet doesn't come back?" Toby asked. Wes just shrugged one wide shoulder and continued working. Toby sat down on a tool box. "I've been thinking…"

"Oh Lord, help us all," Wes muttered. "I bet I can guess what, or who, you've been thinking about."

"No! This isn't about Becca. It's about Nikki. Well, I guess it is sort of about Becca."

"I'm shocked."

"Wes, be serious for a minute." Toby had the temerity to frown at his boss, the former Army Ranger who knew a hundred ways to kill without using a gun. Wes stopped working and put his hands on his hips.

"Okay Toby, I'm seriously listening. What is it that you've been thinking."

"If Vi doesn't come back, who would get custody of the baby?"

"I'm not an expert on this sort of thing, Toby. Nate would probably be able to answer your questions a whole lot better than I can."

"But do you think Becca could keep Nicole? I mean, Violet *gave* Nikki to Becca. So couldn't Becca just keep Nicole and raise her herself?"

"For starters, I don't think Becca has any legal right to that baby. She isn't Violet's next of kin. She isn't even a blood relative. There's no way the state is gonna let her keep that baby, even if she wanted to. Second of all, Becca is only eighteen. She's going to college. She wants to open her own preschool someday. She's got no business being a single mother at her age."

"What if she didn't have to be a single mother. What if someone was willing to help her raise the baby. You know, be a real family."

Wes just stared down at the ground, shaking his head slowly. "I take it that someone would be you." He finally raised his head and pierced Toby with his cool gray eyes. Toby raised his chin a notch.

"Yeah, so what?"

"Toby, you're crazy. No kid in his right mind wants to become a father at your age, much less the father to some other guy's baby."

"Look." Toby jumped up from his makeshift seat. "I care about Becca. A lot. We're both good with Nikki. I think we could make it work."

"It doesn't matter what you think, Toby. There's no way you would get that baby unless Violet signed a legal document of some sort handing over guardianship to Becca. Which I don't believe she's ever going to do. It's a moot point anyway, I'm sure, because I think Vi will come back home, in her own good time."

"And if she doesn't?"

"Then I assume, considering Violet's home life, that Nicole would become a ward of the state. She would go through the system until a family is found for her, however that works."

"Where does that leave Becca?"

"In school, where she belongs," Wes answered adamantly.

"Then where does that leave me?" Toby asked, feeling totally dejected. He felt a strong hand clasp his shoulder.

"On your knees, where you belong," Wes said, giving Toby's shoulder a small shake. "Praying the hardest prayer in the world to pray."

Toby looked into his boss's serious eyes. "And what would that be?" he wondered.

"Not my will but Yours be done, Lord."

CHAPTER ELEVEN

The Weaver farmyard was quiet. The house was still, only a few lights shining from the downstairs windows. Toby parked behind Becca's car and sat looking at the house for several moments before climbing to the ground. He looked up at the night sky. It was clouded over, no stars in sight. A slight breeze stirred the treetops, making the oak leaves rustle. A stronger gust sent dried leaves skittering across the driveway. The smell of wood smoke drifted on the air.

Heading around the house, Toby peeked in the kitchen window. Becca was bent over the table, her pen scratching over the notebook in front of her. Nicole was not in sight. Maybe Violet *had* come home. Toby had to fight off the odd feeling of disappointment that washed over him at the thought. He continued to the back door and gave a soft knock. A minute later Becca stood on the opposite side of the glass.

"Toby," she said quietly, opening the door and staring down at him from the top of the steps. "What are you doing here?"

"Well." Toby shoved his hands deep into the pockets of his hooded sweatshirt. "I thought maybe we could go for a walk."

"It's a little chilly for that, don't you think?" Becca asked.

"Oh, come on. Where's your sense of adventure?" Toby stepped up one step. He glanced down at Becca's feet in fuzzy blue slippers. "But you'll need something else on your feet. Throw those on." He motioned to a pair of large rubber boots sitting next to the door. "And that, too." He pointed to a fleece lined flannel jacket hanging on a hook.

"Look Casanova, if you're going to start spouting about stars and freckles and amour and all that junk…"

"Hey, who said amour is junk?" Toby asked, trying to sound offended. "And look, there are no stars tonight." He motioned to the sky. Becca leaned out the door and looked up. "Come on," Toby coaxed. "I bet you've been locked up indoors all day. When's the last time you got some exercise? A little fresh air will do you good."

Becca heaved a sigh. "You're right about one thing, I have been cooped up indoors all day. But if *you* start getting fresh…" She left the threat hanging between them.

"I know, I know. You'll sick Bobby on me. I get it." Toby waived away her protests. "Seems to me Bobby's the one you need to worry about, if I remember correctly. Come on, throw those boots on and let's go."

Surprisingly, Becca did as she was ordered, slipping out of her fuzzy house shoes and shoving her feet into the boots that looked to be five sizes too big. She grabbed the coat off the hook and stuffed her arms into the sleeves while clomping down the cement back steps.

"I can tell you right now I'm not walking far in these boots," she warned, scuffing along beside Toby as he walked across the yard toward the barn. "Now, what is your real reason for wanting to get me out here alone in the dark? And don't give me all that horse poop about walks and exercise and fresh air."

"Geez Bec, why are you always questioning my motives?" The look she shot him gave Toby his answer. He stopped near the horse pasture and turned to face Becca fully. "You never showed up at Rhonda's this morning. And I didn't see any baby paraphernalia on the kitchen table. I take it Violet showed up and got Nicole?"

"No." Becca shook her head and pulled her jacket tighter as a cold gust of wind kicked up. Toby moved a bit closer, trying to shield her from the breeze. "But she did call. I told her I had tapped out all my babysitters and that Nate was getting suspicious. She arranged for me to take Nikki to her Aunt Connie's while I'm at school and work."

"Oh." Relief flooded Toby, knowing that Becca still had the baby. But he also felt disappointed that he wouldn't be seeing her at Wes and Rhonda's anymore.

"I probably shouldn't admit this to you." Becca peeked up at him through her lashes, making Toby's heart miss several beats. "But I was petrified going over there. Violet's Uncle Joe always put the fear of God in me for some reason."

"Really?" Toby couldn't hide his surprise. "I thought Becca Weaver was completely fearless."

"Don't lie. You always knew I was scared to death of spiders and you used that knowledge to torment me every chance you got!"

"Remember that time at the fair?" Toby started to chuckle.

"Remember? I had nightmares for weeks! You coming over to congratulate me, all chummy, and you put a granddaddy long leg *on my back*! That's when I really started hating you."

"Aw, you don't hate me, Bec. And spiders are harmless. Just like Joe Compton. He's not a bad guy. My dad did some logging with him. He certainly isn't a drunk like his brother. He's just big."

"And hairy," Becca added.

"And loud."

"And domineering," she finished.

"But nothing for you to be afraid of," Toby reassured. He balled his fist and made a playful swipe at her jaw, which she easily knocked away. "You could probably kick his butt."

Becca snorted, unladylike. "Well, I'd rather not find out. Violet told me I had to pick Nikki up before four o'clock or her uncle would blow a fuse. Connie seemed to agree. She reminded me that I had to be there well before Joe got home. After my classes that won't be a problem. But I'm worried about work. Especially this weekend, with the Elkfest going on. The teashop is bound to be slammed and I'm afraid I won't get out of there in time."

"I'll pick her up." The offer was out of his mouth before Toby had time to even think about it.

"Don't be silly…"

"I'm not being silly. I don't mind, really. I'm usually done working for Wes by four. It's the perfect solution. You can't ask Rhonda or Penny and you know your mom won't do it. I'm all you've got left, Becca."

"I really shouldn't accept your offer, but I don't have time to argue." Becca glanced back toward the house. "I need to get back inside. For all I know, Nikki could be screaming her lungs out by now." She turned and started making her way back across the lawn. Toby fell into step beside her. "And as much as I hate to admit you're right…"

"Whoa, whoa, whoa." Toby grabbed her arm, stopping her. "Say that again please."

"Oh good grief! I will not." Becca pulled away from his hand and kept walking. "You heard me perfectly well and you know it. I can't ask anyone else and I can't risk being late to pick up Nicole. That means you are my last resort." She stopped at the back door, one booted foot on the bottom step, one hand on the doorknob. Finally she turned her face up to him and smiled. "I know this is probably more shock than your delicate system can handle in one night, but I really do appreciate you, Toby. Goodnight."

Winning Becca

Toby stood in the dark and watched Becca disappear inside the mudroom. He could tell from the slight light from the kitchen that she was shucking her boots and jacket. Soon he heard the click as she opened the door to the kitchen. With a smile splitting his face, Toby made his way back around to the driveway, pausing next to the Bronco to glance back at the house. It was working. He was becoming Becca's friend. Soon he would be her hero, and eventually he was going to be her husband. Grabbing the door handle, Toby yanked open the driver's side door, and remembered to pray,

"But your will be done, Lord." And he tried to mean it.

As if they had a will of their own, Becca's feet carried her down the hall, up the stairs and across the floor to the second story window that looked down on the driveway. She watched as Toby stopped next to his Bronco and looked back at the house. She saw the flash of his white teeth as he smiled before opening the door and climbing inside. She continued to stare out the window as he backed out of the driveway and disappeared down the road, his taillights quickly fading into the night.

Becca shook herself. What in the world was she doing? Staring after Toby like, like, like *Melissa Mehan!* The realization struck her like a blow to the ribs, making Becca feel slightly ill. She began to turn away from the window, but the flash of headlights caught her eye. A car slowed and paused at the end of the driveway.

Had Toby returned to tell her he had changed his mind about picking up Nicole? But no, the car only lingered for the space of several heartbeats before revving its engine and continuing down the road, leaving Becca wondering. A squeaky cry broke the quiet of the upstairs, yanking Becca from her reverie. Nikki was awake and it was time for her bottle. Becca hurried to her room and lifted the infant from the port-a-crib before the squeak could become a full-blown bellow. With the baby cradled in one arm, she went downstairs and began the now familiar routine of warming Nikki's bottle. It struck her how easily she had fallen into the job of being Nicole's mother.

But I am not her mother! Becca reminded herself forcefully as she offered Nikki the bottle. And furthermore I do not like Toby Sinclair!

"I'm not your mommy, Nikki," Becca spoke to the baby as she carried her back upstairs and settled into the rocker in front of the windows. For some reason she felt the need to convince them both of the facts. "It doesn't mean I don't care about you. But your real mommy, she's going to be home any day now and she's going to take care of you and love you like I never could." Nicole stared up at Becca with trusting eyes. "Please don't look at me like that," Becca begged, setting the rocker in motion. She stared out the windows, trying to avoid the truth that was staring up at her. "And Toby! Can you believe I actually told him he was right? And that I appreciate him? Whatever was I thinking? As if he didn't have a big enough head. Good grief! There'll be no living with him after tonight."

Becca felt the suction lesson on the bottle and looked down at Nicole. The baby was simply staring up at her, a slight smile turning up her rosebud mouth.

"Oh, that's just gas," Becca said, setting the bottle on the floor and lifting Nikki to her shoulder. She patted the baby's back gently and continued to rock. "You save those looks for your mommy. She'll be here soon. Maybe even tomorrow. Oh Lord, please, please, please could it be tomorrow? But as for your daddy. Well, I'm not supposed to fill your head with bad thoughts. That would just be wrong of me. I won't say anything about your daddy except may the Lord have mercy on him! That's what your daddy needs more than anything. Jesus. Even more than he needs you." Becca cradled Nikki in her arms and once more offered her the bottle.

"I wonder why the Lord makes certain people parents," Becca continued her running commentary. "Like why did He choose your daddy and not Nate? Nate would make an awesome daddy. And with his looks! Woo wee, would he make some pretty babies! He and Penny together, man, when they have kids they are gonna be knockouts. Even Toby…" Becca tried to stop the thought, but then with a smile she continued. "Even Toby will make a great dad some day. I mean, look at the way he is with you, little girl." She gazed down at Nicole who's eyes were now drooping shut. "He's been real good with you. So it just goes to show it isn't about age. It's about heart. And as much as it pains me to admit, Toby does have a good heart. That's what I'm gonna pray for your daddy, that the Lord will give him a heart to love you like a daddy should. Now, let's get you changed before you fall all the way to sleep." Becca jiggled the baby for emphasis as she rose to get a clean diaper.

With Nicole changed and sleeping soundly once more, Becca returned to the homework she had abandoned in the kitchen. She sat at the table and stared down at the page in front of her, but the words refused to come into focus. Instead, she found herself remembering how it had felt just a few short nights ago, sitting on the couch with Toby and Nikki. It had felt for a moment like they were a real family. Becca tried to picture the same scene with Violet and Vince as the main characters, but her brain just couldn't wrap itself around the image. Well, that didn't matter, Becca reminded herself. Vi and Vince were Nikki's parents. And the Lord was still in charge of the world. He could bring them back and make them a real family. And even if Vince refused to settle down and become a family man, perhaps the Lord would send Violet a true knight in shining armor. Someone who would love Violet and be a father to Nikki.

Bowing her head, Becca prayed for all those things. Prayed that Vince would find the Lord, that Nicole would have a loving home with her parents, and most of all that Violet would come home soon.

Somewhere a baby was crying. The crying grew louder and more demanding. Becca reached through the dark veil of sleep, struggling for wakefulness. Like a diver breaking for the surface, she woke and took a deep breath. Nicole lay in the port-a-crib, screaming her tiny lungs out.

"Oh my, baby, what is it?" Becca asked in alarm as she jumped out of bed and lifted the distressed infant. She squinted at the clock. It wasn't quite time for Nikki's next bottle yet.

Becca held Nicole to her shoulder and patted her back, trying to comfort her as the baby screamed in her ear. Becca jiggled, swayed, rocked, but nothing calmed Nikki down. Maybe a change of diaper would do the trick. But no, the baby wasn't the least bit wet. Still the crying continued.

"Okay, okay. I'll get you a bottle."

Nikki drew up her knees and let out an ear-splitting scream.

"Goodness, what is the matter little one?" Becca asked, fighting down a wave of panic. She quickly lifted the baby and hurried downstairs to make a bottle. When she offered the nipple to Nicole, she just turned her head away and continued to scream. Any minute now her parents were going to come rushing into the room, wanting to know what on God's green earth was going on.

Flying to the phone, Becca lifted the receiver and clasped it between her ear and shoulder, trying to cradle the howling infant at the same time. She quickly punched in Violet's cell phone number. Soon ringing filled one ear as crying filled the other.

"Come on, come on, pick up Vi. Pick up dadblam it!"

"Hi, it's Vi!" A lilting giggle. "Leave a message and I'll get back to you."

Winning Becca

"Oh good grief!" A beep. Nikki continued to scream. "Vi, it's Becca. You hear this baby of yours? She's screaming to wake the dead. Listen, you have to get home and you have to get home *now*. I'm not kidding!" Becca insisted, desperate. "Get your butt back to Atlanta this minute Violet Compton. I don't know what I'm supposed to do." Tears sprang to Becca's eyes and she fought against the vortex of terror that suddenly threatened to pull her under and drown her. "Today, Vi. Do you hear me? You get home today." Becca held the phone close to Nicole's screaming mouth, making sure Vi's voice mail captured the full effect before hanging up the phone.

"What in the world are you doing to that baby?" Mary Weaver demanded. She came across the kitchen tying the sash on her robe.

"Nothing, Mom." This time Becca allowed the tears to spill over. "She woke up screaming and I can't get her to stop. I've tried changing her, walking with her, feeding her. Nothing helps!"

Nicole was lifted from Becca's arms and Mary held the baby suspended in midair for a moment, assessing the situation. Becca followed as her mother carried Nicole into the family room. Mary turned on a lamp before laying the infant on the sofa. Nikki immediately drew up her knees and continued to scream.

"I'd say she has a bad stomach ache, maybe a touch of colic," Mary decided. She rubbed Nicole's tummy for a few moments before lifting the baby and laying her face down over her knees. Slowly the crying lessened somewhat as Mary rubbed Nicole's back in small, comforting circles.

"What if she needs a doctor?" Becca asked, dashing the tears from her cheeks and trying to regain her composure. How could she ever have entertained any kind of fantasy about being this child's mother? There was no way she was equipped to deal with this kind of crisis.

"If this baby needs a doctor then the jig is up, honey." Mary looked up at Becca who read the truth in her mother's eyes. "Legally, you have no right to authorize medical attention for this child. You know how they are these days about that kind of thing. You can't just walk into a clinic with her and ask to see a doctor. They'll find out quite quickly that you aren't the mother, then they'll start asking questions and when they find out her real mother abandoned her on our doorstep, they'll call in the state authorities."

"I don't want that to happen," Becca whispered, sitting down gingerly on the edge of the sofa. Nikki hiccupped, her head bobbing with the motion of Mary's patting.

"I know you don't," Mary admitted. She lifted Nicole and handed her over to Becca, who gladly accepted the now calmed infant. "I've seen how you are with her, how you've taken over the care for her as if she were your own child. But Becca, honey, she's not your baby."

"I know that!" Becca jumped up and began wandering around the room, bouncing Nicole slightly to keep her pacified.

Winning Becca

"You're too young to be saddled with this kind of responsibility," Mary continued. "I've gone along with it because I know Vi is your friend, but…"

"This isn't about Vi anymore, Mom, it's about Nicole. I don't want her languishing in the system." Becca turned to her mother, pleading with her eyes. "She's a sweet baby, an innocent little girl. She shouldn't be punished because her mother has made some poor choices."

"There are plenty of good people waiting to adopt, or even be foster parents. Maybe even someone in Vi's own family would take care of her."

"Mother, you know just about all there is to know about Vi's family and there's no one who should have the care of this baby. The only one Vi trusts is her Aunt Connie, who's willing to help out with babysitting, but there's no way Joe will agree to raise Nicole."

"But Becca, you just started your college education. You should be concentrating on your studies. And enjoying life. I know Bobby's called here a couple times looking for you. And then there's Toby."

"I have absolutely no romantic interest in Toby, Mother." Becca headed for the kitchen to retrieve Nikki's bottle.

"Be that as it may," her mother's voice followed her. "The point still remains that a girl your age should be having fun, not raising some other girl's illegitimate child."

"Please don't use that term," Becca said, reentering the family room with Nicole securely latched on to her bottle. "It's so negative and I don't think that's the way God sees her. Honestly, sometimes I think you'd be happier if Violet had had an abortion."

"That's not true," Mary protested.

"Well then, you have to give Vi some credit. She may not be the greatest mother in the world, she had no business even becoming a mother at this point in time. But at least she gave her child the gift of life. Anyway." Becca passed a hand wearily over her face. "I'm sure this situation isn't going to last forever. I called Vi tonight and left a very explicit message for her to get home. Until she does, I plan to carry this cross the Lord has given me to the best of my ability."

"Okay honey, if that's what you want." Mary hefted herself from the sofa. "I can't say that I agree with you, but your father and I raised you to be the responsible young woman you're proving yourself to be. Just remember, if she wakes up with another one of those tummy aches to lay her over your knees like I just did. Hopefully it will do the trick."

CHAPTER TWELVE

Heaven smiled down upon Atlanta for one of the town's biggest events, the annual Elk Festival. The sun was shining brightly, the northern Michigan sky was a radiant blue, while nature put on a spectacular display of blazing color in the fall trees that were near peak. Briley Township Park, on the banks of the majestic Thunder Bay River, was the hub of all the grand activities. The park itself was packed with vendors selling everything from French fries to flea market finds, from fine, hand-crafted items by local artisans to baked goods being sold by the Atlanta High School marching band. Main Street teemed with cars, visitors coming from near and far to celebrate the Elk Capital of Michigan. Obviously the glorious weather had brought people out in droves.

The Spot of Tea had been a hot-bed of activity all day. Becca, and her boss Emma McGillis, rushed to and fro trying to keep up with the steady stream of waiting customers. Even Emma's husband, Tyler, had been pressed into service, until he had a to leave to work his shift on the Tri-Township fire and rescue squad. With the town jam packed with people, authorities wanted to have plenty of emergency personnel on hand.

Becca could feel her energy flagging. Nikki had continued to be colicky, waking up screaming nearly every night. Thanks to her mother's advice, and some in-depth searching on the internet, Becca had learned how to deal with the midnight tummy aches, but that wasn't helping her get any more sleep. Of course, Nikki slept like an angel for Vi's Aunt Connie.

Vi. Becca grimaced, shocked that she could detest anyone as much as she did her "best friend" at this moment. Oh, Violet had called *sounding* all concerned. But Becca knew better. For one thing, it sounded like Violet was calling from a whorehouse, the sounds of women's squeals and men's deep laughter filling the background.

"Violet, where on God's green earth are you?" Becca had demanded.

"I'm at my cousin's house, it's near Jackson," Vi answered. "Sam, stop! Give a girl a minute, would you?" Violet's lilting giggle filled Becca's ear while red hot anger curled up her spine. Vi was laughing! Her little girl could very well be dieing of a bowel obstruction and Violet was laughing!

"Who the heck is Sam?!" Becca wanted to know, feeling as if the top of her head was going to come flying off. "And where is Vince? I thought you were going to find him in Kalamazoo."

"Nah, that was a false lead. Hold on a sec." Silence hung suspended over the airwaves while

Winning Becca

Becca's stomach churned with fury. "Okay, I locked myself in the bathroom. Anyway, as I was saying, Vince isn't in Kalamazoo. I was able to call his cousin. They haven't seen or heard from him."

"Then why aren't you home? If you're in Jackson, you can be home in about four or five hours. Nikki needs you. What if she's sick? I can't take her to the doctor. Well, I could and then you would probably never see her again. How would you like those apples?"

"I don't think she's sick. And if she is, you can call my Aunt Connie. Connie's got a sister or a sister-in-law, somebody, that's a nurse. She'll help you out." Violet's dismissive attitude stunned Becca.

"I can't believe you, Vi, I really can't. You've turned into someone I don't even know. Someone I don't think I want to know. You have absolutely no right to be a mother."

"That's not true! I love Nikki. I told you, Becca, I'm doing this for her. I've got one more chance to find Vince. Remember how he was so buddy-buddy with the Westlake boys? They moved away last year, remember?" Becca remained stonily silent so Vi continued, "They live in some little town between Jackson and Ann Arbor. I remembered a few things Vince said before he took off and now I think they may have been clues that he would head there."

"And how exactly are you paying for all this gallivanting all over the state?" Becca wanted to know.

"Oh, I manage." The slight hesitation in Vi's voice had Becca imagining all sorts of sordid ways that Vi was "managing."

"Great," Becca said in disgust.

"Becca, I promise I'm on my way home. If I don't find Vince at the Westlake's, then I'm headed straight back to Atlanta."

"You'd better be Violet, or you may find that when you get back here, Nikki isn't going to be waiting for you."

Pulling her mind back from the distressing conversation, Becca instead tried to concentrate on filling her table's order. She glanced at the clock and grimaced. Three-thirty. The teashop was supposed to close at four and it was still standing room only. She thought about Toby, pictured him picking up Nicole from Connie's house and her heart suddenly went light with the oddest flutter.

Back in the dining room, she placed her customers' order on the table. "Can I get you anything else?" she asked politely.

"No thank you, this looks heavenly," the young woman smiled up at Becca as her husband nodded in agreement. "Okay, enjoy then. I'll be back to check on you shortly."

The silver bell over the door gave out its familiar ring. Becca turned to see Penelope enter the teashop, dressed in her crisp Department of Natural Resources uniform. Her long, blond hair was up in a tidy bun and her golden eyes sparkled as if retaining the fall sunshine.

"Hey Penny, how's it going?" Becca asked. "I hope you don't want a seat. This place is filled to the gills. I keep praying the fire marshal doesn't show up!"

"Oh, that's okay." Penny stepped forward and rested a hip against the glass-fronted counter that separated the dining room from the kitchen. "I've been at the park all day, giving educational talks about the elk herd. I just stopped in to see if I could get a couple chicken salad croissants to go."

"Sure, no problem." Becca jotted the order on a tablet next to the cash register before turning toward the kitchen.

"Hey Becca, um..." Becca turned back to see Penny biting her lower lip. "I was just wondering, you know, about Nicole. You didn't say anything about needing me to watch her again. I was just wondering if, you know, if..."

Becca glanced around the filled restaurant. "Why don't you come in back for a sec." She motioned toward the kitchen with her head. Penny straightened and made her way around the counter toward the more private place to talk. Emma rushed out of the kitchen carrying a full tray. Becca and Penny both backed up to make room for her to pass. Becca headed toward the work counter and began preparing Penny's order.

"I'm going to be straight with you, Penny. Violet hasn't come home yet. I'm frustrated and furious and yet, oddly relieved all at the same time. Nikki's been having colic and at first it scared the living daylights out of me. I think there is no way I can keep taking care of her, but then I'll talk to Vi and she gets me so angry that I think I'm glad she's not the one raising that baby right now. That girl is seriously messed up."

"But why didn't you call me? I would have been glad to help," Penny insisted.

"I know you would have. That's why I'm going to be straight with you. I didn't ask you to baby sit again because of Nate. If he knows what is really going on, you know what he'll do. It's his sworn and bound duty to uphold the law. In his eyes, that baby has been abandoned and I know Nate will see it as his responsibility to contact the authorities. I don't want that to happen. I don't want Nikki in the system. And now I will probably wish I hadn't told you this because if Nate asks, I don't want you to have to lie. That would be wrong. But you know how it is around here, people are going to figure it out sooner rather than later, so you might as well know the truth. I didn't want you to get wind of it and have your feelings hurt that I didn't ask you to watch her. I've been leaving Nikki with Violet's Aunt Connie."

Just then a tapping on the kitchen door had Becca lifting her head. Her heart took wing when she saw Toby on the other side of the glass. He held up Nicole who was dressed in a little pink sweatshirt with ears on the hood. Becca couldn't keep the grin from splitting her face as she rushed to let the two of them in.

"Well look who's here," she gushed, reaching to take Nicole from Toby's arms. "How you doing baby?" She tickled Nikki's tummy and the baby smiled.

"Connie said she was great. No bad tummy aches or screaming fits," Toby answered.

"Of course, she likes to save those for midnight or later," Becca said with a laugh. She looked over to

Winning Becca

see Penny staring at Nicole with hungry eyes and her smile faded somewhat.

"I hate to tell you this Toby, but this place is still a madhouse. I don't know when we'll get all these people out of here and the clean ups done. Is there any way you can watch Nikki until I'm through?"

"I can watch her," Penny immediately piped up.

"Oh Pen, I don't think that would be such a good idea after what I just said about Nate," Becca objected.

"Nate's working the Elkfest and probably won't be home until midnight. He would never even know that Nikki was there for an hour."

"But I can't ask you to deceive him. That wouldn't be right."

"You aren't asking me, I'm volunteering to watch her for an hour. There won't be any deceit involved. If Nate asks, I'll tell him the truth, of course. But there won't be any reason for him to ask or be suspicious because by time he gets home, Nikki will be safely back in your care and all signs of a baby being in the house will be erased."

"What about your mom?" Becca asked, still not completely convinced.

"Mom can't hardly even put an entire sentence together. She won't say anything. And I know she'll be thrilled to see Nicole again. She really enjoyed having her in the house."

Becca felt a light touch on her shoulder and looked up to see Toby staring at her, his brown eyes serious. As if reading her mind he said,

"I think it will be okay, Bec. I'll go out and get Nikki's stuff and then I'll hang around for awhile and help with the clean up if you need it. We can go pick Nicole up together if you want to."

Trying to tamp down her misgivings, Becca agreed, relinquishing the baby into Penny's eager arms. She watched from the door as Toby, Penny and the baby walked to Toby's Bronco. Toby took the baby seat out of his vehicle and soon the three disappeared, going to secure the baby in the back of Penny's SUV, no doubt. Squaring her shoulders, Becca turned back to the counter, only to realize that Penny had left without her order. Obviously, the sight of Nicole had driven all thoughts of hunger from Penny's head.

Toby stood and watched Penny's silver SUV disappear into the throng of vehicles that jammed Main Street. He turned and looked at the teashop, knowing it would be a good while yet before Emma and Becca would usher the last customer out the door and start cleaning in preparation for tomorrow's crowd. He walked to the back of the parking lot and climbed atop the picnic table sitting in the sun, thinking. He had seen the shadow that had clouded Becca's eyes when Penny offered to watch Nicole. With some unexplainable intuition he had felt Becca's inner struggle and knew she was reluctant to surrender the baby to Penny's care. Heck, Toby realized he had felt that same struggle just now, watching Penny drive away with Nicole strapped into the back seat.

Winning Becca

Sighing, Toby leaned back on his elbows and stared up at the clear, blue sky. The afternoon sunlight was fading fast, but there was still enough heat to warm his shoulders beneath his grey hooded sweatshirt. Toby closed his eyes and replayed the look of pure joy on Becca's face when she had seen him and Nikki at the door. She had been happy to see him. Not just the baby. Toby knew that Becca had been happy to see *him*. The knowledge sent a thrill down Toby's back and he nearly shivered from the force of it. Now, it was just a matter of figuring out how to get Becca to agree to his plan.

She had told him about her conversation with Violet. Toby had been taken aback by Becca's fury at the girl who had once been her best friend. He had known Becca all his life and he knew she didn't suffer fools gladly. Violet was being the worst kind of fool in Becca's opinion, a mother who refused to take care of her own child. Toby fully agreed, thinking that anyone who would put Vince Schmidt before Nicole was way beyond foolish. But what struck Toby the most was Becca's vehement desire to protect Nikki at all costs. Even though she may deny it with her last breath, Toby knew Becca was falling in love with Nicole. Just like she was falling in love with him. They could become a family. Toby just had to figure out how.

A car door slammed. Toby started, realizing he must have dozed off in the sun. The parking lot was nearly empty. He could faintly hear the sound of the band warming up in the beer tent down by the park. Soon the party would be in full swing. Hefting himself off the table, Toby walked across the gravel parking lot to the kitchen door and let himself in. Becca was seated on a tall stool looking wilted.

"Hard day at the office?" he asked. Becca just shot him the look he was all too familiar with. A strand of hair had escaped her ponytail and she pushed it out of her eyes half-heartedly. "Anything I can do to help?"

"Can you wiggle your nose and make all these dishes disappear?" Becca asked, gesturing to the deep, double sink where delicate china was stacked to the brim.

"No problem." Toby stepped toward the sink, pushing the sleeves of his sweatshirt up to his elbows.

"Actually Toby, you know what?" Becca laid a staying hand on his arm and he felt the warmth of it pierce right to his heart. He looked down into her cornflower blue eyes and felt himself drowning in their tired depths. "Emma's about wiped out. She's been here since five this morning and I know she really wants to get out of here and pick Tiffany up from daycare. Can you go out in the dining room and put all the chairs up on the tables and help sweep? Maybe take the trash out to the dumpster? I'll get started on these."

"Sure, anything for you sweetheart," he said, doing his best Humphrey Bogart impression. Becca wrinkled her nose and pushed him out of the way.

"You are not Bogart and I am not BaCall. So, just get those romantic notions right out of your brain Toby Sinclair," she commanded, but with less ferocity than she had in the past.

Less than an hour later the two of them were standing outside the locked door of the Spot of Tea watching Emma rush to her car and drive away.

"I don't suppose you're up to walking around the festival now, huh?" Toby asked, trying to fight down his disappointment.

"Ah Toby, I'm awfully tired," Becca groaned.

"Yeah, I know. It's just that I was poking around in the attic and I found this baby stroller. It's just one of those little umbrella things. I figured my mom would never miss it and we could push Nicole around for a bit." Toby realized he was still trying to convince her, even though he knew she was exhausted.

"It sounds nice, but I don't want to raise any more suspicions about Vi and Nikki."

"Oh, I never thought about that," Toby admitted. "You'll be working all day again tomorrow, so I guess you won't get to enjoy the festival at all. That's too bad. They have some pretty cool booths set up."

He saw Becca glance at her watch then up at the sky which was slowly turning from vivid blue to soft lavender. "Well, Penny did say Nate wouldn't be home until midnight. My feet are about to fall right off, but I haven't had a minute without that baby in nearly three weeks except when I'm at class or work. Maybe a quick walk around the park isn't such a bad idea."

Toby's heart soared. He nearly reached out to take her hand as they headed down the sidewalk toward the center of town, then thought better of it. He was still trying to convince Becca he was her friend. Not *boyfriend* yet, although that was surely coming.

The music from the band grew louder as they approached the park, the air reverberating with the steady thump-thump-thump of the rhythm. The beer tent was filled to capacity, the crowd spilling over to the tables set up just outside the entrance. Cigarette smoke mingled with the scent of grilling onions. Bursts of laughter rang out from the tent, which was the hub of all the activity. Toby guided Becca through the crowd, a hand discreetly on her elbow. His lips turned up in a small, satisfied smile when she didn't pull away from his touch.

They stopped at several booths to admire the artwork and handcrafts on display. Most of the vendors had ringed their areas with stringed lights, creating a carnival-like atmosphere that soon infused even Becca's tired frame. She and Toby laughed together over a display of t-shirts sporting funny slogans. Each lifted a shirt and turned to the other, busting out with a belly laugh when they realized they had both picked out the same shirt. Toby moved to one corner of the canvass tent that covered the t-shirt vendor's booth and watched as Becca paused near some infant-sized apparel. He saw her lift a tiny t-shirt and smile before folding it carefully and setting it back down atop the pile. She was moving toward him, looking off across the park, when Toby saw her go suddenly rigid. Her mouth fell open in obvious shock. Toby nearly tripped over his own feet trying to get to her side through the crush of people buying five dollar t-shirts.

"Becca, what is it? What's wrong?" he asked, grabbing her by the arm. Becca blinked several times as if coming out of a daze.

"It's Vince," she whispered.

"Vince? Here? Where?" Toby swiveled his head to scan the crowd beyond the tent.

"Over there." Becca pointed toward the park's shelter house. "He was walking up the path."

Toby took Becca by the hand and pulled her from the crush of people, out to the paved walkway that wound through the park. He craned his neck to peer through the gloom and the crowd. He saw lots of guys wearing dark hoodies and caps, but none that looked like Vince.

"Are you sure it was him? I mean, how could you tell in this crowd?"

"I would know that slouching gate anywhere!" Becca insisted. Toby watched as a look of pure panic filled her eyes. "I've got to get Nicole!" She turned away from Toby. Pulling her hand from his grasp, she rushed from the park, pushing herself through knots of people congregating on the walkway. Toby struggled to catch up, nearly knocking two frothy cups out of a the hands of a large man who was exiting the beer tent.

"Oh, hey, sorry man," Toby apologized as he tried to steady the cups while still continuing his chase. "Can't let my girl get away."

A grin split the man's bearded face and he saluted Toby with a cup before taking a long drink. Toby reached the sidewalk that ran along Main Street, only to see Becca's form running toward the Spot of Tea as if the devil himself were chasing her.

What was Vince doing in Atlanta? The question screeched through Becca's mind as she drove like a mad woman toward Penny and Nate's house. He was supposed to be in Detroit, or Kalamazoo, or some little Podunk town between Jackson and Ann Arbor, not Atlanta! Her foot pressed harder on the gas. She didn't care if she was speeding. Thankfully all the cops were doing crowd control at the festival. Thoughts continued to tumble around her head like clothes in a dryer.

What were the chances Vince knew Becca had Nicole? Had he even spoken to Vi in the past three weeks? Becca tried to recall her conversations with Violet. Had Vi ever mentioned talking to Vince? Becca put a hand to her temple, trying to stop the swirling of her thoughts. No, she couldn't remember Vi mentioning a conversation with Vince. So, did Vince even know Violet was chasing him all over the state? Oh ho yes, Becca was certain he knew at least *that* much. So, if Vince knew Vi wasn't in town, did he also know the baby wasn't with her? And if he knew Vi didn't have the baby, did he have any idea about who did?

"O Lord," Becca breathed the frantic prayer. "What if he knows I have Nicole?" There had never been any love lost between Becca and Vince. She had always made her disgust for him quite clear. Even if Vince didn't care one whit for his own child, he wouldn't want Becca to have her just for spite.

What if he showed up on the doorstep, demanding his baby? "Oh God, I can't give that baby over to him. I can't. Please don't ask me to."

Her car bumped down the driveway leading back to Penny and Nate's log home. Becca threw the car into park and jumped out. Taking the porch step in one giant leap, she had to force herself to knock gently on the front door, not pound the thing down like she longed to do. Taking a steadying breath, Becca tried to calm her racing heart. Penny swung open the door with a smile, a sleeping Nicole in her arms.

"Sorry I'm so late picking her up," Becca apologized as she stepped into the cozy living room. It took an effort to not snatch Nicole from Penny's arms and rush out the door. Instead she immediately began gathering the few baby things that were strewn around the room and stuffing them into the diaper bag.

"That's okay. I told you there was no hurry. I've loved having Nikki here."

Becca glanced up and saw the truth etched so clearly on Penny's lovely face. She ran away from the hunger in Penny's eyes, heading to the kitchen to search for bottles. Coming back into the living room, she rammed them into the side pocket of the diaper bag.

"I hate to rush, but I've still got chores to do at home." The lie slipped out before Becca could even think. Conviction immediately stabbed her conscience.

"Oh, alright." Penny brought Nicole over to the sofa and reached for her sweatshirt. Becca watched as Penny lay the baby on her knees and gently worked the little hoodie over Nicole's head. She tied the hood securely under Nikki's chin. "There you go, sweetheart," Penny cooed, leaning over to touch Nikki's nose with her own. Something inside Becca's heart twisted just the slightest bit. "Her seat's there by the door." Penny motioned with her head and Becca walked over to retrieve the carrier, the diaper bag slung over one shoulder. Soon Nicole was strapped in and ready to go.

"Thanks again for watching her, Penny," Becca said, heading for the door.

"No thanks are necessary." Penny reached around Becca to open the door. "Just let me know if you need anything. I'll do whatever I can."

"Thanks Pen, you're a gem." Becca fairly flew out the door and down the porch step. She buckled Nicole into the back seat and with a sigh of relief, headed toward home.

She was nearly home before reality struck her. If Vince did know that Becca had Nicole, and if he planned to demand her back, the first place he was going to come was the Weaver farm. It would never occur to him to look for Nikki at Penny's house. And even if he did know she was there, he would be far too chicken to step foot on Sergeant Nate Sweeney's porch. Oh well, it was too late to think about that now. And Nate would never agree to such an arrangement anyway. Maybe Wes would let her borrow Ranger for a few nights, Becca thought idly.

As she carried Nicole into the house, Becca met her parents headed for the door. The two were wearing matching quilted flannel jackets.

"Where are you two headed?" she asked.

"Swiss steak dinner at the Elk's Lodge, of course," her mother answered.

"Been our family tradition for how many years now?" her father put in.

"Fifteen," Mary answered absently.

"Oh, that's right, I forgot." Becca maneuvered past them, headed for the kitchen, then nearly froze in her tracks realizing she would be alone in the house. "Well, have fun," she said, trying to mean it.

"We'll miss you baby," David called after her.

"I'll bring you a plate," Mary added.

How 'bout bringing me a gun? Becca thought.

CHAPTER THIRTEEN

There had to be a gun somewhere in this house, Becca thought, wandering through the upstairs. There were hunting rifles, of course, but those were kept securely locked up in the gun safe in the family room. But she was sure her father owned a handgun. Where would it be? She paused in her parents' bedroom door, not quite brave enough to cross the threshold and paw through their dresser drawers. Besides, what would she do with a gun even if she found one? Could she really point it at Vince and threaten his life? Well, she probably *could* but would it be the right thing to do?

She seriously considered calling Wes and asking if Ranger could stay for a few nights, but then dismissed that idea. Wes would start asking all kinds of questions and Becca knew full good and well that she could not lie to Wes like she had so easily lied to Penny. No, she would end up telling Wes the truth and then she'd get a lecture about how she had no legal rights to Nicole and if Vince wanted his daughter back there wasn't anything Becca could or should do about it. So, what options did that leave her?

Prayer. Becca knew that was the only answer. *Do not worry about tomorrow...* The familiar words were like a balm to Becca's raw nerves. She sat down on the top step and bowed her head.

"Lord, forgive me for lying to Penny about having chores to do. Father, believe me, it wasn't intentional. It just came out. But I know it was wrong and I ask you to cleanse me from that sin. I ask, Dear Jesus, that you would protect me and Nikki as we are alone in the house." Becca smiled. "I know Lord, we are never alone because you said you will be with us always, that You will never leave us or forsake us. Thank you for that promise. I pray You will set Your angels over this house to guard it. Be with Violet and bring her home soon. Let her and Vince see the light, Lord. You know where this situation is headed, Father. I don't, and sometimes my heart is so full of confusion and worry and fear. I pray You will give me Your perfect peace and that I can rest in the blessed assurance that You are in control. In Jesus' name, amen."

Feeling a ton lighter, Becca headed down the stairs to the kitchen. She unbuckled Nicole from her carrier and with the baby held securely in the crook of one arm, she headed to the front door and turned the lock, then went to the back door to do the same. Yes, she believed the Lord was watching over them, but that didn't mean she wouldn't take precautions.

"How about a nice, warm bath?" she asked Nicole, who stared up at her with hooded eyes.

"We'll get you all nice and clean and then I'll get your bottles all filled up and then we can cuddle up on the sofa and watch Wheel of Fortune. How does that sound?"

Becca had just pulled the plug on the kitchen sink, allowing Nikki's bath water to drain, when the doorbell rang, practically sending her straight into the beams of the kitchen ceiling in fright. With shaking hands she hastily wrapped the wet, slippery baby in a towel. With Nicole held tightly to her chest, Becca walked on weak knees to the front door. Peering out the narrow window next to the door, she breathed a deep sigh of relief when she saw Toby standing on the front porch holding a flat, white box in his hands. She flipped the lock and yanked open the door.

"For the love of all that is holy, you about gave me a heart attack!" Becca complained, holding the door wide.

"Geez, Bec, what's suddenly got your panties all in a wad?"

"Vince Schmidt! For the past hour all I could think was what if he knows I have Nikki and comes here demanding his daughter?" Becca confessed.

"Do you honestly think Vince is gonna show up on your doorstep and ring the bell?" Toby asked, stepping into the front hall. Becca closed the door and once more turned the lock before turning burning eyes back on Toby who continued, "He'd be way too scared of your dad. If Vince is in town, and *if* he wants Nicole back, which if you ask me is a big if, he isn't going to come here to get her. More likely he'll wait and catch you in some public place where you won't have any choice but to agree. Or he'll get her from Connie, who probably won't think twice about handing Nicole over to him."

"Oh, thanks a lot! I feel so much better now," Becca fumed, pushing past him to head back to the family room where she had laid out Nicole's clean diaper and sleeper.

"I'm sorry, Bec," Toby apologized from behind her. "Believe me, I don't like the idea any better than you do. But I'm trying to be realistic and prepare you for the worst. If Vince really is in town…"

"You keep saying if!" Becca laid the baby on the sofa and looked over her shoulder at Toby, anger blazing. "Why do you keep doubting what I saw?"

"Because you were tired. The park was crowded. It was getting dark. Lots of reasons." Toby's rationality only added to Becca's ire. "The biggest one of all being that if he ran off to avoid his parental responsibilities, why would he come back now?"

"Let me explain it to you, Mr. Smarty pants. You obviously don't know everything, even if you think you do!" Becca said, rubbing Nicole vigorously with the towel. "Because Vince knows I've got Nikki."

"You'll have to explain it better than that." Toby just stood there with the pizza box, looking perplexed. Becca quickly diapered the baby then began wrestling her into a clean sleeper.

"Vince hates me, I hate him. Our distaste for one another has always been quite mutual. He knows how hard I tried to convince Violet to stay away from him, that I thought he was bad news. And look how right I was!" Becca spared Toby a glance. "Vince may not really want Nicole, but he certainly won't want me to have her, either. He'll claim her simply out of spite, not love."

"I think the Bible says something about judging people's motives, that only God sees into a person's heart. You don't know for certain that Vince doesn't love his daughter."

"Actions speak louder than words, and look how he's acted for the past month."

"Then following that logic, wouldn't the simple act of claiming Nicole speak for itself?"

"What are you saying?" Becca stared at Toby, stupefied. "Are you actually suggesting that I should willingly hand her over to that slime bag?"

Toby heaved a sigh and looked down at the box in his hands, shaking his head. "Clean out your ears, Red, and get a grip on your temper. I just told you I don't like the idea any better than you do. But honestly, I don't think we need to worry about it because I don't for a minute think Vince wants anything to do with Nikki. He may not have any love for you, but I can tell you who Vince does love, and that's himself. I doubt he would take Nikki even out of spite if it means inconveniencing himself in any way. Now, how about we call a truce? I brought dinner." He held up the pizza box to emphasize the point.

"I already ate." Another lie slipped out. Toby immediately called her on it.

"Liar."

"How do you know?" Her gaze clashed with his across the room. "My mom fixed a real good dinner."

"Now I really know you're lying. You think I don't know what day it is? Friday night of Elkfest. Your parents are at the Lodge eating Swiss steak same as always. Did you forget that I, too, was forced to go with my parents all the years I was growing up. We used to sit across the table from one another, remember?"

"How could I forget?" Becca muttered. "You ate with your mouth open. You used to stuff your face with mashed potatoes and then open your mouth wide so I could see the whole disgusting mess. Ruined my appetite every year."

"I was trying to impress you."

"Well, it didn't work."

"If it makes you feel any better, I don't eat with my mouth open anymore. Come on, I'll show you." Toby turned and headed for the kitchen.

"Good grief, he has to be the most infuriating guy on the planet!" Becca complained to Nicole. The baby merely gurgled and grinned as if she didn't have a care in the world. "You can laugh now, but just wait. In eighteen years, you'll be finding out for yourself just how annoying guys can be."

Toby set the pizza on the kitchen island and began rummaging through cupboards for paper plates. Becca came in holding the baby in her arms and watched from the doorway.

"What are you doing?" Her tone hadn't softened a bit.

"Looking for paper plates and napkins," Toby answered.

Winning Becca

"Pantry cabinet next to the fridge." Becca strolled into the room and glanced down at the pizza box. "What's this?" She picked up the movie Toby had carried in atop the box and held up the case. Toby smiled and cocked an eyebrow.

"You having trouble reading now?" He walked over and pointed to the title. "Key Largo. See, it's spelled out right there. No wonder I was valedictorian."

"If you remember correctly, I was salutatorian and our GPA's were nearly identical."

Toby could see the fire in Becca's blue eyes and smiled. At least he had gotten her mind off Vince.

"I suppose I should rephrase the question. Instead of what is this?" She rattled the box for emphasis. "I should have asked why is it here?"

"Oh, our little interlude at the Spot of Tea got me thinking. What better to go with the pizza than a good old classic movie?" Toby turned to the fridge and pulled out the carton of fruit punch.

"Our *interlude*? Good grief, Toby, you've got to get that romance stuff out of your head. We didn't have any interlude. And I'm not watching this sappy old movie, I'm watching Wheel of Fortune and Jeopardy."

"Okey-doke." Toby plopped two pieces of pizza on each plate. "We'll keep score and see who wins." Deftly he balanced a plate atop each glass of fruit punch and with the napkins pinched tightly under his chin, headed for the family room.

"I really don't think I like your proprietary attitude," Becca complained. "You waltz in here and act like you own the place. I don't remember even asking you to come in and I certainly never asked you to bring dinner and a movie and now you're just plopping yourself down as if you live here. Maybe I had plans."

"What kind of plans?" Toby carefully set the glasses and plates on the table at the end of the sofa before 'plopping himself down' just as Becca had said. "Plans to hide under your bed until your parents came home?" The question brought the spark of challenge back into Becca's eyes. "You aren't going to send me packing now, you're too worried about Vince. You need me here for protection."

"I already asked for the Lord's protection, so I don't need yours. And you said yourself that Vince won't show up here, so I don't need to be the least bit worried. Which means, you are free to leave."

"But I don't want to leave. I want to eat my pizza and watch Wheel of Fortune and Jeopardy with you. We're gonna see who wins, remember?"

Becca continued to stand stiffly in the doorway, the baby clutched to her chest like a shield.

"Come on, Bec. I called a truce, remember?" Toby heaved himself up from the sofa and went to stand before Becca. He reached for Nicole and gently lifted the baby from her arms. "Take that quilt from the back of the couch and put it on the floor. Nikki will be fine there and you can eat. I bet you didn't get to do more than gulp a couple of bites all day at the teashop."

"Lordy, I hate it when you're right." Becca's shoulders slumped.

"I know you do." Toby smiled down at her. "I'll try not to do it so often, but I can't promise anything."

Becca snorted in response and went to pluck the quilt from the back of the sofa. She spread it on the carpet in front of the couch, folding it to make a comfortable mat for the baby to lay on. Toby knelt and carefully laid Nicole in the center of the quilt. He felt Becca over his shoulder and looked up to see her handing him Nikki's plush, pink blanket. He took it from her hands and covered the baby snuggly. He glanced back up at Becca, a warm glow enveloping his heart. It felt so right. Like they were a family. He stared deep into Becca's eyes, trying to determine if she felt it, too.

"Pizza's getting cold." She spun away from him, toward the end table where their dinner was waiting.

Yep, Toby realized, she must have felt it, too. Now her defenses would be up even higher and he would have to find some way to scale that wall around Becca's heart.

Becca reached for the remote control and the television instantly came to life. Pat Sajak was introducing the day's contestants.

"Sure you wouldn't prefer Bogey and BaCall?" Toby asked, settling himself down on the sofa beside Becca.

"Not in a million, bazillion years," she replied while taking a giant bite from her slice of pizza.

"Suit yourself." Toby shrugged. "I was just trying to give you an easy out. Now you're going to be all torked off at me when I kick your butt at Jeopardy."

"The only way you'll kick my butt, Sinclair, is if all the categories are about math." Becca took another bite of pizza.

"Yeah, with the way my luck's been running these days, they'll probably all be about children's literature and then you'll skunk me good." Toby tackled the pizza on his plate.

"What?" Becca stared at him in mock amazement. "Did the know-all Toby Sinclair just admit that maybe he doesn't actually *know all*?"

"Crazy, huh?" He smiled at her, still chewing. "And cooking. If there's a cooking category you'll definitely edge me out. But, uh..." he lowered his voice to a whisper. "If you do end up winning, don't tell anyone, okay? You see, there's this girl I've been trying to impress and I wouldn't want her to get wind of the fact that I'm not the total genius I've portrayed all these years."

"Oh, Toby," Becca's voice went all sugary sweet. "I don't think you need to worry about *that*."

Both of them turned toward the TV screen.

"Like water off a duck's back!" They yelled the solution to the word puzzle simultaneously.

"I said it first," Toby insisted.

"Oh ho, you so did not!" Becca argued.

"Okay, we'll split the difference. But I'm definitely going to win the next round."

"We'll see about that," Becca replied before turning her attention fully to the television.

Oh, yes we will, Toby thought to himself, glancing at her from the corner of his eye. We most definitely will see who ends up winning. And I don't mean games of chance.

"What are you doing?" he questioned, reaching toward Becca's plate. He snagged a mound of mushrooms she had picked off her pizza. "You're picking off the best part." Opening wide, Toby dropped the mushrooms in his mouth and chewed with relish.

"See, you are still gross," Becca muttered. "Mushrooms are disgusting and if you knew me at all, you would know I never touch the things."

"If you never touch them, how'd you get them off your pizza?" At her stern glance, Toby decided to take the diplomatic route. "Sorry," he apologized before gulping down half his glass of punch. "I'll remember for next time."

"Who says there's going to be a next time?"

"Aw, come off it Bec." Toby leaned over enough to bump her shoulder with his own. "We make a good team. Admit it. You need me to run interference for you with Vi's Uncle Joe, and to help with your math homework, and to protect you from Vince."

"Pa-leeze!" Becca hooted. "I don't need you..."

"Sure you do," Toby interrupted. He looked down at her, so close beside him he could feel the heat of her anger shimmering off her skin. For a moment he thought he would drown in the depths of her blue eyes. He brought his forehead down to hers as his voice softened. "And what's more, for all your bluster, I think you actually like having me around."

Becca pulled away and turned to stare at the television screen once more.

"Kissing the blarney stone!" she shouted triumphantly before slanting a sly glance up at him. "Pay attention Toby," she chided. "That's one-and-a-half points for me, plus I just won a trip to Ireland."

Toby just smiled in response, thinking how Becca was winning more than she could even dream, and when it was all over, she would see that they both came out big winners.

"So, what'd you end up with?" Toby asked. The Jeopardy theme music was fading out as the closing credits rolled across the television screen.

"Seventeen thousand five hundred." Becca said triumphantly, holding the calculator up for Toby to see. "What about you?"

"Twenty thousand even."

"And I'm supposed to just believe you, when you didn't even use a calculator or a piece of paper?"

"Hey, I'm a math whiz, remember? I've got it all stored right up here." Toby tapped his temple.

"Yeah, well, I don't believe for a minute that you actually beat me. I answered way more questions than you did," Becca continued to argue as she rose from the sofa and started gathering up their empty paper plates. "Plus I missed the first two questions of double jeopardy because I was getting Nikki's bottle."

"I don't know what you've got to complain about. You totally whipped my butt at Wheel of Fortune. I think we can call it even."

"I don't want to call it even, I want to win!"

"Really Becca, I think you need to rein in this competitive streak of yours. It's getting a little out of control."

"Oh ho! This from the person who suggested we keep score in the first place!" Becca headed toward the kitchen with the refuse from their dinner. "Is that your guilty conscience talking? I probably did beat you and you just don't want to fess up." Becca shoved the paper plates in the trash can and turned to see Toby lounging easily in the entrance to the kitchen. His hands were shoved into the front pocket of his sweatshirt and his mouth was turned up in a lazy smile. A shiver danced across Becca's shoulders. As if of their own will, her eyes met his across the room. There was a quiet confidence reflected in his soft brown eyes that beckoned to her, encouraging her to walk across the kitchen and step straight into his arms.

She did no such thing. Instead, her fight or flight response kicked in.

"I'd better go check on Nikki." Instead of her feet carrying her into Toby's arms, they carefully skirted around him in the doorway and hurried up the stairs. She could feel his smirk following her the whole way.

In her bedroom, Becca needlessly fussed over tucking the blanket more securely around the sleeping baby. Nicole didn't even stir at her guardian's ministrations, but merely dreamed on, unaware of the storm of emotions that were assailing Becca's heart.

I cannot be falling in love! Becca insisted to herself, hovering over the port-a-crib. *I will not fall in love!* She vowed more sternly. *Not with Nicole and most certainly not with Toby Sinclair.*

How could she even consider such a thing? She was barely over eighteen. She had her whole life ahead of her. It wasn't time to be thinking about a serious relationship. Or motherhood. She had her studies, her plans for the future. And if she was in the market for a boyfriend, Bobby would make a much better choice. Groaning, Becca closed her eyes, realizing that Bobby's laughing blue eyes had never enticed her the way that Toby's gaze just had in the kitchen.

Oh, the whole thing was just sick. Toby was practically like her *brother*! They had known each other their whole lives. Had fought like cats and dogs and competed with one another for every ribbon, award and honor in the county. Becca had never in her life considered him boyfriend material. It must have something to do with having a baby around. Once Violet returned to Atlanta and Nikki was back where she belonged, Becca could get her life back on track and any romantic thoughts about Toby would most certainly disappear.

Unable to dawdle any longer, Becca crept quietly back downstairs, hoping in vain that Toby had let himself out and gone home. She stepped into the kitchen to find it neat as a pin. The empty pizza box and dirty glasses were nowhere to be seen. Toby stood near the scarred table where he had helped Becca with her statistics homework not that long ago, staring out the window to the dark farmyard beyond.

"I've been thinking," Toby said without turning around.

"That's always dangerous," Becca replied, trying to inject a light note into the suddenly serious atmosphere. When Toby turned to face her she saw all humor and teasing were gone from his gaze.

"What if Violet doesn't come back?"

"Of course Violet's going to come back," Becca spluttered. "She loves her daughter. Once she gets over this foolishness about Vince, she's going to come back and take care of her child."

"But what if she doesn't?" Toby pulled out a chair and sat down at the table. He folded his hands atop the worn surface and studied his thumbnails as if all the answers needed in the universe could be found there.

"If Vince is back in Atlanta, then Vi soon will be, too," Becca insisted. She pulled out a chair and plopped down across from Toby. "And even without Vince in the picture, Violet can't gallivant all over the state forever. Eventually she's going to come home and reclaim Nikki. She's a mother, and no matter what happens, her mother's heart is going to want to be with her baby. How could she not?"

"She's been gone this long and it hasn't seemed to bother her," Toby replied with a shrug, his attention still focused on his folded hands. "She could always hook up with some other loser, wind up preggers again. Who knows. Violet hasn't exactly exhibited good judgment in the past."

"Geez Toby, you make her sound like some sort of ho. She's not. You have no idea how rough her life's been. Sure she made a mistake with Vince but…"

"I know she's your BFF, but can we cut the crap?" Toby's hands smacked the table, making Becca draw her head back in surprise.

"What has gotten into you?" Becca asked, feeling alarmed by Toby's intensity.

"I'm sorry." He raked his fingers through his hair, leaving it standing on end.

"Why do you suddenly care so much about Vi or what happens to Nikki?"

"I told you," Toby answered quietly, his eyes once more focused on his hands. "I've been thinking."

"Yeah, and I told you that could be dangerous. I was just joking, but it seems like it wasn't so funny."

"I've been doing some research," Toby continued in the same quiet voice. "Looking into child abandonment and neglect and what the laws are here in Michigan. You know, what it takes to get someone's parental rights terminated."

"Why?" Becca shook her head, truly confounded.

"Because I was thinking if Violet didn't come back, that we…" he stopped to swallow hard and clear his throat. Becca found herself suddenly fearful of what he was going to say next. "That you and I could become her parents."

"Are you out of your mind?!" Becca practically shrieked. She pushed back from the table and stood.

"Yeah, yeah I probably am," Toby admitted with a nod.

"Not probably, definitely! What would make you ever think we could become that baby's parents? We're only eighteen, we have no way of supporting ourselves much less a baby. Not to mention that we aren't married!"

"We could change that." Toby finally looked up and met her gaze head on.

"You are certifiably insane." She spun away so she could no longer see the look in his eyes, the look that had her almost believing his idea wasn't so crazy. After all, hadn't she harbored the same, brief daydream a time or two. She went over and began filling the coffee maker for the morning, just to give her hands something to do. "You're the genius, you know the statistics as well as I do. Fifty percent of marriages end in divorce and that's when the couples start out supposedly loving each other. That would leave us with what, um, about zero chance of success?"

"You're assuming we don't love each other." Toby stood and came to stand at the end of the kitchen island, a mere arm's length away.

"Toby, you're way too smart to be this stup..." Becca felt a firm hand on her shoulder, turning her around. Toby took the coffee pot out of her hands and set it on the island before pulling her into his arms. "...id." She finished lamely before his lips covered hers in a gentle caress. The feather-light kiss lasted mere moments, but it was long enough to send Becca's heart crashing against her rib cage.

"I'm not stupid," Toby said softly when he lifted his head. "I was valedictorian, remember? And I've loved you since I was four years old."

"Oh, get out of town!" Becca put her hands on his chest and tried to push away, but Toby linked his hands behind her back and held fast.

"I'm serious. When I was four years old I told my mom I was going to marry you when we grew up. She wrote it in my baby book, so I have proof."

"We all say rash things when we're four," Becca said, reaching behind her to grab Toby's wrists and pull his arms from around her. "No one holds us to it." She stepped resolutely away from him, putting the island between them as a safety precaution. "Most of our lives we haven't been able to stand each other."

"We just had a friendly rivalry going, that's all. Look at all we've achieved competing against one another," Toby continued in a persuasive tone. "Just think what we could do if we joined forces, got on the same team. For Nikki's sake."

"It doesn't matter," Becca said firmly. "I told you, Vince is in Atlanta. Soon Violet will be, too. Nicole will be back with her parents where she belongs and you and I are going to concentrate on school and our jobs so we can make something of ourselves. We've worked too hard for the past few years to ruin it by making a stupid mistake now."

CHAPTER FOURTEEN

At least she hadn't said no. Toby clung to that small comfort throughout the next day as he finished putting a fresh coat of paint on Wes Cooper's barn doors. He couldn't believe he had actually suggested they get married and Becca hadn't laughed him to scorn. Sure, she had rejected the idea in theory, calling him crazy, insane and stupid, but she hadn't actually said no. That meant there was still hope. And Toby was clinging to that hope with every fiber of his being.

He stood back to admire his handiwork. The double barn doors were now a glistening white that contrasted nicely against the rust-red of the barn. With the vivid fall colors, the Cooper farm looked like something right off the pages of a glossy magazine. Toby ran his gaze over the neat farmyard, amazed at the transformation he and Wes had accomplished in just a few short weeks. Cooper Orchard and Pumpkin Farm was just about ready for its grand debut. Toby tried to picture the place teaming with customers in just a short week's time. He could see children picking their pumpkin out of the patch, could hear the squeals of laughter as families made cherished memories. Maybe he and Becca and Nikki could make a memory, too.

Squatting down, Toby carefully replaced the lid atop the can of paint then grabbed up his supplies and headed toward the house to clean up. From the look of the sky, it was nearly time to go pick up Nicole from Connie's. As he stepped through the door of the back porch he set the can of paint down and fished his cell phone out of the front pocket of his jeans. Yep, he just had time to wash the paint off his hands and get out to the Compton place before Joe got home from work.

The farmhouse was oddly quiet. Brendan must be napping, Toby thought as he stood at the sink lathering his hands. He scrubbed at a spot of paint on his knuckles and whistled between his teeth.

"You're sounding awfully chipper today."

The tune died on Toby's lips as he spun to see Rhonda lounging in the doorway. Realizing he was dripping dirty water on her clean kitchen floor, he quickly turned back to the sink and stuck his hands under the tap.

"What's got you whistling Dixie?" Rhonda asked, coming farther into the kitchen. "It's the end of the work day. I know Wes has been driving you like an Egyptian slave. I would think you would be dead tired and yet here you are practically bouncing up and down."

"Maybe I just love my job," Toby said with a smile. He ripped a paper towel off the roll and turned to face Rhonda.

"Oh, I think I know what you love and I'm not so sure it's your job." Rhonda grinned and tucked a stray, red curl behind her ear. "You been seeing a lot of my sister lately?"

"Hmmm, quantify a lot." Toby dried his hands carefully, rubbing at a splotch of paint he had missed. "I've been helping Becca out with Nicole some, which means I get to see her regularly but not nearly as much as I would like." He chewed the inside of his cheek and continued to work the paper towel over the paint stain on the back of his hand.

"Wes tells me the two of you have had some very grown up conversations about your future."

"Your husband thinks I'm out of my mind, as does your sister." Toby shrugged and tossed the paper towel into the wastebasket with a basketball player's flourish. "Maybe I am."

"You're a smart kid Toby. You've got a good head on your shoulders. I trust you'll think things through and make the right decision."

"I appreciate the vote of confidence but I doubt you'd be saying that if you knew what I've been thinking about." Toby stepped away from the sink and headed for the back door. He hesitated with one hand on the knob. "Can I ask you a question?"

"Sure, you know you can ask me anything," Rhonda answered.

"Do you think Violet is coming back?"

Rhonda leaded back against the edge of the table and cocked her head to the side.

"I don't know, Toby, I truly don't. As a mother I can't imagine being away from my baby for as long as Violet has. If I leave Brendan with a sitter just for an evening I miss him like crazy and can't wait to get back home. But I've got a husband and a home and a stable family life. Violet's awfully young and she's had it hard. I have a feeling that when she ran off, she was running away from something more than she was running toward Vince." Rhonda shrugged a slim shoulder. "All we can do is pray she comes home."

"I don't," Toby admitted. He looked across the kitchen and met Rhonda's gaze. "I don't pray she comes back. I pray she stays away. Maybe that's wrong of me. Maybe it's selfish. And for Becca's sake I probably should be praying that Vi comes back. But I can't. I won't. I think Nicole is better off without Violet and Vince. She deserves to have two people that truly love her and put her first."

"Like you and Becca?" Rhonda's straightforward question surprised Toby. He shrugged a shoulder.

"Yeah, maybe."

"Toby, I…"

"I've gotta go. I'm supposed to pick Nikki up before four, and if I don't get out of here I'll be late. See ya after church tomorrow."

Toby rushed out the door before Rhonda could launch into the lecture that he knew was coming. He didn't have time for her well-intentioned advice. Besides, he knew what she was going to say. The same thing Wes had already said. The same thing

Becca had said. It was crazy, it was insane, it was *impossible*. Well, wasn't the Bible full of stories about God making the impossible possible? So what was so crazy and impossible about two people who loved each other making a home for a little girl who needed parents?

And Becca *did* love him. She had even allowed him to kiss her. Toby replayed the kiss in his mind as he backed the Bronco from Wes and Rhonda's driveway. A little shiver danced across his shoulders. That little kiss had been one of the most amazing experiences of Toby's life. Better than winning four grand championships. Better than being valedictorian. Having Becca in his arms was just right. It was where she was meant to be. And if the Lord smiled on him, maybe tonight she would be there again.

Marry him!! What was Toby thinking to even suggest such a ludicrous thing? Becca wondered as she scooped chicken salad onto a croissant. As if two eighteen-year-olds just out of high school had a snowball's chance of making it in the first place. Then add a newborn to the mix, one that wasn't even theirs, and the probability sunk well below zero.

The din from the dining room full of customers barely registered in Becca's brain. Her mind had been consumed all day with thoughts of Vince and Nikki and Toby, her emotions fluctuating between abject terror that Vince would walk in the teashop any second and demand to know where his child was, to disbelief that Toby would actually *propose* that they get married and raise Nikki themselves, to...

Becca slapped the top on the chicken salad sandwich, unwilling to delve too deeply into the other emotion she'd been feeling rather frequently lately. The one that made her knees go weak from something other than fright. The one that made her heart feel like it was beating with butterfly wings when she looked down at the sleeping angel in the port-a-crib. Grabbing up her full tray, Becca headed toward the dining room. No, it was best to leave those emotions unexplored. She would much rather feel terrified that Vince Schmidt was going to walk into the Spot of Tea any second than even consider the possibility that she may be falling in love. Girls her age didn't even know what love was! Hadn't she told Violet that a thousand times?

"Whew! What a day, huh?" Emma asked several hours later as she turned the key in the front door, locking it behind their last straggling customers. She turned to look at Becca, reaching up to tuck a stray lock of dark hair back into her slightly frazzled French braid. "This has been the best weekend we've had since the Fourth of July. Maybe I'll actually be able to survive another winter. But then again, if I can't I guess it won't be the end of the world."

"Aw Em, you've been in business how many years now? You're a pillar in Atlanta. Folks around here will keep you in business. I can't imagine the town without the Spot of Tea. And I'm not saying that just because I need this job." Becca laughed and began stripping soiled linens off the tables. Emma pulled a chair out and sat down tiredly.

"Yes, well, I've been thinking a lot about the future lately."

Haven't we all? Becca thought. "Any reason in particular?" she asked aloud.

"Oh, you know." Emma shrugged noncommittally and gazed out the plate glass window. "With a growing family and a business, it just gets harder to keep up."

"But I thought Tiffany was doing well in daycare and won't she be starting kindergarten next fall?"

"Yes, but…" Emma folded the tablecloth in front of her into tiny pleats.

"But what?" Becca pulled out a chair and sat down across from Emma. "Spill it," she demanded. "You're making me a nervous wreck!" As if thoughts of Vince hadn't been doing a good enough job!

"There's a possibility that I…" Emma broke off again and bit her lip.

"That you might be what?" Terror gripped Becca's stomach. "Geez Emma are you dieing or something? You're scaring me half to death here!"

"No, no, I'm not dieing." A small smile tipped up Emma's lips and she shook her head slightly. "Actually, you're the first person I've told this to, besides Tyler. I think I'm pregnant."

"Sheesh, is that all?" Becca threw the wadded up tablecloth she had been clutching at Emma's head. It fell harmlessly to the floor. "You practically gave me a heart attack! Not that it isn't great news. I mean, it is great news, right?" she asked, feeling somewhat uncertain.

"Of course it is." Emma's smile suddenly lit up the room. "As long as you look past the puking and the exhaustion and the weight gain. But like I said, I don't know for certain yet. It's too early to get an official test. I just have my suspicions. And I've found over the years that my instincts are fairly reliable. Just don't go telling anyone yet. After all it could be a false alarm."

"Wow, so I'm the first to know besides Tyler?" Becca stared wide-eyed at her boss. "I feel so...like we're...I mean...it's almost like we're friends."

"Of course we're friends, silly." Emma reached across the table and squeezed Becca's hands. "And I felt you should be one of the first to know. You need to be prepared for what could possibly happen. Talk to Rhonda, she'll tell you. It was a nightmare the first couple months I was pregnant with Tiffany. Plus, I was serious when I said I've been thinking about the future. I'm not sure how I can juggle two kids and running a restaurant. Not with Tyler's schedule. And my kids have to come first."

"I understand." Becca nodded. "But I guess it's best to just take it one day at a time. After all, doesn't the Bible tells us that's all we're promised anyway? Today? None of us knows what the future holds." She stood and gathered the tablecloth that had fallen to the floor, unable to tell Emma that by spring, she may have her own baby to take care of.

Wait a minute! Becca brought herself up short. She wasn't actually considering Toby's preposterous idea, was she? No. No way. She would not marry Toby Sinclair, not in a million, bazillion years.

Winning Becca

"Too bad your admirer didn't show up today," Emma commented, as if reading Becca's mind. "I'm beat. It would have been nice to have the extra pair of hands."

Becca glanced at the clock above the cash register, suddenly realizing it was well after four and Toby hadn't shown up yet. Unease tiptoed up Becca's spine but she tried to shake it off. Toby had to have picked up Nikki on time. She was counting on it. And if Vince had gotten there first, wouldn't Toby have high-tailed it to the teashop to let Becca know? Of course he would have. She trusted him. The truth of that thought struck Becca fully in the heart. She trusted Toby, more than she had ever trusted anyone outside of her immediate family.

"So, what's the latest on Nicole?" Emma's question startled Becca from her woolgathering.

"Nothing new." Becca gathered china onto a large tray. "No word from Violet in days, or should I say nights." Becca contemplated telling Emma that she thought Vince was in town, but decided against it. "I'm just taking it one day at a time, putting one foot in front of the other. But I'm getting in deep and by time this is all over with, I'm gonna owe favors to just about everybody I know. Plus there's the added stress of trying to keep the truth from Nate."

"Why don't you just talk to him, Becca? Tell him the truth. He would be able to help, I'm sure of it. Whatever you've imagined in your head would happen to Nikki, I'm sure the reality isn't anywhere near as bad. There's lots of wonderful people working as foster parents. Responsible, loving, hard working people. Nikki would be well cared for. You're too young to be dealing with such a heavy burden by yourself."

"I'm not doing it by myself. Like I said, lots of people have been helping out. And, and I've got Toby. He's been a godsend and is really good with Nikki. I want to give Violet a little more time. I don't know, I can't explain it, but I keep feeling like if I just wait a little bit longer, she's going to come home and everything's going to be alright. All our lives will go back to how they were a few weeks ago."

"That's a nice thought Becca, but something in my spirit tells me that things are never going to be the same."

Toby had managed to pick Nikki up just in the nick of time. As he was turning off McMurphy road onto the main highway headed back toward Atlanta, Joe Compton came from the opposite direction and turned his rusty, blue pickup truck onto the road headed toward home. Toby quickly spun his head away, hoping Joe hadn't recognized him, and if he had that he wouldn't suspect that Toby had just come from the Compton homestead. He sent up a quick prayer that Connie wouldn't have to answer any questions.

Please Lord, give us just a little more time. I know it's wrong to deceive people, but we aren't doing it to hurt anybody. The exact opposite. We're trying to keep Nikki safe. And Lord, if You'll help me out here, Becca and I could give Nicole a real home and parents that love her. But not my will but Yours be done, he remembered to add.

As Toby passed the Spot of Tea he saw that even though it was four o'clock nearly on the dot, the parking lot was still full of cars. The second day of the Elk Festival was in full swing and downtown Atlanta was packed with people. It could still be another hour or more before Becca was finished. No point in taking the baby inside and distracting her from her work, or making her worry that Vince would somehow stroll by and see Nicole. Without a moment's hesitation he continued on through town and drove toward the Sinclair ranch.

Whispering Pines Ranch was nestled on 60 acres northwest of town in the pine-covered approaches to the Rattlesnake Hills. The cedar siding on the low slung ranch house was weathered to the softest shade of grey. Looking like a piece of driftwood washed up on the shore of one of the great lakes, it blended perfectly into the surrounding hills. Over the years Whispering Pines had evolved from a rustic hunting camp to a dude ranch of sorts until finally Toby's parents had groomed it into a highly respected equine facility that produced some of the finest Arabian horses in the state, his Rocky being merely one of the offspring they had bred and trained.

Jeb and Anita Sinclair had been thrilled when their youngest son exhibited so much talent and promise in the show ring. But the couple quickly had their hearts broken when after a short stint on the Arabian show circuit Toby had returned home, steadfastly refusing to step a hoof outside Montmorency County ever again. He turned down every opportunity that presented itself to strut his stuff on a broader stage, content instead with local grand championships. A fact that frustrated his parents to no end. Although proud of their son's intellectual accomplishments, they nonetheless took every opportunity to encourage him to reach for the gold that could be won in the show ring.

Gravel crunched under the Bronco's tires. Toby pulled into his favorite parking spot in the driveway, facing the horse pasture. Rocky and several other horses stood close together, their rumps turned toward the cold breeze that was blowing down out of the hills. Turning off the engine, Toby sat for a moment staring out the windshield at the horses in the pasture beyond. He allowed himself the briefest trip down memory lane, to the last Arabian show he had competed at in Columbus, Ohio. The competition had been stiff but he and Rocky had held their own. For a split second he almost regretted his choice to quit. Almost.

A soft mewling sound from the backseat reminded Toby why it was a good thing he had hung up his spurs and returned to Atlanta. If he hadn't, who would be helping Becca right now? And if his dream came to fruition, his horse show days would be over for good. Class A showing was an expensive hobby and if he had a wife and daughter to support, there wouldn't be money for even feeding Rocky, much less showing him.

Nicole squeaked. Toby opened his door and climbed down from the Bronco, folding the seat forward and reaching into the backseat to unlatch Nicole's carrier. He carried the baby, seat and all, through the breezeway and into the house where all was dark and quiet. He stood for a moment, letting his eyes adjust and listening for his mother's familiar humming before heading toward the back of the house. The west-facing windows filled the paneled dining room with fading light. Toby set Nikki on the polished surface of the dining table then reached to unbuckle the straps that held her securely in place.

"Alrighty, here we go," he said, lifting the baby from the seat and cradling her in his arms. Nikki stared up at him with wide eyes. The ears on her pink hoodie made her look like a little teddy bear. With one hand Toby untied the hood and pushed it back from Nikki's head. "What do you think of this place, huh?" he asked, taking the baby over to the French doors that led to a brick patio. "See the horsies?" He held Nicole up to the glass. "When you get a little bigger, Becca and I will teach you to ride. Yep, I can see it now. You'll be a future grand champion for sure."

Cradling the baby once more, Toby headed for the kitchen. Opening the large refrigerator, he reached for a Mountain Dew then took both baby and soda into the spacious family room where he collapsed on the overstuffed sofa.

"How much time you think we've got to kill?" he asked Nikki before glancing at the clock over the stone fireplace. "Half an hour? We should be able to handle that, don't ya think? Just don't go screaming, or dirtying your diaper, okay?"

Toby leaned back into the corner of the sofa and propped his feet on the coffee table. He reached for the remote control, but before he could click the television on, the front door slammed. Clicking of heels sounded on the hallway floor, then were muffled by the family room carpet. Toby glanced over the back of the couch to see his mother standing behind him.

"Hey Ma." Toby greeted, quickly removing his booted feet from the coffee table and sitting up straight.

"Hey yourself," his mother returned, staring at the baby in her son's arms. She came around to stand in front of the sofa. "I would ask who our little guest is, but I think I have a pretty good idea already."

"You've been talking to Mrs. Weaver." It was a statement, not a question.

"We missed you and Becca at the Swiss steak dinner last night. Of course, since the two of you weren't there, Mary had plenty of time to fill me in on what's been going on. Any word yet on when Violet will be coming home?"

"Nope."

Anita perched herself on the arm of a nearby chair. Toby continued to stare down at the baby, refusing to meet his mother's eyes.

"Toby."

"Yeah?" Toby finally looked in his mother's general direction, but let his eyes rest on the fireplace beyond instead of her face.

"Mary says you've been coming around a lot."

Toby shrugged. "I helped Becca with some homework. Now I'm giving her a hand with the baby. So what?"

"So, I've always known how you feel about Becca. You're sitting there holding that baby as if it's the most natural thing in the world and I can see the wheels turning in your head. What kind of crazy scheme are you cooking up?"

"Look, I'm just sitting here waiting for Becca to get off work. What makes you think I'm cooking anything up?"

"I'm your mother. And you are your father all over again. I always know when your dad is gnawing on a bone and now I can see it plain as day that you are, too. And I have the distinct feeling that I'm not going to like it."

"Geez Ma, can't a man keep a few things to himself?" Toby rose from the sofa and went to stand next to the fireplace.

"Man now, is it?" Anita swiveled on her perch to level her serious gaze on Toby.

"I'm eighteen. Old enough to vote. Old enough to serve my country."

"Is that what you're considering, joining the service?"

Toby quickly glanced her way.

"No, I didn't think so. So, let me guess." Anita tapped her chin and continued to pin Toby with her serious, dark eyes. Her gaze dropped to the baby in Toby's arms. Nicole had drifted off to sleep. "I would bet this ranch that you are trying to figure out how to get Becca to marry you and settle down. Maybe even with that little girl right there."

"Aw, come on Ma!" Toby spun away from his mother's prying eyes and went to stand before the bank of windows at the far end of the room. The horses in the paddock continued to graze, unconcerned. Oh to be out there with them and not here getting the third degree from his mother! Man, Nate Sweeney could take lessons from the woman.

"You know, for the longest time I could never understand it," Anita continued quietly. "Why you quit the circuit after such a short time when you were doing so well. And then community college? With your SAT and ACT scores you could have gotten into any college or university in the nation. It all seemed like such a waste to me. Stupid. And stupid is something you've never been. So why? Then it finally hit me. Not why, but who. It's all because of Becca."

"Don't say it like that," Toby commanded in a low tone he had never used with his mother before.

"I'm sorry Toby, but you are making a terrible mistake. If you and Becca are meant for each other, then she'll still be here when you are finished with college. Don't you think you have a much better chance with her, to make a good future for you both, if you take advantage of the opportunities you've been offered? Two years in community college and then what? I can see it now, you'll be stuck in Atlanta forever in some dead-end job. You've been blessed with a brilliant mind and an awesome talent and what are you doing with either? Throwing them back in God's face, that's what. Refusing to use them to the best of your ability. Do you think that's going to impress Becca? And now you're actually thinking about getting married and raising a baby? On what?"

"You said it yourself Ma, I've got a brilliant mind. I'll think of something."

"Well, I have something that just might change that brilliant mind of yours." Anita stood and strode to the fireplace. She lifted a heavy, beige envelope from the mantle and held it out to Toby. Slowly he came closer and reached to take the letter from her hand, his eyes quickly scanning the embossed return address. "One more opportunity God is placing in your lap. Heaven help you if you throw this one away, too."

Turning on her heel, Anita quickly left the room. With his eyes still glued to the return address on the envelope, Toby walked to the sofa and sat down. He laid the letter on the coffee table. Chewing the inside of his cheek, he continued to stare at it as if he could read the contents right through the thick paper of the envelope. Finally he put Nicole on the sofa beside him and picked up the letter, finding that his hands were trembling slightly. Did he really want to know what was inside? He flipped it over, only to find the seal was already broken. Of course, his mother had read it already. She knew what "opportunity" was being put in his lap. Toby extracted the paper and slowly unfolded the page, still unsure that he wanted to know what it said. Unable to resist, his eyes scanned the words while his heart thudded heavily against his ribs and his breathing grew shallow.

The letter fluttered to the floor. Toby dropped his head into his hands and pressed his fingers into his eyes. He had to think. A once in a lifetime chance had landed literally right on his doorstep. What was he going to do with it? What did God want him to do with it?

O Lord, don't ask me to make this kind of choice! It's not fair!

A buzzing against his thigh made Toby sit up straight. He reached into his jeans pocket and pulled out his cell phone, flipping it open.

"Yeah?"

"Toby, where are you? Where is Nicole? Is everything alright?"

CHAPTER FIFTEEN

Okay, now things were getting really weird, Becca fumed as she sat at the kitchen table the next morning, sipping a cup of hot tea. First Toby doesn't show up with Nicole at closing time. Then she gets tailgated all the way home by the same black car that practically ate her bumper on her way to class several days ago. At least, she was fairly certain it was the same car. In the dim half-light of dusk it was hard to tell if it was the same driver behind the wheel or not. Then when Toby finally does show up, he practically shoves Nikki at her then leaves with barely a fare-thee-well! To top it all off, Violet finally calls and actually sounds contrite and worried about her child. Something definitely was going on! Had there been a full moon the night before?

Becca shook her head, unable to remember. All she knew was that Toby's odd behavior had kept her up half the night, tossing and turning. To think she had actually given some thought to his proposal! She was nearly as crazy as he was. Even worse, her sleepless night had kept her from attending church, something she needed now more than ever. Becca felt the guilt creep in. She really should have forced herself to get up, get dressed and go. But Nikki had been sleeping so peacefully, Becca hated to disturb the baby, especially since sleep had been such a rare commodity for the past month.

With a sigh Becca pushed the hair back from her face and reached for her Bible. Since she wasn't in church, the least she could do was have her own little study right here at the kitchen table. What would be a good Scripture to set her mind on for the day? Becca wondered. She could re-read the Book of James. That was the one Becca always turned to when her mouth got her into trouble. All those Scriptures about taming the tongue and the comparison to bridling a horse. Yes, James was always a good choice. Becca flipped her Bible open, but before she reached the Book of James, her eyes fell onto a Scripture in Hebrews that she had previously underlined.

Therefore, do not cast away your confidence, which has great reward, she read in Hebrews chapter 10. *For you have need of endurance, so that after you have done the will of God, you may receive the promise.*

Stunned, Becca sat back in her chair, chewing over the words she had just read. Was God trying to tell her that she really was doing His will by caring for Nicole? She certainly had need of endurance for *that!* But if she held on to the end, God would reward her.

Her eyes fell once more to the Bible and she continued to read the next verse.

"For yet a little while, and He who is coming will come and will not tarry."

Becca's heart stilled. She understood that the writer of Hebrews was referring to Jesus in this passage, but was the Lord trying to send her a different message? If so, she hoped the Lord meant that Violet was coming and would not tarry and not Vince! She shut the Bible with a resounding thud. She was reading far more into the Word of the Lord than He had ever intended, Becca was sure.

After a long, hot shower, Becca felt much more refreshed. The sky beyond the farmhouse windows remained leaden, a chill wind blowing straight out of the north. Fall was definitely here, with winter not far behind. She sent up a quick prayer that the Lord would bless Wes and Rhonda with good weather for the opening of the orchard. Maybe there was something she could do to help them get ready, Becca thought. She quickly bundled up Nicole then pulled a heavy grey sweatshirt over her head.

"Maybe Rhonda will even take pity on us and offer us lunch," Becca said as she strapped Nicole into the backseat.

Becca remembered how life had been just a few short years ago after Wes and Rhonda got married. How she had spent nearly every weekend at the Cooper farm, sleeping in the white iron bed in Wes' old room. Rhonda had almost always made blueberry pancakes for breakfast, allowing Becca to slather them in as much blueberry jam as she wanted. She had been such a child! It seemed like eons ago now.

"Hello! Anybody home?" Becca called a few minutes later as she entered Rhonda's kitchen. The smell of oven-fried chicken hung on the air. Oh, maybe she would be offered lunch! Becca's mouth watered at the thought as she made her way into the living room.

"I'll be right down," Rhonda called from upstairs. Within moments Rhonda's slender form came bouncing down the steps. She wore faded jeans and a blue checked flannel shirt over a white t-shirt. "I just got Brendan down for his nap. What brings you here?" she asked, giving Becca a brief hug before taking the baby carrier from her hands. With practiced ease she removed Nicole from her seat. "We missed you at church."

"Yeah, sorry. I was wiped out," Becca said with a shrug.

"No need to apologize to me, and I'm sure the Lord understands. Didn't see Toby there either."

"No? That's weird." Although the way Toby had acted last night, Becca figured she shouldn't be surprised at anything Toby did!

"He's here now though, sitting down in the orchard." Rhonda motioned with her head toward the window. "Wes had to run to Hillman and I didn't really know what jobs he wanted done. Not that it would matter anyway. I don't think we'll be getting much work out of Toby today. Something's definitely up with that kid."

"Really?" Becca tried to sound unconcerned. "Maybe I should go talk to him."

Rhonda gave her a knowing look. "Yeah, maybe you should. Go ahead. I'll watch Nicole."

As Becca trotted down the back porch steps, Ranger came running up to her, barking playfully. She patted his head and reached down for a stick, which she threw across the yard. Ranger chased after it like a shot. The brown grass crunched under her tennis shoes as she made her way down the hill to the orchard. Toby's back was to her, his head down. He didn't acknowledge her approach. Becca lowered herself to the ground.

"Rhonda says you weren't in church this morning. Seems we were both playing hooky," she said, watching his serious profile.

"I took Rocky for a ride up into the Rattlesnake Hills this morning," Toby said quietly.

"See any rattlesnakes?" It was an age-old joke around Atlanta. Toby merely shook his head.

"Saw four elk though."

"That's cool." Becca glanced down, noticing the piece of paper Toby held in his hands. "What's that?" she asked, bumping his shoulder with her own.

"A letter," Toby answered without turning his head.

"Thank you Captain Obvious." Becca slapped her forehead mockingly but Toby didn't even crack a smile. "What's it say?" she asked, all kidding aside.

Toby offered her the letter then sat staring off across the orchard. Becca's eyes scanned the paper, her gaze falling immediately on the lovely photo of a snow white Arabian horse at the top of the letterhead.

"This is from Desert Sands," she said stupidly.

"Alonzo Ferrera is offering me the chance to come train at his stable and show his horses," Toby explained.

"Alonzo Ferrera?!" Becca repeated, taking a closer look at the letter. "*The* Alonzo Ferrera, the horse trainer? He's one of the biggest names out there right now. He's in all the horse magazines. How'd he hear about you?"

"That judge at the fair, I guess. Seems he talked to my parents. Told them to send a video of me and Rocky and he'd make sure it got in the right hands."

"So your parents *did* stack the deck!" Becca accused.

"I don't know." Toby shrugged and stared down at the ground. He pulled up tufts of grass. "If they did I didn't have any knowledge of it at the time, I swear."

"Oh, it doesn't matter now anyway." Becca waved the letter in the air. "Alonzo Ferrera," she said again, trying to digest the reality. "Desert Sands is in what, Flagstaff?" She glanced at the letter once more.

"Phoenix."

"Phoenix. Wow, that's like a million miles from Atlanta."

"Actually it's two thousand, one hundred fourteen point three seven miles." Becca gave him a stunned look. "I Mapquested it," he explained with a shrug.

"This is unbelievable." Becca shook her head, trying to let the truth sink in. "When do you go?"

Winning Becca

"Who said I'm going?"

"Who said?" Becca spluttered. "Of course you're going. Toby, this is like winning the lottery. A one in a million chance. A one way ticket out of Hicksville. How could you not go?"

"I tried the circuit thing before, remember. I didn't really like it."

"Oh come off it. You love to win, and you won a lot on the circuit. Didn't you know your parents made sure your picture got in the Tribune every time you took a blue ribbon? Trust me, I got to see your ugly mug plenty while you were gone."

"It wasn't the same." His brown eyes finally met hers.

"What do you mean, it wasn't the same? That doesn't make any sense."

"It wasn't the same without you there."

"Oh ho, so winning was only fun if you could beat *me*? That's just great! I always knew you were a first-class jerk!" Becca pushed herself up from the ground, but Toby grabbed her arm, forcing her to stay put.

"That's not what I meant. It wasn't about winning ribbons or trophies or scholarships. It was about you. Do you know I was offered a full ride to at least three universities? I turned them all down. Know why?"

"Because you love nothing more than to make my life miserable?"

"Well, you're partially right. Because I love you, period. And I knew if I went off to Harvard or Yale or MIT, somebody like Bobby Fitzgerald would come along and snap you up in a heartbeat." Toby snapped his fingers. "Just like that, you'd be gone. So I stayed."

"Are you saying that you threw away your future because of me?" Becca stared at him, flabbergasted. "When I didn't even like you? And to think all these years I thought you were a genius."

"For one thing, I didn't throw anything away. I'm still going to college. I can transfer to a bigger school whenever I want. And for another thing, I didn't see much of a future without you in it."

"Stop!" Becca grabbed his arm and shook him as hard as she could. "Toby, you have got to stop this romantic nonsense right now! Listen to yourself. Your so saccharine it's sickening. Get your head out of the clouds and start dealing in reality. I'm not marrying you. I'm not marrying Bobby Fitzgerald. I'm not marrying *anybody* for a good long while yet. Believe me, if I had gotten a full ride scholarship to Timbuktu I would have accepted it and never looked back. Not that I'm complaining, mind you. What I was offered is a blessing and I'm forever thankful. Plus I save a ton living at home. My point is that I know this is all part of God's plan. I stayed in Atlanta for a reason, and now I know Nikki is a big part of that reason. She needs me for this period in time and God is using me to take care of her. But I know in my heart I am not meant to raise her. As much as it pains me to say it, I cannot be that baby's mother. I've prayed, Toby, I've prayed and I've sought God's will. Can you say the same?"

"I've tried," he said in a choked voice.

Becca's hand became gentle, stroking his arm in a near caress.

"Toby, look at me." He turned his face to hers and she saw the devastation etched so clearly there. She touched his cheek. "I'm not trying to hurt you. I'm not saying I won't ever love you, or that there's no chance for us. We've come a long way in the last month. But we both have a lot of growing up to do, physically, emotionally and spiritually. If we're meant to be together, don't you think God will make that clear, to both of us?"

Toby looked away and cleared his throat. "I suppose."

"We both need to grow in our faith and trust the Lord for our future." Becca placed the letter back in his hands and stood. "Pray about Desert Sands, Toby, and if you feel it's the Lord's will, then take that leap of faith and go. And if it's the Lord's will, I'll still be here when you get back."

Toby listened as Becca's footsteps faded away. A moment later Ranger ran up and sat before Toby, his tongue lolling. The German shepherd wore a perpetual smile. Toby reached out and stroked the dog's silver fur.

"What are you so happy about, huh?" he asked, pushing the dog's head playfully. Ranger barked in reply. "Easy for you to say. Your world isn't falling apart. Guess that's why a dog's life is so appealing."

Toby stood and folded the letter, shoving it into the back pocket of his jeans. He'd better get to work. Man, he would like to pound something! Too bad

Wes didn't have any nails to be driven. Toby could pretend they were his mother's head. He hated her right now for meddling in his affairs. Why couldn't she have left well enough alone? Why couldn't she see that he was happy with his life the way it was?

But was he really?

The question brought Toby up short. Okay, let's be truthful, he thought. Becca was right, he *did* love winning. And more than once he had wondered where he would have ended up if he had stayed showing on the circuit. He could have ended up at the Grand Nationals, his picture on the front cover of magazines. And then there was school. Nothing against community college, but the courses were not nearly as challenging as what would be offered at a major university. Not to mention the fact that people around town looked at him funny. It was obvious they were all wondering what he was still doing around here when he could have his pick of any college in the country. His mother and Becca weren't the only ones who thought he was crazy. Everyone in Atlanta probably thought he had lost his mind.

Toby glanced toward the stone farmhouse. Not his mind, just his heart, which was probably worse. At least they were making great strides with psychotic drugs these days, but there was not a cardiologist in the world who could fix what Becca had just done to him.

His misery mounting with every step, Toby headed toward the barn. He had noticed a couple loose boards on the farm wagon that needed to be secured before the hay rides started on Friday. Maybe he could pound a few nails after all.

When Wes returned from Hillman, Toby was hard at work on the wagon. He had removed several loose boards and replaced them with new, making sure all the others were tight and secure. Power tools were strewn near his feet on the barn floor. Toby was just considering if he should try to give the wagon a coat of paint when Wes walked through the barn doors.

"Looks like you've been busy," Wes said in greeting, glancing around at the proof of Toby's labors. "You didn't have to come today you know. It's the Lord's day, it should be a day of rest."

"Yeah, well, I didn't think you would want people falling out of the wagon during the hay rides. Might put a crimp in business," Toby explained. He grabbed one of the side boards of the wagon and shook hard, proving it was now secure. "And I figure there will be plenty of time for rest after October thirty first."

"True enough."

"I was wondering if I should try giving it a coat of paint. What do you think?"

Wes stood back, assessing the wagon. He gave a brief shake of his head. "Nah, I think it's good the way it is. Rustic looking."

"Yeah, that's what I thought." Toby bent to gather the tools.

"Rhonda says Becca was here after church."

Toby's hands stilled.

"And that after talking with you, she left in a hurry," Wes continued. "Everything okay?"

"It would be a heck of a lot better if people would keep their noses out of our business," Toby growled. He picked up the drill and stalked to the workbench where he forced himself to place the tool carefully back in its heavy plastic carry case. He could feel Wes' eyes boring into his back. Toby's heart began to thump erratically as he realized the giant mistake he had just committed, mouthing off to a man who was highly trained in the art of killing.

"Usually when someone sticks their nose in your business, it's because they care." Wes' voice was tightly controlled. "And I shouldn't have to remind you that Becca is family and if anyone hurts her..."

"It's far more likely to be the other way around." Toby spun around. Leaning back against the workbench, he crossed his arms over his chest.

"You want to explain yourself or should I just fire you on the spot?" The coldness of Wes' words chilled Toby to the bone.

"You probably won't have to. There's a good chance I'll be going away soon."

Wes cocked an eyebrow in question. Toby dug the letter from his back pocket and handed it to Wes, who scanned the missive quickly before offering it back.

"I know less than nothing about this kind of thing, but that seems like a pretty impressive honor," Wes acknowledged. "I would think you would be excited about an opportunity like that, not angry. And what's this got to do with Becca?"

"She thinks I should go."

"Of course she does. She's your friend, right? Anyone who cares about you would want you to have a chance to succeed at something you're good at."

"These shows take place all over the country." Toby glanced down at the letter before folding it and returning it to his pocket. "Who knows when I could get back home. Anything could happen in the meantime."

"Ah, I see." Wes nodded knowingly. "You're afraid you'll win in the show ring, but lose the girl."

"Something like that." Toby set his jaw and swallowed hard. "I thought I knew what I wanted. Going away again wasn't part of my plan."

"There's this Proverb you should look up when you get home. It says something like a man's heart plans his way, but the Lord directs his steps. Seems to me you've been letting your emotions run your life. You're making plans with your heart and leaving the Lord out of it. You been praying that prayer I told you about?" Wes asked. Toby nodded once. "Well, pray it again, this time like you mean it."

"What's got you looking like the world is one day away from coming to an end?" Mary Weaver asked as she entered the kitchen.

Becca sat at the kitchen island, chin in hand.

"Just thinking," Becca answered idly as she flipped through the pages of her textbook.

"About psychology?" Mary asked, glancing over Becca's shoulder at the book. "Or something else?"

"Do you think I made a mistake, not going away to school?"

"Guess that answers my question," Mary responded wryly. She went to the sink to wash her hands before taking items out of the refrigerator to start dinner.

"I mean, I was *salutatorian* for Pete's sake. I had a 3.99 GPA. I won the Michigan Competitive Scholarship, the Michigan Merit Award, the Rebecca Lodge scholarship. Good grief, even Heath Everett is going to CMU and I'm going to community college!"

"It seems a little late to be regretting that decision now." Mary began tossing vegetables together in a salad bowl. "We had this discussion months ago. Your father and I never discouraged you from going away to university. Central Michigan and Eastern both accepted your applications. You were the one who said you didn't want to live on campus, that Alpena had an excellent early childhood program and that you wanted to stay close to home so you could still be involved at church and with the family."

"Brianna Kincade was salutatorian at Johannesburg and she's going to Michigan State for pre-med," Becca said, forlorn.

"The sight of blood makes you throw up," Mary quipped. She put the salad in the fridge then filled a pot with water and put it on to boil.

"Only that one time!" Becca argued. "This family never lets you live anything down."

"I thought your plan was to get your associate's from Alpena, then go on to Central for your bachelor's. You said that was the best use of your finances. If you've changed your mind then I'm sure you can still get into Central at the start of the new semester, that is if Violet has reclaimed her child by then."

"That's another thing." Becca sighed and tucked a strand of hair behind her ear. "I think it's time I talked to Nate and find out what the options are for Nicole."

"Glory hallelujah!" Mary praised. Becca glowered at her mother.

"Try not to sound so happy about it."

"I'm sorry honey, but look at yourself. You're pale as a ghost. Your worn out and I swear you're losing weight. And that's after having the baby for a month! Can you imagine what kind of shape you'll be in if this thing keeps dragging out? It's time you let the authorities take over and move on with your life. Live a little, go on a date, *have fun*."

"Yeah, I suppose." Becca slid down from the stool and picked up the psychology book. "Guess I'll finish this homework later," she said with a decided lack of enthusiasm. Feeling a hundred years old, she left the kitchen and trudged up the stairs. At the top of the steps she looked out the window, noticing the steel gray of the sky. The weather perfectly matched her mood. Gloomy.

In her room, Becca tossed the textbook on the bed then threw herself down next to it, burying her face in her pillow. Toby would be going away. Nicole would be going away. Everyone was going away. Becca would be left to plod through the dreary days of winter alone. Turning onto her back, Becca stared up at the ceiling and finally allowed herself to imagine life without Toby in it. To think he had actually turned down full ride scholarships because of her! How stupid was that? All because he was afraid she would fall for someone else while he was gone.

Would she have? Becca wondered. Probably. She tried to imagine how her life might have been if Toby had gone away to college, if Nicole hadn't been left on her doorstep. She probably would have continued to date Bobby, maybe even fallen in love with him eventually. After all, she hadn't given Toby a second glance until a month ago. And now here she was, on the verge of throwing caution to the wind and falling in love with him, and he was going to leave.

Feeling the tears gathering, Becca covered her eyes with the back of one hand. Telling Toby to go had been one of the hardest things she had ever done. Amazing, considering that six weeks ago she had tried to convince him to never speak to her again. Becca smiled despite the tears. What a pair they were! Him professing his undying love, she telling him to fly away to Arizona. The ache in her heart told Becca just how much she was going to miss Toby when he left. She had come to trust him, to rely on him. Who would help her with Nicole? Who would bail her out when she couldn't make heads or tails of her statistics homework? Who would make her laugh in spite of herself?

And what kind of girls lived in Arizona, anyway?

The thought had Becca brushing the tears away roughly. They were probably all blond and tan and wore string bikinis. Did riders on the Arabian circuit have groupies like rodeo cowboys did? And Toby thought he had to worry about *her*!

In one fluid motion, Becca rolled off the bed and stood. She went to look down at Nikki, who slept peacefully in the port-a-crib.

"And what about you, little girl?" she whispered. "Where will you end up?" The question cut like a knife, slicing Becca to the heart. The tears came again. "Guess I'd better take my own advice huh, and pray and trust the Lord."

Becca closed her eyes, trying to recall the Bible verse she had read just that morning.

"Do not cast away your confidence, which has great reward," she murmured. "For you have need of endurance so that after you have done the will of God, you may receive the promise." Becca took a deep breath. "Oh Lord, I hope this is your will. I don't know anymore. Show me the way. Show Toby the way. In the meantime, I will cling to my confidence, which is found only in You."

Opening her eyes, Becca stared out her bedroom windows. What was that old saying? She had seen it at least a million, bazillion times. Something about if you wanted something, to let it go. If it came back to you, it was meant to be yours. If not, you were never meant to have it in the first place. That's what she had to do with Toby, and Nicole. Let them go. If they were meant to be part of her life, God would bring them back to her.

CHAPTER SIXTEEN

Bone weary, Becca dragged herself across the community college parking lot to her car. She unlocked the door and threw her backpack and purse into the passenger seat before lowering herself behind the wheel. Tiredly she pushed the hair back from her forehead and sat staring out the windshield. Nicole had been spitting up a lot and not sleeping well again. The baby was fussy and cranky, making it nearly impossible for Becca to get her homework or anything else done. Violet, after that one, brief heartening conversation had once again gone incommunicado, refusing to answer her phone or return Becca's calls.

Today, Becca told herself. Today she would talk to Nate. She could no longer avoid the inevitable. She would pick Nikki up from Connie's and go straight to Nate's house and unburden her soul. Nate would know what to do. He would take care of everything and soon Becca would be free.

The thought should have brought a lightness to Becca's spirit, but it just increased her despondency. To make matters worse, she hadn't seen or heard from Toby in two days. Maybe he was just trying to make it easier on them both, now that he was going away.

With a heavy sigh, Becca started the engine and drove out of the parking lot. She had to pick up Nikki. She had to talk to Nate. She had to tackle her English comp homework. Suddenly it all seemed too much for an eighteen-year-old girl and she had to fight back the tears. All she really wanted to do was saddle up Bailey and ride. Ride far, far away and leave all these grown-up responsibilities behind. How ridiculous it had been to have daydreamed for even a moment about marrying Toby and raising Nicole. Nikki would be much better off in the care of adults who actually knew what they were doing.

M32 was the main artery between Alpena and Gaylord and was sparsely traveled at this time of day. Becca had driven the route so many times in her short life she could almost do it with her eyes closed, which considering her state of exhaustion she was nearly tempted to try. The well-maintained road was two lanes, except where it climbed a steep hill and then a passing lane appeared so that faster-moving traffic could get around the logging trucks and other slow vehicles that often traversed the route.

As Becca's little compact climbed the hill just outside of Alpena, she automatically moved into the left-hand, passing lane even though there was no traffic in front of her. A black car pulled out onto the road, keeping pace next to her. Becca pressed the gas harder. The driver of the dark car did the same.

"Okay buddy, either speed up or slow down," Becca muttered. "That lane isn't going to last forever." She glanced over at the other driver. Her heart went cold when she saw dark glasses and a ball cap pulled low. She took her foot off the gas, slowing somewhat, hoping the car would speed on ahead of her. No luck, the dark car slowed to the same speed.

With sweaty palms, Becca stared at the top of the hill, knowing that one car or the other had to make a move or risk getting hit head on when the right hand lane came to an end. Her heart pounded furiously as she stomped on the gas, trying to pass the car on her right, which merely sped up again. As they neared the top of the hill, Becca's eyes went wide as she saw the logging truck, fully loaded, barreling towards her. The right-hand lane began to narrow as the road sign warned to merge left. Becca glanced once more to her right. The black car was inexorably crowding into the left lane, forcing Becca into the path of the oncoming semi. The logging truck, now traveling at full-throttle, came on at alarming speed. Becca could hear his horn blaring. At the last possible second, she turned the wheel sharply, barely skimming across in front of the oncoming truck. Gravel dust filled the air as the semi blared past. Becca's car came to a skidding halt in the empty parking lot of an abandoned gas station.

Trembling from head to foot, Becca sat clutching the steering wheel. Her frightened eyes scanned the road. The black car was nowhere to be seen. But there was no doubt in Becca's mind that the driver had purposely forced her into the oncoming lane. He had tried to kill her! The thought left her feeling weak and sick to her stomach. What if he was simply waiting up ahead for another try? How was she going to get home?

With shaking fingers, Becca rubbed her temple and tried to think. She would have to take another way home. It would take longer, but it wasn't impossible. She knew every back road and two track between Hillman and Lewiston. The question was, did her would-be killer know them as well? And more importantly, who had just tried to take her life? The question plagued Becca as with jelly in her knees she pulled back onto the road and headed toward home.

The shaking increased as she pulled into the Compton's driveway. Her legs felt like over-cooked spaghetti as Becca climbed out of her car and up the steps to Connie's front door. All she could see was that semi loaded with logs coming straight at her windshield. Her stomach tightened and Becca put a hand to her belly, trying to calm the roiling that had bile rising in her throat. Before she could lift a hand to knock, the door was swung open.

"Becca, is everything okay?" Connie stood there with a worried look marring her features. She held the door wider and Becca attempted to cross the threshold, one hand on her stomach, the other clamped across her mouth. She swallowed hard.

"Yes, no, um, someone just tried…" A sob overtook the words as tears poured from her eyes.

"Oh, honey, what is it?" Connie's arms came around her, giving Becca something solid to lean on. "What happened?"

"A logging truck almost..." she gulped. "I almost got..." She couldn't untangle the words enough to make any sense. Then the nausea came again. "Oh Lord, I'm gonna be sick." She slapped a hand over her mouth once more and Connie quickly steered her toward the bathroom. All Becca saw was the powder blue commode as she rushed toward it and lifted the lid. Kneeling, she was violently ill.

Water ran. A cold cloth was pressed into her hand. Grateful, Becca took it and wiped her face. She flushed the toilet then sat and leaned back against the bathroom wall. She buried her face in the washcloth, trying to block out the sight of the semi that nearly took her life. With a ragged breath, she finally looked up. The quaint, old-fashioned bathroom slowly registered in Becca's brain. The fixtures were all powder blue. There was a crocheted-covered tissue box on the back of the commode and she was sitting on a fluffy, baby-blue rug that covered linoleum that had to be at least twenty years old. Connie, her eyes filled with concern, still stood near the bathroom door.

"Are you okay now?" she asked kindly. Becca nodded slowly. "Can you tell me what happened?"

"Someone tried to run me off the road on my way here." The shuddering began again and Becca had to clench her teeth together to keep them from chattering. "They almost ran me right into the path of a logging truck," she managed to choke out. She pressed her face into the cool cloth once more and fought back tears. "I thought I was a goner." Becca reached for the toilet seat and unsteadily pushed herself up. She waited a moment to see if she would be sick again.

"Do you think they did it on purpose?" Connie asked, bewildered.

"It sure seemed that way to me," Becca answered. Still wobbly, she made her way toward the door. Connie stepped aside and Becca moved toward the sitting room, lowering herself onto the edge of the settee. "I was in the passing lane, but he wouldn't let me pass, and he wouldn't let me get behind him either. Then the logging truck was coming and I..." Hot tears pressed against Becca's eyelids as she closed her eyes, seeing the semi once again. "He tried to push me right into the path of the truck. It's a miracle that I was able to turn before it hit me." The tears made their way slowly down Becca's cheeks and she didn't have the strength to wipe them away. "I was so…. I was so scared," she hiccupped.

"Of course you were." Connie sat beside her and put a motherly arm around Becca's shoulders.

"I've never been so frightened…in my…life," Becca said between sobs. Shaking overtook her again. She was so overwrought that she failed to hear the creaking of the porch steps. Then the front door was flung wide and Joe Compton filled the doorway. "Until now," she squeaked.

"Connie, who's here?" Joe bellowed just as Becca's world went black.

She was floating on a cloud. The scent of roses hung on the air. Becca's eyes fluttered. Fading light filtered through lace curtains. She relaxed deeper into the marshmallow-soft cushion that enveloped her, straining to hear angels singing the hallelujah chorus.

"Am I dead?" she whispered.

A quiet squeak answered her. Becca turned her head slightly to see Toby sitting in a whitewashed wooden chair beside the bed. She frowned.

"I guess that would be a no," she answered her own question then asked another. "What are you doing here?"

"Connie called me." Toby shifted himself from the chair to the edge of the bed. His brown eyes, overflowing with concern, roved over her face. "I had given her my cell number that first time I picked up Nikki. Just in case there was an emergency. You shook her up, passing out like that."

Becca swallowed hard, remembering Joe Compton's intimidating form that had nearly scared the life clean out of her. She raised her head slightly, realizing she was laying on what was apparently a guest room bed. The downy soft twin bed, with its white wicker headboard was covered with a patchwork quilt of lavender and green material.

"How did I get to this bed? Did you carry me in here?"

Toby chuckled low. "I wish I could take credit for such a heroic act, but no. You were here when I arrived, so I assume that means Joe carried you in here."

"Oh good heavens." Becca covered her face with her hands. "I might as well be dead cuz that man's gonna kill me anyway." She felt a gentle clasp as Toby drew her hands away from her face and held them.

"No he won't. Everything's okay." Toby ran his thumbs over her knuckles and Becca drew strength from his touch. "Connie and I explained the situation to Joe. He took it pretty well. Actually he was more upset that we were scared to tell him the truth. He felt bad that he frightened you to the point of fainting."

"Yeah, well, the state I was in, it didn't take much." Becca took a shaky breath and pushed herself up to a sitting position. Sliding her legs over the side of the bed, she sat beside Toby. Their shoulders bumped together in easy familiarity.

"You want to tell me what happened?"

Breathing deeply, Becca grasped her knees and tried to think where to begin.

"Someone's been following me. The first time was…" She screwed her face up, trying to remember. "Two or three weeks ago I guess. On my way to class. I've seen the car a few other times, always tail gaiting me."

"What kind of car? Who was driving?"

"I dunno." Becca shrugged a shoulder. "The car was black. Older. Medium size. The driver is always wearing dark glasses and a ball cap pulled low over his eyes. I can never get a good enough look to tell who it is."

"And today he was tail gaiting you on your way home from school?"

"No." Becca shook her head. "He just pulled out on the road next to me. I was in the passing lane and he pulled out of a driveway, I think. I don't know really. I was so tired, I wasn't paying very good attention. I tried to get past before the lane ended, but he wouldn't let me. I sped up and so did he. So I tried to slow down and get behind him, but he slowed down. He kept crowding me over into the oncoming lane and by then there was this logging truck…" Becca broke off, feeling the terror once more. Toby put an arm around her shoulders and she automatically leaned into him, gathering strength and comfort from his nearness. "Oh Toby, I was so scared. What if Nikki had been in the car? We could have both been killed." Her hand clutched the front of his sweatshirt.

"Shhhh." Toby laid his cheek against the top of her head. "You're safe, Nikki's safe. Thank the Lord. But I think we should tell Nate."

"Tell him what? That some guy in a black car is going around driving like a maniac? I can't even give him a decent description of the vehicle. Not even a partial license number. What could Nate do?"

"I still think you should tell him," Toby insisted. Becca pulled out of his arms and stood.

"I was going to talk to him today about Nicole," she admitted. "But I don't feel up to it now. It can wait one more day."

"Is that really what you want?" Toby asked.

"Yes." Becca tried to sound definite, even though her heart rebelled. "And now, after what just happened here this afternoon, I don't see where I have any choice. Connie won't be able to keep watching

Nicole. I'm exhausted and stressed to the max. Nikki will be better off in foster care and Violet will just have to deal with the consequences of her actions when she gets back to town."

As if on cue, a lusty cry broke the stillness of the farmhouse. Becca hurried out of the bedroom, following the sound to the kitchen where she found Connie offering the baby a bottle while Joe leaned back against the stove, his dark brows lowered, arms crossed against his massive chest.

"I'm terribly sorry Mr. Compton." Becca rushed across the room to take Nicole from Connie's arms, surprised that her voice came out relatively steady. "Please don't take your anger out on Connie. She was just trying to help me out."

"I don't abuse my wife," the bear of a man growled.

Maybe not physically, Becca thought, nearly quaking in her tennis shoes. Toby entered the kitchen and Becca felt an odd reassurance at his presence, even though Toby was dwarfed by the massive man standing by the stove.

"Connie tells me Violet skipped town awhile back," Joe's deep voice rumbled through the room. His onyx eyes pinned Becca to the floor.

"Ye...Yes sir," she stuttered. "She's been gone nearly a month now."

"Her daddy's a drunk," Joe stated. Reaching for a long-necked, amber bottle on the countertop, he took a long swig. "Can't blame the girl for getting out of Dodge, but she shouldn't have left the kid behind."

Maybe she was imagining it, but Becca thought the man's gaze softened somewhat when he looked at the baby held in her arms.

"She's coming back." The quaver in Becca's voice belied her conviction.

"Huh," was Joe's reply as he took another pull from his bottle.

"The truth is Mr. Compton." Becca squared her shoulders and spoke with sudden confidence. "If Violet doesn't come home soon, someone is going to have to raise this baby. I'm just a kid myself, and not even any blood relation. Vi's mom and dad…"

"Ain't fit to raise a hamster," Joe interrupted.

"You and Connie are probably next of kin then."

"I done raised my own. Don't have no desire to do it again." His eyes swiveled to his wife. "So don't go gettin' any ideas, woman."

"No, Joe, of course not," Connie replied with a small smile, her hands fluttering nervously.

"So if I contact the authorities and start a child abandonment investigation, you won't object?" Becca asked.

"You won't hear a peep out of me," Joe agreed.

"Okay then, well, I'll get out of your hair." Becca moved toward the sitting room to retrieve the baby's things. "Again, I'm sorry about all this and, and about fainting earlier." She risked a glance over her shoulder at Joe's intimidating figure. Crazy as it seemed, she thought the man nearly quirked a smile.

"Don't figure you planned on that."

"N…No sir, I sure didn't."

"The wife here says you nearly had a run in with a logging truck."

"Ye...Yes," Becca stumbled over the admission, seeing once again her near brush with death.

"That's enough to shake anyone up," Joe admitted, almost kindly. "Want a beer? That might settle your nerves." He held the bottle out to her in invitation.

"No thank you." This time there was no stutter to Becca's reply. "We really must be going. My parents will be worried."

Becca hurried to the sitting room. Nicole fussed when the bottle was pulled from her grasp. Becca ignored the baby's protests as she pushed Nicole's arms into the sleeves of a pink crocheted sweater. Nikki would survive a few more minutes without her bottle. Becca just wanted to get out of this house and get home, home where she would be safe and could take an easy breath. Home where she would be surrounded by people who knew what love was.

Toby followed Becca home, driving her car. He had convinced her it was safer if she drove the Bronco, just in case her would-be assailant was waiting someplace up ahead. Toby knew a thing or two about defensive driving. He had plenty of family members and friends who had taken part in the bump-and-run races at the fairgrounds who had taught him a few tricks. If anyone tried to run him off the road, they had a surprise coming.

Toby's mind was a boiling cauldron of thoughts and emotions. He was furious that anyone would try to hurt Becca. If he got his hands on the jerk who had nearly killed her, watch out! When he had gotten Connie's call, Toby's heart had nearly come undone at the thought of Becca's brush with death. If anything happened to Becca, Toby didn't know how he would handle it.

Then there was worry. How could he keep Becca safe? If she wouldn't go to the police, how could he assure himself that there wouldn't be a repeat of today's near tragedy? Becca had to go to class and if it were true someone was watching her, just waiting for the next opportunity... Toby's blood ran cold at the mere thought, but he knew Becca well enough to know she wouldn't stay holed up in her bedroom, crouched in a closet.

Mixed in with his anger and anxiety, Toby felt some elusive sense of urgency that he couldn't quite comprehend. Like something was about to slip from his grasp, but he didn't know what or why or how. Was it Becca's sudden determination to turn Nicole over to the authorities? Despite Wes and his mother's and Becca's assumption that Toby would jump at the opportunity to train and show out west, Toby himself wasn't at all sure he was going to accept the invitation. He still held tight to his hope, his dream, of winning Becca's heart and making a home for Nikki. He was praying to know God's will but so far he still didn't have a definite answer. He wished God would give him a sign, like those big arrows the road crews used that blinked on and off, pointing a person in the right direction. Or maybe a billboard. Something big with bright colors that shouted, "hey Toby, God wants you to..."

Do what? Toby didn't have the slightest idea. And worse, he wasn't sure how he was supposed to find out. Pray, sure. Well, he'd been doing a lot of that lately. But how was he supposed to *know* what God wanted him to do? How did other people seem to figure out the will of God so easily?

And there, in the middle of this knot of emotion and concern was the biggest question of all. Who would want to hurt Becca? And why? It didn't make any sense. Becca was sweet, well, at least most of the time. To most people. She was thoughtful and helpful and kind. She didn't have an enemy in the world. So who would try to run her into the path of a logging truck? Toby shook his head and sighed. Another question he couldn't answer. Another dilemma to pray about, seeking answers that Toby wasn't even sure he would recognize if they were given.

By the time the two vehicles pulled into the Weaver driveway, Toby was about wrung out from all his mental gymnastics. Somehow he had to clear his mind, and his heart, so he and Becca could think rationally and come up with a plan for the future.

Toby quickly got out of Becca's car and hurried to help her with Nicole's baby seat. The child was screaming fit to kill.

"That couldn't have been a very pleasant ride home," he commented. Becca threw him a look of pure exasperation.

"No," was her short answer. Becca headed for the house. Toby reached for the carrier and took the baby from her grasp. Becca relinquished her burden without an argument. "I took her bottle away at the

Compton's and she let me know all the way home that she wasn't pleased. She's hungry, and probably tired, too. And most likely wet. It never ends."

The trio trooped down the hall to the kitchen which was filled with the reassuring smell of homemade bread. Mary Weaver looked up from her dinner preparations. She raised an eyebrow when she saw Toby enter the room carrying Nicole.

"We were getting worried about you," Mary said, turning to stir a pot on the stove.

Toby glanced at Becca, curious as to how she would explain her tardiness. Would she tell her mother what had transpired on the road from Alpena? He watched Becca swallow hard.

"Sorry Mom, I didn't mean to worry you."

Toby set the baby seat on the kitchen table and Becca moved to lift the squalling infant. She rummaged in the diaper bag and removed a half-full bottle which she quickly offered to Nikki who latched on as if she hadn't eaten in a month of Sundays.

"Did you have car trouble?" Mary questioned over her shoulder. "Did Toby have to come to your rescue?"

"Something like that," Becca hedged. "Everything's okay now."

"I'm glad to hear it. Maybe your father should take a look at your car. You're putting a lot of miles on it, driving back and forth to school."

Toby and Becca's eyes met. He smiled, trying to ease the tension that still marred her features.

"Like I said, the car's okay. But if it will make you feel better to have Daddy look at it…"

"We'll mention it when he comes in for supper," Mary promised. "Toby, would you like to stay and eat with us? I'm making pepper pot stew. And I just took a loaf of bread out of the oven."

Becca frowned at him and shook her head in an almost imperceptible movement. Toby smiled again.

"Sure, Mrs. Weaver, that sounds great," Toby gleefully accepted the invitation. "Just let me call my mom and let her know I won't be home." Toby dug his cell phone from his front jeans pocket.

"Oh look Becca, a cell phone," Mary observed. "You know, that wonderful technological advancement that you refuse to use. If you had one maybe you could have called to let me know you were having car trouble."

"Mom, don't start," Becca warned tiredly.

"Well, soon you won't have any choice. When you go away to CMU next semester, you'll have to have one."

Toby froze, his phone flipped open, thumb on the send button. He swiveled to stare at Becca who had taken a seat at the kitchen table.

"Since when are you moving down to Mt. Pleasant?" Toby asked slowly.

"Didn't she tell you?" Mary interjected. "She's decided to go away to school after all. Your mom told me you're headed to Arizona to train at some big horse stable. Looks like Atlanta will be losing both its top students."

CHAPTER SEVENTEEN

"Nikki needs to be changed." Becca slapped the baby bottle down on the table and bolted from the kitchen. She hurried up the stairs but she hadn't made her escape fast enough. Toby was right on her heels. "You shouldn't be in my room," she flung over her shoulder.

"I've seen it before," Toby retorted.

"Mom and Dad don't approve of boys in my bedroom," Becca continued to argue.

"The door's open."

Becca went to her dresser and snatched a clean diaper and the box of baby wipes. She laid Nikki on the bed and tried to concentrate on the task at hand, all too aware of Toby's presence behind her.

"When did you make the decision to go to Central next semester?" he asked, his voice low.

"I haven't decided," she ground out. "Mom spoke out of turn. I've just been considering my options." Becca took great pains with snapping Nikki's sleeper. She lifted the baby then turned to sit on the edge of the bed. "What do you care anyway? You'll be away in *Arizona*." The word came out with much more sarcasm than she intended.

"I never said I was going." Toby crossed his arms and stared at her, his eyes as hard as cinders.

"Don't be a moron." Becca stood and went to her bookcase. Kneeling, she rummaged one-handed through the stack of magazines until she found what she was looking for. Standing she went to Toby and thrust the magazine in his face. "See that? That's the Class A amateur Arabian champion for this year. Don't tell me you don't recognize the picture. You're parents raise Arabians for Pete's sake! So you know darned well who's horse Carson Delany was riding and where he trained."

"Alonzo Ferrera's," Toby whispered.

"That's right. Carson Delany trained at Desert Sands. The very same stable that's courting you. Now don't you dare stand there and tell me that you wouldn't love to have your picture on the cover of Horse Illustrated." Becca shook the magazine for emphasis before she tossed it on the bed.

"Okay, sure." Toby shrugged a shoulder. "It would be cool to be on the cover of a magazine, but I'm not that good."

"Oh pa-leeze!" Becca turned away and threw herself into the rocker by the windows. "Toby, you've *always* been that good. Why do you think I hated you so much?"

"Hated? Past tense?"

"Don't try to change the subject," Becca muttered.

"You're the one who changed the subject. I didn't come up here to talk about Desert Sands. I came up here to talk about you going to CMU."

"To talk me out of it, you mean."

"You know what kind of people go to CMU. Jocks like Heath Everett. Football players with their chiseled physiques and empty heads."

"Heath Everett is a dung beetle. I never understood why you were friends."

"Teammates," Toby corrected. Becca just shrugged. "Or you have the Farmer Fitzgerald types," he continued.

"Nah. They go to Michigan State." Becca looked at Toby, smiling wickedly.

"That's true," Toby conceded with a grin of his own.

"Besides, what kind of girls do you think hang around the horse show circuit?" Becca asked. "That's a stupid question. You already know what kind of girls are there. Vacuous, bubble-headed bleach blonds who probably throw their panties in the show ring."

"Are you saying girls who show horses are vacuous bubble-heads?"

Becca glowered at him in response. Toby chuckled.

"Anyway, I don't go for blonds, I prefer redheads."

"Well then, I guess that means I'm safe, because I am not a red head."

"Close enough," Toby replied, his eyes roving over her strawberry blond hair.

"Maybe I really do prefer muscular, empty headed jocks like Heath Everett," she said, trying to ignore the odd shimmy that fluttered in her stomach at Toby's close perusal. She set the rocker in motion with her toe and sent Toby a coy look.

"If Heath Everett so much as looked at you…"

A light bulb went off in Becca's brain. She set both feet on the floor, stopping the rocker with a jerk. Nikki started awake.

"I think that's it!" she exclaimed. Toby looked at her in bewilderment.

"That's what?" he asked.

"Not what, but who." Her eyes locked on Toby's as reality sank in. He shook his head, clearly confused. "You asked me earlier when was the first time I saw the car that has been following me, and who was driving. I just realized the first time I saw that car, it wasn't on my way to school. It was in the parking lot of the IGA. That day that Heath and Mike were harassing me about Nikki. I've never known why, but Heath has always hated my guts. Maybe he's the one who was driving the car."

"But Heath's away at school," Toby countered, confusion digging a deep furrow in his brow.

"No." Becca shook her head, adamant. "That day I ran into him and Mike, they should have been at a game but they had been in some kind of trouble. Then Mom was telling me just the other day that the gossips at the quilt shop were all atwitter because scuttlebutt says Heath got kicked out of school for drugs. Of course, I don't know that for sure because I haven't seen him and I just put it down to the same old Atlanta gossip mill. But maybe, maybe it's true. Maybe Heath *is* back in Atlanta and maybe he's gunning for me."

"But why?" Toby asked the age-old question.

"I dunno."

"Becca, Toby," Mary's voice called up the stairs. "Supper's ready."

Becca stood and laid the sleeping Nicole in the port-a-crib. Toby came to stand beside her and they both looked down at the baby, so peaceful in slumber. Becca felt Toby's hand, gentle on her shoulder. She risked a peek up at him.

"I know this sounds trite, Bec. But everything's going to be okay. I'm gonna make sure of it."

Toby sat at the dinner table and tried to concentrate on the conversation going on around him, but his thoughts were as jumbled up as a tangled string of Christmas lights. He was having trouble straightening them out. Start at one end, he told himself, and work your way down.

The first thing he latched onto was the fact that Becca was jealous. That thought brought him nearly as much comfort as Mrs. Weaver's delicious stew. Sure, Becca might talk a good game, telling him he was an idiot for not jumping at the chance to show Alonzo Ferrera's horses, but she really didn't want him to go. She was just as concerned about who he would meet as he was worried about her going away to a big university and falling for some stud muffin.

Toby took another bite of stew and chewed thoughtfully. Okay, Becca didn't really want him going away to Arizona and he certainly didn't want her moving down to Mt. Pleasant, straight into the arms of some genius chemistry major who would like nothing better than to show her his "experiments." The thought made Toby scowl.

"Is the stew okay, Toby?" Mrs. Weaver asked.

"Hmm?" Toby looked up. "Oh, yeah, it's great Mrs. Weaver, really good."

Mary gave him an odd look. "More bread then?" She passed him the basket.

"Sure. Thanks." Toby took a slice and buttered it absently, his mind still on the dilemma of Becca going away to college.

It all seemed rather ridiculous to Toby. Becca didn't want him going. He didn't want her to go. So why were either of them thinking of leaving Atlanta? Why didn't they both just stay here and focus on what really mattered, their growing relationship and doing what was best for Nikki?

That settled in his mind, Toby moved on to the next knotty problem that was nagging at his brain. Heath Everett. Was Heath really the one tailing Becca? Toby thought back over the years to all the snide comments Heath had made about Becca. It was true that the guy always seemed to have a burr in his butt about Becca, but Toby always thought that was because Heath secretly had a crush on her and was mad that she never gave him the time of day. Well, if Heath had gotten kicked out of school and was back in town, Toby would be able to find out easy enough. Atlanta was a small town. No one could hide out around here for long. Not to mention that the grapevine was always bearing juicy fruit for the gossips' consumption. A few phone calls and Toby would know where Heath was and what kind of car he was driving these days. If it was black, well then... Toby hand clenched around his spoon, imagining it was Heath Everett's neck.

When supper was over, Toby helped clear the table. Mary rinsed the dishes and stacked them in the dishwasher while Becca stored the leftovers in the refrigerator and Toby brought things in from the dining room. He took a washcloth from the kitchen sink and wiped the table, his mind now clear. He knew what he had to do. It was the only way that made any sense. And why put it off? Tonight would be as good a time as any.

He returned to the kitchen just as Mary closed the dishwasher. He set the washcloth on the sink and turned to look at Becca.

"I have to go feed the horses," she abruptly announced.

"I'll go with you."

Mary gave them both a knowing look as they passed, going from the kitchen to the mud room at the end of the hall. Toby stood and watched as Becca shoved her feet into a pair of ancient, curly-toed cowboy boots. She took a quilted jacket off a peg and shrugged into it as she pushed out the back door and headed across the lawn to the barn. She entered the barn from a side door and immediately went to the opposite end, pushing open a large sliding door to reveal three horses standing patiently on the other side of a hot-wired gate. Instincts took over as Toby unlatched the wires and held the gate open while Becca went to open the stalls and secure each animal inside. Silently the two worked together to fill the feed boxes, hay racks and water buckets. Finally there was nothing left to occupy their hands. Becca shoved hers in the pockets of her jacket. Toby leaned against a stall, looking down at Becca's aging pony, Smokey.

"You going to tell your parents about what happened today?" he finally asked.

"No." Bailey stuck his head over his stall gate and Becca reached out to run her fingers through his forelock. "It would just worry them."

"I think you should take the Bronco to school tomorrow. We could meet at Wes and Rhonda's to switch vehicles. Your parents wouldn't have to know."

"But what excuse would I give to Rhonda? I don't want to start telling a bunch of lies. You know that wouldn't be right."

"Then I guess I'll just have to follow you to class to make sure you get there okay."

"It doesn't matter. I'll have to miss class tomorrow anyway because there's no one to watch Nikki now. My mom will never agree to do it and Rhonda would kill me if I asked her to baby sit the day before the orchard is due to open." Becca rested her cheek against Bailey's and closed her eyes. Toby could see tears glittering on her golden lashes. "Maybe it's for the best. I'm so tired."

Stepping forward, Toby reached out and clasped a handful of her jacket sleeve, pulling her gently into his arms. Becca immediately stiffened.

"Relax, would you," Toby commanded, trying to nestle her more comfortably in his arms.

"No." Becca put her hands on his chest and leaned back. "I can't keep leaning on you. I have to stand on my own two feet."

"I like it when you lean on me." Toby smiled down into her upturned face. His gaze roved over the freckles sprinkled like pixie dust across her cheeks. "And you don't have to face any of this alone. I told you, I'm going to make everything okay."

"Toby, you're a good friend, really you are. I'm shocked at just how much I've come to rely on you. But you can't make everything okay. You just can't. It's not possible."

"I can try, can't I?" Toby asked. "Like tomorrow for instance. It's Thursday. Isn't Penny normally off on Thursdays and Fridays? Why don't you call and ask her to baby sit? She's really good with Nicole and I know she enjoys having her. Plus, you've already said you were going to talk to Nate, so it's not like you're trying to hide Nikki from him anymore."

A tiny little dagger twisted in Toby's heart at the thought of Nicole being put into the hands of strangers. Well, he still had hope that was never going to happen. Becca sighed and pushed from his arms.

"I suppose I could try," she agreed reluctantly, heading for the barn door. "We'd better get inside before Daddy comes out here with a shotgun to defend my honor."

Toby trailed her to the house. Once inside the mud room Becca shucked her boots and jacket.

"I'd better go up and check on Nikki," she said over her shoulder, entering the house.

"Okay." Toby watched her disappear down the hallway then stood and listened to her tread on the stairs. He glanced into the family room and saw Becca's parents sitting in their familiar spots. Her father, dressed in a navy blue sweat suit, was in his armchair half-hidden behind the newspaper. Mary had changed into her pajamas and a fleece robe and now sat on the sofa working the crossword. Toby chewed the inside of his cheek. It was now or never. With one more glance down the hallway he wiped his hands on his jeans then stepped down into the family room. Mary glanced at him over the top of her reading glasses.

"Toby," she greeted.

"Mrs. Weaver." Toby nodded and cleared his throat. "I would like to speak to you and Mr. Weaver if I might."

"This sounds serious." Mary observed. David lowered his paper a fraction, looking at Toby over the top of the business section.

"It is," Toby agreed and swallowed hard. "I would like to, that is..." He swallowed and tried again. "I would like to ask permission to marry your daughter."

"Excuse me?" Mary asked, dropping the crossword on her lap. Toby's heart pounded.

"I said I would like to ask for your daughter's hand in marriage," he repeated.

"Toby!" Becca's shocked voice sounded behind him. "What in the world are you doing?"

Winning Becca

Becca stomped across the carpet. Grabbing Toby by the arm, she pulled him from the room while her parents looked on in shocked silence. Her fury building with every step, Becca pushed through the door to the mudroom, storming across to the glass door on the far end and out into the cold back yard. As soon as she had cleared the cement steps, she turned the full force of her anger on Toby.

"What in the world were you doing back there?" she screeched.

"I was asking your parents permission for us to get married," Toby's nonchalant answer only heightened Becca's rage.

"Married?! Married?! Toby, are you *insane*?" Becca clutched her hair, trying to keep her head from exploding.

"I've been thinking…"

"No." Becca cut him off with a slice of her hand. "You obviously have not been thinking! I swear you don't have a working brain cell left in your head! I told you, I'm not marrying you. I'm not marrying anybody at eighteen."

"I told you I would make everything okay. Just hear me out," Toby pleaded. "I'm a genius remember? I've got this all figured out."

"You may be a whiz at math, Toby, but when it comes to common sense, every day life you don't have a clue." Becca shivered in a gust of cold wind. Looking down she realized she had stormed outside wearing her fuzzy blue slippers. "It's freezing out here. We should go back in." She turned to mount the steps.

"Wait." Toby laid a staying hand on her arm. "I really want to talk this out with you, but I don't want to do it in front of your parents."

"Because then they'll realize you aren't the genius you've portrayed all these years?" Becca asked, eyebrows raised. Toby didn't rise to the bait.

"Come on Bec, cut me some slack here, okay? Let's go sit in the Bronco for a minute. Let me argue my case. Please?"

Against her better judgment, Becca allowed herself to be led around the house to the driveway. She climbed into the passenger seat of Toby's Bronco. He fired up the engine and cranked up the heat.

"This is a terrible waste of gas," she grumped.

"Oh shut up a minute and just listen." Becca glowered at him but clapped her mouth shut. "I don't think you really want me going to *Arizona*," he mimicked her earlier sarcasm perfectly. "And I don't want you going away to school where the wolves would love nothing more than to eat you alive."

"I've been doing a pretty good job of taking care of myself long before you appointed yourself my protector."

Toby snorted. "That's what you think."

"What's that supposed to mean?"

"Kirby Moulton," Toby said the name with some satisfaction.

"What?" Becca spluttered. "What on God's green earth does Kirby Moulton have to do with anything?"

"He had a terrible crush on you. I remember how he used to crowd you at the lunch table." Toby's mouth set in a grim line.

"How do you even remember that? That was way back in elementary school."

"Yes, and heaven knows that was sooo long ago." The words dripped with satire. "So I guess that means you have no clear recollection of what he did to you at sixth grade camp."

"Oh ho, I do too." Becca shivered. "He filled my sleeping bag with crickets. Ugh. I didn't sleep a wink the whole rest of camp. But why would you bring that up? It just proves my point that I can take care of myself. I reamed Kirby up one side and down the other. He never came near me again."

Toby began to chuckle. "Bec, he never came near you again because the next day when we went canoeing I tipped his canoe over and held him underwater until he swore he would never so much as look at you again for as long as he lived."

"Oh good grief!" Becca slapped a hand down on the vinyl seat. "Are you telling me that you nearly drowned poor Kirby Moulton, who wore bottle-thick glasses and had the worst case of acne in the entire school, because of me?"

"He never bothered you again, did he?" Toby asked, one eyebrow raised over a glittering brown eye.

"No, that was left entirely up to you."

"That's okay," Toby said with a grin. "I'm allowed. I staked my claim to you way back in preschool, remember? Which brings me back to my original point. We're meant for each other Becca. You have to know that by now. Why should I go clear out to the desert when all I want is right here? We can get married and still go to school. We can pursue our dreams and maybe even make a home for Nicole. I know you don't really want to hand her over to the state anymore than I want you to do it."

"People don't just up and get married on a whim. Marriage is a serious commitment between two people who love each other. We've never even dated."

"Because we've always been in the same group. From preschool all through grade school and high school, we've pretty much done everything together. We know just about all there is to know about each other."

"Yeah, and if you remember correctly, because I knew you so well I couldn't hardly stand you. You ate with your mouth open. You farted in public. And you beat me at just about everything. You were disgusting."

"Were, being the key word," Toby returned. "I don't do those things anymore. Well, except I do still beat you an awful lot."

Becca frowned at him. Toby merely smiled that self-satisfied smirk, making Becca shake her head. She relaxed back against the seat.

"Okay, Toby." She nodded. "Awhile back you said we both like playing the game. So, lets play it. Let's play the what-if game. All the way to the end."

Toby looked at her with a puzzled frown. "What's the what-if game?"

"It goes like this. What if we got married?" Becca asked. Hope lit Toby's eyes. "Where would we live?"

"There's plenty of places for sale around here, or we could rent."

"Okay, so what if we found a place to live. How would we pay for it?"

"Jobs."

"I work two days a week at the Spot of Tea, and mostly I get paid in tips, which are going to go way down over the winter as business falls off. That's hardly enough to make a house payment on. And your job with Wes is probably about over for the year."

"I can find another job. If I have to work at the Home Depot in Gaylord…"

"What if you did get hired somewhere else," Becca cut him off. "How would you balance working full-time, if you could even got hired full-time, with going to school?"

"People do it all the time, Becca. None of this is impossible," Toby argued.

"Maybe not impossible, Toby, but it would be very, very difficult. Marriages have a hard enough time surviving without the added stress of financial worry or class loads. We're young. We have our whole lives ahead of us. Why would we want to start out setting ourselves up for failure?"

"Neither one of us have ever failed at anything. And then there's Nikki."

"There isn't a judge on this planet that is going to give that baby to two teenaged kids to raise. It's just not going to happen, Toby."

"Violet gave her to you. There's plenty of people who will attest to that, that she wanted you to have Nicole. Plus possession is nine-tenths of the law."

"I don't think it works that way with children," Becca answered. "Besides, Violet is going to come back. She isn't dead, she just left town. And it doesn't matter anyway. Even if she didn't come home, I've thought a lot about it. I've prayed and I honestly don't think I'm meant to raise Nicole. I believe God put her in my life for this time. I'm serving some sort of purpose. But I don't believe it's His will that I keep Nikki."

"But how do you *know*? You keep talking about God's will. Wes keeps telling me to pray for God's will. But nobody tells me how I know what God's will is," Toby's voice rang with frustration.

Feeling his anguish in the depths of her heart, Becca reached out and touched Toby's arm.

"It's not that hard really but I'm not sure how to explain it. It's just a, a *knowing* inside. A feeling of peace. When I would look at Nikki and wish she were my baby, there would be this odd tug inside me, like a struggle. But when I thought about giving her up, even though there's a hurt there, I also had a feeling of relief, like I knew this was the right decision.

"That's why I can't agree to marry you, Toby. I don't have peace about that either. I'll be honest with you, I *have* thought about it. I allowed myself the briefest time to fantasize about what it would be like for you and I and Nikki to be a family. But dreams and reality seldom match up and in the deepest part of my being I know it's not right. At least not at this time in our lives."

Toby's shoulders slumped and he looked down at his lap. Becca found herself scooting across the seat to lean against his side.

"I'm not saying never," she stated quietly. "After all, you nearly drowned Kirby Moulton for me. But the Bible says there's a time and a season for all things. This isn't our time yet, not for marriage anyway. There's too many other things we need to do first."

"I suppose you're right," Toby said, sounding defeated.

"Oh ho, I'm right for once?" Becca asked, playfully slapping his arm. She quickly turned serious once more. "I can't tell you what to do about Desert Sands. It's not for me to decide God's will for your life. But I think you need to explore the possibility a little more, Toby. Just like God laid Nikki on my doorstep for a reason, He put this opportunity on yours. And you can't use me as an excuse. That's just not fair. You're going to have to learn to trust me a little bit, and then let go. Just like I have to do with you, and with Nikki. Open my hands and just..." she opened her fingers wide and spread her arms. "Let go."

Becca slid back across the seat and opened the door.

"What about tomorrow?" Toby questioned as she hopped to the ground.

"I called Penny when I went up to check on Nikki. She said yes she'll watch her."

"I still think we should switch vehicles. We don't have to lie, but if your parents already think you were having car trouble they wouldn't question it if I came and gave you the Bronco in the morning."

Becca hesitated for just the slightest moment before agreeing.

"Okay, sure. You've wasted enough gas for one night. I don't want you wasting even more following me to Alpena and back. You're a good guy, Toby. Too bad I wasted so many years despising you."

Lifting a hand in farewell, Becca hurried around the Bronco and up the front porch steps. As she opened the front door, a lusty bellow echoed down the stairs. Sighing, Becca leaned back against the door for a moment and closed her eyes. Soon and very soon her life would be back to normal.

CHAPTER EIGHTEEN

True to his word, Toby was there bright and early the next morning. He helped Becca secure Nicole in the back seat of the Bronco, then the trio set off down the road where Becca dropped him off at the end of Wes and Rhonda's driveway, artfully avoiding the necessity for any explanations. If Toby wanted to give one, then let him come up with his own story. Becca didn't want any part of deceit.

A soft smile turned up Becca's lips as she remembered how their bodies had brushed when she walked around the Bronco to get behind the wheel. How Toby's eyes had shone as he smiled down at her from beneath the brim of his ball cap before bending to place the lightest kiss on her lips. Becca placed a fingertip where his mouth had been, still feeling that feather-light touch. How bizarre to think that Toby Sinclair had kissed her and she hadn't gagged. No, she had sighed like some chick in a romance novel.

What was odder still was that the two of them had sat right here in the front seat of this Bronco and talked about marriage almost as if it were the most normal thing in the world. They had discussed where they would live and how they would support themselves, even talked about raising a baby, but they hadn't talked about love. Oh sure, Toby had said on several occasions that he had loved her since he was four. He had nearly drowned Kirby Moulton for her sake. How many other boys had he put the fear of God into? Becca wondered. No wonder she never had a date for the prom. Not that she cared. It had always been more fun going with a group of friends. And Becca had never really even looked at boys *like that* until a couple months ago at the fair after Bobby had kissed her and made her toes curl.

She tried to compare Bobby's kiss with Toby's, but it was a impossible because Bobby's had been a full-contact kiss and Toby's had been more like chaste pecks. Almost brotherly. Well no, she amended, not exactly brotherly, but certainly not passionate embraces that made her want to cross any lines like Bobby's had done. Maybe Toby wasn't really attracted to her in a physical sense. He claimed to have loved her since they were children, but why? Because she always gave him a run for his money at Quiz Bowl?

As Becca drove to Penny's, she took a quick inventory of her physical attributes. She knew she was passably attractive. She had good hair. Not too red or too curly like Rhonda's. It had enough red highlights to make her look fiery without being subjected to cruel names in school. It was thick and fairly straight. Becca glanced in the rearview mirror.

She had inherited the same blue eyes as most of the other Weaver children. Her lashes were light but they were long and thick and had never been touched by mascara. Becca had no use for makeup. Of course, she was stuck with these stupid freckles. She returned her eyes to the road. Maybe she should try some foundation to cover them up, although Toby had made that comment about them when they were up on the Ferris wheel. At the time she thought he was being purposefully stupid.

Becca sighed. Her face was definitely her best asset. She didn't have any chest to speak of. She had been flat as a board until her junior year which made Becca wonder what had ever attracted Kirby in the first place. At least she had something there now, but certainly not enough to make a guy's eyes bulge out of his head. And besides big breasts, didn't guys like girls with long legs? She was barely five two. But she was in pretty good shape. Years of riding horses had seen to that. But she wasn't a knockout, which brought her back to her original question. Was Toby attracted to her in a physical sense or did he just love her for her brain? The thought made Becca laugh out loud. How ridiculous. A man might *say* he loved a girl for her intelligence, but every intelligent woman knew it was really about her body.

Maybe not, a little voice tried to argue. Maybe Toby really did love her for her brain. And it wasn't like she would give little kids nightmares or anything like that. She wasn't hideous. And it wasn't like Toby was some kind of Adonis. He was... Becca chewed her lip thoughtfully. He was cute. And when they were together she felt safe and secure, which was probably a lot better than raging hormones anyway. But did she love him? They had talked about getting married but could Becca honestly say she loved Toby with a head-over-heels, heart-all-aflutter kind of love? Not yet. Which is why she knew it wasn't right for them to rush into marriage and a baby. But maybe, given time, her feelings for Toby would blossom into the kind of love that made her heart pound and palms sweat. Right now she was satisfied with the *goodness* she felt when they were together. Like the way it had felt when she got behind the wheel of the Bronco and he closed the door and just stood there looking at her through the window. Okay, so maybe he did make her heart pound just a little.

Thoughts of Toby fled as Becca turned into Penny and Nate's driveway. Now her palms truly did start to sweat as she tried to think what she would say to Nate. Was today the day they would contact the authorities and place Nicole in the care of the state? Becca glanced in the rearview mirror to the carrier in the back seat and sent up a little prayer.

Guide us, Lord. For this baby's sake, help us make the right decisions.

Once inside the house, Becca soon found her worry had been for naught. Nate wasn't home.

"He got called out a couple hours ago," Penny explained when Becca inquired as to Nate's whereabouts. "I guess there was a big drug bust up near Clear Lake State Park. Nate figured he'll be tied up all day."

"Oh," was all Becca managed to say.

"Did you need to talk to him about something?" Penny looked up from where she sat on the sofa cradling Nikki in her arms. She looked so contented and happy that Becca didn't have the heart to bring up the subject of Nicole going into foster care.

"No. Nothing that can't wait," Becca finally answered.

Maybe Nate wouldn't be tied up all day, she tried to reassure herself. Maybe he would be home when she returned for Nicole, and he'd be so suspicious that she still had Violet's baby he would ask all sorts of questions and it would be the perfect opening for Becca to confess she was ready to call in a higher authority. She said none of these things to Penny.

"I've got to get to class." Becca moved toward the door. Penny made to rise but Becca held out a hand. "Don't get up. You two look comfortable. I'll be back to get her around three-thirty. Thanks again, Penny."

Out on the porch, Becca was faced with her next dilemma. She had to face the drive to Alpena and all she could do was pray she didn't see a suspicious black car along the way.

Toby flipped his cell phone closed and stood in the doorway of Wes' barn, staring down the driveway but not seeing the pickup trucks parked there. He had his answer and it had been far easier to obtain than he had imagined. Once he had stopped complaining about the early hour, an obviously hung over Brad Archer had been a fount of information when asked about Heath Everett's whereabouts.

"Man Tob, what time is it?" Brad complained, not bothering to stifle a yawn.

"Eight o'clock," Toby answered.

"It the morning?!" Brad's dismay reverberated across the satellite airwaves.

"Well, if it were eight in the evening you would be well on your way to another hangover," was Toby's response.

"Yeah, that's true enough." Brad chuckled, sounding like he had swallowed a bucket of gravel.

"Some of us actually have jobs. You know, responsibilities. We can't lay around in bed all day."

"Hey, a farmer's work is never done," Brad said. A loud belch sounded in Toby's ear. He grimaced.

"Uh huh," Toby responded. "Sounds like you're working hard there Brad. But that's not why I called. I heard a rumor and I was wondering if you could confirm it for me."

"A rumor? In Atlanta?" Brad tried to sound shocked. "No way!"

"I know, hard to believe, isn't it?" Toby responded, keeping it light. "Anyway, this rumor I heard was about Heath, that um, maybe he isn't actually in school down at CMU anymore."

"That, my good friend, would not be a rumor but an actual fact," Brad confirmed. "I know first-hand cuz I partied with Heath all night last night."

"Really?" Toby waited, holding his breath.

"Yep." Brad was obviously relishing his role as talebearer. "Heath done got in trouble with a capital T down there at college. Seems the football coach doesn't take well to the use of illegal substances. Not to mention cutting class. Heath and me had a good old time last night. Man, he had some good shi…"

"How long has Heath been back in town?" Toby cut off Brad's colorful commentary.

"Couple weeks maybe."

"A couple weeks?! He's only been away at school a little more than a month." Toby shook his head in disgust.

"I know. Hard to believe isn't it? But that Heath, he works fast. Think he set a new world record for getting kicked out of college."

"So, Heath's been back in the area for a couple weeks," Toby repeated, letting the news settle in his brain. That would mean he could easily be the one tailing Becca. "What kind of car is he driving?"

"Man Toby, you are just full of questions," Brad complained. "Why do you need to know what kind of car he's got?"

"Just curious. You know?"

"Yeah. He's been driving his brother's Pontiac Grand Am. Do you need to know the year, cuz that I can't help you with."

"Nah. But I would like to know what color it is," Toby said slowly. His heart settled into a dull thud waiting for the answer.

"Black."

"Black huh?" Toby's hand tightened on the cell phone. "That's interesting."

"Really, I can't see why," Brad said.

"Doesn't matter," Toby answered shortly. "Thanks Brad. Go back to sleep." With that he flipped the cell phone closed, ending the conversation.

Wes approached the barn and gave Toby an odd look.

"Everything okay?" Wes asked.

"I'm not sure." Toby continued to stare at a distant spot on the horizon.

"Toby?" Concern rang in Wes' voice. Slowly, Toby turned to face his boss.

"What would you do if you thought someone was threatening Rhonda?" As soon as the question had cleared Toby's lips, he knew the answer. Everyone in town knew what Wes Cooper would do if the woman he loved was put in danger.

"I think we both know the answer to that," Wes stated in a quiet voice. "It got me in a lot of hot water."

Toby could see that Wes was re-living the moment when Blake Dalton had held a knife to Rhonda's throat, threatening her life because of jealousy and greed.

"But looking back, would you have changed anything? If you could go back in time, would you do things differently?" Toby wanted to know. Wes shrugged one broad shoulder.

"That's impossible to say. Now that Nate and I are friends, it's easy to say I should have trusted him from the beginning, should have confided in him. But at the time I didn't trust anyone. So I guess the answer to your question is no, I probably wouldn't change the way I handled it. A man's got to do what a man's got to do. And one of the most important things a man's got to do is protect the woman he loves."

Toby nodded and swallowed hard.

Winning Becca

"Toby, what's going on?" Wes asked.

"I told you, I'm not sure."

"Do you think Rhonda is in some kind of danger?" Wes asked skeptically.

"No, no, not at all," Toby rushed to reassure and watched as Wes visibly relaxed. Then he tensed again.

"Becca then?"

"I told you, I don't know. It's probably nothing. But you don't have to worry. I'll protect her."

"Toby, listen." Wes laid a heavy hand on Toby's shoulder. "When Rhonda was in trouble, I was trained to handle it. I was trained to kill if need be. You, you're just a kid. If Becca's in trouble, you'd better tell me. Let me and Nate deal with it."

Toby considered Wes' words before dismissing them. No, Heath Everett was his problem. He would deal with his former teammate. He had been protecting Becca all her life, he wasn't going to relinquish that job now.

"I told you Wes, you don't need to worry. I've got it covered. And if it comes down to it, I'll do what I have to do."

Turning, Toby entered the shady interior of the barn, his mind still on Becca. Wes had told him the best way to win her over was to be the best friend she could ever ask for, then be her hero. Well, hadn't Becca confessed just last night that he was a good friend? So that battle was already won. And now Heath Everett may have just presented him with the perfect opportunity to be her hero.

Breathing a sigh of relief, Becca parked Toby's Bronco behind Penny's SUV. She had managed to get to Alpena and back without ever sighting the menacing black automobile. She sat for a moment, trying to absorb the peace of the setting into her very being. It was a glorious fall day in northern Michigan. The sun reflected off the rainbow hues of the trees, which shimmered against the backdrop of the azure blue sky. Becca stared past the house, to the silver ribbon of the Thunder Bay river. The red streak of a cardinal flying past the windshield caught Becca's eye and she smiled. Oh to be a carefree red bird, unbound by the chains of this world. Her eyes once more roved over the sky. A few puffy, white clouds hung suspended on the horizon. She sent up a brief prayer that the Lord would bless Wes and Rhonda with as perfect a day tomorrow.

Becca opened the door and jumped to the ground. Leaves crunched under the soles of her little suede boots as she walked to the front porch. She knocked briefly on the door, then let herself in.

"Penny? It's me," Becca called softly.

"In the kitchen," Penny answered.

Becca made her way through the house, noticing how Nikki's paraphernalia seemed to blend perfectly into the surroundings. She found Penny standing at the kitchen sink, peeling potatoes.

"Hey. How'd it go today?"

"Perfect." Penny's smile nearly lit up the kitchen. "Nikki's upstairs sleeping."

"Where's your mom?" Becca asked, looking around.

"She's laying down taking a nap, too. She had her physical therapy today. It always wears her out."

Penny turned and opened the oven. Pulling out a roasting pan, she lifted the lid, sending a cloud of steam laced with the aroma of roasting meat into the air. She dumped the chunked potatoes into the pan before returning it to the oven. Becca pulled out a chair from the dining room table and sat. Her gaze was caught by the bird activity around the deck and she simply stared, her mind feeling like mush.

"Everything okay?" Penny asked. Wiping her hand on a towel, she came to stand near the table.

"Mmm hmm," Becca answered absently, drawing her eyes away from the birds beyond the sliding glass doors. "I'm just tired, I guess. I haven't been getting a whole lot of sleep."

"Most people don't when there's a baby in the house." Penny pulled out the chair across from Becca and sat down. Her golden eyes looked straight at Becca. "Any word from Violet yet?"

"Not since Saturday." Becca passed a weary hand across her brow and pushed her hair away from her forehead. "I don't know what to think. I keep praying she'll come home. I keep holding on to hope, but…" She shrugged.

"So what are you going to do?" Penny asked.

"Oh," Becca drew the word out, her gaze sliding away from Penny, back out to the bevy of birds that flew to and from the feeders. "I have a few options." None of which she wanted to discuss with Penny right at this moment. A change of subject was in order.

"Can I ask you a question?" she asked, her eyes still trained on the scene beyond the windows.

"Sure."

"How did you know you were in love with Nate?" Becca finally turned to look at Penny once more. Penny's eyes had gone wide at the question.

"Wow. Uh, I wasn't expecting that question." She gave a little laugh and tossed her long blond hair back over her shoulder. "That's a pretty tough one to answer."

"Was it love at first sight?"

"Are you kidding?" Penny waved a hand and smiled. "It was more like loathe at first sight. We couldn't get within twenty yards of each other without sparks flying."

Becca smiled in return. She could relate to that.

"So, how did he finally win you over?" Becca truly wanted to know. Penny shrugged and sat back in her chair.

"Persistence. Kindness. Caring. Thoughtfulness. All those things. I, I had some trust issues, so Nate didn't have an easy time of it. I treated him pretty terrible, making him pay for what somebody else did to me."

"Some other guy broke your heart?" Becca asked with a smile. Her smile slowly faded at the painful look that crossed Penny's lovely face. Penny looked down at her lap.

"It was a bit worse than that," Penny said quietly. "It's not something I normally talk about but you're all grown up now so I guess you're old enough to know. I was raped several years ago by someone I worked with."

Becca's stomach lurched. She reached over and touched Penny's hands that were folded on the table.

"Oh Penny, I'm so sorry. I had no idea."

"Of course you didn't." Penny sat up straighter and tried to smile. "You were just a kid when I came to town. Emma's the one who dragged the truth out of me. She saw how badly I was hurting and persisted until she got to the bottom of it. She was the only person I confided in, until I was finally able to tell Nate the truth. Rhonda didn't even know until about a year ago. It's not exactly something you talk about in polite company." Her eyes went wide as if she just realized she had confided her deepest, darkest secret to a near stranger. "Please," she whispered. "Don't tell anyone I told you."

"No." Becca shook her head adamantly. "Of course not. I wouldn't tell a soul. You have my word. You know, you and Violet have something in common."

"Violet was raped? Everyone just assumes she and Vince..." Penny let the thought trail off.

"It wasn't Vince." This statement elicited a look of surprise from Penny. Becca bit down hard on her lip. "I shouldn't have said anything. It's Vi's secret. Nobody knows about it but me." She was going to have to re-read the Book of James again. Maybe someday she would actually think before she spoke.

"Don't worry." This time it was Penny's turn to pat Becca's hand reassuringly. "I won't tell anyone."

Becca breathed a sigh of relief.

"Thanks. Now." She pushed herself up from the table. "I'd better get Nikki and head home before people start getting worried about me."

Penny rose, too, and headed toward the stairs.

"I'll go up and get her. Wait a minute." She paused at the bottom of the steps, her narrow-eyed gaze pinned on Becca. "Why all the questions about me and Nate and how I knew I was in love?"

"Research." Becca gave a shrug, trying to appear nonchalant. "I'll be asking Rhonda the same questions in the near future."

"Does this have anything to do with Toby? He sure is sweet on you."

Becca turned and stared back out the sliding glass doors at the dusk that was quickly falling.

"Up until a month ago, Toby and I couldn't get within twenty yards of each other without sparks flying," she said. She heard Penny's soft laugh behind her.

"Yeah, well, that's not such a bad thing. Look how Nate and I turned out."

Penny's light tread sounded on the stairs and Becca was left alone to contemplate what Penny had confided. She wished she had more time to talk to Penny about it. What had Penny done afterwards? Had she run away? Because now Becca had the distinct feeling that perhaps Violet taking off really didn't have that much to do with chasing after Vince. Maybe it had more to do with running away from the ugliness of her past.

CHAPTER NINETEEN

The Lord answered the prayers of His saints and Friday morning dawned bright and clear, the perfect backdrop for the opening of Cooper Orchard and Pumpkin Farm. As she drove slowly past, Becca gazed with longing at the stone farmhouse, its sparkling windows reflecting the early-morning sunlight. Toby, Wes and Rhonda were all scurrying about the yard, preparing for the first customers of the day. How Becca wished she could be there! She pressed harder on the gas and continued down the road. She had to get Nikki to Penny's and then get to work. All Becca could do was pray business at the teashop would be slow this afternoon and Emma would let her off early.

Becca parked her green compact behind Penny's SUV. Since she wasn't going all the way to Alpena today, she had decided it was safe to drive her own vehicle, although Toby had disagreed and kicked up a fuss. What could possibly happen to her, Becca had argued, when she was driving to the home of a police officer? Finally, Toby had reluctantly agreed. Becca had to admit it was sweet the way he was so concerned about her, but honestly, she could take care of herself.

"Today's the big day," Penny greeted when Becca entered the house.

"Yep. Rhonda was cracking the whip when I drove past," Becca said with a smile.

"I'm so thankful the Lord blessed them with such a glorious day," Penny continued as she unbuckled Nicole from the baby carrier. "We've all been praying they would have good weather. I so hope the orchard will be a big success."

"I think it will be. We've been passing out flyers like crazy at the teashop, and the Tribune did a real nice article. I just wish I could be there for the kickoff. It kills me that I have to work."

"I bet." Penny nodded. "But I'm sure Rhonda understands. Nate and I will be there sometime today. It's such a lovely day that we're going to take Mom over. I think she'll really enjoy it."

Becca's heart went still. She swallowed hard.

"But what about Nicole?" she managed to say around the lump in her throat.

"Oh, we'll just take her with us." Penny rose from the couch, cradling the baby in her arms.

"Take…Nikki…with you?"

"Yeah." Penny removed the bottles from the diaper bag and headed for the kitchen. Becca followed on her heels.

"But what about Nate?" Becca questioned. She watched as Penny carefully put the bottles in the fridge. Penny closed the door and stood for a moment staring at a photo of Brendan that was stuck there with a magnet. Finally she turned to look at Becca. The bottom dropped out of Becca's stomach. "Penny, what's going on?" she whispered.

"I talked to Nate about Nicole," Penny confessed. She hitched a lock of hair behind her ear as she walked toward Becca. "Yesterday I asked you what you were going to do, and you said you had a few options. I figure the only option you really have is to call in the state and turn Nikki over to the authorities."

"So you told on me?" Becca wailed. "Penny, I trusted you!"

"No, Becca, it's not like that." Penny shook her head in denial. "Hear me out. This wasn't about getting you in some kind of trouble. It's about Nikki and what's best for her. You've been so good with her Becca, but I can see it's wearing you down. But I know you don't want to turn her over to strangers, either. I talked to Nate because, well, because I want us to take Nikki. I want us to become her foster parents."

"You want to take Nikki away from me?" Hurt rang in Becca's words.

"No! Sweetheart, it's not like that." Penny put an arm around Becca's shoulders and gave her a squeeze. "I'm not trying to hurt you. Honestly. I'm trying to help you. And Nate, with his job, he knows all the right people to talk to. He can steer all this through the system with the fewest amount of obstacles. It will be perfectly painless and you'll have the peace of knowing who will be taking care of Nikki, that she'll be loved."

"But I told you I still have hope Violet's coming home. She could be here today for all I know." Becca moved out from under Penny's arm, fighting the twin feelings of betrayal and alarm that were squeezing off her breath. She had decided to talk to Nate, but it was supposed to be in her own time! And now, Penny and Nate were going to take Nikki to the pumpkin patch like they were a family, when Becca had been planning that she and Toby...

Becca cut off the thought. No, not she and Toby. She and Toby and Nicole were *not* a family and Becca had made it plain to Toby that they couldn't be. So why was she upset at Penny? Wasn't this the solution she had been praying for? Maybe God was stepping in and removing the decision from Becca's hands so that she wouldn't feel like she was stabbing Violet in the back. And Penny and Nate, they'd been wanting a baby for so long...

"I'm sorry Becca," Penny's voice was small. "I never meant to hurt you. It was wrong of me to talk to Nate without discussing it with you first. I know you're very attached to Nikki and..."

"No." Becca spun, cutting off Penny's words. "No, you don't need to apologize. You're right. It's time a decision was made. I've been putting it off, feeling like I'm caught in the middle between Violet and Toby and my mother. But I've known for awhile that something needed to be done. And really, you and Nate would be an answer to my prayers. I take it he's agreed?"

"Well..." Penny drew out the word. "Not exactly. He's still concerned about me getting hurt. That's why I wanted us to go to the orchard today, all of us, to see how we fit together. But Becca, I've been doing a lot of praying and I honestly think God is in this. Truly I do."

"Yeah." Becca gave a short nod and cleared her throat. "I think you may be right. But can I at least ask for the rest of this weekend? Can we wait until Monday to start the process? I'd like a little time to adjust to the idea."

"Of course! Oh, of course," Penny rushed to reassure. "I don't want you to think I'm trying to steal Nikki from you."

"No, I don't." Well, maybe she did just a little, Becca admitted to herself. "It's just that, oh, I know it's silly." Becca shook her head. "I guess I harbored my own fantasies, even though I knew it could never be."

"That's not silly, it's natural," Penny said quietly.

"Honestly." Becca took a deep breath and straightened her shoulders. "I'm relieved. Now that the initial shock has worn off, I can't understand why I didn't think of this sooner. It's the perfect solution for everyone." She glanced at the clock on the stove. "Now, I've got to get to work before Emma fires me."

The first car pulled into the orchard right on the dot of nine. It seemed to open the floodgates and soon a non-stop parade of cars began filling the Cooper driveway. Toby was glad he had arrived at the crack of dawn to help Wes and Rhonda put the finishing touches on the pumpkin patch. He was amazed at the results of their weeks of hard work. Wes had driven him like a drill sergeant, but Toby could now admit that it was worth all the pain, sweat and yes, sometimes even blood.

Bales of straw were artfully arranged around the farmyard so families could sit a spell if they desired. Bushel baskets of apples filled the barn with their redolent fragrance as customers partook of donuts and cider under the barn's protective shade. Wes and Toby had constructed large display bins on wheels for the Indian corn and smaller gourds that were for sale. These were placed near the piles of pre-picked pumpkins on the lawn above the orchard. While customers roved through the orchard and pumpkin patch, Toby was kept busy driving the farm wagon around the apple trees and down a path that had been cut between the golden corn fields and back around the pasture to end once more in the circular driveway near the barn. He smiled as he listened to young and old alike laughing, throwing hay at one another, and simply enjoying the fresh air and spectacular fall day.

A young couple arrived pushing a baby stroller. Toby watched from his perch atop the tractor as the couple parked the stroller near the barn and the mother bent to unbuckle the baby from the seat. They approached the hay wagon and Toby turned in his seat, watching as the young man settled his wife and baby on a bale of hay before sitting close beside them. He put a protective arm around the woman. Toby felt a painful tug at his heart and realized he missed Becca. He wished she were here and that it was them in the back of the hay wagon, snuggled up close together with Nikki in between them. Cold reality was like a dash of ice water on his warm emotions. Becca had made it clear that the three of them were not going to be a family. Toby spun back around to face the front of the tractor. It wasn't too late, he told himself. Becca still had Nikki. There was still time to convince her they could make it work.

But God's will be done.

The words echoed hollowly in Toby's heart and he was assailed by guilt. Becca had told him she knew it wasn't God's will for her to raise Nikki, so why was he still so set on changing her mind? He wasn't being fair.

I'm sorry, Lord. Toby bowed his head and quickly prayed. *I wish I understood Your will as well as Becca does.*

The passengers in the hay wagon were singing a rousing rendition of "She Thinks My Tractor's Sexy" as Toby pulled into the farmyard. Several teenaged girls, who must have skipped school for this occasion, squealed with laughter as the tractor came to a stop in the circular drive near the barn. The girls continued to giggle, throwing flirtatious looks Toby's way, as they hopped down from the wagon and sauntered toward the barn. Toby nudged his cowboy hat back on his head and smiled. Maybe he did resemble Kenny Chesney just a little bit. He pictured Becca laughing hysterically at that then wondered how amused she would be if she could see those girls in their tight fitting jeans sashaying away from him, their hips swaying in obvious invitation.

"Hey Toby." Wes approached the tractor, making a motion for Toby to cut the engine. Toby quickly obeyed. His ears hummed with engine noise even after it had died away.

"Yeah?" He looked down at Wes.

"Why don't you take a break," Wes suggested. "You've been at it all morning. Go on up to the house and get yourself some lunch and something cold to drink. We can start up again in a half-hour or so."

"Okay."

Toby jumped down from the tractor and resisted the urge to rub his behind. He had been sitting on that hard, metal seat a long time. It would feel good to move around a little bit. Toby turned toward the house then stopped dead in his tracks. Coming across the lawn toward the barn was Nate Sweeney, pushing a wheelchair, and walking beside him was Penny who held a tightly wrapped pink bundle in her arms.

"Hey guys!" Wes moved forward to greet them. Toby watched as the former Army Ranger bent to place a kiss on Penny's mother's cheek. The woman smiled up at him lopsidedly. "Hey Rhonda, look who's here!" Wes called. Rhonda hurried across the lawn carrying Brendan on one hip.

"Well, look at you out and about," Rhonda greeted with a welcoming smile as she bent to hug Ms. Scott. She stood and looked down at the baby in Penny's arms. "I didn't expect to see you here today, especially with Nicole." Rhonda shot a questioning look toward Nate.

"We're getting a feel for the family business," Penny said. Toby watched as Penny slanted a loving look up at her husband. "Nate and I have talked it over and we'd like to become Nicole's foster parents."

The bottom seemed to drop out of Toby's world. His knees went so weak he had to reach out to steady himself against the corner of the house. He quickly pressed his back against the cold stones, hoping the two couples hadn't seen him standing there listening. He squeezed his eyes shut. Penny and Nate were going to take Nicole? How had Becca let this happen?

"Wow! I never saw that one coming," Rhonda laughed.

"Neither did I," Nate responded drolly.

"I talked it over with Becca this morning," Penny interjected. Toby came alert once more at the mention of Becca's name. "She didn't see it coming, either. I feel bad because I think I hurt her feelings. But once she got over the shock of me suggesting it, she said it's actually an answer to her prayers."

"So, you guys can get her just like that?" Rhonda asked, snapping her fingers.

"Well it won't be quite that easy," Nate answered. "There's still protocol that has to be followed."

"But Nate knows all the right people to contact to make it happen, and with Becca in agreement it should be a pretty smooth transition," said Penny.

"What about Violet?" Wes wanted to know.

"Unless she's home by Monday, there's a good chance she won't be seeing her daughter again." There was steel in Nate Sweeney's voice.

Feeling sick to his stomach, Toby crept quietly to the back door and entered the cool interior of the house. All thoughts of lunch had fled. Dejectedly, he threw himself down in a kitchen chair and tossed his hat on the table. He stared unseeing at the fall centerpiece in the middle of the table. Toby knew he should be rejoicing. The fact that Penny and Nate were going to take Nicole should be good news. Nikki would have two people who loved and cared for her, parents who could give her everything a little girl could ever want. But Penny and Nate and Nikki's gain was Toby's loss. He sat silent, his dream laying in pieces around him like shards of shattered glass.

Eventually Toby roused himself and stood. He went to the refrigerator and pulled out a bottle of Mountain Dew. Unscrewing the cap, he tipped his head back and gulped half the twenty ounce bottle in three big swallows, wishing for the first time in his life that it contained something stronger. Anything to dull the ache that had settled in the region of his heart. Snagging his hat off the table, Toby strode out the back door. Maybe the chug-chug-chug of the tractor engine would soothe his wounded soul.

Rhonda had pushed Penny's mother into the shade of the big red barn and now the two women stood talking animatedly. Wes and Nate stood near the hay wagon. Neither man seemed to notice Toby as he approached.

"Heard there was some big happenings up near Clear Lake," Wes commented.

"Yeah." Nate nodded agreement. "Big drug bust. You wouldn't believe the stuff we bagged. Seems terrible to say, but even I didn't know kids around here were doing some of that stuff. Big city narcotics, you know, stuff I thought only Detroit cops had to worry about, not us little peons here in mid-America nowhere."

"I guess you aren't truly safe anyplace nowadays," Wes said, shaking his head sadly.

"And worst of all is the kid we busted," Nate continued. "I can't say a whole lot due to the investigation. But geez, this kid had it all. Athlete. Big time scholarships. The world at his feet and he blows it all."

Toby froze next to the tractor's large tire, puzzle pieces clicking into place. Was Nate just describing... Heath? Heath was an athlete who had earned scholarships. Heath had just gotten kicked out of CMU for drugs. And he lived near Clear Lake.

"That kid lost everything. We even impounded his car. With all the evidence we collected, he won't be seeing daylight again for awhile."

Toby climbed stiffly into the tractor seat and sat facing forward, stonily silent. Self-pity and fury played tug-o-war in his heart as he tried to digest reality. Heath Everett was in jail and the cops had his car. So, not only were Nate and Penny taking Nicole from him, but now Nate had also stolen Toby's chance to be Becca's hero.

Something about this whole thing just didn't seem right. Becca sighed and plunged her hands into the hot, soapy dishwater. Her seeking hands found a delicate china tea cup and she carefully ran her rag along the inside rim.

Once more Becca went over the conversation she had with Penny just that morning. Penny's idea that she and Nate try to become Nikki's foster parents *seemed* perfect. After all, Becca was certain that she was not to raise Nicole. But still, something about this whole idea wasn't setting right in Becca's heart. There was still some small strand of loyalty to Violet that tugged at Becca's conscience. After all, Vi hadn't been gone *that* long. Yes, Violet had made some very bad decisions, but did she really deserve to lose her child? Violet had already suffered an awful lot in her young life. What would losing her baby do to her?

"You've been awfully quiet today," Emma observed. She set a full tray of dirty china on the counter next to the large, stainless steel sink.

"I've had a lot on my mind." Becca dipped the cup in the sanitizing rinse water before placing it carefully on the drain board. She picked up another piece of china.

"Anything you want to talk about?" Emma asked. "I know you have Rhonda to confide in, but she's been awfully busy for the past few weeks. I'm here for you, too, if you need me."

"Thanks." Becca threw a grateful smile over her shoulder. Emma pulled a tall stool up to the sink and began drying teacups. A comfortable silence fell between them. Becca stared down at the mounds of bubbles in her dishwater and swirled her rag around. "There might be someone who is willing to take Nicole," she quietly confessed.

"Ah," Emma responded and reached for a plate that was resting on the drain board. "And you aren't sure how you feel about that."

"I'm confused," Becca admitted. "On one hand, I'm tired of playing house. Do you know I haven't gotten to go riding in three weeks? That's got to be the longest I've ever gone. Bailey's going to be a nutcase by time I get to ride him again. I'm exhausted all the time. I can barely keep up with my homework."

"But?" Emma prodded.

"But, I've gotten rather attached to the little stinker, despite the colic and the spitting up and the dirty diapers." Becca shook her head in wonder. "Then there's Violet. She's my friend. You have no idea how bad she's had it. She used to beg to stay the night at my house, just to get away from…" Becca bit down on her lip, stopping the flow of words.

"I know it could get pretty ugly at their house."

"You don't know the half of it," Becca muttered. "I'm the only one Violet's ever been able to count on. She trusted me with Nikki. And think about it Em, how would you feel?" Becca turned to look at her boss. "If you had an emergency come up and you had to leave Tiffany with a friend, how would you feel if the state just came in and took her away while you were gone?"

"I'd be devastated," Emma conceded with a nod.

"Maybe instead of being so quick to take Nikki away, it would be better if the state got Violet some help. I know she's showed really poor judgment, but if people just understood why she's done some of the crazy things she's done, they could get her the help she needs. You know, break the cycle that's been going on in that family for years."

"I'm no expert on this stuff, Becca, but I think the state tries very hard to keep children with their mothers. Except for in cases of terrible abuse, I think they'll do everything in their power to keep Nikki and Violet together. Even if they deem her unfit, they'll probably work with a family advocate to get Vi the help she needs so she can raise her baby."

"You think so?" Becca asked. Emma nodded. Becca breathed a sigh of relief. "I hope you're right. As much as these people who want Nikki would be great parents, I still feel Violet deserves a chance. As angry as I've been with her, the truth is she's not a bad person, you know? She's just lost."

"She needs Jesus," Emma stated.

"That's for sure," Becca agreed heartily. "I've been praying for her. And for Vince, too. As much as it pains me to do so. The Lord is their only hope. I mean, the state can only do so much."

"But with God all things are possible."

"Yeah." Becca nodded, letting the truth sink in. "With God anything's possible."

Emma glanced at the clock that hung on the wall above the door leading to the dining room. She hopped down from the stool.

"I need to go get Tiffany from daycare. The dining room's all done. Can you finish up these dishes then lock up before you leave?"

"Sure."

Emma came over and put an arm around Becca's shoulders, giving them a quick squeeze.

"You're a good friend Becca. Violet's blessed to have you in her life. You've got a loyal heart. That's a rare find these days. The Bible says a friend loves at all times. You've stuck with Violet through thick and thin. That shows a depth of character you don't often see in girls your age."

"Thanks. It hasn't always been easy. There's been a few times in these last few weeks I wanted to kill Violet."

"That's your human emotions. But deep down inside you want what is right and best for everybody. The Lord's going to reward your faithfulness." Emma went to retrieve her jacket from the hooks near the door. "I'll see you tomorrow."

"Bye."

The door slammed. The kitchen became quiet. The monotonous tick-tick-tick of the clock echoed in the now silent kitchen. Becca was lost in thought as she washed the last of the dirty china. Funny that Emma should tell her she would be rewarded for her faithfulness. Isn't that what God was trying to tell her in the verse from Hebrews?

"Therefore do not cast away your confidence, which has great reward," Becca recited to herself. "For you have need of endurance, so that after you have done the will of God, you may receive the promise."

She carefully dried each piece of china before putting them away in the cupboard. She knew what she had to do. It wasn't going to be easy. Penny was going to be hurt. But Becca felt confident she was doing the right thing. She had to tell Penny and Nate that Violet deserved a little more time.

Her mind made up, Becca headed for the door. She made sure it was locked behind her, then headed across the gravel parking lot to her car. Stones scattered as she came to an abrupt halt, a scream ready on her lips. There, leaning casually against the driver's side door, was Vince Schmidt.

CHAPTER TWENTY

Shaky legs carried her closer. Becca glanced around. They were in the middle of downtown Atlanta. Traffic continued to pass by on Main Street. It was broad daylight. She was perfectly safe. But oh how she suddenly wished for a cell phone! She glanced over her shoulder at the back door of the teashop. Maybe she should just go back inside and call Nate. And tell him what? Becca asked herself.

"What do you want?" she asked, trying to keep the tremor from her voice.

"Where's the kid?" Vince responded with a question of his own.

"Obviously not with me," was Becca's quick retort. "Where's Violet?"

"How should I know?" Vince shrugged.

A slow anger began to burn through Becca's veins. "Supposedly she's been chasing you all over the state."

Vince laughed. "She never was any too bright."

"Yeah, and we all know you're a freaking genius," Becca spat.

"Smarter than you think." A greasy smiled turned up Vince's lips. "Smart enough to figure out who has the baby." He pinned her with his pig-like stare.

"What makes you think she's not with Violet?"

"She's been chasing me all over the state, remember?" Vince said with a smirk. "I've got people keeping tabs."

"Oh yeah, I'd trust your peeps." Becca crossed her arms and met Vince stare for stare.

"My peeps would love to get a hold of you." The look he shot her nearly made Becca shiver. He fished a pack of cigarettes from his t-shirt pocket and shook one out. Relaxing back against the car, he put the cigarette in his mouth and lit it. He took a long drag and blew the smoke out slowly. "You still haven't answered my question. Where's the kid?"

"Look." Becca held her arms out wide. "No baby here. Now get away from my car before I call the cops and have you arrested for loitering. Nate Sweeney happens to be a good friend of mine. Besides, I'm in a hurry to get home and call Violet. I'm sure she'll be very interested to know where you are."

"That chick's been a millstone around my neck for the past year," Vince growled, taking another drag on his cigarette.

"Yeah, well, for reasons way beyond my comprehension, that chick loves you. Now vamoose before I go in and call the cops."

"You're not going to tell me where the baby is?"

"Not in a million, bazillion years," Becca vowed.

"That's okay." Vince pushed himself away from her car and strode toward her. Becca's heart thudded painfully with each step he took. When he came abreast of her, he halted. "You've always thought you were so much better than me. But I told you, I'm smarter than you think. I'm gonna have the last laugh. Nate Sweeney won't be able to protect you."

Becca watched as he scuffed across the parking lot and headed down the sidewalk. When he was out of sight, she hurried to her car and unlocked the door with trembling fingers. Once inside she slammed the lock back down. She took a shaky breath.

"Okay Lord, what was that all about?" she asked as she started the engine.

Her quaking had finally abated by the time she reached Nate and Penny's driveway, only to begin again as she contemplated the task at hand. She was going to have to disagree with Nate and hold her own against his extremely forceful personality. Becca sent up a quick prayer that she was doing the right thing.

"And if I am Lord, then You'd better send Violet home quick. The sooner Nicole is back with her mother, the safer I'll be. Vince will leave me alone once Vi is back in town."

Her fist shook slightly as she knocked on the door. *Fear not,* Becca reminded herself. The door swung open. Nate stood on the other side, Nicole asleep in his arms.

"Come on in, Becca." Nate held the door wide. Becca took a deep breath and crossed the threshold.

"Hey, Becca," Penny greeted, coming into the living room from the kitchen. She slung a dishtowel over her shoulder and perched on the arm of a chair.

"How was the pumpkin patch?" Becca asked.

"Crazy busy." Penny laughed. "I don't think we need to worry anymore about it being a success."

"Oh, that's good." Her gaze shot nervously between Penny and Nate.

"Have a seat," Nate ordered. "I think we all need to talk about Nicole."

"Yes, yes we do," Becca agreed, sitting on the edge of the sofa.

"Penny tells me she talked to you about what we would like to do."

"Yes." Becca nodded and tried to swallow past the lump in her throat. "But I've changed my mind."

"What do you mean?" Penny asked. Hurt and bewilderment rang in the words.

Becca stared at the carpet and wiped her palms on her thighs.

"What do you mean, Becca?" Nate repeated the question, steel in his voice. She felt his laser-blue eyes burning into the top of her head.

"I mean…" Becca cleared her throat and tried once more to swallow the knot of fear that was choking her. "I asked Penny if we could wait until Monday to start the proceedings. But I've changed my mind. I would like to ask for a week. To give Violet a little more time to come home." There, she'd said it.

"She's already been gone nearly a month," Nate said coldly.

"I know that. But Nate, I've been thinking a lot about it and I believe she deserves more time. I mean really, when Val and Steven went to Hawaii a couple of years ago, they left the kids with us and no one said they were bad parents."

"That's totally different," Nate argued. "They were taking a vacation. You knew when they were coming back. They didn't just dump their kids on your back doorstep and leave."

"I'm just saying that I think Violet deserves the benefit of the doubt. She's been through a lot." Becca risked a look at Penny and saw the disappointment shining in her golden eyes. "It's just a week. That's all I'm asking for. I'll call Vi as soon as I get home and tell her she has a deadline. If she really thinks you're going to take Nikki away, I know she'll hurry home. But if she doesn't, you guys can start the process to get custody. But..." Becca hesitated.

"But what?" Nate prodded.

"There's another reason I think Vi will get back to Atlanta soon."

"What's that?" Nate asked.

"Vince is back in town. I saw him today. As the father, doesn't he have a right to his baby?" The mere thought made Becca ill, but the law was the law.

"You're sure he's the father?" Nate was clearly skeptical.

"Of course!"

"You've seen the birth certificate?"

"Well, no. But of course he's the father. Everybody knows that."

Nate merely shrugged. "Birth certificates are registered with the county courthouse. It will be easy enough to find out. Everybody knows Violet's been a little loose."

"Don't say that!" Becca reprimanded sharply. "You don't know anything about her. You really shouldn't judge."

"I'm just saying…"

"Nate, don't," Penny commanded quietly.

"I'm sorry Penny," Becca said trying to convey the depths of her sincerity. "I just feel as a Christian I need to make sure about this. I feel Violet deserves a second chance. And if she blows it, then you and Nate are free and clear to do whatever you have to do to get Nikki. Give it one more week. Please? After that, I'll cooperate completely."

"I suppose a week isn't all that long," Penny hesitantly agreed. "And I did spring this on you out of the blue this morning. It's normal you would have second thoughts."

"Not second thoughts about you," Becca stated with conviction. "You guys would be the perfect parents for Nikki. I just think her real mom deserves a second chance."

"Well, don't think I'm going to be sitting around twiddling my thumbs for the next week," Nate said, placing Nicole in Becca's arms. "I plan to use every means at my disposal to investigate this whole mess and discover Violet's whereabouts. You know what kind of car she was driving?"

Becca shook her head. "It was dark when she left Nikki, and I didn't go around front to the driveway.

When we were in school she used to drive a little blue Taurus. I don't know if she still does."

"Well, I'm sure I can find out," Nate stated.

"I'm sure you can," Becca replied, bundling Nicole into her sweatshirt. Penny stood and retrieved the baby carrier, which she brought over to the sofa. Becca quickly secured the baby in the seat. Standing, she headed toward the door. "I really am sorry if I upset you," she looked up at the couple standing in the doorway. Nate's arm was protectively around Penny's shoulders. "I appreciate you giving me a little more time."

"I just hope you know what you're doing," Nate said.

"So do I," Becca murmured as she stepped out onto the porch. "So do I."

"Whew, what a day huh?" Wes commented.

"Yep," Toby answered shortly and threw another bale of hay down from the loft. Wes easily lifted the bale and hefted it over the side of the hay wagon.

"Better than I ever could have hoped for," Wes continued. Toby didn't respond. "Sorry you got stuck on the tractor all day. That couldn't have been much fun for you. Tomorrow I'll take a few turns to give you a break."

"Doesn't matter." Toby shrugged. "I don't mind. Gives me plenty of time to think."

"Yeah, driving a tractor sure does give you plenty of time for that. You want to share what you were thinking about all afternoon?"

"God's will," Toby stated simply. He sat on the edge of the loft, his legs dangling over the side.

"Hmph. God's will, huh?" Wes stood looking up at him, hands on his hips. "That's pretty deep. To think when I was your age, driving the tractor around, all I ever thought about was girls."

"I've been doing too much of that lately," Toby confessed. "I decided it's time I get serious about my future."

"I see." Wes climbed into the hay wagon and began spreading the fresh hay around. "And did you experience a great epiphany about God's will for your future?"

Toby merely stared down at Wes.

"What?" Wes asked, glancing up to where Toby still sat.

"Did you just use the word epiphany?" Toby questioned. "I didn't know Army Rangers used words like that."

"Hey, you aren't the only smart one around here," Wes defended.

"Oh yeah, that's right. Becca told me recently how you used to help her with her algebra homework."

"Good Lord Almighty, don't remind me about that!" Wes ordered with a laugh. "I'm glad those days are over."

"They might not be," Toby stated, climbing down from the loft.

"What do you mean?" Wes shot him a questioning look.

"Becca's taking statistics this semester. I've helped her with it some, but when I go away, she might need someone to explain things to her if she gets stuck."

"Well, it isn't going to be me," Wes stated firmly. "So, you've decided to go to that horse place?"

"Yes." Toby went over to the workbench that was now covered with material in a fall leaf pattern. He needlessly rearranged a display of small pumpkins. "I'll probably be leaving sometime in November."

"Well try not to sound so excited about it."

"I'm sure I'll be excited when the time rolls around."

Wes sat on one of the hay bales in the back of the wagon. "So this is what you were contemplating while you were driving around all day?"

"Man Wes, you've got to stop using such big words. You're freaking me out."

"Now you're being evasive. And that's an army word." Wes pinned Toby with his cool, grey eyes. Toby leaned back against the workbench. He chewed the inside if his cheek for a moment.

"Sorry. And to answer your question, yes, that's what I was contemplating while I drove around. You kept telling me to pray for God's will to be done. Becca kept telling me about doing God's will. But I couldn't seem to figure out how a person knows God's will. Until today. I realized that all the things I kept trying to plan, there's always a roadblock. You told me about that Proverb, and I did look it up. A man's heart plans his way, but the Lord directs his steps. My heart was making plans, but the Lord wasn't directing me down the way I wanted to go. It took…" Toby hesitated. "It took me awhile to see it, but now I do. I believe the Lord wants me to go to Desert Sands."

"Good for you." Wes jumped down from the wagon and patted Toby's shoulder in a brotherly fashion. "You're showing a real maturity, Toby. A lot of people go through their whole lives without ever figuring out God's will for them."

Wes headed toward the barn doors. Toby fell into step beside him, pausing as Wes flipped off the lights. Each man grabbed a barn door and swung them shut, securing them together with a padlock.

"Now go on home and get some rest," Wes ordered. "Tomorrow will be an even bigger day."

Toby climbed tiredly into his Bronco but as he backed from the driveway, he knew he couldn't go home. Not yet. He had to see Becca first and tell her of his decision. And also tell her she didn't have to worry anymore, the man who had nearly ran her into the path of a logging truck was now behind bars.

"Becca?" A knock sounded on the bathroom door. Becca sank deeper under the layer of thick bubbles in her bathwater.

"What?" she answered her mother's summons.

"Toby's downstairs. He wants to talk to you."

Oh good grief! Becca rolled her eyes. First Vince, then Nate and now she had to deal with Toby, too? It really was too much to ask of a girl.

"I do hope we aren't going to get another unexpected marriage proposal," Mary complained from the other side of the bathroom door.

"Mother!" Becca reprimanded.

"Well really Becca, maybe I should get dressed this time, just in case."

"Mom, I'm not getting married." Becca pulled the plug from the drain with her toe. "Tell him I'll be down in a minute, okay?"

With a sigh Becca hefted herself from the tub and rubbed herself dry with a towel. She tugged on a pair of flannel pajamas before wrapping herself in a thick, fleecy robe. She pulled out the ponytail that she had secured high atop her head and let her hair fall carelessly around her shoulders. Slipping her feet into her fuzzy blue slippers, Becca opened the bathroom door and marched down the hall toward the stairs. Toby stood at the bottom of the steps looking up at her. His brown eyes were serious beneath the brim of his straw cowboy hat. Becca's heart lifted like a feather blown in the wind before settling back into its normal rhythm.

"Toby," she greeted, walking slowly down the stairs. She stopped one step from the bottom.

"I'm sorry to come by so late," he apologized, removing his hat.

"That's okay." Becca glanced around the banister and saw her mother standing in the hall outside the family room, watching them closely. "Come this way." She hopped down the final steps and led Toby toward the little-used living room at the front of the house. "Have a seat." Becca motioned toward the sofa with its faded floral print. She sat on the edge of a small side chair covered in royal blue velvet. "I heard the grand opening was a huge success."

"Yep." Toby sat on the sofa. Becca watched as he ran the brim of his hat round and round through his fingers. "Saw Penny and Nate there. With Nikki," he finally added.

"Yes. Penny told me they were planning to go," Becca replied quietly.

"And Penny also told you they want to get custody of Nikki," Toby stated. His eyes held a look of such deep hurt and sadness that Becca had to glance away.

"Yes." She took a fortifying breath. "I don't know why you're so upset. I told you I was going to talk to Nate. I wasn't necessarily planning on doing it *today*, but sometimes things are taken out of our hands. It's happened. We both have to accept it and move on."

"I know." Toby sat forward. With elbows on his knees he continued to fiddle with his hat. "I guess I just held out some hope, you know?" He shrugged. "Is she still here? Can I go up and see her one last time?"

"You make it sound like the world's ending." Becca tried to chuckle but failed. "Nikki's not going anywhere yet. I convinced Nate and Penny to give me one more week to get Violet to come home. I think she deserves that much. I called her and left a very strident message on her voice mail, telling her that not only is Nate on the verge of calling in the state authorities, but also my little coup de grace."

"What?" Toby looked up at her intently.

"That Vince is back in town," Becca said triumphantly.

"Bec, you don't know that for sure," Toby began to protest.

"Yes I do. He confronted me today in the parking lot of the Spot of Tea."

"Tell me he didn't." Toby's lips tightened.

"He did. First he asked me where Nicole was at. Then he intimated that he already knew. He pretty much admitted to sending Vi off on a wild goose chase. Then..." She swallowed hard, not sure she should add the rest. "Then he threatened me."

"Threatened you how?" Becca could see the fire burning in Toby's eyes. It put a warm glow in her heart.

"Nothing specific. He just said he would have the last laugh, and that when he did, even Nate wouldn't be able to protect me."

"I don't like the sound of that, not at all."

"Oh, I'm not really worried. Once Vi gets my voice mail, she'll be back in town in a heartbeat. Vince is all she cares about, except for Nicole. Once she knows he's back in Atlanta, she'll come home and Vince won't have time to be concerned with me anymore."

"I hope you're right." Toby relaxed against the back of the sofa.

"It happens once in awhile." Becca shot him a grin.

"At least I have some good news for you."

"What's that?"

"I did some checking. Found out that Heath did get kicked out of college. A couple of weeks ago. And he drives a black Grand Am."

Winning Becca

"That's good news?" Becca's hand went to her throat where she fiddled with the collar of her robe.

"He also got busted for drugs a couple of days ago. He's in jail and they impounded his car. At least that's one less thing you have to worry about. You won't be getting followed anymore."

"That's a relief."

"Now for the bad news. You were right."

"My being right is bad news?"

"No, that's not what I meant."

"Then say it again, slowly."

"Say what?"

"That I was right," Becca demanded with a smile.

"Come on Bec, this isn't a competition. I'm trying to be serious."

"Okay." Becca tried to rearrange her facial features into an acceptably serious expression. "I'm being serious. What's the bad news?"

"I had a lot of time to think today, and to pray. And I've decided to go to Desert Sands and train with Alonzo Ferrera. I have to call and set everything up, but I'll probably be leaving the middle of November."

Becca's word tilted crazily for a moment. "Oh," she said softly.

"You'll be going away to CMU. You'll never even know I'm gone."

"I haven't decided for sure that I'm going to transfer."

"You should. You're smart. You'll do great at Central. And now that I know Heath isn't there, and Fitzgerald will never leave the farm, I'm not so worried."

"Yeah, well, what about me? I've still got those groupies to worry about," Becca said with a sad smile. Toby looked up and his eyes burned into hers.

"I've never looked twice at another girl."

"Oh, Toby." Becca fell to her knees in front of the sofa and wrapped her arms around Toby's middle. She pressed her face into his shoulder. It felt so right to have his arms go around her and pull her close.

"I don't want to leave Atlanta, leave you," Toby whispered the admission against her hair. "But... oh man I can't believe I'm going to say this again."

Becca felt him smile. She leaned back a little so she could see his face.

"Is this going to have something to do with me being right? Again?" she asked with a grin.

"Now who's going to get the big head?" Toby ran his hands through her hair, causing a little shiver to twirl down her back. "Okay, yes. It has to do with you being right...again. We both need to grow up. We both need a chance to explore the world a little bit, see what's out there. Although I already know there isn't another girl alive who can hold a candle to you."

"There you go with that romantic nonsense again," Becca protested weakly.

"Oh come on, Bec." Toby's mouth lowered until it hovered just a breath above her own. "Admit it. You like that romantic nonsense."

"Well." She swallowed hard. "Maybe just a little." She saw the self-satisfied smirk turn up his lips just before they descended on her own. And this time it was no brotherly peck, but a hot branding that had Becca thankful she was kneeling so she didn't collapse right there on the living room floor. Slowly he raised his head.

"Just a little?" he asked.

Becca tilted her head back, asking for another kiss. Toby quickly obliged, leaving her brain as fuzzy as a summer peach. What had they been talking about? Oh, yes, Toby was going away. Reality had her pulling back. Toby broke the kiss off with obvious reluctance.

"How long will you be gone?" Becca asked breathlessly. Toby shrugged.

"I don't know for sure. But I can tell you this much. When I come back, I'm going to ask your parents again for permission to marry you."

"Can you make sure my mother is dressed next time?" Becca asked. "She's mortified that the last time you asked for my hand she was in her bathrobe."

"I'll see what I can do," Toby answered with a chuckle, pulling her hard against his chest.

"And then are you planning to ask *me?*" Becca wanted to know.

"And give you the opportunity to turn me down?" Toby responded. "Not a chance. I'm just going to throw you over my horse and ride off into the sunset."

"Oh ho, that's what you think!" Becca tried to push out of his arms, but Toby held fast. He ran his hands through her hair once more.

"I love you, Becca," he stated quietly, causing Becca to go still. He stared deeply into her eyes. "I know you think we're too young to know what love is. But I love you. I always have and I always will. I'd kill anyone who hurts you, which means I never will because I don't think too much of suicide."

Becca bit her lip to keep from smiling.

"When I get back, I'm going to set myself to winning you, the old fashioned way. We're going to date and I'm going to be so romantic it makes you sick. Before you know it you'll have such a bad case of me, you'll never be cured. Then I'll ask you to marry me and you won't have any choice but to say yes."

"You can't win me like some blue ribbon," Becca protested.

"Becca, honey, you're better than any trophy." Toby framed her face lovingly. "You're my grand prize. And I told you before, we both like playing the game. And love's the best game of all because it's the only one where both of us will end up winning."

CHAPTER TWENTY ONE

Well, here goes nothing, Becca thought as she raised a fist to knock on the Compton's front door. The smell of frying bacon hung on the early morning air. She was sure Joe was probably just sitting down to his Saturday morning breakfast of bacon and eggs. He would not be pleased at this interruption, but Becca had no choice. She swallowed hard, reminding herself one more time to *fear not*.

The door swung open. Connie stood on the other side. Surprise made her eyes go wide when she saw Becca on the front porch, baby carrier in hand.

"Becca. This is a surprise."

"I know Mrs. Compton, and I'm sorry. But could I please speak with you and Mr. Compton?"

"Oh, Joe's having his breakfast." Connie's hand came up to fiddle with the collar of her plaid blouse. "I'm not sure how he'll…"

"Connie, who is it?" Joe's bellow echoed through the farmhouse.

"It's Becca, Joe," Connie called the answer over her shoulder.

Becca was shocked that such a big man could move so fast. In a mere moment he was standing behind Connie's shoulder. He eyed her, then the baby.

"What do you want?" he asked, his voice gruff.

"Can I please come in and talk to you both?" Becca asked, trying to stifle the fear that rose up in her breast at the sight of the giant on the other side of the door.

Connie looked up at Joe.

"Thought you were giving that baby to the state," Joe said, motioning with his ham-like hand toward Nicole.

"I am." Becca swallowed hard. "It's just, well, these things take time. Can I please come in?"

Joe heaved a sigh before giving a nearly imperceptible nod. "My breakfast is getting cold." He turned on his heel and headed back toward the kitchen, while Connie held the door open for Becca to enter.

Becca followed the couple through the house, into the warm kitchen where Joe now sat at the table, shoveling fried eggs into his mouth. She set Nicole's carrier on the end of the table and shook her arm. Man, that thing was heavy!

"So, what is it you want?" Joe asked again, taking a gulp from his coffee cup.

"Truthfully? I'm here to ask a favor."

Joe's hard eyes came up to meet hers. Becca took a deep breath, determined to stand her ground. She had gotten herself into this mess, asking for another week before handing the baby over to the authorities. Now she had to deal with the consequences. If that meant begging Joe Compton on her knees, so be it.

"I have talked to someone about Nikki. There is a couple who desperately want to become her foster parents. They're good people. Hard working. They're Christians who love the Lord and already love Nikki. I'm sure the state will be more than willing to make them Nicole's guardians."

"Then what's the problem?" Joe took a huge bite out of his toast.

Becca sat down on one of the cracked vinyl kitchen chairs. "I feel Violet deserves a little more time. Mr. Compton, you know yourself what a rough time Vi's had of it. You told me you weren't surprised she left town. Her life wasn't anything like mine. Or like the life you gave your own children."

Okay, that was laying it on a bit thick, Becca thought, but she would do what she had to in order to win Joe Compton to her side. Joe sat back in his chair and picked up his coffee cup.

"I've asked, um, these people who want Nikki, to give me one more week. One last chance for Violet to come home. She never meant to leave her baby forever, I'm sure of it. As her friend, I think she deserves every chance to make things right. If she comes home in the next few days, we can give her the opportunity to get her life straightened out. Get her some help. Don't you think Nikki would be better off with her mother than in foster care?"

"Not necessarily," Joe replied, slurping his coffee.

"I think having Nikki taken away from her would be the straw that broke Violet's heart," Becca replied.

"It would be devastating for a mother," Connie commented, her voice quiet. Becca threw her a grateful look.

"And I think Violet will be home soon. She told me she left to find Vince. Well, he's back in town now."

"That kid's a first-class creep," Joe muttered.

A smile split Becca's face. "I'm glad to know we agree on something," she said with a laugh.

"You've been doing a lot of talking here, girl, but you still haven't told me why you're here. What do you want?"

Becca's smile slowly faded. "When I asked to give Violet another week, I was thinking with my heart, as a loyal friend. I was thinking about Nikki and how she needs her mommy. I wasn't thinking about myself. I still have my job, and my classes. And now I don't have anyone to watch Nicole. Unless…" She chewed her lip. "Unless you agree to let Connie watch her," she finished in a rush.

"I'd be happy to do it, Joe," Connie said in her soft voice.

"You always were a pushover," Joe admonished.

"I miss the grandkids," Connie confessed.

Joe looked at his wife with narrowed eyes. "You never said so."

"It's so far to go, and you've always got so much work…" Connie's voice trailed off.

"It's only for a week, Mr. Compton. At the most. I have to work today. Tomorrow I'm off so I don't need a sitter. Violet will probably be home before I have to go to class on Monday."

Joe gave a beleaguered sigh and shook his head. Setting down his coffee cup he rose from the table.

"I've got to get to work. Connie, you do whatever you want. But only for a week, no more. You understand me?"

"Yes, Joe," Connie answered submissively.

"Thank you Mr. Compton," Becca said with relief.

"You can thank me by brining me some of those muffins from the teashop," Joe replied, stomping out of the kitchen. "Blueberry!"

"Will do," Becca agreed, chuckling. She smiled at Connie who gave a timid smile in return. "He's not so bad."

"No." Connie shook her head. "I think he likes you."

"Well, I'll bring him a whole bag of muffins just to be sure."

Toby took a swig from his bottle of Mountain Dew and stood staring out the dining room's French doors to the pasture beyond the patio. It was empty of horses at this early hour. Toby was still trying to stir up the gumption to go out and feed them and turn them out for the day. He heard a cupboard door open in the kitchen, knew his mother was pouring her first cup of coffee of the day. He raised the bottle of pop to his mouth and took another long swallow.

"Morning, Toby," his mother said softly as she entered the dining room.

"Morning, Ma," Toby answered, not turning around.

He heard her set her mug on the table, pull out a chair and sigh as she sat down.

"Going out to feed?" she asked.

"In a minute."

"Going to be another beautiful day," Anita observed.

"Looks like it." Toby's eyes scanned the horizon, clear of clouds. The evergreen-covered hills glowed in the early morning light and the aspens shimmered in their crowns of golden leaves. It would be another boon day for the pumpkin patch, Toby was sure.

"Something wrong, Toby?" his mother finally asked.

"Nope." Toby finally turned. His mother's dark hair was still rumpled from sleep and she wore a silky, pink robe wrapped around her trim frame. "I guess I should tell you that I've made a decision about Desert Sands. I plan to call them Monday and make arrangements for going out there."

"Oh, Toby, that's wonderful!" Anita's dark eyes glowed up at him.

"I'll talk to the college, too. I'm sure I'll be able to keep taking my on-line courses. I'll need a laptop. I don't want to swap college for the circuit. I want to do both."

"Of course. We'll help you however we can." Her steady gaze stayed on Toby. "You aren't entirely happy about this, are you?"

"It's an amazing opportunity," Toby replied. "I hope I can live up to it."

Winning Becca

"You will," his mother said decisively.

Toby pulled out a chair and sat across from his mother. "I guess what I'm not happy about is that you went behind my back to arrange all this. You didn't talk to me first, ask me what I wanted."

Anita picked up her mug and took a sip of coffee, observing Toby over the rim of her cup.

"And if I would have asked you, what would you have said?" she finally asked, setting the mug back down on the table. She didn't give Toby time to answer. "You would have said no. Just like you said no to the circuit the last time. Just like you said no to going away to college. I knew the only way we would ever get you out of Atlanta was to set the stakes so high, make the prize so attractive, you wouldn't be able to resist. That judge at the fair gave me just the opportunity I'd been looking for. I knew right then it was a godsend. Something I could never have orchestrated on my own."

"My life isn't something you can orchestrate, Ma," Toby said, his voice low, his anger barely constrained. "I'm not a puppet on a string, somebody you can manipulate."

"I know you're not." Anita reached across the wide table for Toby's hands. "Your father and I love you, Toby. We want to see you make something of yourself. We want to give you the world, that's what parents do for their children. You have so much potential, I didn't want to see you waste it. Truly, I wasn't trying to manipulate you, just open a door, that's all. You're an adult now, and if you had chosen not to go, I would have accepted it."

"I think you were just trying to get me away from Becca."

Anita withdrew her hands and sat back in her chair. Once more she picked up her coffee mug and took a sip.

"Becca's a lovely girl. Smart, loyal, a hard worker. I couldn't ask for anything more for you. But you're too young to be getting married and settling down with a family."

Toby twirled the soda bottle around and around on the table, leaving dewy rings on the wooden surface.

"Then you'll be happy to know Becca said the exact same thing. She encouraged me to go to Desert Sands."

"See." Anita raised her cup in a silent toast. "I told you she was a smart girl."

"My going away doesn't change the fact that I love her," Toby insisted. "And I'm going to marry her. Maybe not next month, maybe not even next year. But eventually I will. You're just going to have to get used to it." Toby pushed back his chair and stood. "I'll say thank you, this time, for giving me this opportunity. But Ma, from now on, don't be orchestrating my life anymore."

Becca pulled the back door of the Spot of Tea closed and hurried across the parking lot to her car. In her arms she carried a white sack filled to the top with goodies from the teashop. Not just blueberry muffins to satisfy Joe, but also bear claws, poppy seed scones and pecan pralines. She didn't think

Connie got sweet treats very often, and she owed the woman big time.

All Becca wanted to do was hurry to pick up Nicole then get home and tackle her psychology homework so that tomorrow she could spend the whole day at the orchard. Maybe even hitch a hayride with Toby. Becca's heart did a little pirouette when she remembered the kisses she and Toby had shared the evening before and her stomach felt like she was once more on the Ferris wheel at the fair. He loved her. He really did love her. Becca had no doubts. And the scariest thing of all was that she was pretty certain she loved him back. Why did she have to go and fall in love with him just as he was getting ready to leave Atlanta for God only knew how long? Toby was right, she should transfer to Central. Get a full class load so she wouldn't have time to think about how many millions of miles stood between Phoenix and Atlanta. Or about bubble-headed bleach blondes in string bikinis.

Gravel crunched under her tennis shoes as she approached her car. She couldn't help looking cautiously around, expecting to see Vince slinking from the late-afternoon shadows any minute. Becca breathed a sigh of relief as she reached her car. Vince was nowhere in sight.

"Praise the Lord for small kindnesses," Becca muttered.

She glanced down to fit the key in the door. What was that? Something was wedged under her front car tire. Balancing the full sack on one hip, Becca reached down and tugged the object free. She stood and examined the doll she now held in her hand. Weird. What would a baby doll be doing under her car? Becca couldn't remember running over anything when she came to work that morning.

This wasn't just any doll, Becca realized with a shiver. The face was bashed in. Looking closer she saw it wasn't really a baby doll. It had long hair, like a girl doll. Long, *red* hair. Becca shivered again. Her hand opened, dropping the doll to the ground. She quickly looked right and left, searching for any sign of Vince. Had some child lost their doll in the parking lot, or was someone trying to send her a very threatening message?

No, that was just silly, Becca reassured herself as she unlocked the car door and slid in behind the wheel. Vince might talk big, but he wasn't that smart. Some child simply must have dropped their toy in the parking lot and Becca had unwittingly run it over when she came to work. It had been early and she hadn't really been paying attention, too intent on hurrying inside and getting to work.

Satisfied with that explanation, Becca pulled from the parking lot, determined to not give the doll another thought. Ten minutes later she was at the Compton's, exchanging the bag of baked goods for a baby who Becca was certain grew heavier by the hour. With Nicole safely strapped in the back seat, Becca headed toward home, anxious to get started on her homework. And maybe, just maybe, Violet would be there waiting for her, anxious to reclaim her daughter.

As she turned down the dirt road headed toward home, Becca glanced into her rearview mirror. Another car had turned as well and was now directly behind her. The driver suddenly turned on his bright headlights, even though it was only dusk. The light bounced off Becca's rearview mirror and into her eyes, nearly blinding her.

"Nice buddy. Turn off the brights, will you?" Becca complained.

She lifted a hand to shield her eyes from the light, then pushed the mirror up so the light didn't shine directly in her eyes. Pushing harder on the gas pedal, she sped toward home. A glance in her side mirror showed her the car was still right behind her, practically taking a bite out of her back bumper. Becca's heart leapt into her throat as she slammed the gas pedal to the floorboard. The little car fishtailed on the washboard road. She was nearly home. In just a moment she would be pulling into her own driveway, safe and sound. She gripped the steering wheel with white-knuckled hands, her mind spinning as quickly as her tires.

If Heath Everett was in jail, then who was following her?

CHAPTER TWENTY TWO

The computer screen glowed in the tiny downstairs office. Becca clicked on another link, searching the internet for sources for the psychology paper she had to write. Her father's leather desk chair creaked as Becca shifted her weight. The air was tinged with the musky smell Becca would always associate with her dad, an odd combination of leather, aftershave, sawdust and a hefty dose of sweat. Farm smells. Becca smiled sadly, wondering how it would feel to sit and do homework in a dorm room, a hundred or more miles from home. At least going away to school would force her parents to finally buy Becca her own computer.

The phone on the desk jangled. Becca automatically reached out to snag the receiver, wedging it between her ear and shoulder as she typed a heading into the Google search engine.

"Weaver farm," she answered absently, her eyes glued to the computer screen.

"Becca?"

Though the caller sounded like she was crying, Becca immediately recognized the voice. She shoved the chair back from the desk and clutched the phone.

"Vi? Is that you? Where are you? Are you home?"

"No. No. Not yet." Violet sniffled.

"Why not? Did you get my message?"

"Yes. Is it true? Is Vince back there?"

"Yes. He is. So why aren't you?" Becca got up, wanting to pace, then realized the office phone cord was too short. She plopped back down in the chair.

"Did you talk to him?" Vi asked.

"Yes," Becca gritted out between clenched teeth.

"What did he say?" Vi wanted to know.

"He wanted to know where Nikki was. I wouldn't tell him."

"What else did he say?"

"It doesn't matter!" There was no way Becca was going to tell Vi about the threats. "Why are we talking about Vince? We should be talking about your daughter. I left you that voice mail on Friday. It's now Monday night and you're just now getting around to calling me back? Do you realize you are just a few days away from losing your child? I've done everything in my power to keep it from happening, but Violet, I can't do any more. If you get home now, we are all willing to help you. Whatever you need to make a home for yourself and Nikki, we're all in agreement we'll do whatever we can. You can get help from the state. Whatever it takes. But if you aren't home by this weekend, I'm handing Nikki over to Nate Sweeney and you'll have a heck of a time getting her back, I'll make sure of it."

Silence greeted this declaration.

"Violet, did you hear me? Do you understand what I'm saying?"

"Yes," Vi answered weakly. She sniffed again. "It's, it's so complicated."

"No, it's not," Becca was adamant. "Do you love Vince?"

"I, I thought I did."

"Well, do you love Nicole?"

"Yes!" Finally a spark of conviction.

"Then come home!"

"I'm trying. This... it's, it's all so hard." Vi's voice sounded tired.

"Yes, Vi, sometimes life is hard. But I'll help you. I promise." Well, until I go away to school, Becca thought with regret. She pushed her hair back from her face. She wouldn't think about that right now. "And you know, you have someone bigger than me who will help you."

"Who's that?" Vi asked, sounding mildly curious.

"God. You know God loves you. He's your help and your strength when you need Him. You just have to turn to Him and ask Him to be Lord of your life."

"We've had this discussion before, Becca. If God is the lord of life, He's made quite a mess of mine."

"We have free choice," Becca argued. "You can't blame God for all the messes in your life when you've made some poor choices."

"You know darned well that I had no choice in some things," Vi said. Anger rang in the words.

"I know that Vi," Becca softened her tone. "I'm on your side, remember? And God is, too. I know that's hard for you to believe, but He is. If you'd just let Him in. Come home, please. I don't have all the answers for you, but I know people who do. We can help you if you let us."

Silence hung once more on the airwaves. Becca sighed, knowing she was not getting through. *Help me, Lord,* she silently prayed. *Help me say the right things.*

"Free choice, Vi. You can make the choice to come home. I'll hand Nicole over to you and you can start making a life for you and your baby, no questions asked. It's up to you. Her fate is in your hands. If you choose to stay away..." She let the sentence trail off, waiting for Violet's response. Her friend remained mute. "Vi, you there?" Becca looked questioningly at the phone in her hand. Reaching down, she pressed the disconnect button. A dial tone rang in her ear. Violet had hung up. And Becca still had no idea if she was coming home or not.

Toby stood on the front porch of the Weaver farmhouse, feeling almost giddy. He clutched the small, wrapped parcel in the pocket of his letterman jacket and grinned. Becca was going to be so surprised, and hopefully thrilled, by the gift he had gotten for her. He pressed the doorbell, listening as the chimes echoed down the hallway. Within minutes the door swung open.

"Toby," Becca greeted quietly.

She smiled softly and Toby wondered if she was remembering the heavenly time they had spent together the day before, riding with Nikki in the hay wagon, lazing in the orchard beneath the warm fall sunshine, drinking cider standing shoulder to shoulder in the barn. It had been a day of bliss. One that Toby knew he would remember for the rest of his life, the colors, the smells, the taste of Becca's kiss.

"Come on in." She held the door wider and Toby crossed the threshold. "What brings you here?"

"You," he answered. Snagging the sleeve of her sweater, he pulled her into his arms and dropped a quick kiss on her mouth. "Where are your parents?" he whispered, glancing around.

"In the family room watching Jeopardy. You want to join them?" she asked, looking slyly up at him.

"Hmmm. Sounds inviting, but I'm thinking no," Toby answered. Unable to resist the temptation, he kissed her again. "How about we go into that nice, cozy living room? I've got a present for you."

"A present?" Becca's eyes sparkled with interest. "What kind of present?"

"Come on, I'll show you." Taking her hand, Toby quickly led her to the living room. He sat on the sofa, pulling her down next to him. He tried to kiss her again, but Becca pulled back.

"Present?" she demanded.

"Boy you're pushy," Toby complained with a laugh. "Okay, here." He reached into his pocket and withdrew the small box wrapped in sparkling blue paper.

Becca sat, hands clasped between her knees, staring at the package.

"Toby?" she questioned hesitantly.

"Go on, take it." He held the box out to her. "It won't bite."

"What is it?" She still made no move to take the gift from his hand.

"Open it and find out. You'll like it, I promise."

"I'm not so sure."

Slowly she reached out and lifted the small box from the palm of Toby's hand. Holding it to her ear, she shook the package suspiciously.

"It's not a bomb or anything," Toby assured. He rested an arm on the back of the sofa, watching as Becca removed the tiny blue bow from the top of the box then carefully turned it over to peel away the tape one piece at a time. "You don't have to be so careful."

"I'm savoring," Becca replied, concentrating fully on the task at hand.

"Is that what you call it? I thought you were just being obsessive compulsive."

Finally she had the box unwrapped. She lifted the lid.

"A cell phone?" Her voice was filled with bewilderment as she lifted the slim phone from its bed of tissue paper.

"Yeah, a cell phone." Toby sat forward, nearly bursting with excitement. He took the phone from her hand. "Look, it's sparkly blue, your favorite color."

"How did you know blue was my favorite color?" Becca's eyes, still filled with questions, met his.

"Well, you always preferred blue ribbons, didn't you?" Toby asked with a grin. "And you wear blue a lot. I pay attention to these things," he said, tapping his temple. "I had it put on my plan, unlimited text, so when we both go away, we can talk all the time. Between the phone and the internet, it will almost be like we aren't apart."

"Toby," Becca began to protest. Toby cut her off.

"Since I'm the only guy you're going to be talking to, I programmed it with my number. I'll show you how the speed dial works. And best of all, look." He flipped the phone open and held it up for Becca to see. "I took a picture of myself. So every time you open up your phone, I'll be right there."

"Toby, I can't accept this."

"Can't accept it?" Toby looked at her, stunned. The joy he had been feeling slowly oozed away. "Why not? If it was a ring, sure, I could understand you being unwilling to accept it. But this isn't an engagement ring, it's a cell phone."

"I know, and it was very sweet of you to think of it. But I can't afford a cell phone bill."

"You don't have to." Toby waved away the argument, relieved. "I told you, I put it on my plan. It hardly costs anything extra, as long as you don't go running up minutes talking to some other guy." He smiled, though the thought of Becca falling for someone else while he was gone was like a mule kick straight to his gut. "Right now my mom's caught between elation that I'm making her dream come true and guilt that she went behind my back to do it. I can pretty much get anything I want at this point. And like I said, it doesn't cost hardly anything extra to add a line to my plan. Look." He put one arm around

Becca and drew her tight against him. Holding the phone out in front of them, he pressed a button. "It even takes pictures, see?"

"That is pretty cool," Becca finally admitted, looking at the picture on the tiny screen.

"Told you you'd like it," Toby boasted, bumping her shoulder with his own. "It's your favorite color, it's got a picture of your favorite guy right there, and if you need to reach out and touch someone, that would be me, you just do this."

He pushed 1 on the phone, then hit send. A second later Kenny Chesney was singing "Everywhere we go" in Toby's jeans pocket. He fished the phone out and opened it, cutting the music off.

"That's your special ring, because no matter where I go, I'm still going to love you, Becca." He gazed into her eyes, saw them go all soft.

"There you go with that romantic stuff again."

"It's your own fault," Toby said. "I've never acted this way with any other girl."

"You haven't dated any other girls," Becca retorted.

"Well, there is that." Toby chuckled, then drew back before he could start kissing her again. "Anyway, it works in reverse, too. Of course, you're number one on my phone as well." He pushed the button. Becca's phone began playing some electronic sounding music.

"I need a hero?" She asked, laughing up at him. "I didn't realize you watched Shrek 2, or listened to the soundtrack."

"Is that where that song's from?" He tried to act innocent. "It took me a long time to come up with that one. This ring is perfect because every time I call you you'll be reminded that I'm your hero."

"Hmmm. What if I want to change the ring tone?"

"I'm not going to tell you how."

"I'm pretty near to being a genius myself, I'm sure I can figure it out," Becca argued.

"Now why would you want to go and do a thing like that, when I spent so much time finding the perfect songs for both our phones?"

"Maybe I'll just leave it on vibrate."

Toby opened his mouth to argue, then saw the smile playing across Becca's lips. He bent his head and placed a quick kiss there.

"Can you show me how to program Violet's number in?" she asked, looking up at him with shining eyes.

"Sure." Toby pressed the menu button then hit 'contacts.' The phone beeped as he typed Violet's name in. "What's her number?" Becca rattled it off and he quickly entered it in. "Now to call her all you do is hit this button. Go to contacts then scroll down to Vi's name. Hit enter and it will call her."

"Cool." Becca nodded, taking the phone from his hands. She ran it through her thumb and forefinger again and again. "She called me tonight," she stated.

"Violet? Really?" Toby pulled back to get a better look at Becca's face. She was suddenly so serious, and almost sad.

"I'm worried about her, Toby." Becca shook her head and tucked a strand of hair behind her ear. "I don't think she's coming home."

Becca allowed Toby to pull her close. Felt him drop a kiss on the top of her hair.

"I tried to talk to her about the Lord, but I'm afraid I botched it up." She hung her head, feeling an overwhelming sense of failure. "Somehow, I've missed something along the way. I don't know what, but I feel it, deep in my heart. Something else in going on and I don't know how to get through to Violet, or if I even can."

"Hey." Toby's arm around her shoulders gave a gentle squeeze. "You've been an amazing friend to Violet. The best. You've stood by her through thick and thin. When she got pregnant and a lot of girls at school distanced themselves from her, you didn't. You were loyal. You've tried to set a good example. You brought her to youth group, tried to show her there was a better way to live her life."

"But it obviously wasn't enough."

"You planted seeds, Bec. The rest is up to God. He waters. He gives the increase. Violet is God's responsibility, not yours. You have to leave her in the Lord's hands. If she doesn't come home, then God will take care of Nikki. See how He's providing the perfect home for her? You reminded me not all that long ago that God's eye is on the sparrow. Doesn't that mean His eye is on Vi? He knows where she is. He knows where she's going. You've done more than enough just by taking care of Nikki for all this time. Whatever happens from here on out is up to God."

The bonging of the doorbell made Becca jump.

"Sheesh, Grand Central Station around here all of a sudden." She stood, leaving the protective circle of Toby's arm. "I got it!" she yelled as she went to answer the door.

Becca couldn't hide her surprise when she saw Nate Sweeney standing on the porch. He was dressed in civilian clothes, black jeans, a red and black checked flannel shirt and a scarred, black leather jacket. His vibrant blue eyes were serious as he greeted her.

"Becca." He nodded. His gaze shifted beyond her shoulder. "Toby."

"Is something wrong, Nate?" Becca asked.

"Not wrong exactly, no. I just have some information I thought you'd want to hear."

"Okay. Come on in." Becca stepped back as Nate came inside, his tall frame filling the entryway. "Is this something my parents need to hear?"

"No, I don't think so."

"Becca, who is it?" Her mother's voice came down the hallway.

"It's Nate, Mom. He just has something he wants to tell me. We'll be in the living room." Becca motioned with her head toward the living room then turned to lead Nate that way. Entering the room she flipped on the overhead light, dispelling the atmosphere of cozy intimacy. "Should I be sitting down for this?" she asked, turning to face Nate fully.

Nate shrugged a broad shoulder. Toby moved closer and Becca gained strength from his quiet presence.

"I checked with the county's vital records," Nate began. "I found Nicole's birth certificate."

"Oh. Okay." Becca shook her head slightly, puzzled. "So?"

"So, Vince Schmidt isn't listed as Nikki's father."

"He's not?" Dropping onto the edge of the sofa, Becca looked up at Nate, stunned. "You're sure?"

"Positive." Nate gave a definitive nod of his head.

"Then who?"

"Nobody."

"What do you mean, nobody?" Becca's voice hitched up an octave. "Nikki has to have a father."

Toby sat down next to her. She felt his hand touch the middle of her back, knew he was trying to keep her calm.

"It's possible she doesn't know who the father is," Nate said. The words held a hard, biting edge.

"No." Becca bit out the denial. "I know what you think, but Vi wasn't like that. It has to be Vince. They were always together. We joked and called them V and V nation. You know, like the band? They were going to get married. She told me so. We were best friends. I would have known if there was somebody else."

"Well, the fact remains that she didn't list him on the birth certificate. That means she either didn't want him in the baby's life, or he isn't the father.

Since she didn't list the father at all, that makes me think she doesn't know who the father is."

"Or." The shocking truth hit Becca like a hammer blow. The room suddenly felt hot and cold at the same time. She looked up at Nate, a sick feeling twisting in her stomach. "She knows who the father is, but didn't want anyone else to find out."

CHAPTER TWENTY THREE

"Bye Mrs. Compton. I'll see you tomorrow. Just a couple more days and you'll have your life back. I hope Mr. Compton enjoys those honey buns. It's a new recipe Emma decided to try."

"I'm sure he will," Connie assured, following Becca to the door. "You really don't need to spoil him so."

"Sure I do." Becca grinned. "It keeps me on his good side. And I could never repay all you've done for me and Nikki."

"It's been my pleasure." Connie reached for the door and pulled it open. Becca stepped out onto the porch. "Still no word from Violet, hmm?"

"Not since Monday." A cold wind blew up, causing Becca to shiver. "I've lost hope. I just have to believe it's for the best."

"You've done all you could. It's out of your hands now."

"Yeah. Toby said the same thing. But for some reason it doesn't make it any easier. I've gotta run.

Nikki needs diapers and formula and I want to drive over to Lewiston to do my shopping. The supermarket's bigger over there and I need to stop at the drug store, too."

"Drive careful now," Connie warned. "See you in the morning." The woman ducked back inside the house as Becca hurried to her car and strapped Nicole in the back seat.

The October sky was turning the color of crushed grapes as Becca drove west toward Lewiston. Oh, how she missed the long, lazy days of summer, Becca mused. Here it was barely four o'clock and night was already falling. Soon the hibernation days of winter would arrive. It seemed they rarely saw the sun between November and March. At least Toby wouldn't have to worry about that. He'd be out in Arizona where the sun always shone. Becca envied him just a bit.

She took her time perusing the well-stocked shelves of the large supermarket in Lewiston. She had no reason to hurry home. Her mother was busy with her evening quilting class and her father was up to his neck with the corn harvest. He wouldn't come out of the fields until nearly ten, most likely. Becca glanced down at Nicole who was cooing and gurgling, laying in her baby seat in the back of the cart.

"This is the last time I have to buy your milk and drawers," Becca informed the infant. "Come Monday you'll be someone else's responsibility." Becca found the statement didn't hurt this time. It was time for Nicole to be with a real family. And time for Becca to get her life back.

Winning Becca

Becca paid for her purchases then drove the short distance across the supermarket parking lot to the Rite Aid. She was out of her favorite bubble bath, plus she was considering experimenting with a little makeup. Maybe. If she was going to attend university at Central she didn't want to look like a country hick.

The bright lights of the drug store dispelled some of the gloom that had been weighing Becca down all day. She kept trying to give the situation with Violet over to the Lord, but it seemed she no more than laid it on the altar before she was worrying over it again. She knew she should be relieved that Vince was possibly not Nicole's father. That should be good news, and Becca did silently rejoice in the fact that Vince would have no claim to Nikki, wouldn't be able to interfere with Nate and Penny getting custody. But, if Vince wasn't Nicole's father, that only left one possibility, as far as Becca knew. And it was a possibility so awful, so ugly, that she dared not even think it, much less say it aloud. Besides, Vi had forced her to swear an oath on the Bible that she would never breath a word of it to another living soul. A vow Becca had nearly broken on several occasions.

As she stood contemplating the wide array of foundations and eye shadows, the hair suddenly stood up on the back of her neck. Becca slowly turned her head, feeling the creepy sensation of being watched. Only two other customers could be seen from where she stood in the makeup aisle and both of them were busy flipping through magazines. Shaking her head

Winning Becca

to dispel the unsettling impression, Becca went back to selecting a shade of concealer.

It was nearly six before Becca headed back toward Atlanta. Her stomach grumbled and she pushed the gas pedal a little harder, eager to get home and eat some dinner. Nikki began to fuss in her seat. She's probably hungry, too, Becca thought. Full dark was quickly settling over the land. Becca slowed somewhat as she took the series of treacherous curves between McCormack Lake and Big Rock. Almost home, she thought with relief as her stomach growled once more.

Bright lights shone behind her. Becca kept her eyes steadily on the road, her thoughts occupied with what she would eat for dinner once she arrived home. Nikki squeaked in protest in the back seat, working herself up to a full-blown bellow, Becca was sure. The curves safely navigated, Becca once more pressed hard on the gas. The bright lights grew closer in her rearview mirror until Becca was nearly blinded by the light. What was with people not knowing how to drive? she fumed.

Slowing to make the turn onto the road that lead toward home, Becca expected the car to go around her and head on towards town. Instead, it turned with her, crowding her bumper. Not again! Becca fought the feeling of déjà vu. This could not be happening again! Without thinking, she pulled into Wes and Rhonda's driveway. Relief flowed sweet as honey as the car sped on by.

"Idiot," Becca muttered, pulling back onto the road. "Probably got his license from a vending machine." Nicole's cries ratcheted up a notch. "Okay baby, just a couple more minutes and you'll have your dinner. I promise. I know how you feel. I'm so hungry I could cry, too."

She pulled into her own driveway and cut the engine. Nikki continued to protest as Becca unbuckled the carrier from the back seat and pulled the baby from the car. Standing on the porch in the dim glow of the porch light, Becca fumbled for her house key as the baby squalled.

"Daddy can probably hear that all the way out in the back fifty," Becca complained.

She fit the key in the lock and gratefully pushed open the front door. She quickly padded down the hall to the kitchen. She set the baby carrier on the island and dumped her purse, keys and cell phone next to it before hurrying to the fridge for a bottle.

"Okay, okay. Hold on. I know we don't normally microwave these things but I think this time we just might make an exception since we're both star..." The words died on Becca's lips as she turned toward the microwave, a bottle clutched in one hand. There, standing in the kitchen, stood Vince, and in his hands was a tire iron.

Becca had a sudden flashback to the doll she had found under her car. Its face had been bashed in. Had it been a warning after all, of what was going to happen to her?

"Get out of my house!" Becca ordered, unable to keep the quiver from her voice. Why on God's green earth had she not re-locked the front door behind her?

"I'll get out," Vince growled. "But I'm taking the kid with me."

"Over my dead body!"

"That's the plan."

Before Becca could blink, Vince had rushed around the island and raised the black iron bar. The bottle went flying as she instinctively raised her arm to shield her face from the blow. The shaft of cold, hard metal glanced off her wrist and into her temple. Shooting arrows of fire burned into Becca's head and arm. She kicked out. Vince swung again, this time aiming for her knee. Becca fell to the floor with a cry of pain. She barely managed to twist away before the next blow fell, leaving a gouge in the hardwood floor. Becca scrambled backwards, finding herself trapped between Vince and the refrigerator door. Adrenalin pumped through her body, temporarily numbing the piercing pain that raced from her knee to her head. She screamed as the tire iron came down once more, but this time she managed to raise her left hand and grab a hold before it found its mark. The two wrestled. Becca held on for dear life with both hands, the pain in her right arm bringing tears to her eyes. She kicked out with her feet. With one mighty tug, Vince pulled the bar free and raised it high. Putting both hands over her head, Becca rolled to her side. Shafts of knife-like pain pierced her shoulder as the iron connected with flesh and bone. Stars danced in front of her closed eyes as she braced herself for another blow.

Winning Becca

Nikki screamed. Becca opened her eyes and raised herself up on her hands just in time to see Vince grab the baby carrier and run down the hall. Groaning, Becca tried to rise and follow him. She limped toward the kitchen door, catching a glimpse as Vince vaulted off the front porch. Grabbing her keys and phone, Becca hurried down the hall, making it to the front door just as Vince's car squealed out of the drive. A black car. He's the one who had been following her! The truth drove Becca off the porch to her own car. She quickly got in and started the engine, ignoring the pain that throbbed throughout her whole body. As she punched the gas, trying desperately to catch up to Vince, her other hand clutched the cell phone. She flipped it open, grimacing at the pain that shot up her wrist, before quickly hitting '1' then 'send'.

"Come on, come on, come on," she whispered as she heard it ring.

"Hey Bec, miss me?" Toby's jovial voice greeted.

"Toby," Becca said on a sob. She had to swallow the hysteria that was bubbling to the surface.

"What is it? What's happened?"

"It's Vince," Becca managed to get the words past the tears. "He's got Nikki."

"Got her where?"

"In his car. I'm following him. And you know he probably doesn't have her car seat in right! He probably doesn't have her strapped in at all. O Lord, what if he gets in an accident? He drives like a lunatic!" The panic crept in once more as Becca envisioned Nikki being thrown from the vehicle. "Toby, he has a black car. He's the one that's been following me.

He's the one that tried to kill me on my way home from class, not Heath!"

"Okay, okay. I'm coming. Where are you?" Toby demanded.

"We just turned north on 33."

"Okay, just keep talking. How did Vince get her?"

"I was in the kitchen fixing her bottle. I just turned around and there he was." Becca gulped, remembering the weapon in Vince's hand. "He had a tire iron. He hit me."

"Hit you where?" Toby's voice was tight.

"My head, my arm, my knee, my shoulder," Becca listed her injuries.

"I'll kill him," Toby vowed. "I'll kill him with my own two hands."

"He's turning. Onto Voyer Lake Road. Where's he going?"

"Becca be careful. Did you get his license plate number? Just get his license plate and back off. We'll call the cops. Let them deal with Vince."

"No. He's got Nikki. He's going to hurt her, I just know it. He just turned down Stevens Spring," Becca informed Toby. "Where are you going?" she muttered. "Oh, God." Becca let her car slow.

"What is it?"

"He just turned down the two track that leads back to Sportsman's Dam," Becca whispered.

Sportsman's Dam was a small lake in the middle of nowhere. It had once been owned by a fisherman's club that used it to breed and raise fish. Until one year when the dam got washed away and all their fish ended up downstream in Voyer Lake. It was located in prime elk herd country so eventually the state took it over, cultivating rye grass fields along its edges to help sustain the elk population. It was isolated and remote.

"There's only one way out of there, and that's the way he went in. Hang up and I'll call the police. All you have to do is block the entrance so he can't get back out."

"I can't do that, Toby. You didn't see the desperation in Vince's eyes like I did. There's no way he's coming out of there with Nikki alive."

Becca flipped the phone closed, cutting off the conversation. With both hands tightly gripping the wheel, she turned down the overgrown two track and hit the gas. The little car shot forward. Branches scraped against the sides as Becca navigated the narrow trail. The meager light from her headlamps was soon swallowed by the darkness of the woods.

"Help me, Lord," Becca cried out. The adrenalin that had sustained her until now began to ebb and terror took a firm hold. Pain throbbed in her wrist, knee and shoulder with every beat of her heart. "I don't know what I'm going to do, Lord. Help me. Send Toby, send Nate. Fast!"

The trail veered sharply to the left, leading into a large field. The track continued to the water's edge where a spot was worn from countless boats being launched from the shore. As Becca drove into the clearing, Vince stomped on the gas, doing a doughnut so that his car now faced hers. She watched in horror as the black car careened toward hers. She barely had time to brace herself for the head-on collision. Metal crunched. Glass shattered. Still reeling from the impact, Becca dazedly saw Vince throw his car into reverse and back away before jumping out, dragging Nicole's baby seat behind him. Nikki's cries pierced the darkness.

Becca threw her car into park and shoved open the door. She fell to the ground as her knee gave out from under her. Shoving the pain aside, Becca pushed herself up and limped after Vince who's figure was quickly disappearing in the darkness.

"Vince, stop!" she screamed. "What are you doing? Stop!"

Vince was forced to stop at the water's edge. He spun to face Becca.

"Stay away from me or I'll kill her," he ordered.

"How can you say that? She's your daughter," Becca pleaded, hoping Vince didn't know any better. His high, hysterical laugh told her otherwise.

"Ha! That's what Vi wanted everyone to think. What she wanted me to think. Trying to saddle me with a kid. Wanting me to be her ticket out of that hellhole she lived in. But I told you, I'm not stupid. I didn't flunk out of high school. I didn't fail math class. Shut up!" he screamed down at the baby as she continued to cry.

"Vince, listen," Becca began in a reasonable tone. "You aren't on the birth certificate. No one will hold you responsible for Nikki. There's a couple who wants to adopt her. You won't be saddled with her at all. So, just put her down and walk away."

"Did you figure it out then?" Vince asked, his tone sharp. "You're smart. And you and Vi were tight. You had to have known the truth all along."

"No. I didn't," Becca denied. "I thought you were the father. Vi never told me any different. It wasn't until I found out you weren't listed on the birth certificate that I began to wonder."

"Well, I'm sure you came to the right conclusion. And if you did then you know why the kid has to die. She'll be a freak and everyone will think she's *my* freak!"

Vince spun, swung his arm back and launched Nicole, baby seat and all, out into the lake. Becca screamed. Leaping forward, she rushed headlong toward the water. Vince grabbed her by the arms, squeezing until Becca cried out in agony. Headlights bounced into the clearing, followed by the roaring of an engine. Becca fought like a trapped grizzly bear, desperate to get to her young. She bit down as hard as she could on Vince's forearm.

"Ahh!" He screamed, loosening his grip enough for Becca to yank free. She lifted a knee, connecting with his groin. Vince fell to the ground. Ignoring his yowls of pain, Becca rushed toward the lake and into the icy water. Muck sucked at her shoes as she ran in up to her knees. Everyone knew this lake had a deadly drop off just a foot or two off shore. Becca tried not to think about mucky mud, swimming things or the frigid temperature of the water as she dove under, searching with her hands for Nicole's heavy carrier.

Tall weeds and rye grass scraped against the bottom of the Bronco as Toby bolted into the clearing, maneuvering around Becca and Vince's cars that blocked the track. In the beam of his headlights he saw two figures grappling near the water's edge. Vince and Becca came into clear focus as he drove closer. Shoving the gear shift into park, Toby, slammed open the door and dropped to the ground at a run. He barely registered the fact that Vince had fallen to the ground until he heard the splash and saw Becca dive into the lake.

Vince was attempting to rise. Toby's football training kicked in. He threw a tackle right at Vince's knees that brought both boys to the ground, rolling in a knotted ball of flailing arms and legs. Tossing Vince onto his back, Toby straddled his middle and pounded punch after punch into Vince's face, taking morbid pleasure in the feel of bones crunching under his knuckles.

"Toby, help!" Becca's desperate plea broke through the red haze of rage that had Toby blinded. He spun to see Becca thrashing about in the water. "I can't find Nikki!" she cried.

In a heartbeat Toby rocketed up. Launching himself into the cold lake, he dove under just as Becca did the same. He could feel the water stir around him as he went down, down, his hands searching the blackness of the lake's bottom. Reaching through the tangle of aquatic plants, his searching hand encountered something hard just as Becca's did the same. Struggling for the surface, the two of them came up, fighting for air. It took every once of strength for Toby to lift the baby seat out of the water. In the reflective light of the Bronco's headlamps, Nikki looked like a sleeping angel. With a last superhuman effort, he propelled himself toward the boat launch. Finally feeling mucky ground beneath his feet, Toby dragged himself and the saturated carrier onto the shore. Becca crawled up beside him, fighting to unbuckle the seat's harness.

"I don't think she's breathing," Toby choked out.

"I know CPR," Becca responded, her teeth chattering. Toby saw how badly her hands shook as she finally released the buckle and pulled Nikki from the seat. "Come on, little girl, come on," Becca urged, placing her mouth over Nicole's. Toby watched, helpless as Becca searched for a pulse on the baby's neck. Siren's wailed, coming closer. "Call 9-1-1," Becca ordered. "Tell them we need an ambulance."

"My phone, it's in my pocket," Toby said with a groan.

"Mine's on the front seat of my car. Go!"

Toby shot up, nearly tripping over Vince who still lay sprawled in the grass. He sprinted to Becca's car. The damage from the collision with Vince's vehicle finally registered in his panicked brain. The door hung open, the interior light burning. He grabbed the phone and was just dialing 9-1-1 when a patrol car careened into the clearing, siren blaring, red and blue lights flashing. Toby wasn't surprised to see Nate spring from the car.

"We need an ambulance," Toby ordered into the phone. "The baby's not breathing! Becca's doing CPR. Sergeant Sweeney's here now. Hurry, please."

"Toby, what's going on?" Nate demanded.

"Vince, he threw Nikki into the lake. Becca and I got her out but she's not breathing." Toby could barely keep up as the deputy's long strides carried him to the lake's edge. Tears coursed down Becca's cheeks as she breathed into the baby's mouth then pressed three fingers against the tiny chest.

"Becca, let me," Nate reached out. Becca slapped his hands away.

"No! I'm doing it. Leave me alone," she sobbed.

The radio on Nate's shoulder crackled. He spoke into it in staccato phrases.

"Dispatch I have a 10-62 at Sportsman's Dam. What's the ETA of the ambulance?"

Toby couldn't understand the garbled response.

"10-4 dispatch, copy that. The ambulance will be here in just a minute Becca. You're doing great," he encouraged. "I'll take over any time you need."

The baby spluttered. Becca quickly flipped her over as water came gushing out of Nikki's mouth.

"She's breathing," Becca announced, weeping. "Thank You God, she's breathing."

Toby dropped to the soggy ground and put his arms around Becca, giving her a fierce hug as Nicole began to cry.

Vince moaned, snagging the deputy's attention. Nate reached down and dragged the man to his feet, silently perusing the damage Toby had done to Vince's face. Toby watched as Nate mercilessly twisted Vince's arms behind his back and slapped handcuffs on his wrists.

"Vince Schmidt you are under arrest for attempted murder and kidnapping. You have the right to remain silent." The rest of the Miranda warnings were lost to the night as Nate led Vince to his cruiser and slammed him inside. Another siren split the night and Toby breathed a prayer of thanks as the ambulance bounced across the ground toward the little group huddled on the lake's shore. The door opened and Tyler bounded out, hurrying towards them.

"It's okay now Bec." Toby's teeth clattered together as he shivered spasmodically. "Tyler's here."

CHAPTER TWENTY FOUR

Wrapped in blankets, Becca and Toby sat huddled on a gurney in the emergency room of Otsego Memorial Hospital in Gaylord. Her hair hung lank as seaweed around her face. Periodically her body gave an involuntary shiver, a result of the cold or shock Becca couldn't tell. She stared morosely at her squishy tennis shoes. One hand clutched the blanket to her chest while the other held an ice pack to the side of her head.

"We've called both your parents," Nate announced, entering the cubicle. "They'll be here shortly with some dry clothes for you." He touched a finger to Becca's chin, his laser-blue eyes roaming over the plum colored goose egg on her temple. "They check you out real good?"

"I'm fine." She pulled away from his grasp. "How's Nikki?" The tears flowed once more as Becca thought of Nicole drowning, or being brain damaged.

"They took her up to ICU. But so far things look good. You saved her life."

"Saved her life?" Becca looked at Nate in disbelief. "I'm the one who nearly got her killed! It's my fault Vince took her. If I hadn't insisted on giving Vi one more week, none of this would have happened." She dissolved into sobs. Toby put his arm around her but it brought no comfort.

"She should have been with you," Becca hiccupped. "She would have been safe. What if she's brain damaged? How am I supposed to live with that for the rest of my life?"

"Based on the estimated time that she was possibly underwater, and how quickly you were able to do CPR, the doctors don't think she will be," Nate reassured. "We're all praying and believing God for the best."

"It still never should have happened." Becca swiped the blanket under her nose and tossed the icepack into the trashcan.

"Your heart was in the right place, Becca. No one blames you for any of this."

"Well, they should. I screwed up. I knew Vince was back in town. He came around with his threats. But I thought it was me he was after, not Nikki, and once Vi was back he would leave me alone. Someone had been tailgating me everywhere I went, but I didn't know it was him. I didn't put it all together until tonight."

"We all make mistakes. Some more grievous than others," Nate said solemnly. "Especially when we're young. You did the best you could. And in the end, you did save Nikki. You fought with everything you had and then some."

"I could never have gotten her out of that lake without Toby. He's the real hero." Becca laid her head on his shoulder.

Nate rocked back on his heels and crossed his arms over his broad chest.

"Yeah, well, your hero and I will have to have a little talk later about the condition of my prisoner," he admonished.

"Charge me with assault if you want to." Toby set his jaw stubbornly. "I don't care. You see what he did to Becca? He nearly broke her wrist and her knee. If she hadn't yelled out for me to help her find Nicole, I probably would have killed him."

"Then you'd be the one in jail," Nate stated simply. "Considering the charges Vince is facing, I don't think you need to worry."

"I should call Vi." Becca looked around desperately for her cell phone. "If she knows that Nikki's in the hospital, she'll come home. I know she will."

"Um, Becca." Nate dropped his gaze to the floor. "There's something I need to tell you about Vi. But it can wait until your parents get here and you've had a chance to clean up a bit."

"What? What about Vi? Why can't you just tell me now?" Becca insisted. Nate raised his head and she saw the seriousness in his eyes. "Something's happened to her." The bottom dropped out of her stomach and she felt the truth of it down to the deepest part of her soul.

"I'd rather wait until your parents are here. You've had enough trauma already."

"Just tell me, Nate. I can handle it." She reached for Toby's hand.

"No, I think we should…"

"Just tell me!" Becca ordered. Grimacing, she put a hand to her head. Yelling made the pain worse.

"Okay, okay. Calm down. Monday, when I searched for Nikki's birth certificate, I also checked DMV records to see if I could find out what kind of car Violet drives. You were right, there's a blue Taurus registered in her name. I put out an APB on the vehicle. Are you sure you want me to tell you this now? It won't be easy for you, Becca."

"Yes, please," Becca whispered. "Just tell me and get it over with."

"Man, I hate doing this." Nate shook his head sorrowfully. "We got a call from the state police this morning saying the car was found abandoned on the Zilwaukee Bridge. There was a suicide note on the seat. Along with another note addressed to Becca Weaver."

"No! No!" Becca cried out.

Toby wrapped his arms around her before she could collapse. She sank against his chest, sobbing. Not knowing what else to do, Toby merely held on as tightly as he could. Hot tears soaked through his already wet t-shirt.

"Shhh," he whispered against her still-damp hair.

"She's not dead. She can't be dead," Becca moaned against his chest.

"They've been searching the Saginaw River all day," Nate said quietly.

"Why? O Lord, why?" Becca's wrenching question hung on the air. Suddenly she pushed out of Toby's arms and dropped her head into her hands. "Oh, I know why," she groaned.

"The suicide note revealed some pretty horrendous details," Nate admitted. "Do you know what they were?"

"Yes," Becca whispered with a sad nod of her head. Slowly her hands slid away from her face. "I promised her I would never tell."

"And Nicole's father? Do you know who he is?"

Toby watched Becca closely. Saw her swallow hard and nod once. She closed her eyes.

"Her brother."

It was a tortured admission that left Toby reeling. He stared at her in disbelief.

"Bec, come on," he began to argue. "That's just sick."

"It is sick!" Becca agreed sharply. "You have no idea just how sick. Vi told me about it. Every last gruesome detail. It was the grand finale for a life that had been filled with nothing but suffering and pain. Oh, people around town could judge. They whispered behind the family's back. But no one ever tried to help. Then her brother started drinking, just like their dad. Came home one cold November night totally plastered and ended up in the wrong bedroom. It wasn't the first time Violet had been abused in that house, I can tell you. I begged her to go to the police,

Winning Becca

but she wouldn't. Next thing you know her brother has a job downstate."

Becca heaved a tired sigh and shook her head. Her hands nervously knotted and unknotted the corners of the blanket that was still draped around her shoulders.

"When Vi turned up pregnant she told everyone her due date was early September. I mean, by then she and Vince had been, you know." Becca shrugged. "For quite awhile. So we all assumed he was the father. Honestly, I never questioned it, even when Nicole was born three weeks early. It never crossed my mind that Vince wasn't the father until you told me about the birth certificate. But then I knew. If Vince was Nikki's father, Vi would have put his name on the birth certificate. And if Vince wasn't, there was only one other possibility. I'm not sure how, but Vince figured it out, too. Violet must have told him about the rape and when Nikki was born early..." Becca shook her head sadly "That's why he said Nikki had to die."

Tears seeped from Becca's eyes. Toby's heart broke as he watched her grieve.

"I should have done more. I should have told someone. But I promised." Once more she dropped her head into her hands as her shoulders heaved with silent sobs. "I tried to be a good friend. I took her to church a few times. I tried to tell her about Jesus. But it wasn't enough. And now it's too late."

"No, Becca. It's not too late." Nate's gentle words had Becca lifting her gaze to his.

"What do you mean? Is Vi alive?"

"I don't know. Like I said, they're searching the river and it's my estimation that they're looking for a body. But I told you, Violet left a second note, addressed to you."

"You read it?"

"Not the actual note, no. But they transmitted the contents to the Sheriff's office. She spoke of you in glowing terms. She obviously held you in very high esteem. Whatever you may think, you did have an affect on Violet's life. She said she had prayed and asked God to forgive her for what she was going to do. And she also left a declaration of intent, saying it was her final wish that you be given legal custody of Nicole. She even had it signed by two witnesses. Not exactly a legal document, but I'm sure the court will take it into consideration."

Toby's heart soared as his dream of he and Becca making a home for Nikki once more flared to life. But his hopes were smothered when he saw Becca shaking her head adamantly.

"I've already made a big enough mess of Nikki's life. If the court honors Vi's wishes and gives Nicole to me, I'll gladly give her over to you and Penny. That is if you still want her, now that you know the truth."

Wearing dry jeans and a thick pullover hoodie, Becca sat in the ICU waiting room along with her parents, Penny and Nate, and Toby and his parents. She cradled a hot cup of tea in her hands.

"Well, when I drove up to the house and saw the front door standing wide open, you can just imagine how frightened I was," Mary Weaver explained to Toby's mother. "And then when I walked in the kitchen and there was baby formula everywhere and no sign of Becca or Nicole!"

"It must have been terrifying for you," Anita murmured, her deep brown eyes on Becca.

Becca tried to disappear into the dark navy cushions of the couch. Toby stood abruptly.

"How about we go down to the cafeteria and get a bite to eat," he suggested. He removed the Styrofoam cup from her hands, setting it carefully on the end table before taking her hand in his and pulling her up. "We're going to find the cafeteria," he announced to the room at large as he led Becca out into the brightly lit corridor.

"Your mother hates me," she sighed.

"Nah, she doesn't hate you," Toby replied, putting an arm around her shoulders. "She's just jealous. I'm her baby boy and I've given my heart to someone besides her. It's just taking her awhile to get used to it, that's all. She actually thinks very highly of you."

"Hmph," Becca responded as Toby reached out and pressed the call button for the elevator. The whirring of machinery broke the silence of the hallway. The bell dinged as the elevator doors slid open.

"I don't actually think the cafeteria is open at this time of night," Toby said as they stepped into the elevator. "But I think there's some vending machines down there somewhere. I'll buy you a bag of chips or something."

"Funny." Becca leaned back against the side of the elevator, feeling exhaustion sweep over her. "A couple of hours ago that's all I was thinking about, how hungry I was. Now I don't care if I ever eat again."

"You have to keep your strength up, for Nikki."

"Nicole's not my responsibility anymore. Someone from CPS will be here in the morning."

The elevator doors opened and the two stepped into the hospital's lobby. Toby led the way to the alcove of vending machines outside the dark cafeteria.

"You know, I don't have to go to Arizona," Toby stated. He dropped some change into the vending machine and hit a button. A bag of cheese puffs dropped to the bottom and Toby reached in. Pulling out the bag, he handed it to Becca.

"Don't be stupid. Of course you have to go to Arizona. You've already made all the arrangements."

"I can call and cancel."

Toby steered her toward an empty group of chairs where they both plopped down. Absently Becca opened the bag of cheese puffs and munched one. It almost took more energy than she had. All she really wanted to do was curl up and sleep for a week.

"Violet wanted you to have Nikki," Toby continued, making Becca's mind cramp. "If you're having second thoughts about giving her up, we can always fall back on my original plan. We can get married and raise Nicole ourselves."

"Good grief, we've had this conversation a million, bazillion times." Becca squeezed her eyes shut and nearly threw the bag of cheese puffs at Toby. "I'm not having second thoughts. And after nearly getting that child killed, I think I'm the last person on God's green earth who should be raising her."

"Don't get so hostile. I just wanted you to know my offer still stands, that's all."

"I'm sorry," Becca murmured, rubbing a finger over the knot on the side of her head. "I shouldn't have snapped at you."

"Apology accepted. I just think you're being way too hard on yourself. A big part of living life is learning from your mistakes, and then forgiving yourself when you make them."

"Really?" She took a careful bite out of another cheese curl. "And what mistakes have you made that you had to forgive yourself for?"

"Well." Toby sat back in his chair and propped one cowboy booted foot on his knee. "Funny you should ask since most of them involve you."

"Me? How so?"

"Well, for starters there was that time in Mrs. DeArmond's English class when I failed to spell 'disadvantageously' and you ended up winning the class spelling bee. I beat myself up over that for a *week*."

Toby grinned. Becca rolled her eyes.

"Then there was that little episode at the fair a couple of years ago."

"Which one? There were always *episodes* at the fair involving you and me."

"Oh, the one where I got the bright idea to switch out all the ribbons you won on your arts and crafts projects to make it look like you got reds and whites instead of blues. But I got caught before I had even switched a hand-full. They nearly took *all* of my ribbons away because of that. I had to do some really fast talking to save my butt."

"So, are you sorry you did it, or that you got caught and didn't get to finish the job?" Becca questioned.

"Hmm. That's a toughie." A smirk turned up one corner of Toby's mouth.

"You are impossible," Becca declared. Wadding up the empty snack bag, she threw it at Toby's head. He easily ducked. "I'm going back upstairs," she announced. Her knee throbbed as she stood and made her way to the elevator.

"Wait a sec." Toby quickly caught up with her. He grabbed her hand before she could punch the call button. Leaning a shoulder casually against the wall, he carefully studied her profile. "I didn't get to tell you the most important one. The one thing I regret more than any other."

"What's that?" Becca asked quietly, feeling herself being pulled into the depths of his brown eyes.

"That I waited so long to tell you how much I love you. That I spent all those years trying to win ribbons and awards instead of trying to win your heart. I guess it was my ego and pride that made me think I was doing both."

"So, are you telling me that you would have blown the championship this year if it had meant assuring my undying devotion?"

"Not a chance." Toby grinned and Becca couldn't help but smile in return.

"I didn't think so." She jabbed the elevator call button. "I wouldn't love you as much if you were the kind of guy to just let me win." Becca stepped into the elevator.

"Wait a minute!" Toby stood, staring at her. The doors began to slide closed and he reached out a hand just in time. They slid open once more and he quickly stepped across the threshold and hit the 'close doors' button. Turning to Becca, he pulled her into his arms. "What did you just say?"

"I said I'm glad you didn't let me win."

"No, not that part." Toby nuzzled her ear. Becca pulled back.

"Stop that. I probably stink like dead fish."

"You could smell like horse manure and I wouldn't care," Toby insisted, keeping his arms tight around her.

"A lot of times I do."

"Me too, it's something we have in common." He kissed her cheek, his lips traveling down to her neck. "Now back to what you were saying."

"I don't know what you're talking about," Becca protested weakly, fighting to keep her painful knee from collapsing out from under her.

"You just admitted you love me."

"Did I? I don't really remember. I do have a head injury, remem..." The words were cut off as Toby's lips settled over hers. Becca was lost in the tenderness of the kiss.

"Did that jog your memory," Toby asked, raising his mouth a fraction from hers.

"I love you, Toby," Becca whispered. "As much as an eighteen year old girl with a bum knee and a bruised shoulder can love someone."

"'Bout time you admitted it!" Toby crowed with delight, crushing her against him. Becca squealed out in pain causing Toby to immediately loosen his grip. "Sorry." His mouth covered hers once more.

The elevator bell rang and the doors slipped open.

"Excuse us. Are we interrupting something?" Nate asked.

Toby lifted his head. Becca stared with embarrassment at the audience that stood in the hospital corridor, obviously waiting for the elevator.

"We were just coming to find you two," Penny informed.

"The doctor says they think Nicole will be fine," Mary put in, trying to hide her smile. "They want to keep her a couple of days for observation. But they told us all to go on home and get some rest."

The three couples crowded onto the elevator, squashing Becca and Toby into one corner. He kept his arm protectively around her.

"So Toby, something we should know?" Nate asked nonchalantly, staring straight ahead at the closed elevator doors.

"Oh, just the same old, same old, Nate." Toby grinned down at Becca. "I won, just like I always do."

"But just remember, Toby." Becca smiled sweetly. "The game's not over yet."

CHAPTER TWENTY FIVE

The two horses scrambled over the rocky ground, lurching to reach the crest of the hill. Saddle leather creaked as Becca and Toby sat on the horses' backs, taking in the view. Undulating waves in varying shades of brown and evergreen stretched before them, as far as the eye could see. A few lazy snowflakes spiraled down from the pewter sky. Becca glanced at Toby. He had the collar of his sheepskin coat turned up. His profile was serious beneath the brim of his felt cowboy hat.

"Even with all the trees bare, this is still the prettiest view around," Toby observed. Rocky tossed his head as if in agreement. The Arabian mare Becca was riding danced to the side. Becca quickly reigned her in and brought the horse back alongside Rocky. "I doubt there's this many trees in all of Arizona, much less in one place."

Becca felt the pinch in her heart when she thought about Toby's departure the next day. She shivered as a gust of bitter wind blew across the top of the hill.

She reached up to tug the knit cap she wore down over her ears.

"At least you know it will be warmer than twenty degrees," Becca said, trying to accentuate the positive.

"Thanksgiving's going to be a total bummer."

"I'm sure they serve turkey and stuffing there, too. After all, Arizona is still part of the United States."

"I'm gonna miss you so bad." Toby finally turned his eyes to hers and she saw the misery in their brown depths. She reached out one gloved hand and Toby took it in his own.

"I know. I'm going to miss you, too."

They sat still in their saddles, staring into one another's eyes. Toby grimaced and turned away, staring back over the sea of hills dressed in their winter drab.

"Man!" he bit out. "Why did I ever think this was the will of God? This is the hardest thing I've ever done in my life."

"I think a lot of the times doing God's will is difficult. We wouldn't learn anything or grow if it was a cake walk. And the Bible says do not cast away your confidence, which has great reward, for you have need of endurance so that after you have done the will of God you may receive the promise. That should appeal to your competitive streak."

Toby tugged her hand, causing Becca to lean sideways in the saddle, then dropped a quick kiss on her lips.

"Can you be my reward?" he asked, finally smiling.

"I think the Lord has much greater things in mind for you than just little old me," Becca said with a laugh.

"Nope. Can't be. I don't really want anything else."

"Toby, you really need to expand your vision. God is laying the whole world at your feet." She gestured to the endless forest stretched out for miles before them. "His Word assures us He has a plan for us, a plan for our future. You need to open your heart and your mind to what that might be."

"But what if I don't want the whole world?" Toby argued. "What if all that I want is right here?"

"I think once you see more of the world, you might change your mind." Becca chuckled and turned her horse's head to start back down the hill. Toby grabbed the reigns, stopping her.

"Never!" He insisted fiercely.

"Toby." She laid a gloved hand on his cheek that was chaffed red by the cold. "I wasn't talking about me. I know you love me. I don't doubt that. But you're going to be experiencing things I can only dream of, seeing new places, meeting new people. A whole cornucopia of opportunities will be given to you. Once you've had that, you might not want to settle down in boring old Atlanta." She patted his cheek then nudged her horse forward. "Who knows, you could become a world-class trainer yourself. But it doesn't matter because I'm going to have a degree in early childhood education, which means I can teach preschool anywhere."

"So, are you saying you'd be willing to leave Atlanta?"

Becca shrugged. "If we knew the Lord was leading us elsewhere, then sure, I suppose so." She gave her horse its head, allowing the mare to pick her way carefully down the hill.

"Us?" Toby questioned hopefully from behind her.

"Well yeah, us. I thought that was a given." She reigned in the mare and turned in her saddle to look at Toby. "Unless you plan to fall for some tanned, bleach-blond bimbo in a string bikini."

"Not in a million, bazillion years, Bec." Toby grinned. "Not in a million, bazillion years."

Toby steered Rocky toward the hitching rail in the ranch's stable yard. He threw a leg over the saddle horn and hopped to the ground, leaving the reigns trailing in the dust. Rocky didn't move a muscle. Becca reigned her mare to a halt beside him and Toby lifted his arms up.

"I'm perfectly capable of dismounting on my own," Becca announced.

"I know. But it's so much more fun this way," Toby said, smiling as she slid from the saddle into his arms. Their mouths met, their breaths making puffs of steam on the cold, November air. The brim of his cowboy hat bumped Becca's forehead and Toby lifted one hand to sweep the hat off his head. The hat was nearly crushed against Becca's back as he drew her as close to him as their heavy coats would allow.

Breaking off the kiss, he rested his forehead against hers and tried to catch his breath.

"Man, I'm going to miss you."

"It's going to be okay," Becca assured, giving him a hard squeeze. "We're going to call all the time. And text, and e-mail. We can even do pictures, remember?"

"But I won't be able to hold you. To kiss you," Toby complained.

"Maybe that's a good thing." Her cheeks were rosy, and Toby had a feeling it was from more than just the cold. Bits rattled as the horses grew impatient. Becca pulled from his arms. "We'd better get these guys untacked."

Toby sighed. "I suppose you're right."

They led the horses around the shining silver horse trailer that was parked in the stable yard, filled to the gills with all of Toby's best tack and show clothes. The horses' hooves clopped on the cement of the wide barn aisle. Within moments the two horses were secured in cross-ties. Toby and Becca worked in companionable silence as they uncinched the saddles, tossing them over a stall gate before setting to currying both animals that were fluffy with winter coat. Periodically Toby glanced over at Becca, his gut clenching with the thought that after today he wouldn't see her again for months.

When the horses were turned out in the pasture, Toby took Becca's hand and led her toward the ranch house. Gravel crunched. Toby turned to see a patrol car coming up the long driveway. They waited outside the breezeway for the car to come to a stop. Nate Sweeney got out.

"Becca," he called, slamming the car door. "Your mom told me I'd find you here."

"Something wrong?" Becca asked. Toby tightened his grip on her hand.

"No, actually. Something is right for once. I thought you would want to know that Vince took a plea deal. He'll be going away for 25 years and you won't have to testify."

Relief flowed over Toby, nearly making him dance a jig. He had spent countless sleepless nights thinking of Becca having to face down Vince in a courtroom, having to relive every moment of that terrifying night, while he was two thousand miles away, unable to give her comfort or support.

"That's great news," Becca agreed. "But I wasn't afraid to testify."

"I know you weren't. You've been very brave through this whole thing."

"Yeah, well, I would have liked to see him get more than 25 years."

"That's a minimum, without any chance of parole before that. He'll be doing hard time and you'll be living your life without having to look over your shoulder. You can forget all about what happened."

"I'll never be able to forget," Becca insisted. "Every time I see Nikki I'll be reminded of that dreadful night."

"That will ease over time." Nate patted Becca's shoulder. "She's doing great, by the way. We've decided to take the state's advice and have some

DNA testing done before we consider adoption. The case worker thinks we should have a clear picture of what we may be getting into. Well." Nate hitched up his belt. "I'd better get back to work. I hear you're leaving us," he said, turning his attention on Toby.

"Yep, we pull out first thing in the morning," Toby answered. Nate held out a hand and Toby shook it.

"Good luck to you then, and God bless." Nate turned and strode toward the police car. "Becca, stop in soon and see the baby. She misses you I think, and so does Penny," Nate called over his shoulder before opening the driver's side door and lowering himself inside. They watched him back around before heading slowly back down the driveway.

"You haven't gone to see Nikki?" Toby asked, his eyes still on the disappearing patrol car.

"No," Becca answered, her voice quiet. "Not since she got out of the hospital."

"Why?" Toby slid his gaze down to hers.

"I could say because I wanted her to have time to bond with Penny without interfering. But the truth is it's just too hard right now. I see her and I'm overwhelmed with guilt. Guilt that my stubbornness nearly got her killed. Guilt that I didn't do enough for Violet. I think of our last phone conversation, how I yelled at her, never having any idea that she was about to toss herself off a bridge." Becca shook her head sorrowfully. Toby put an arm around her shoulder and pulled her close.

"There is now no condemnation for those who are in Christ Jesus," he reminded.

Winning Becca

"I know that in my head," Becca admitted. "Maybe in time I'll believe it with my heart."

Becca stood on the front porch and watched Toby's taillights fade into the darkness. Her heart felt like a boulder in her chest as she turned and opened the front door. All those years she had wasted being Toby's enemy when it was so much sweeter being his ally. And now he would be so far away.

Standing in the entryway, Becca was struck by the quiet. Even after nearly three weeks she still wasn't used to the absence of Nicole's cries. She padded down the hallway, shucking her heavy coat and hat as she went. In the kitchen she found her mother sitting at the island sipping a cup of tea and working the crossword puzzle. Mary glanced up as Becca entered.

"You and Toby have a good day together?" her mother asked.

"Yeah." Becca tossed her coat onto a chair then climbed up on the stool next to her mom. "We went riding up into the Rattlesnake Hills. Toby took me to this spot that has the most amazing view."

"I bet," Mary snickered.

"Mother! Anyway, when we got back Mrs. Sinclair made us hot cocoa. I think she's starting to warm up to me."

"Anita thinks the world of you. She just always worried that Toby's feelings for you would prevent him from achieving his full potential."

"Well then, I guess she was right to be concerned. I can't understand how someone so smart can be so stupid about some things." Becca shook her head.

"Honey, he's a man," Mary commented. The two shared a secret smile. "Oftentimes they will do things that make absolutely no sense to us females."

"You've got that right." Becca looked over her mother's shoulder. "Eighteen down is taxidermist," she informed.

"Oh, thanks." Mary penciled in the answer. "Did Nate find you?"

"Yes. He told me Vince pled guilty and will be going away for at least 25 years."

"That's a relief. Now you can start working at putting that whole ugly mess behind you. I think this might help." Mary slid an envelope toward Becca.

Becca picked it up, looking at the CMU logo in the upper left hand corner. She slid the flap open and unfolded the letter.

"They've accepted my application to start with the spring semester in January," Becca stated quietly.

"I figured as much," Mary said with a shrug. Becca shuffled the sheaf of papers.

"There's an awful lot I have to take care of before then." Becca felt a growing sense of excitement mixed with a healthy dose of dread.

"Good. You'll have plenty to keep yourself occupied so you won't be mopping around missing Toby."

"I don't mope!" Becca denied. "Gosh, I guess I have to give Emma notice."

"I heard that Carolynn and Ed are going to be moving back here now that Emma's expecting again."

"Really? I thought they didn't like the winters up here."

"Oh, grandkids will make you change your mind about things like that. Plus, now that Milt's passed away and Mable's in that assisted living place, I think they're bored and want to be closer to family. Mable's got all of Tyler's family keeping an eye on her, so she really doesn't need Carolynn and Ed to take care of her."

"I'm happy to know Emma will have some help with the teashop. Hopefully she won't have to close it up once the new baby comes. And I'm sure I can think of a couple girls who would love to waitress there. Well." Becca slid off the stool and gathered the sheaf of papers. "I stink like horse. I'm going to go up and take my bath."

"Okay honey."

As Becca left the room she heard her mother's pencil scratching away at the crossword puzzle. Upstairs, her bedroom still seemed oddly empty, bereft of the port-a-crib and other baby paraphernalia. Plopping down on the bed, Becca let her gaze rove around the room. Her textbooks were stacked neatly on her desk. A snapshot of her and Toby was tucked into the mirror above her dresser. The worn rocker sat in front of the windows.

Two months, Becca thought. Only two months and she wouldn't be sleeping in this room anymore. Instead she would be crammed into a dorm room with some stranger she'd never met. What if her roommate was a partier? Someone who smoked and drank and *didn't believe in God*?!

The distressing thought brought Becca up short. No, she would not dwell on possible negatives. This was an adventure. A new beginning. Limitless possibilities opening before her. She was going to pray and believe that her new roommate would become her new best friend. And if they didn't believe in God, well then, Becca would just be a witness and a testimony. She had botched it with Violet, but maybe God would give her a second chance.

Grinning, Becca reached for her sparkly blue cell phone. She flipped it open, gazing longingly at Toby's picture before hitting 1 then send. It took only moments for Toby to pick up.

"Hey Toby, guess what!" Becca greeted, excitement ringing in her voice. "I'm going to Central!"

EPILOGUE

The sun broke out from behind a cloud, doing little to dispel the chill of the cold March wind. Becca strode from the Montmorency County Courthouse behind Nate and Penny. In her arms Penny held Nicole, dressed in a frothy pink dress and matching bonnet. Waiting on the steps below were Emma and Tyler along with Wes and Rhonda, who broke into a rousing round of applause as the new family stepped into the weak spring sunshine.

"Let's hear it for the new family!" Rhonda cheered before splitting the air with a shrill whistle.

"She's all ours," Nate crowed. Taking the baby from Penny's arms, he held her up for all to see. "Ladies and gentlemen I present to you Nicole Anne Sweeney."

Emma snapped a series of pictures. Becca scurried to get out of the way.

"Wait a minute!" Penny grabbed for her arm. "I want some with Becca, too. After all, if it wasn't for her, we wouldn't have Nikki." Penny pulled Becca into the circle of her arm. Becca smiled for the camera. "And we want you to be Nicole's godmother. That way you'll always be an integral part of her life."

"I'd be honored," Becca murmured, giving Penny a hug.

"Okay gang, we're all headed over to the steak house in Alpena. It's the place where Penny and I had our first date, so it's only fitting that it should be the first place we take Nikki now that she's officially our daughter. Lunch is on me."

The whole group cheered. Laughter filled the air as they skipped down the courthouse steps and headed toward the parking lot. A figure wearing a tan Stetson careened around the corner of the building, nearly bowling into Tyler.

"Whoa, partner, slow up there," Tyler warned, putting his hands out to prevent a head-on collision.

"Sorry." The cowboy glanced at the group. "Oh man, am I too late?" he wailed.

"Toby?" Becca squealed. She pushed through the crowd and launched herself into Toby's arms. Winding her arms around his neck, she stared up in amazement at his deeply tanned skin. "Good grief, could you get a little more brown?" she asked.

"Well, the sun has a tendency to shine a lot out there in the desert," Toby replied. His teeth flashed white against his dark skin. "Let me get a look at you." Holding Becca away from him, his appreciative gaze roamed over her as the rest of the group flowed around them headed toward their cars. He let out a low whistle. "I like the dress."

"Then you'd better take a picture because you probably won't be seeing me in another one for a long time," Becca retorted.

Toby glanced around at the departing couples before placing a lingering kiss on her lips.

"I guess I missed the big event, huh? I got here as quick as I could."

"The adoption papers were signed about ten minutes ago," Becca told him. "But you aren't too late for lunch. You want to come with? Nate's buying."

"Sure," Toby agreed. "Gives me more time to ogle you in that dress." The familiar smirk turned up one corner of his mouth. Becca's heels clicked as they made their way across the parking lot to Toby's Bronco. "And is that makeup you're wearing?" he asked, holding the passenger side door open for her.

"Yep. I'm a co-ed now, you know."

"Don't remind me," Toby groaned. Becca smiled as she watched him hurry around the vehicle's hood and climb behind the wheel. "So, how's your spring break going?" he asked, starting the engine.

"It's going too fast!" Becca laughed. "But I miss my job at the café, and my roommate Kelsie. I would say you would love her, but if you did then I would have to kill you both."

"Well, I have seen pictures. She is pretty hot. Ow!" Toby complained when Becca slugged his arm. He rubbed his bicep. "Anyway, I guess in the fall we'll have a chance to find out." Toby pulled out onto Main Street and headed toward Alpena.

"Find out what?" Becca looked at him quizzically.

"Find out if I'll love your roommate." Toby took his eyes off the road long enough to throw her a mischievous glance.

"What are you saying?"

"I'm saying that I'm applying to CMU for the fall."

"But," Becca spluttered. "But what about the circuit?"

"I've won enough ribbons to last a lifetime," Toby confessed. "Don't get me wrong. Alonzo's been fantastic and his horses are a dream. I've learned so much. But there's still this emptiness inside me. A restlessness I can't explain. I've done a lot of praying and spent a lot of time in God's Word and I've decided to leave the circuit at the end of the summer. I feel so good about this, Becca." The air nearly buzzed with his enthusiasm.

"I really do feel like God's given me a vision. Remember how you told me I would make a good teacher? Well, I've thought a lot about that and you're right. I would love to come back to this area some day and start up a camp for disadvantaged youth. You know, give riding lessons and things like that. I know that's all a long way down the road but I'm just so psyched about it."

"I can tell," Becca chuckled.

"What do you think? I mean, is this something you think you could get excited about?"

"Absolutely! I love the idea. We could have preschool activities. Arts and crafts and games. Oh Toby, I've learned so much in these past few months. There are thousands of hurting kids who are just

Winning Becca

languishing in the system. Scores of little Violets out there. Wouldn't it be awesome if we could have a positive impact on their lives before they turn tragic like Violet's did?"

"Yea," Toby agreed.

They continued to dream and discuss different ideas until they hit Alpena's city limits. Toby swung the Bronco into the parking lot of the restaurant. Cutting the engine, he turned toward Becca. His brown eyes overflowed with emotion. "Before we go in, there's something I'd like to ask you."

"Okay," Becca replied seriously.

Toby took her hands in his, fiddling with her fingers.

"I've won a lot of things in my life, Becca. But the thing I want more than anything is to win your hand. Becca, will you marry me?"

"Oh Toby," Becca sighed.

"Not right now, of course," Toby amended. "We have to get through school first. But you would make me the happiest man on earth if you would agree to wear my engagement ring." He reached into his jeans pocket and pulled out a tiny box. He placed the box in Becca's hand. With trembling fingers she lifted the lid.

"Oh Toby," she repeated. Staring up at her was a sparkling sapphire set on a slim circle of twisted silver. "It's beautiful."

"Blue, like first place." Toby removed the ring from the box and slipped it on Becca's left hand. "To remind you you're always first in my heart."

"Oh Toby."

"I didn't think it was possible, but I do believe I've rendered you speechless." Toby laughed and dropped a quick kiss on her lips. "You really need to expand your vocabulary a little bit, Bec. Come on, let's go share our good news with the others." Toby opened his door and made to step down from the Bronco.

"Wait a minute!" Becca commanded. "Did I say yes? I don't remember saying yes."

"It was implied in the way you said 'oh Toby,'" Toby mimicked in a falsetto voice. Becca frowned at him. "Okay," Toby sighed. "Let's try it this way. Becca will you marry me?"

"Yes!" she shouted, throwing her arms around his neck.

"Geez, it's about time," Toby groused good naturedly. His pressed his lips to hers. "Now lets get inside. I'm starved. Plus I want to brag to everyone how I finally won the real grand prize."

For this reason we also, since the day we heard it, do not cease to pray for you, and to ask that you may be filled with the knowledge of His will in all wisdom and spiritual understanding. Col. 1:9

THE END

Dear Readers,

Thank you for going on one more adventure with me! I do so hope you've enjoyed Toby and Becca's little romance, although it was somewhat of a departure from my other novels. Once they came to life in my mind, I couldn't rest until I had given them their own story. But, the Northwoods Adventures Series now comes to a close, and I mean it this time! I continue to work on my historical set during the Indian uprising at Fort Michilimackinac prior to the American Revolution. Also, I've decided to put my obsession with WWII to good use and write a novel set during that era. So, I will have plenty to keep me writing in the future.

Please e-mail me at amycorron@northwoods-novels.com. I LOVE hearing from you! You would be amazed at how God uses you, because often I receive an uplifting e-mail from a happy reader just at the point when I am ready to give up, or am struggling with a plot line. Your words of encouragement mean so much to me. Also, visit my web site at www.northwoodsnovels.com to see a list of my book signings and author events. I also have a web store where you can purchase autographed copies of my books. I'm also trying to get my web designers (namely my husband and son) to post pictures on the web site so that you can "take a walk through the northwoods."

Thank you again and God bless!!

Amy A. Corron

Printed in the United States
125101LV00001B/2/P